Menopausal fairy Mischief

Menopausal fairy Mischief

Tina Scott

Foutz
Fables & More
Mesa, Arizona, USA
Foutzfablesandmore@gmail.com

Cover design by: CMI. Cover artists: Laura Tolman, Dillon McGaughey Cover pic: Lana Langlois/ Shutterstock

Published by Foutz Fables & More 2016

ISBN: 978-0-9891581-4-5

Many thanks to my dear husband who encourages my writing, brags about me at every opportunity, and who thinks I'm brilliant.

Thanks to my children who seem to like my stories, who encourage their friends to read them, and who cheer me on when I get discouraged.

A special thank you to the numerous women of the American Night Writers' Association (ANWA) who have critiqued, edited, and helped guide my writing.

My warmest grattitude to Cecily and to my niece, Shannen, who liked Angela from the very first, and to Jennifer and Valerie for their editing skills. Thanks also to the LDSStorymakers who first acknowledged Angela's possibilities.

And, to Angela: Thank you for letting me tell your story:
After all these years, I believe.

FIFTY YEARS AGO

Five-year-old Angela Benoit stirred in bed, her eyes fluttering beneath her eyelids as she awakened to the static of a magical energy filling her room.

Something or someone was in her room. Something magical, she hoped. Afraid for it to go away, yet curious as to what it was, Angela peeked an eye open.

A light darted away from her, and from it trailed golden sparkles. A fairy! Angela squeezed her eyes shut and held perfectly still—if the fairy knew she was awake, it might leave. She waited almost an eternity, and was ready to get out of bed when something tickled her cheek like a miniature kiss.

Both eyes flew open as she sucked in a breath, and sat abruptly up in bed. The shimmering light disappeared through her open window. She giggled. Joy and happiness crawled around her insides. She'd never had this feeling before. It was as if she was filled with ice cream and cotton candy. Or bubbles. Angela touched her tingling cheek and then jumped out of bed.

"Mama! Mama!" She called, running to her parents' room.

"What is it?" Mama leaned toward Angela.

"I feel so happy!" Angela shivered and rubbed her arms. "It was a fairy, Mama. Just like you said!" She bounced on her tiptoes. "It kissed me. Here." She felt her cheek with her fingertips.

"A kiss," Mama said reverently. She sat up and drew Angela near. "Are you sure?"

"I feel warm and happy. What does it mean, Mama? Will I be a fairy now, too?" Angela snuggled into her mother's warmth. Love glowed brighter there. With that love and warmth, the edges of sleep tried taking over, but Angela forced herself to stay awake. "Will I be able to fly now, and grant wishes?"

"*Snor-splnt!*" Daddy rubbed his nose and turned, reaching for Mama.

Mama peered back at him, patting his arm, her eyebrows creased. When Daddy settled, she put a quieting finger to her lips. "A fairy vvvvvkiss is special indeed, but we mustn't wake your father." Mrs. Benoit stroked Angela's auburn hair, a big smile growing on her face. She whispered, "A kiss means the fairies have granted you a wish."

Angela drew her clasped hands to her chin. "I wish—"

Her mother put a finger to Angela's lips. "Don't speak hastily, my daughter. A fairy wish is a tricky thing, and once wished cannot be *un*-wished." She looked at Angela sternly.

"But I know what I want, Mama." Angela bounced on her toes.

"I will help you form the exact words in the first light of dawn." She kissed Angela's forehead. "Now, we mustn't wake your papa. He has a busy day tomorrow." She yawned and patted Angela's head. "Think about it, yes. It is nearly dawn now. Decide what it is you truly want, but do not speak your wish until it's time."

Angela started to protest but her mother stopped her.

"Hush now. Don't speak a word." She touched her fingers to Angela's lips. "Go in and go potty." Her eyebrows lifted. "And I'll meet you back in your bedroom. You can be a big girl and wait that long. Can't you?"

"Yes, Mama." Angela frowned and then turned toward the bathroom. She was a big girl, but she didn't need to wait. She'd known what to wish for since forever ago when, early one morning, she had secretly witnessed her mother change from fairy to human.

"My wish is to have wings and fly just like Mama does," Angela muttered as she climbed into bed. "Why does that need to wait until dawn?"

Her room brightened with a flash of lightning followed by a thunderous boom. Angela screamed and drew the covers over her head.

Mrs. Benoit ran to Angela's bedside. "Oh, my dear baby, what has happened?"

"I was thinking of my wish, like you told me to." Angela whimpered, her heart thrumming like a hummingbird's, and tried hiding in the comfort of her mother's gown.

Mrs. Benoit rushed to the window and peered through the curtain. "It is just as I feared. The sky is clear." She came back and hugged Angela tight. "Did you think of what you wanted out loud?" She knelt before her. "Tell me what you said. What was your wish?"

"I wished for wings, just like you."

"You know?" She took Angela's hand in hers and gazed kindly. "How?"

"I didn't mean to." Angela hung her head and tried remembering. It felt as though she had known forever. "I'd had a dream and it woke me up." Her shoulders lifted.

"Yes. Go on," her mother encouraged.

"I went to your room." Angela worried her lip. "Papa was sleeping alone. When I started to come back to bed, I heard a noise and hid behind your door." Angela peeked up at her mama. "And then I saw you come in the window," she whispered.

"Well, there is nothing we can do about that now." Mrs. Benoit stroked her daughter's hair. "Tell me exactly what you wished."

Angela thought for a moment. "I said that I wanted to have wings and fly just like my mama — like you."

"Did you mention when you would like this to happen?" She sat on Angela's bed.

"Don't wishes come true when you make them?" Angela looked

hopefully into her mother's eyes.

"No, dear, I'm afraid not." She clasped Angela's hands and squeezed them.

"When will my wish come true then?" It wasn't fair that she couldn't get wings right now.

"I'm sorry, sweetie." Her mother gave her a half smile. "Since you didn't specify a time, the fairies can grant your wish whenever they want."

"I wish for my wish to be granted right now." Angela gazed expectantly around the room. When nothing happened, she drooped her shoulders and hung her head. "What can I do?"

Mrs. Benoit pulled Angela onto her lap. "For starters, you need to remember this moment forever, and always believe."

"I do, Mama. I believe in fairies." She adored her mama.

"Next, when you're much, much older you must find someone. Like Papa." She lifted Angela's chin with her finger. "Your papa is a good man who also believes in fairies. This is very important." She smiled at Angela and gave her a squeeze. "He allows me to be who I am and loves me for it."

"Yes, Mama. I will always remember." How could she forget? "When I grow up I'll marry someone just like Papa." She would be a fairy-human long before then. "He'll believe in me just like Papa believes in you." She clasped her hands and sighed. "We'll live in a big house and have twenty kids—and they'll all grow up to be just like you."

ONE

PRESENT DAY

Angela groaned with frustration. If only she could get some sleep. Leg cramps. Hot flashes. They were having a heyday with her tonight—and that familiar ache in her shoulder. massaging it, she tried alleviating the pain, but something was there—unfamiliar, foreign. Angela swept her hand across the sheets underneath her thinking to remove a stray candy wrapper.

Nothing.

Puzzled, she rubbed her shoulder again. Something was stuck to her back. Only able to reach so far, she fingered the edge. It felt satiny. She tugged. It didn't come off. Curious and sitting up now, Angela arched backwards, reaching.

It felt strangely like ... wings. Wings?

Shaking the sleep away, Angela leaned forward, elbows on her legs, chin in her hands, and rubbing her cheeks. What month was it? Had she forgotten to take off her Halloween costume again? No, it was September. Chills surged down her spine and sparkled down her arms, making the hairs stand on end.

"My wish is finally coming true," she whispered. "But why now?"

She glanced at her sleeping husband. This wasn't some misguided joke. Was it? Angela shook her head at the improbability. But wings?

It seemed like too much to hope for. That didn't stop a hopeful grin from spreading across her face.

"M' you okay?" Ted mumbled as he rolled to face the wall.

"I ... I'm going to walk around a bit." Her reply was unnecessary. He'd already gone back to sleep.

Angela felt lightheaded as she walked through their family room, heart thumping, occasionally reaching for the soft form on her back yet not succeeding. She went out the arcadia door and then stood in the grass just off the patio. The security light came on. Angela stepped onto the porch, wincing against the bright light flooding the back yard and waiting for it to shut off.

All she needed was the Denalis waking up and seeing her from their second story bedroom window. Angela glanced up. Their house was dark.

Angela arched again, reaching, stroking bits of rich satin and looking at her reflection in the sliding glass door.

They *were* wings. They suited her and came through her T-shirt without a rip or pucker. If the wings didn't feel like a natural part of her body she would have believed they were a part of her shirt. They were light and delicate with a luminescent quality to them, their color shifting from deep sapphire, to turquoise, to emerald, with an occasional flicker of purple.

She had been a fairy for Halloween every year since she was five, and now through some stroke of luck, she would finally be a real one. A smile stole across her face.

Thirty-four years ago last October, she'd purchased her exquisite fairy costume to celebrate Ted's getting on with Braxton & Braxton, the hottest new accounting firm in Phoenix. The sales clerk's cryptic message had Angela up nights and planning her first fairy adventure. (Thinking, of course, that the costume was her link to becoming a true fairy.)

Angela huffed. Nothing had ever happened. Nothing except alienating herself from several of the neighbors.

Five kids later, she could barely pull the spandex and sequin outfit up and over her ample hips and stomach. It didn't matter. Such silly details didn't keep her from wearing the costume. They certainly didn't keep her from dreaming that one day her family would believe. She smiled again.

Vindication. Finally!

For the last fourteen years since Hannah was born, her husband and children had taken turns hiding the precious costume. Each time she found it and put it on, Ted rolled his eyes and her children moaned their disapproval.

Well, no more—her fifty-year magical famine was at an end.

A light breeze stirred the air and Angela rubbed her arms. The hot flash now gone, she felt chilled. The corners of her mouth turned upwards into another smile—she just couldn't help herself. What would Ted think when she showed him her new set—her *real* set of wings? A giggle escaped her lips that mirrored her girlish glee.

An overwhelming desire to fly consumed her. Angela chewed her lip while forming a plan. She wouldn't be hasty like a five-year-old. She would learn how to make her wings work, and then show Ted and the kids in the morning. Yes, a short flight around the neighborhood was in order. Angela pressed her fingertips against the smile she couldn't hold back. Then, looking into the night sky, she wondered how these things—these *wings*—worked.

"Fly, wings!" she commanded.

Nothing happened.

"Go, wings, go!"

They remained lifeless against her back.

Maybe her wings were just an elaborate dream. She'd had them before. After all, according to Ted, fairies weren't actually real. Her childhood fairy kiss—an overactive child's imagination. Her mother being a fairy-human and going on countless missions that she later shared the details of with Angela—the result of a generous and compassionate mother who wanted to keep her good deeds anonymous. Ted didn't believe any of it was real — not that he hadn't played along while they were dating.

She pinched her arm. "Ouch!" She looked at the red mark. That felt pretty real.

So, it wasn't a dream. Hm. Angela ticked her finger against her lip.

It would be just her luck to sprout wings only to have them faulty and unusable. Yes. Exactly her luck. She shrugged her shoulders. Her family was right. She was a housewife. Not a fairy.

Nothing special.

The wings made her feel special, though. Angela turned to look once more at her reflection in the glass door.

The wings were beautiful, glistening with the moonlight. But how could they possibly lift her middle-aged frame even a foot off the ground? Angela peered down at her flabby mid-section with a frown.

Dang it! If she could just lose that extra thirty-seven pounds she'd been packing around — maybe then she could fly. She took a shaky breath. *I'm swearing off of fudge brownies forever.* First thing tomorrow they were going in the trash.

Discouraged and ready to go back to bed, Angela shrugged again and trudged toward the back door. That's when she felt it, the slight twinge of life in her wings. She paused and looked behind her. They had expanded.

Wahoo! Angela jumped into the air, her heart flipping with excitement.

She rushed back to the lawn. The security lights clicked on once again and flooded the yard with light.

Heck with it. Who cared? The Denalis probably had blackout blinds anyway.

"Whooee!" With arms outstretched, Angela ran in circles around her backyard feeling five again, flapping her arms and trying to fly. "I'm a fair — oops!" Her feet slipped out from under her. She landed on the grass with a thud. Angela winced and rubbed her derriere. There was a little too much to rub. Not at all like when she was five.

With heart pounding in her chest and knees aching from overexertion, Angela stood and gazed into the night sky with renewed hope and determination. She stretched her hands upward, reaching toward the moon in an exultant act of celebration, then pulled her fists back to her chest. "Yes!"

She would fly!

She moved her shoulders back and forth methodically, breathing slow, even breaths—back and forth, back and forth. Angela needed to get this right. She had to. As she wiggled, a tingling sensation moved from her head to her toes and back up again sending a shiver in its wake. Her wings fluttered excitedly at the exercise, but didn't take flight.

Angela chewed her bottom lip and creased her brows, concentrating. What was the key to flight?

Closing her eyes, Angela pictured her wings and what she wanted them to do—just flutter a little. In response, she felt a tremulous ripple—they did it! The secret to flight wasn't verbal commands. A smile of satisfaction spread across her face. A small test, and then she'd go in and show Ted. Sha-bam! Angela would shake Ted's two-dimensional world.

But he hated getting woken up. Angela made a face. It'd have to wait.

Eyes still closed, she pictured her wings lifting her a foot into the air—nothing more. After all, she didn't want to end up in the hospital. Her wings fluttered in response to her pictured thoughts. Angela peeked to see herself hovering a foot above the earth. Total elation!

She could do it—she could fly!

No more would she be considered a joke. Her husband and children, the neighbors—they'd all have to take notice of her now. Fairies were real, and she was one! Now her daughter, Leanne, would certainly buy a fairy charm for her baby when it came and continue Angela's fairy-loving legacy. Angela nodded, satisfied, and imagined herself on the ground again.

Something went wrong, however. Instead of floating gracefully back to earth, her wings seemingly developed a mind of their own and flew her across the yard. Aaaak! Yes, something was definitely wrong! Angela flailed her arms and legs, trying to stop, trying to gain direction. The speed left her dizzy. "Oh," she moaned. "How did Superman do it?"

She was too old for flying — too old to be a fairy. Her doctor had explained this to her with as much clarity and tact as doctors ever did. Menopause — the mysterious change of life. It meant her body was shutting down — preparing for old age — preparing for death. Ugh! Preparing to make her sick at the thought.

Hovering fifteen feet in the air, Angela bent over, her stomach retching out the remnants of dinner. She had never been good with heights. Angela wiped perspiration from her forehead. Luckily, she'd had a light dinner.

She looked around, frantic. Had anyone seen her? The backyards of all her neighbors were visible from this height. Momentarily forgetting her dilemma, Angela eyed them critically. The Madisons' backyard looked like a weed patch. Who did they think they were fooling? Well, everyone apparently. But not her. Angela smiled sardonically.

Ah, but back to her problem. She couldn't get down. Would she be stuck in midair all night?

"Ted!" she called. How would she explain it — her floating in air? She looked down again. Sucking in a breath, she closed her eyes. Why had she ever wanted to fly?

"Sweetheart, help me!" Angela shouted at their bedroom window. It was no use. Ted didn't own a rope. Not that he knew how to use one. If she yelled louder, she'd wake the neighbors and that presented a different disaster altogether.

Closing her eyes with hopes of landing on the back patio, Angela formed what she deemed the proper mental picture, and tried once again.

Her wings sprang to life and, satisfied, Angela opened her eyes. Instead of landing safely, the wings darted her toward their house. Her eyes widened in alarm. Her mouth opened, but the scream froze in her throat.

Too high for landing—she was headed for the second floor. She would hit it, too, and splat against it. Too big to be a bug, her impact may very well shake their foundation if she didn't gain control—quick!

Concentrate. Concentrate. Concentrate. Forcing herself to erase the mental picture of her impending doom, she pictured a safe flight up and over her rooftop. She didn't want to wake Hannah. That was her bedroom wall flying nearer at an alarming rate.

Angela grimaced, and shut her eyes, preparing for the moment of impact. Instead, she felt a whoosh of air pull her upward and she now hovered over her home. Her stomach convulsed again. Their roof became the recipient of her latest bout with vertigo.

This fairy thing was not going well.

She needed sleep. She needed sanity. More than anything at the moment, she needed down. Closing her eyes again, Angela strained against exhaustion to form a picture in her mind—the one of her floating slowly and safely to earth. The lack of sight, the lack of quick movement helped calm her troubled stomach.

Was she descending? One eye peeked open and squeezed shut more tightly than before. She wasn't touching ground yet. In her mind, she forced herself down slowly and pictured her feet planted on the cement. After waiting with her eyes closed a moment, she peeked again and found herself standing solidly—other than her quivering knees—on the ground.

In the front yard.

Angela tilted her head forward and groaned. The front door was locked. Of course. She hobbled over and checked it just to make sure. The gate to the backyard was of no use. They had kept it padlocked since the town of Gilbert's rash of burglaries last year. Until tonight, they had never needed the gate anyway.

She limped to the front of the house and stared at the door. Should she ring the doorbell? No, no, no, she would not. Angela wanted them to see her wings, yes, but not as a fairy failure. A laughingstock. Angela needed just a minute. She would figure things out and show them in the morning. Ah, yes. Morning. Hopefully, she would get some sleep before then.

Ugh. She groaned, looking at the sidewall. She didn't dare use her fairy wings to flit her up and over the fence. That could prove disastrous. No, she'd had enough airtime for one night and would do it the old-fashioned way. Climb over. The wall was only six-feet high after all, and she used to climb trees as a kid. How hard could it be? (She tried convincing herself of this.) Luckily, the block fence began as a two-foot-tall structure by the sidewalk.

Angela pushed against the block, making sure the wall wouldn't collapse beneath her weight. It seemed sturdy enough.

Oomphing herself onto the short, stub of a wall separating the Anderson home from that of her malevolent neighbor, Rebecca Helman, proved more difficult than she'd anticipated, but after climbing the two-foot section of cinder-block, Angela climbed onto the four-foot-tall middle layer of wall.

Her knees wobbled. The cinder block moved slightly beneath her. She bent further, her knees popping, and straddled the edge. It was the most exercise she'd had in ages. She wiped the sweat off her forehead with the hem of her T-shirt and eyed, doubtfully, the next two-foot precipice she needed to overcome in order to access the backyard. It may as well have been the Superstition Mountains.

Clutching tightly to the fence, and with a leg dangling over each side, Angela paused. What insanity had led her to this moment— How could she get up and over that wall—What would happen if someone drove by and saw her? Angela trembled at that thought. Yet, as if in answer, a brand new sage-colored Lincoln Navigator pulled into the Helmans' driveway on the other side of the block fence.

"Drat! What're the Helmans doing out this time of night?" Angela could see the headlines now. "Aging woman found on wall," she mimicked. "Angela Anderson, wife of Ted Anderson, partner at Braxton & Braxton and beloved president of the Gilbert High School Booster Club was caught trying to break into her own backyard—at two a.m., no less." She stiffened, hoping they wouldn't see her. "I do look wall-like. Don't I?" she muttered.

"Good morning, Ms. Anderson. Preparing for Halloween so soon this year." A statement, not a question, Rebecca Helman cooed. Her charm was all a charade—the woman was a cobra. After seeing Angela in her fairy costume last July, Rebecca insisted Angela be removed from the Homeowners Association Neighborhood Committee, and Angela was one of the founding members of HANC.

Angela shifted, trying to hide her wings. "Oh, hello, neighbor. I . . . um . . . couldn't sleep." It wasn't a lie. "Nope. I couldn't sleep." She smiled sheepishly at them, avoiding any mention of her newly sprouted wings at all cost.

Mr. and Mrs. Helman stood beside their vehicle, appraising her.

She needed to think of something good—fast. "The block wall here, it's the perfect height for my new exercises." Angela stood uneasily, lifting a leg up and down as proof.

They stared at her in blatant disbelief.

Frantically, she switched legs, lifting the other in what she hoped was a graceful attempt at serious exercise. Unfortunately, graceful she was not. Angela failed to place her left leg securely onto the narrow fence before lifting her right leg.

"Aack!" She screamed as she fell, straddling the block wall at first, then sliding down the length of it with one leg leaning uncomfortably upwards and over her head.

TWO

"Oh, ha, ha," Angela tittered. "My bad." She heaved herself up onto her forearms and tried stopping her head from spinning. She was grateful, at least, the Helmans hadn't caught her suspended above ground in the backyard.

"That was quite a stunt. You okay?" Jeff Helman peered over the fence.

"Yeah, yeah. I'm fine." Every bone in her body ached. "Everything's fine." Angela plastered a smile on her face. She hated this conversation, having to convince the Helmans of her wellbeing — smiling and chatting and pretending she was okay while trying to ignore the throbbing pain emanating from the general area of her lap. She winced, pushing her leg down to the ground with the rest of her bruised body.

"Is there some way we can help you?" Jeff stepped over the two-foot section of wall and offered his hand.

"Naw. I don't need help." She avoided his outstretched hand and placed her own on the wall. With herculean effort, she heaved herself onto her knees and then into standing position. "I could use a ladder, though. Do you have one?" Angela grimaced. Did she just ask for a ladder? Sheesh! It was late. She wasn't thinking clearly. But she wouldn't try climbing that wall again.

"A ladder?" Jeff frowned. "If you're locked out, we should call Ted." Jeff pulled out his cell phone, eyeing her with one raised eyebrow, and flipped the phone open. "Maybe an ambulance is in order."

"No!" Angela screeched, then cleared her throat. "I mean, please don't. I'm not locked out. I just need to get into the backyard." She touched Jeff's arm hoping a bit of neighborliness would soften him up. "Ted has to work early tomorrow. I hate to wake him. And an ambulance, well, that's totally unnecessary." She would die first.

"What are you doing out here?" Rebecca interrupted. Of course she wouldn't believe Angela's 'exercise' story. The woman was always suspicious.

"Ha, ha." Angela smiled haplessly. "It's the funniest thing. Have you got a couple minutes? It's a really funny story." To stall for time, she rubbed her sore knees and hips, then straightened and un-kinked her neck.

"Get her the ladder." Rebecca pursed her lips. "It's two a.m. We don't have time to listen to some freaking pointless story."

Her ploy had worked. Angela smiled to herself. Who wanted to chat in the wee hours of the morning? Not her, and not ever with Rebecca Helman.

Jeff came back with their ladder and put it against the wall.

Angela hobbled forward, peering up at it. "Wow. It's tall." She chewed a fingernail. Even worse, the ladder kept going forever after it touched, ever so lightly, the fence.

Perhaps a call to Ted was in order.

"That's our wall." Rebecca grumbled. "What if she breaks it? Who's going to pay?"

"It's not your wall—it's our shared wall," Angela said. Did the woman have no sense of neighborliness? Frowning, she eyed the ladder ominously. Waking Ted still seemed less practical. She could climb the stupid ladder. Ted needed his rest.

"This most certainly is our wall." Rebecca thrust her hands to her hips. "Your wall is over there." She pointed. "On your side—the apparently inaccessible side."

Angela hadn't climbed a ladder in nearly forty years. It hadn't gone well for her then. Too clumsy, always too clumsy. But she wasn't a chicken or a crybaby — and she wouldn't let the Helmans know. "Never show weakness in front of your enemy," she muttered to herself.

"What did you say?" Rebecca glared.

"It's all the same wall." Angela shook away the painful memory of ninth-grade gym class. Her 'friends' had dared her to climb the custodian's ladder in order to retrieve their stuck basketball. Halfway to the top, she and the ladder had toppled backward. Angela had cried. They had laughed and teased and called her, "Crybaby Benoit."

Angela heaved a breath and stepped onto the first rung. It creaked. She looked down at the aluminum step. How old was this ladder anyway?

"She'll break our ladder, too." Rebecca pursed her lips.

Choosing to ignore the insidious witch, Angela took another step and coughed, hoping to cover up the creaking of the second rung. It didn't work.

"What do you expect me to do?" complained Jeff.

"I just don't know why she is suddenly our problem."

Did they think she was deaf, or what? Angela looked apprehensively from the ladder to the wall. All she had to do was lift her derriere and move one foot's distance. But how?

"Ted is a great guy and a good neighbor. I can't leave his wife out here." Jeff held fast to the ladder.

Yep. Ted the Terrific. Everybody loved him. She did too, of course. Peering over the fence, she gazed down to her lawn below. Six feet looked a lot different from this angle. Rappelling the Grand Canyon couldn't be more dangerous.

Angela could break her neck.

"Why doesn't she get on with it?" Rebecca tapped her foot impatiently.

"Yes, well, this is the easy part." Angela shrugged, wanting nothing more than to stick her tongue out at the she-devil. She gripped the cement blocks, smiled half-heartedly and began the silent countdown that would mark the end of her life — one — two — three. Then, holding her breath and squeezing her eyes shut, she pushed down hard with her hands and heaved herself over and onto the skinny little wall.

The brick held fast.

Oh, yeah, I did it, I did it — Angela jigged a mental victory dance while breathing a sigh of relief. But, thinking she felt the wall wobble beneath her, she clutched it, heart racing, and opened her eyes.

"Are you going to keep us out here all night?" Rebecca was right under her, with Jeff trying his best to silence his wife's constant hiss.

Always the gentleman, or at least more polite than his wife, Jeff Helman heaved the ladder over the fence for her. Angela scooted closer, not daring to bring attention to her wings by touching them. Hopefully they weren't damaged. She looped her leg over a rung of the ladder, loosened her grip on the wall, and flung herself to the aluminum steps, and then made her way down into her yard. The ladder groaned its complaint every step of the way. Her exercise-starved body groaned its complaint every step of the way as well. She and the ladder made quite a team. Musical even.

As soon as she stepped onto her lawn, the ladder disappeared up and over the fence without her ever saying she'd made it down. Angela leaned against the grey brick, exhausted.

"Did you see that?" Rebecca asked. "You'd better make sure the ladder is still straight."

Angela heard a muffled reply and tittering. She shook her head, and winced at the pain. "It's time to get into the house and away from those creeps."

The echo of her neighbors' amusement got louder with each step Angela took. By the time she walked the few steps to her back patio, the Helmans' loud riotous laughter filled the otherwise silent neighborhood.

One day she'd get even.

No. Angela shook her head. She was a Christian woman. What she meant was, forgiveness is divine.

Whatever.

With her pride currently nonexistent, Angela hobbled inside and went to her bathroom, standing a moment in the dark and then leaning against the sink. What was she going to do? Tylenol—that would work for now.

She reached into the medicine cabinet, got herself a couple, and chugged them down with water from the sink. The tepid water dribbled down her chin and felt good against her warm face so she splashed a little more on her cheeks and forehead.

Her feet were hot like she'd walked on coals. So, keeping the water on, she hefted a foot into the sink and let the water run over it. She could almost see the steam rise. Angela grabbed the hand towel and dried her foot and, taking care not to slip, she repeated the process with the other foot.

"Helmans." Angela gritted her teeth. Their unkind judgments were so aggravating, and everything seemed mixed up. She wanted to cry. In fact, she did shed a silent tear or two. Sleep deprivation—that was her problem—it always made her an emotional wreck. She cried about every little thing when the least bit tired.

"Sleep." Yes. "I need sleep." Angela limped to the bedroom. Nervous for the morning's reveal to Ted, she touched the edge of her wings and slipped in to bed beside her loving husband of thirty-two years, feeling more alone in her fairy life than ever.

"Good morning, sunshine."

Angela could have sworn she had barely closed her eyes.

She did swear.

Angela had never been a morning person—even less so when she didn't sleep at night. She kept her eyes closed and tried to ignore her husband's insufferable cheerfulness. Why did she have to get up?

"Rise and shine, sleepyhead."

"Just a few more minutes," she croaked. Ugh! She'd meant to say just a few more hours. She was so sleep deprived she couldn't even get time straight.

"I let you sleep as long as I could." Ted straightened his tie in the mirror. "Breakfast doesn't make itself." He pulled her out of bed and kissed her forehead. She stood limp and lifeless, refusing to open her eyes. Then she remembered the night before—the good part.

Opening her eyes, Angela smiled. "Hey, do you notice anything different about me?" Her stomach fluttered with anticipation.

Ted squeezed his eyebrows together with his mouth pulled to one side. "Um, you haven't showered yet?" He grinned broadly at his joke. She was never showered by six.

"No. That's not it." Angela frowned. "Try again." She turned her back toward him, blinking timidly over her shoulder.

His impatient frown witnessed his dislike of her 'what's different' game. Unfortunately, it was one of her favorites.

"I'll give you a hint." Gyrating her shoulders she stepped closer. Maybe the wings had flattened against her during the night. Her nerves bubbled wildly and she hoped finally for his acceptance of her fairy culture. "Feel my back." Angela wiggled her eyebrows.

"Anj, you know I've got to get to work." He frowned and stepped away. "And the kids need a ride to school. Quit horsing around and get breakfast ready. If you want to, we can do it tonight."

Knowing his meaning, a wave of hurt washed over her. It was Mother Nature's cruel joke. They'd had a blissful first year of marriage, making love regularly—then the kids came. She'd been too worn to a frazzle changing diapers and cleaning crayon off the walls to appreciate his needs—until now.

Now her body was changing. For whatever reason, all those changes increased her desire for passion. Angela couldn't get enough of Ted. She always wanted him touching her, kissing her, making her feel desirable.

He didn't seem to want any of those things anymore. All he wanted was to watch television and fall asleep in his recliner.

She felt needy.

He hugged her and kissed her cheek. "I'm sorry. I didn't mean to upset you. It's just that the kids are waiting."

She wiped the angry tears from her eyes and tried again. "But don't you feel them?"

"Feel what?" He looked at her now, questioning.

"My wings!" Sheesh, sometimes he could be so obtuse.

He clenched his jaws together, upset.

When they'd first married, he'd found her "fairy fixation," as he'd later termed it, endearing. As the years passed, however, he'd grown less tolerant of fairy culture, and even less so of her immersion in it.

Now she was curious. Why hadn't he felt them? She stormed to the mirror, turning to the side.

They were gone!

She gasped, tears spewing from her bloodshot eyes. "I had wings last night. I saw them! I felt them!" Angela cried alone at the mirror until Ted took her hand and brought her back to their bed. He helped her in and covered her with the sheet.

"I think you deserve a rest. You just stay here and sleep as long as you need."

"What about breakfast?" she bawled. It couldn't have been a dream.

"We'll have cold cereal. Your famous waffles can wait until tomorrow." He squeezed her hand reassuringly.

"I had wings," Angela wailed. "I even flew." Her heart hurt.

"Sure you did." He kissed her forehead and left the room.

What was going on with her? Were her fairy wings merely a dream? Angela didn't understand how it could be—but if not, why hadn't the fairies welcomed her?

Angela didn't intend to rest for long. She wanted to compose herself, shake the bizarre episode from her memory, and at least send her children to school with an "I love you," but as soon as Ted pulled the curtains shut, she fell into complete oblivion.

THREE

Not knowing how long she'd been content in her blank oblivion, Angela discovered herself, all too soon, standing somewhere strangely familiar although she couldn't imagine when she had ever been there before. "Is this another dream?" She rubbed her eyes with her fists and looked again. With extensive lawns and myriad trees, the place was enchanting.

Early morning light shining across the umbrella of an Arizona ash cast a fiery glow to the area. Angela wondered, vaguely, how she'd gotten there.

Others, small and magical were nearby. Her heart skipped a beat—the fairies had come for her! Finally. They were only fifty years late, but that didn't matter anymore. Completely forgetting her dream theory, Angela nearly floated as she stepped toward the miniature women.

"Yoo-hoo! Hello!" Angela hurried forward. She must have gotten there late, and not wanting to miss a thing, she headed toward the front.

Sitting cross-legged on the ground, they were listening to someone speak.

"Pardon," she said, maneuvering through the group. "Don't mind me." She stepped forward, felt a sharp pain on her foot, and looked down. "Oops. So sorry. Did I tear your dress?" Angela knelt. "I can sew. Let me take this home. I'll fix it right up." The outfit was pretty small though and she'd never been good at making doll clothes. Not even for Barbies, which were significantly larger than these women. "I can fix this." She gave a determined nod. "I can." She reached toward the fabric.

A fairy whipped out her wand and struck Angela with a sharp jolt of electricity.

"Ouch!" She pulled her hand away and stood. "What'd you do that for?" She looked around at the frowning and impatient sprites.

The speaker at the front motioned for Angela to sit.

"Oh, my apologies." And, even though it had been years since she'd sat on the ground on purpose, she started downward to join the fairies. Pausing midway, she glanced around. "Can't one of you whip me up a lawn chair?" She lifted her eyebrows.

Holding their hands to their ears, they looked to the woman at the front.

The wait was too long.

Angela's knees creaked and popped, giving way completely — her derriere slamming to the earth with a reverberating thud, knocking several nearby fairies into the air with a puff of dust.

"Ow," she groaned.

"Angela fairy-human," said the fairy at the front with an air of disdain. "For fifty years you have made a mockery of our culture—"

"I have not." She jerked back at the insult. "If anything—"

"You have joined yourself to a man who refuses to believe. You have raised children who do not believe."

It wasn't for lack of trying.

"We would not have called on you, blessed you with our cherished wings, had you not made that rash and ill-formed wish fifty years ago." She looked into the distant shadows. "The expiration date is near and we have no choice but to grant it. At least for a short time."

"Oh." That was blunt. "But why'd you grant me the wish at all if you didn't want to fulfill it?" She'd always wondered why they hadn't made her a fairy right after her mother passed away. Her spirits sank at the revelation they hadn't wanted her.

"Your mother was an amazing woman. It was her desire." She put her hands to her hips. "We granted the wish against our better judgment, and see where it has gotten us." She flipped her hand dismissively. "Silly costumes, plastic wings, a house-full of fairy statues, and a family who doesn't respect our culture."

"But I'm here now," Angela said, trying to regain her sense of hope. "There must be some way I can prove myself—show you that I am my mother's daughter. I can be amazing. I can." She chewed her bottom lip, hoping they'd agree.

The lead fairy didn't speak right away.

Angela worried. Her knees hurt. She fidgeted and finally lifted her leg, rested her arm on her thigh, and pushed herself to stand, no easy feat. She stumbled and stepped back to gain her balance, immediately looking down. "I didn't squish anyone, did I?"

The lead fairy arched an eyebrow. "There is the matter of the green-eyed pixies."

"Yes, yes. Green-eyed pixies," the others cheered, and winked at one another.

"Wait. Lead fairy? Are you ... Are you the fairy queen?" Angela's eyes widened. She must be.

The others flitted to Angela. "Let us teach you about those horrible green-eyed pixies." Fairies pulled her clothes, trying to get her to move to the front.

"I am," the lead fairy said.

She was! This diminutive royal was the fairy queen! Angela's mind buzzed with thoughts, questions, ideas. She broke away from the other fairies and hurried forward unaided. As she did so, a name floated in the air and seemed to descend, taking hold in her mind. *Tatiana.*

"You're Tatiana, the Fairy Queen." Angela stopped abruptly,

pressing her fingers to her mouth. All of Angela's books on fairy lore suggested it was against the rules for humans to meet the queen herself. Even sightings of regular fairies were rare.

"It is an honor, O Queen." Angela bowed.

All the fairies grimaced, covered their ears, and flew to the nethermost corners of the magical land. Only Tatiana remained.

"Angela, fairy-human — that is what you are. For now. You need not use your human voice to address us. Our ears are sensitive." She brushed against her left ear with her fingers. "And your voice is too loud."

"Shall I whisper then?" Angela whispered. This was so exciting!

"There is no need. Your whispers jumble together like the rushing of great waters, making you difficult to understand. Address us with your thoughts and we will hear you."

"*Wow!*" Angela clapped her hands. "*Monumental!*" In all her years of believing in and hoping to be a fairy, here she was talking to the queen herself! She would rock their world with her amazing skills and make them regret not granting her wish sooner.

"You are pleased to meet us, then?"

"Oh, yes!"

The queen grimaced.

Angela, realizing her mistake, thought, "*Oh, yes!*"

"Will you join us, then?"

"*It has been my life's desire. Yes, O Queen. I am honored that you ask.*" And that was putting it mildly. Angela's wings appeared and without her knowledge or permission, she found herself floating in air.

The fairies surrounded her, singing and dancing and praising her name. Had it been that easy? Had they already accepted her? Angela laughed in an attitude of pure bliss while the other fairies, none bigger than six inches tall, adored her.

Yeah, she could get used to this.

At home, she felt more like Cinderella — all housework and no fun — and definitely under-appreciated. Angela basked in their attention, thinking briefly of her family, of Ted, and of Leanne who carried Angela's first grandchild. If only they believed in her.

"Silence!" Tatiana glared at Angela.

The tiny fairies rushed back to the lawn, once again sitting cross-legged. Angela rubbed her temples. What in the world? It felt as though the queen was burning a hole through Angela's head. She wasn't prone to headaches, but this was a doozy.

"I am not used to being interrupted."

"*Of course.*" Angela nodded. She needed a book on fairy etiquette.

Tatiana glared at her.

Angela bit her lips together. No thinking.

"As I was saying, the green-eyed pixies have come to our city. Do we want them here?"

"No!" the other fairies shouted.

"They're using their spells to cause a multitude of anger and discontent," Tatiana said. "Will we allow them to continue?"

"No!" they shouted.

Anger? Discontent? Yeah, Hannah and Derek were way moodier than usual. Come to think of it, she had been too. Angela wiggled closer. That doctor of hers — what did he know? Angela wasn't old. Pixies, not menopause, were the reason for those stupid mood swings.

Oh, whoops. Angela was missing stuff. She floated closer to hear.

"Will we let the pixies steal our homes?"

"No!"

"Then let us cast the pixies out and keep our kingdom safe."

"Yes, O Queen, we will!"

Kingdom? Was she in England? Angela looked for something that might give her a clue as to her surroundings. A castle, maybe — but everything still resembled Arizona — the lighting, the long block wall, houses in the distance. The palo verde and mesquite trees especially were a dead giveaway.

Duh! Angela whacked the side of her head — she was in Freestone Park a few miles from home. She hadn't been here in years, but no one could have torn her away if she'd known this was some magical kingdom.

There was a long pause. The fairies glared at Angela, and Angela felt that same piercing sensation at her temples. She held the side of her head. *"That's right. No thinking. Sorry."*

"I'm counting on my faithful subjects to thwart those dratted pixies."

Thwart? Who says that? It must be some kind of joke. Angela bit back a smile, peering at the miniature women more closely and wishing she had glasses. Were they the fairy police?

Tatiana paused again, appearing annoyed. The backs of the others stiffened.

Angela tucked her head down. They'd heard her. That would be hard to get used to. She stared toward the front.

"Your fairy breath," Tatiana continued, "gives the pixies amnesia and makes them harmless."

A pixie with amnesia? How would that work? Angela's lip twitched. They were making this hard for her. Would a pixie know she was a pixie with amnesia? Would they take her to a pixie hospital – in a toy ambulance? Angela barked a laugh.

Everyone turned, glaring, hands over their ears.

She zipped her lips. Clearly these fairies hadn't had any fairy juice; they were a bit on the angry side.

One of the other fairies, prodded a fairy next to her. "Look how big she is," she said, and stuck out her tongue. They pushed each other forward, others joining them.

Angela's lips formed a dissatisfied smirk.

The chattering fairies were shapely and cute. Their wings shimmered all the same beautiful colors as hers, but were smaller and translucent.

Angela was more like Gulliver mingling with the Lilliputians, and not at all like a cute fairy. It kind of ruined her moment and Angela frowned at the sensation of feeling more ginormous than usual.

Everything about her was thicker, why not her wings too? She sank slowly back to earth. Would she ever fit in to anyone's world? One size did not fit all. She was too big for fairies, too quirky for humans.

"Silence!"

The tiny fairies rushed back to the lawn.

Angela rubbed her temples, watching the fairies obey, and trying to alleviate the pain. Whatever Tatiana's trick to cause the headache of obedience, she needed to learn it and try it on Derek and Hannah.

Tatiana's left eye twitched. "Angela fairy-human, if the pixies triumph, our world will be no more. Our colony will be forced back to our motherland never to return. If left to their own devices, the pixies will wreak havoc on both of our worlds." Tatiana lifted her eyebrows. "Will you help us?"

They needed her. It warmed Angela's soul, and she bowed. "*Yes, O Queen. I said I would help, and I always keep my promises.*" She rose and made an X over her heart.

"Just like when you were five." Tatiana tsked. "Always rushing into things and not weighing the facts before you decide." The corner of her lip turned up.

"*Decide? Weighing the facts?*" Angela peered at Tatiana. "I *decided fifty years ago.*"

"As you wish." She swirled her wand over Angela's head. "We fairies are born to bring about peace and joy—but this is war!" The gathered fairies cheered.

"*War? Wait, what?*" Angela bent closer. Had she missed something?

"Angela fairy-human, you have until All Hallow's Eve"

"*For what?*" She frowned.

The other fairies joined hands with Angela. "We like to feast and party every day." They floated into the air in unison, and danced in circle.

"*Feasting? Partying?*" Angela threw Tatiana's warning to the back of her mind. *"This is the life!"* To heck with vacuuming and dusting and all the mundane chores at home.

As they danced, Angela sank to the earth. Tatiana's cryptic message worried a hole in her chest. All Hallow's Eve was seven weeks away. What would happen then?

Something shiny and green flew past the corner of her eye. The other fairies saw it too and, leaving Angela on the grass, rushed for cover.

"What's going on?" Angela wanted to help, to prove herself to her new friends.

"The green-eyed pixies have come. Help us!" several of the fairies chimed in unison.

"Of course." But how? What did they want her to do? She hoped they wanted her to stay safe. Angela ran behind a nearby rock and cowered there. If something terrible happened, what would Ted do? How would he even find her? She chewed her fingernail.

Tatiana stood forward. Wand in hand, she flicked it masterfully. A flash shone like a prism. The many colors flared, and then faded. Tatiana hovered above while putting her wand away. Angela inspected the spot. Nothing was there but charred earth.

That was something. Angela furrowed her brows. But what? Had there been pixies? If Tatiana could get rid of them that easily, what did they need her for?

"A celebration is in order. The pixies are gone," Tatiana said. "For now."

Before Angela knew what was going on, she was sitting in front of a large feast spread out on the lawn. The fairies drank nectar and ate little bits of fruit. Their names came occasionally to her mind just as Tatiana's had. Fai'la, one of the queen's helpers, offered her a cup shaped like the bell of a miniature daffodil. It reminded Angela of her birthdays as a young girl.

Someone took her hand. *"Brai'la"* They joined another group and danced on the soft grass. This was the best time ever, even if she was big! They spent the magical hours in merriment, and that was plenty fine with Angela.

The sun shone through the bushes, and the other fairies seemed to tire. One by one, they walked to a nearby body of water, beckoning her to join them as they took rest among the bushes. The idea thrilled her and she started to follow, but stopped mid-step. Hello. She was married. She needed to get home. Ted would miss her, and she would miss him.

"You have done well as a fairy." Tatiana's lips lifted. "Meet us back here tomorrow night and we will see how you fare."

How had she gotten there to begin with? The thought of leaving this bliss to return to a life of cleaning toilets made the pit of her stomach heavy.

Suddenly, Angela heard a sucking noise like water circling down a large drain. Something tugged at her head, her body stretched, and she felt the bizarre sensation of being squeezed through a vortex. She opened her mouth to scream, but nothing came out.

FOUR

Her head spun as though she'd spent the last hour twirling in circles. When her vision cleared, she was back in her bed. "Oh," Angela groaned. Her stomach churned as though she had the stomach flu. It took a moment before her body settled down into her mattress and she was able to think. What just happened had been epic.

She had gone to Freestone Park and come back again. Without her car.

Had she gone in person or was it some wacky out-of-body experience? She pressed her hand against her spinning head, held her churning stomach. Yeah. She'd been there with her whole self — like she'd teleported or something. Who in their wildest dreams could have imagined such a thing?

Despite her unsettled stomach, a smile stole across Angela's face. She had almost given up hope, almost decided to quit wearing her aging fairy costume, and had even considered living a dull, ordinary life. Like Ted.

Other than the times when her children were born, Angela didn't remember a time when she'd felt so complete. She lay there for a few minutes basking in her own glow. Ted didn't currently believe, apparently that was an issue, but he would soon. He had to.

When her stomach settled, she got up and danced through the

house cleaning every corner. Fairies were real! And she had been a miniature sprite all night! But wait ... night? The dust rag dropped from Angela's hand. What day was it?

Ted had put her to bed just before he went to work. He would have woken her up if she was still sleeping when he got home. The kids' banging in the kitchen and scrounging for leftovers would have awakened her before that. Something wasn't right. Angela rushed into the den and brought their computer to life. In the monitor's bottom right-hand corner, she saw the truth.

It was still Monday.

Stunned, Angela walked to the kitchen. It was lunchtime. Is this what it felt like to lose your mind? That dream was lifelike. Real. Like it actually happened. If it was a dream, did that mean fairies weren't real? That could not be a possibility. Not after last night and whatever this latest episode was. It had happened. It had.

She opened the refrigerator out of habit and stared inside.

The sound of bell-tones filled the air.

Angela had specifically chosen their doorbell chime because it sounded like fairy twinkling — whatever that was. She was reluctant to speak to anyone, and irritated that someone — probably a salesman — was imposing on her perplexing day. She pressed her hand against a sudden headache, and went to answer the front door.

"Hello, Ms. Anderson."

Rebecca Helman. This day was not going well. Any day with Rebecca Helman in it was not a good day. Angela started to close the door.

Rebecca put her foot in the way. "Ted, um, your husband," Rebecca straightened and pulled at the shirttail of her designer blouse. "Mr. Anderson came by this morning and asked me to check on you." Rebecca smiled sweet as sugar as she thrust a bowl of ramen soup into Angela's unwilling hands. "I made this especially for you."

Rebecca had made offhand efforts to be friendly before. Those efforts always ended with Angela being the focus of gossip. She didn't trust that barbaric bat. The soup looked good, though.

"Jeff and I were just so surprised to see you last night, perched on our—"

"Our fence. Jointly," Angela growled, finding her voice.

Rebecca should have forgotten that whole episode by now, and besides, the Helmans' complaint about the conjoined fence was a moot point. The fence hadn't sustained any damage whatsoever.

"Yes, well. I suppose you're right." Rebecca grimaced and continued. "But, like I explained to your husband—I'm surprised he didn't know anything about it—I thought you two were so close. The perfect marriage and all." Rebecca trailed off for a second with a faraway look. "Anyway, you hadn't told him about your little escapade in the neighborhood last night in your fairy costume?"

Rebecca ended it in a question as though hoping Angela would make her day by doling out all the juicy details. As if. But something startling occurred to Angela—Rebecca's eyes were green. Angela shut hers quickly—before being zapped into oblivion. Then she formed an O with her lips, and taking a deep breath, she exhaled into Rebecca's face.

"Aak!" Rebecca Helman coughed, spat (which was highly uncustomary for her), and sneezed. "How rude! Angela Anderson, whatever did you do that for?!"

Angela didn't answer. She didn't open her eyes, but kept them shut tight until she heard the stomping sound of Rebecca Helman's departure. Angela dared to look just as the faux-friend disappeared into her own home.

She heaved a sigh. "Crisis averted," she said, and closed the door. In the safety of her kitchen, Angela tasted the soup.

"A hint of nutmeg." It was delicious.

She was instantly ravenous and couldn't shovel it fast enough. That was until she got near the bottom of the deep bowl. There was something there. Something black and crunchy with legs.

"I'm such an idiot!" Angela screamed.

Barely making it to the bathroom, Angela's stomach voluntarily emptied itself of the soup. She brushed her teeth, threw the toothbrush away, and then gargled five times with antiseptic mouthwash to make sure.

Angela stormed back to the kitchen, took the bug out with a spoon, washed the bowl, wrote, "Thanks for the treat," on a pink sticky note, and then placed the bug carefully back inside. What kind of cancerous toad put bugs in people's soup?

She marched next door, grateful to see their car gone, and thrust the bowl on Rebecca Helman's doorstep. That wildcat's last name should be Hell-woman instead.

Special soup indeed.

Turning from the Helmans' front step, Angela stumbled to hers feeling unusually exhausted. Her eyes kept closing. She wasn't in the habit of napping during the day, but she barely had time to shut the front door and get to her bed before falling asleep.

She dreamed of pixies chasing her, with a glaring, green-eyed Rebecca Helman leading the way; of Tatiana saving her at the very last minute; and of Ted shaking his head in disapproval.

Three hours later, Angela looked at the clock with bleary eyes. Had she really been napping the afternoon away? It was past time to start dinner. She crawled out of bed. What had caused her to sleep so long?

Holding the wall for support, she went to the kitchen and gazed in the refrigerator. The package of ground beef screamed of spaghetti and meatballs. She had the perfect recipe, and set to work.

Pixies indeed. She'd been hallucinating. Her life was here — as a culinary queen and homemaker extraordinaire.

FIVE

"Dinner was great." Ted kissed Angela's forehead.

"Thanks." Angela put her elbows on the table, and with her chin resting in her hands, stared into space.

"No, I mean it," he said. "If you had only cooked the noodles for a minute less, they'd have been perfect."

"Noodles overcooked?" She liked them tender. Did fairies eat spaghetti?

"You seem kind of distracted. Is something wrong?" Ted sat in the chair beside her. He brushed his fingers across the side of her face, pushing a lock of hair gently behind her ears. "I'm here if you want to talk."

"Hmm?" Angela looked up. "I'm just tired."

"Didn't you have a good nap this morning?" Ted took her plate and put it in the sink.

"Nap?" Indignation roiled inside—someone should arrest that neighbor. She should file charges. "Yeah, I had a nap, all right. Thanks to that rat next door." She stood and started pacing.

"Oh, good. Mrs. Helman brought the soup over then?"

"Soup?" She flung her hands into the air, then let them rest on her hips. "More like poison in a bowl."

"Is she not a good cook? Talk to me." Ted rested his hand on the counter. "What's going on?"

He sounded concerned. Angela sat beside her husband. Could she tell him? Ted inches from her face, his blue eyes a song to her soul. How could she not?

"I have wings," she said. "When I sleep, the fairies take me to their magical world." She smiled. "It's at Freestone Park."

"Right. If you want help with the dishes all you have to do is ask."

Scratching her forehead and combing her fingers through her hair—her graying hair, she criticized—Angela tried thinking of something Ted might want to hear.

"Help with the dishes would be great." Nothing else came to mind.

"You're worrying me, Anj." Ted took her gently by the arm. "Let's get you to bed." He pulled her up and she snuggled his chest. "You'll feel better after a good night's rest." He walked her into their bedroom

"Yeah. I bet I won't even have dreams tonight." She plopped down on the bed. Her dreams weren't usually as vivid as they'd been last night. She could still remember every moment as though it had actually happened.

"Bad dreams?" Ted raised his eyebrow. "Or good dreams?"

He hadn't believed her. "Um, fairy dreams." Had she not just mentioned it? She sat up, hating the patronizing look on his face. Why could he not believe?

"You've spent your whole life dreaming about fairies." Ted sat her on the bed. "You need to find a hobby or something." He lifted her chin. "Why don't you join Rebecca Helman's sewing group. Crochet. I think that's what she called it. She said she'd love to have you. I think they call themselves the Happy Hookers." He forced a smile. "Funny, huh."

Angela plopped back on the bed directly under the ceiling fan, cooling her overheated pores. She didn't knit and she certainly didn't hook. "When did you become such great friends with Rebecca?" The hateful wench.

"She joined the Booster Club last week." Ted sat on the bed beside her and began pulling off his shoes and socks. "It was the meeting where we voted for new officers. Everyone voted her in as secretary. Didn't I tell you?"

"No." Angela sat up, shaking her head. She would have remembered that.

"Rebecca's willing to teach you how. To crochet, I mean." Ted grabbed his satin tiger-paw pajamas from the nearby drawer and put them on.

Angela folded her arms against her stomach. "I can't believe you want me to be friends with that woman. She had me kicked off of HANK, and I was one of the founding members. And that soup." Angela jumped to her feet. "She tried to poison me!" Angela's hands went to her hips as she scowled. "I am not going to be friends with that wretched excuse for humanity!"

"Poison you?" Ted smirked incredulously. "Don't be ridiculous. You haven't been part of the homeowners neighborhood committee for a year. Why would she have done it? What's her motive?" He went into the bathroom and grabbed his toothbrush.

"She's a green-eyed pixie, that's why." Angela stood in the bathroom archway. "And she put a bug in that soup you told her to bring over." She went to the cupboard and took out a new toothbrush while remembering her unexpected afternoon nap. "It had to have been something in the soup," she muttered. "Or maybe the bug was poisonous."

Ted rinsed his mouth and then put away his toothbrush. "There are a couple of flaws in your theory. You know that, right?"

"It's not a theory, and there are no flaws in my perfect reasoning." Angela put toothpaste on her toothbrush and began brushing her teeth. Ted always had to be right. He always had to have the last word. Sure enough, he faced her and started speaking again. *Blah, blah, blah!*

"For one, pixies are only a figment of your beautiful imagination."

He fluffed her hair.

Angela scowled. That was Ted's nice way of saying quirky or eccentric.

"For two, why would anyone put a bug in your soup? It's ridiculous."

"Why was there a bug in my soup, then?" He could shove that up his perfect reasoning.

"I don't know." Ted shrugged, his eyebrows scrunched together. "Maybe they haven't paid the exterminator. Maybe it fell off the tree in our front yard."

"Or maybe she's a pixie and did it on purpose to poison me." Angela took a clean washcloth, got it wet with the tepid sink water, and washed her face. Sometimes Ted was so single-minded.

"If she did it on purpose, which I don't think she did, you need to be the bigger person."

"Bigger, Ted?" She indicated her midsection. "Really?" She pulled the bedspread back with a flick.

"I didn't mean it like that, and you know it." He stood behind her and gave her a squeeze. "Take the high road, Angela."

Angela pulled away and sat on the bed.

"It's time to forgive and forget. Rebecca has offered you an olive branch, so to speak, and I think you should take it." Ted sat back on the bed and put his arm around her shoulder. "She does a book club once a month on Wednesdays. You could go to that if you'd rather."

Oh joy.

"Rebecca thought you might not be up to learning the crochet-thing, but she says the books her group reads are all easy."

"What?" Angela frowned. "She actually said that?" Angela flipped off her shoes. They accidentally landed across the room. "I don't crochet or knit because I've never been interested. Not because I'm not smart enough to learn. And easy books? Please." Angela stormed across the room and grabbed a pair of pajama bottoms. "If you'll recall, I majored in English!" She fumed as she finished getting ready for bed. "I'll join her silly book club if that'll make you happy. But don't be surprised if I end up sprawled out on the lawn, poisoned. She hasn't changed."

Ted took her in his arms and kissed her. "I don't care if you join any of her clubs. I just think it's time for you to get involved in something else — learn something new."

Angela nodded, and then slipped between the covers. Ted headed toward the bedroom door.

"Aren't you coming to bed?" she asked.

"I think I'll watch the news first." He closed the door behind him.

Of course Ted would let her fall asleep before joining her — no chance of hanky-panky then. Angela stared at the ceiling. When they were first married, Ted would never have let an early-to-bed evening go to waste. She turned onto her side and stared at the wall. Apparently, the nightly news was infinitely more interesting than an aging housewife.

All Ted's talk about Rebecca Helman, and thinking Angela might actually join a club with her — for a brilliant accountant he was occasionally obtuse.

Rebecca had acted superior the night before — and it had actually happened — Pea-head Helman had actually referenced it in the soup debacle that morning. Sheesh! The woman was ridiculous — and the bug poisoning — that had been on purpose.

Angela crept out of bed and tiptoed to her purse. If she so much as dreamt of wings tonight, there would be no upsetting the neighbors with her news. With a sly smile, Angela took her key ring, slipped it into her pocket and then climbed back under the covers.

SIX

Sweat dripped down Angela's forehead, her shoulders ached, her joints ached. She rolled onto her back and groaned, "Why, oh why?" If her body's inner thermostat would just correct itself, she could get some sleep. Just maybe. She had never been able to sleep on her back before, she wouldn't now, but the pain in her shoulder had returned (aching joints being another casualty of age).

She felt a lump underneath her. The covers, thrown to the side during her nightly sauna routine, were not the cause. And now, suddenly chilled, Angela pulled the sheets up and around her. Rather than disappearing, the lump increased in size and wiggled underneath.

They didn't own a cat.

Did she want to feel her back? If she did, and the wings were there again, what would it mean? She reached. Of course she reached, and a multitude of feelings coursed through her—fear, trepidation, skepticism, anxiety. They all melted together with anticipation and hope.

A thrill warmed her body (or maybe it was another hot flash) as she felt the soft and growingly familiar form of her wings. Extreme jubilation, it was time to fly!

"Ha!" She threw the covers off and sat up. No longer would she merely be thought of as Ted's wife, the invisible appendage who cooked and cleaned. Tonight she, Angela Anderson, was about to follow in her mother's footsteps as a human-sized fairy on her first fairy mission. And it was well before Halloween.

Ted, the dear, had fallen asleep in his TV chair again. Taking the remote, she clicked the power off, covered him, and then hurried out the back door.

It didn't take long to remember how she had flown the night before. Angela pictured herself shooting into the night sky like Superman, and the wind rushed past her ears as she did so. As she ascended, something flew from the tree in their backyard. Before she could even think about redirecting herself, a bird flew smack into her chest.

"Oh!" Ouch. Didn't birds sleep at night? A shrill screech escaped her lips as Angela plummeted toward the general direction of her backyard. She flailed about frantically, grasping for something to brace her fall, but found only air.

Mere seconds before Angela spattered on the ground like so many bird droppings, her wings whooshed her away from certain death and toward her home.

"Wahoo!" Angela shouted excitedly. "I'm alive." Now she could show Ted her wings. She latched onto the patio's large supporting beam before crashing into the sliding glass door. The force of her movement swung her up to the ceiling with a slam and then down to the patio floor with a thud.

The security light flashed on.

Angela lay there like a bug under a microscope, waiting for the moment her head quit spinning. The cement was cool at least. If Ted saw her wings — saw her fly — he'd have no choice but to believe. He would think she was gifted. Not weird. And she could become a full-time fairy. In between cleaning house, of course.

Think of her monthly savings on gas alone.

Angela rolled to her side and, reaching for the post, pulled herself up — a feat more difficult than climbing that ladder the night before.

Letting go of the post, she tried to fly inside (her legs were of no current use for standing), but her wings began flying her backward and away from the house.

"Oh, no you don't!" Angela shouted to her misbehaving wings. "I'm going to show you to Ted." She lunged forward and grabbed the post again.

Her wings wanted to fly away. Angela wanted to fly into her house.

This was how she ended up in a tug-of-war between her will and her magical wings, her wings pulling against her like a spoiled child. Angela holding on to the post, shouting, "You'd better start behaving and let me in!"

"Anj?" Ted appeared in the doorway.

"Yes?" Without her immediate knowledge, Angela won the tug-of-war. The wings disappeared, and like a snapped rubber band, the power of her thrust landed her neatly at Ted's feet.

"Oomph!" She looked up into the face of her puzzled husband.

"What are you doing?" Ted knelt and extended his hand, helping her up.

Still woozy from the ordeal, Angela's knees wobbled. Ted wrapped his arm around her shoulder and helped her into the house.

"I thought you were asleep," he said. "What were you doing outside?"

There was no proof of what she'd been doing. Angela only had a few options: sound as though she was absolutely out of her mind, and say something like, "*I was coming in the house to show you my new wings, but they disappeared. Sorry.*"

That would never work.

Angela chose the second option: appearing sane. She said, "Ow." It was all she could come up with. Besides, her face and arms hurt.

"You're pretty scraped up." Ted helped her into their bathroom where Angela kept the first aid supplies. "So, are you going to tell me?" Ted glanced up at Angela as he helped cover her scratches in ointment.

"Ow, ow, ow! I'd rather not talk about it." She clenched her teeth and winced. She did need to talk to that fairy queen, though.

By the time Angela climbed into bed, she was slathered in first aid ointment. Between the ointment and another hot flash in full force, she felt somewhat like a roasting pig. Oink.

SEVEN

With hands joined, the fairies circled a tree trunk, dancing. The gurgling sounds of water, the backdrop for their play.

Angela gazed at the scene with more than a little trepidation.

The fairies bid her forward. "Come and join us."

Yeah, they were a jolly lot. Sure she'd join them. What would they do to her next, string her up in the tree? That fairy queen had a wicked sense of humor.

She had always wanted to be a fairy, though, so she would put up with their little games. For now.

Pretending nothing was wrong, Angela hurried to greet them. First item on her agenda: Figuring out what was supposed to happen on All Hallows' Eve. Were they warring with the pixies that night? She would stay the heck away if that was the case.

In her haste, she tripped over a tree root.

"Fairy-human Angela, you are too clumsy." Tatiana offered a small smile.

She sat on the earth rubbing her bruised knees, feeling foolish. How rude for Tatiana to mention this life-long problem of hers.

A flicker of anger flashed across Tatiana's face.

"*Clearing the mind of all thoughts.*" Angela put on a happy face. She would beat these fairies at their own game.

"Oops. Clearing all thoughts." All thoughts. She wouldn't think about how beautiful and shapely the other fairies were. Nope. She wouldn't think of it. Not at all. She especially wouldn't think of her flabby, 5'7" body sitting there with the lot of them. Trying to be one of them.

If she hadn't been body shy before (which she had been) hanging out with those shimmering beauties would give her an even bigger complex. Nope. *"I refuse to think about it."*

All of the non-thinking was hard though. Angela's head bobbed up and down as she fought sleep. Fought sleep? She was asleep. Wasn't she?

Bryn'ee, a blue-eyed fairy, nudged her.

"Not thinking here. Don't interrupt." Angela stared ahead.

Bryn'ee nudged her again. Reluctantly, Angela peeked over. The fairy gave her a small bag.

"Angela." Tatiana tilted her head upward. "You are only the second human to receive our magical gifts. You are to use them wisely."

"Dang straight." She was wiser than the wise in regards to magical stuff. Angela opened her miniscule bag and peeked at the quivering, shimmering mass inside. Fairy dust. This was too good to be true.

Tatiana nodded her approval.

The fairy dust looked thick, like gel, and rippled with her touch, but when she pinched it, it fell back into the bag in thousands of golden flecks. *"Awesome!"*

"You will use it sparingly."

Angela nodded, and shivered excitedly. *"I have my own bag of fairy dust."* This was even better than a banana split.

Tatiana glared.

"Right. No thinking."

"We have another tool." Tatiana raised a small, white pearlescent stick.

"A wand?" Angela's heart flip-flopped with glee.

A rumble of discord rose from the other fairies. What did she care? They would appreciate her soon enough.

Tatiana raised her hands and silenced them. "Fairy-human, do you accept these gifts, and vow to aid the fairies' every need?"

"*Yes, oh, yes, oh, yes! Yes! Yes!*" Angela jumped up and ran to the queen, fell to the ground with bowed head, and thrust her hand outward waiting for her wand. As soon as the wand passed into Angela's hands, she felt a powerful surge of magic course through her. "*This is it! I'm a full-fledged fairy!*" The others rushed to her side and danced around her.

"Silence!"

The fairies sat with their hands in their laps, looking forward.

Angela rubbed at the pain in her temples. She really needed to learn how to do that. Derek and Hannah could use a lesson on obedience.

"Silence!"

"*Silence,*" Angela repeated.

"There are a few rules and regulations you should be aware of." Tatiana then began speaking faster and quieter, her words garbled together like a hum.

Angela picked out, "believer" and "Ted" and "All Hallows' Eve." This would not do. "*What was that again? Speak slower, and louder.*" She worked her jaw around. "*Just a tad.*"

"Fairies cannot be married to non-believers." Tatiana put her hands to her hips. "Your husband must believe in fairies by All Hallows' Eve. And you must rectify the damage you've done with your children regarding our culture. They must believe as well by All Hallows' Eve. And you must perform one successful mission of our choosing."

"*By All Hallows' Eve?*" She'd always liked Halloween. But getting Ted to believe in fairies in seven weeks' time? That was a huge assignment.

Tatiana's brows pinched together. "Surely you can manage to

not bungle one mission."

"*Or?*" she asked. What would happen if she failed?

"That, you do not want to know." She made a small motion with her hands, and the fairies gathered around Angela. They were trying to distract her. Nevertheless, Angela had developed quite a taste for fairy nectar, and strawberries. Just as before, in the distant shadows, Angela saw green and glaring eyes.

"*Do you see that,*" she asked Ti'ana.

"What?" The fairy turned in the direction of Angela's pointing finger. "I don't see anything." This happened over and over again, with each of the fairies denying the presence of green-eyed pixies. Angela saw them, and became increasingly distressed, but she tried not to look. Perhaps it was a rodent. Her insides shivered.

EIGHT

How long had the alarm been buzzing? Angela opened her eyes. Ted was up. The shower was on.

The memory of green eyes flashed before her. Why had the fairies not seen them? Or had they? Those magical sprites were as clever and tricky as the pixies were. Angela needed to figure out what they were up to. She shook her head and yawned.

If her family didn't need her anymore, could she just roll over and go back to sleep? She did, in fact, lie there with her eyes closed, and then remembered—she had promised her family waffles for breakfast. Angela groaned. Derek and Hannah would expect her famous homemade waffles. She forced herself up.

Her eyes were dry and fuzzy. Her mind was too, but ever the dutiful mother, she got out the ingredients—flour, eggs, milk, oil. There was something else. Angela scratched her chin, and then beat the ingredients together. Salt. That was the missing ingredient. Grabbing the salt, she poured some into her hand and added it to the mixture.

She poured batter into the heated waffle iron and waited for it to cook. When the light turned green, Angela opened it and took the waffle out with a fork. At least she tried to. The waffle, neither crisp nor brown, was a rubbery, sticky alien glob.

"Baking powder." Angela heaved a sigh. "I forgot the baking powder." She grabbed it from the cupboard, added a tablespoon-full to the batter and tried blending it in. It didn't want to blend. At all. She smashed at it with a fork, whipped at it with a whisk, and then made pancakes out of the mess.

"Breakfast is ready." Angela placed the plate of slightly-alien pancakes on the table.

The kids came in first. "Where's the waffles you promised?" Derek asked while piling pancakes on his plate.

"I thought you'd like a change today." She handed Hannah a plate.

Hannah took a pancake, examined it closely, wiggled it and then plopped it onto her plate. The teens sat at the table, slathering syrup over their food.

"Ew! You need glasses, Mom." Hannah pulled something from her mouth. "You forgot to take the eggshell out."

That child was always so perceptive — budding chef that she was. (This was tongue-in-cheek. The only thing Hannah ever cooked was frozen corndogs.)

"I don't need glasses." Angela frowned, knowing she did. "And there are no shells in the waffles." None she saw, anyway. Angela got the milk from the refrigerator and put it on the table. "Now, eat your breakfast."

Hannah made a face. "I'm not eating that."

Ted came in. Angela watched as he glanced around the kitchen. His eyes stopped at the waffle iron — still open with batter smeared across it. He glanced at the batter-encased eggshell hardening in the sink.

"We saved you some," Angela said brightly, and brought him a plateful.

Ted looked past Angela to the kids. She turned in time to see them shaking their heads.

"You didn't sleep well last night." Ted took the plate and kissed

Angela on the cheek.

"No, I didn't. But I promised breakfast, and here it is." She smiled, hoping there wasn't any shell in Ted's pancakes and hoping his also had a little leavening.

He slathered butter over each one and drenched them in syrup.

Angela waited for him to take a bite.

He did.

She heard a crunch.

He stopped chewing.

"Gross!" Derek exclaimed. "You're eating eggshell."

Angela waited for Ted to spit out the mess and go to work hungry.

Ted gulped the food down and took another bite. "I don't know what you're talking about." He raised his eyebrows. "These are good." He took another bite. "Eat up, kids." Ted lifted his pancake-filled fork. "Your mother is a superb cook, and you should appreciate her efforts." He put the pancake in his mouth. Chewed. And crunched.

Pancakes shouldn't crunch. Angela closed her eyes, resting her hand against her mouth.

After he finished, Ted poured himself a tall glass of milk, paused for a moment and then went to the cupboard and pulled out a container of chocolate mix. He scooped some into his cold milk and stirred. "You work too hard keeping this place clean." Ted chugged the milk down as though he was a thirsty camel. "This stuff's pretty good." He wiped his lips. Would you like some?"

"No thanks." Angela shook her head.

"It's chocolate," he said in a sing-song voice, and left the container on the counter. "Promise me you'll take a nap again today." He waited for her reply.

"Fine," Angela said, though she had no intention of complying. Only old people and babies took naps.

"We've gotta go." He pecked her on the lips, hurried the kids out the door, and left.

The messy house was all hers. Yay. Clean it now or clean it later—

no one would do it for her. She surveyed the damage — later.

Angela opened the can of chocolate mix. It was an odd-looking can. But, whatever. Maybe it was a gift from one of Ted's clients. Too tired to care, Angela stirred some into a mug of cold milk.

It was yummy.

Ted was right. It was thicker and richer than their regular chocolate mix, with just a hint of a foreign spice. "What is that flavor?" It had a familiar taste. She would ask Ted where the mix came from and buy more. Angela sipped her first cup, trying to figure out the exotic flavoring, and then started another. She really should have something to eat, but a liquid breakfast, well, it was perfectly delicious.

With her mug in hand, Angela decided to work on the kitchen before taking on the family room — but her bed called to her. Beds don't really talk, but if they did, hers would have said:

"You're tired. I'm soft. Come lie on me."

She ignored the bed while taking dishes to the sink. For some reason, her kids and even Ted didn't know that's where dirty dishes went. She ignored the bed while washing the table and kept ignoring the enticing call of that bed clear until she took hold of the waffle iron to clean it. It was a mess.

After prying the waffle grids loose, because, yes, they had cemented themselves to the part that reads, "Do not submerge in water," Angela put them in the sink to soak and followed that dreamy little voice into the bedroom.

"Anj?" She felt Ted's warm touch. "Anj. What's going on?"

She opened her dry and scratchy eyes. Her mouth, dry like cotton. "Ted?" She saw the blurred form of her husband. He looked upset about something.

The kids.

"Something happened to the kids." Angela bolted up. Her

swimming head took her back down.

Ted was home early, and upset.

"Is it Derek?" She sprang from bed to save her son, twisted in the sheet, and fell.

Ted caught her and sat her on the mattress.

"Did he get in an accident? I knew we shouldn't let him drive." She clung to her husband's waist, heart thrumming, and sobbed into his shirt.

"Anj. Settle down." He rubbed her back. "Nothing's wrong with the kids." He petted her hair and turned her face upwards. "It's just that it's six o'clock and the morning dishes are still in the sink." He kissed her forehead. "I came in here to change, and you were in bed." He kissed her nose. "You haven't even dressed for the day, and the day's nearly over." He smiled. "I guess you had a good nap."

Angela ran her hands through her tangled hair. "I drank some of that chocolate milk for breakfast. That's all I remember."

"It worked, then." Ted nodded and smiled thoughtfully.

"What worked? What are you talking about?" Angela pinched her eyebrows into a frown.

"Huh?" He rubbed his whiskered jaw and looked away. "I just didn't know if you'd lie down. I'm glad you did." He quirked a smile and tugged on her hand. "The kids are gone for the evening. Let's go get a hamburger."

NINE

Steam rose from the bed. Angela rolled to her side, hoping to cool the fabric underneath. Keeping her eyes closed, she pretended not to be awake. But, as had become customary, once her mind arose to consciousness, like it or not, the rest of her body woke up too.

She worked to ignore the pressure on her bladder. Ironic. As large as her stomach had become—stretched out balloon that it was, it seemed that with the passing years, her bladder had become smaller. This was something her doctor had explained.

"The womb is like a balloon, small and elastic when new, but each time you blow it up, it and your surrounding organs lose some of that elasticity. It'll never be the same."

Poor balloon. Stupid doctor. As if she needed someone to tell her that. It was her body after all—she was living the dream, baby. All she had to do was look down. She could see her body. Nope, it hadn't snapped back into its pre-pregnancy shape. Ever. How long had the poor guy gone to school before learning that priceless tidbit?

Now, because of her bladder's minute holding capacity, sleeping through the night had become virtually impossible. And, when it wasn't that need waking her up, she woke up anyway for a variety of other reasons that all led to the same result—her having to get up in the middle of the night.

She heaved a sigh. Well, she knew what she had to do next. Go pee. Why, oh why did she have to wake up? She hated doing that little bit of business at night. Grudgingly she got out of bed, urged by her bladder's complaint, and went to the bathroom.

Angela glanced up while washing her hands, and saw the shadowed form of wings reflected in the mirror. This wasn't a dream. "I'm not crazy," she whispered, dried her hands hurriedly and felt around her — air — not a mattress. She was awake!

"Go-m Tigers," Ted mumbled from their bed.

Angela peeked around the corner to the sleeping form of her husband. Age and gravity had taken its toll on him too, but not like her, and it just wasn't fair. She had no idea how he could possibly still find her desirable.

Maybe he didn't.

Nevertheless, she couldn't go back to bed now. She had a mission to perform, and as she thought it, the command descended into her mind: "Fly around the neighborhood and find pixies."

She could do that. Angela bounced excitedly, and her knee popped. "Ow," she mouthed, rubbing the sore spot. Patting her pockets, she made sure her keys were still there, and tiptoed to the sliding glass door. She flipped off the security light and headed outside.

Angela Anderson would not blunder things. She would be the master of her own fate. She would conquer her fear of heights and be the hero in her own life at least. Tatiana had given her fairy dust and a wand. She patted her pockets again. Only her keys were there. She must have put her magic stuff somewhere safe. Should she go inside and get it? Angela drummed against her lips. Risk waking Ted? She shook her head.

It didn't matter if she had the magical stuff. The mission was to fly around and look for pixies. Angela didn't need a wand or fairy dust for that. She had her wings. The corner of her lip lifted, and she leapt into the night sky with only one goal in mind — German chocolate ice cream with extra coconut and pecans. Okay, so she had two goals—Angela would look for pixies on the way there and back.

Determined to avoid her green-eyed neighbor, Angela flew east. There was an open-all-night ice cream shop near Power Road. Don't ask how she knew. She squealed. Flying was fun when the heights didn't bother her. The night air blew through her hair and rippled her clothing as she flew toward Chillers Ice Cream for All Occasions.

Her weightless bliss was short lived when, in her peripheral vision, a fleck of green flashed past. The shock of it caused her to lose altitude. It was nothing. She was seeing things. *I'm being a fraidy-cat.* Why would the pixies bother her? Notwithstanding her pep talk, another flash of green, and another flashed by.

"Ouch!" She felt a pinch on her arm, swatted at it but there was nothing there. She felt another pinch, and another. This was too much. "This isn't my imagination."

Heart pounding, Angela turned and headed home. "Mission accomplished. I found the pixies," she called into the air.

A veritable curtain of green, all pixies, wands out, flew toward her wearing sardonic smiles.

"That hurts! Cut it out!" Angela ducked, lost her balance and plummeted downward. "The pixies are after me!" she screamed hoping Tatiana would hear. "I'm going to die!"

Angela cringed, waiting for the moment of impact. It would only hurt briefly. But—she couldn't die yet. She still had a family to care for. She peeked below. Someone's pool was getting closer and, remembering her wings, she wiggled them. They swooped her up and out of the strange backyard nanoseconds before plummeting to the pool's depths.

"There'll be no ice cream tonight." Angela headed for home. It was safer there. She sighed a tremor of relief at the sight of her wonderful beautiful home, and flew to the top of their tree, clutching it and looking around. Had the pixies followed her? Did they know where she lived? Was her family in danger?

The Helmans were home and the lights were on. Regardless of the fact that Tatiana had told her to use her gifts sparingly, Angela could do something to make that noxious weed regret the hateful rumors and vicious lies she liked to spread. Angela envisioned Rebecca cowering in the corner of her lawn, begging for mercy. "Please don't zap me with your wand," Angela squeaked in a falsetto-like imitation of the Hellcat. "I promise I won't gossip about you anymore!"

Yes. A wonderful dream. But Angela didn't have her wand.

Speaking of dreams, Angela was tired. She exaggerated a yawn. It was time for bed. Her going inside had nothing to do with two green eyes peering over the fence.

TEN

Angela lay blinking in bed and trying to gain her bearings. She looked at Ted's vacant pillow, frowning. Had the pixies stolen her husband? Where was he?

"Good morning, sunshine!"

"Aak!" Angela jumped.

Ted kissed her forehead. "Kind of tense this morning. Don't ya think?" He grinned. "Pixies? Really? You're so weird. Have you given up on the fairies then?"

She wasn't weird. Angela sat up ready to protest. It made her head swim. She closed her eyes and rubbed her face. "Did I say something in my sleep?"

"Did you say something?" He chuckled. "You kept me entertained for most of the early morning." Ted stepped into the bathroom and brushed his teeth. "The way you carried on, it sounded like a whole battalion of pixies were after you." He scoffed. "As if." Looking around the corner at her, he smirked. "You kept talking about your fairy dust and your wand." He flipped his head sideways with an air of drama. "If only I had my wand."

"I did not." Clearly she hadn't gone anywhere, had never been in any real danger. "You're just playing with me." She searched the recesses of her mind, trying to figure out the puzzle.

"It's the honest truth." Ted held his right hand up as though taking an oath. "I bet you're pretty exhausted after all that fighting, though. I thought you were going to rip the sheets in half." He disappeared into their walk-in closet and came back with a tie. "I told the kids they could go one more day without your yummy waffles and sent them over to the Helmans' to catch a ride to school."

"Helmans?" Angela pulled the covers to her chin, frowning. "You didn't."

"Oh, I did." Ted came close and lifted his tie out for her to see. "You like the color? It's the color of green and glaring pixie eyes. Oooooo!" He chuckled, and then kissed her forehead. "Well, I've got to get to work, but I'm thinking that you should probably stay in bed a while longer. Love you," he said, and left the room.

Angela sat in bed sulking and listening to his high-pitched and playful banter as he walked through their house. "I'm a fairy, and you'd better watch out. No! No! Don't zap me. I have magical powers but I left them somewhere. Ooooo! It's a green-eyed pixie."

Angela didn't move a muscle until after she heard Ted close the door to the garage, and then heard the garage door open and close.

Had she really just been in bed the whole time?

That stupid fairy kiss had happened when Angela was five. She pretended to remember it, but she didn't, and her parents were no longer around to ask. Recent memories rushed into her mind like waves in the sea — the fairies adoring her, Angela as their special guest — the banquet and dancing. She looked down in disbelief at her flabby, full-sized torso. "What's the likelihood of me being a fairy?" She frowned.

Rebecca Helman had green eyes. Was that where her deranged mind got the idea for the pixies? But, Rebecca had also mentioned Angela's wings. Angela reached back, trying to feel. Did she have wings at least? Of course not!

There was nothing there. They had never been there! Rodent Rebecca was a liar. Angela was worse than quirky — she was bizarre!

The worst kind of oddball! Her shoulders drooped — she was pathetic. None of it was real — it was all some crazy, three-dimensional dream. And Ted, her supposed knight in shining armor, was having a big laugh at her expense.

"Aaagh!" Angela screamed and flounced backward in bed. She hated that Ted laughed at her — she hated being deserving of his laughter.

But wait. She was supposed to have a bag of fairy dust, and a wand. Ted had indicated as much. Clinging to her last glimmer of hope, Angela sat up in bed and felt around in her tangled sheets searching for any sign of the dreamt of fairy dust and wand. There had to be evidence somewhere, anywhere. She searched the corners at the foot of the bed increasingly frantic. Nothing. The corners at the head of the bed. Nothing. Under her pillows? Nothing. Her shoulders slumped in defeat. The sheets were empty other than her.

Her lifelong desire to be a real fairy, with real wings, had finally sent her overboard, sanity-wise. Ugh! She was the weirdest of the weird. No wonder Ted had made fun of her. She was a laughingstock. What grown woman still believed in fairies — believed that she was one? She would call Leanne and forbid her to buy a fairy charm for the baby when it came.

Angela jumped up angrily. Her sheets were buttercup yellow, the color of all fairies' favorite flower. It was a blossom with a nicely shaped bell where fairies could cuddle into the soft petals and rest.

Well not this fairy — not anymore!

With a guttural roar, Angela ripped the sheets from her bed and marched to the closet for replacements, something pink or possibly blue.

She stood, dumbfounded. Every sheet set was the same color: Buttercup yellow. Angela slid down the wall with a groan. How long had she been living this fantasy?

ELEVEN

She blew into a brown paper bag. Angela needed to get a grip, and she needed one now! Her whole life was based on fantasy. Ted was right. She needed something else, something to bring balance back to her life. The corner of her mouth turned up in a wry smile. Something like getting dear hubby's romance gene sparked. Angela tossed the bag aside.

The cause of all her troubles was that old bed of theirs. Every time she got in it, she dreamed she was a real fairy. If she bought a new bed, her magical dreams would disappear, and Ted would use it for something other than sleeping. Hopefully.

She got up and flipped through the phone book, and then dialed Legendary Furnishings.

"Hello. Yes. This is Angela Anderson. I need a king-sized bed. I don't care what the frame looks like, but I'd like one of those nice pillow-top mattresses. Yes. Super deluxe would be wonderful. I need it delivered to my house. STAT." She'd always wanted to say that.

"No, tomorrow won't be fine!" Angela screeched. "I need it right away." What part of *STAT* did they not understand? "I'll pay double the delivery fee, and I'm willing to tip the driver."

"Yes. One p.m. would be wonderful." Angela sighed with relief. She gave the man on the other end of the phone her address and credit card number. Angela had a little money tucked away and would pay the card down tomorrow.

Then she remembered something. "Um, do you sell sheets? No?" Angela's heart sank. She needed to get rid of all evidence of her pathetic fairy weirdness, and those fairy-yellow sheets. Ted would laugh at her no longer. One quick glance at the clock assured Angela that she had time to run to the mall. "Okay, I'll see you at one then? Thank you." She grabbed her purse and raced off to J.P. Bauchman's Home Store.

Human-sized fairies? Ha! Fairy queens? Fairy dust? Wands? Hogwash! After a life of hoping, dreaming and endless waiting, Angela was done pretending. She needed to get a life! One without the dream of fairies unsettling her—and one with Ted feeling amorous. She ran her hands through her graying auburn hair—maybe she'd color it. Ted would look at her like she was twenty-five again.

For the most part, Angela stayed away from the mall. Just too much walking coupled with the irresistible desire to buy things she didn't need. Ted was an accountant, after all. He couldn't have his wife out spending the paycheck every week.

As luck would have it, Bauchman's was having a sale—fifty percent off. Today was the last day. The store looked like Christmas with all the banners and lights. Angela loved the way they had miniature rooms set up at every aisle showing off the different bedroom styles. She went from one to the other while trying to decide which one she liked best. They were all so elegant.

"Sheets, though. I need sheets." She forced herself away from the beautiful bedspreads and perused the sheets, picking a midnight blue set, a striped pink and burgundy set and a brown set with crazy geometric designs. Ted would like that one, maybe. Nothing at all fairy-like, she noted with satisfaction.

With her arms full of sheet sets, and on the way to the cashier, another new bedspread caught her eye with its rich earth tones. It was on clearance—ten percent above the fifty percent off—and she remembered the frayed bedspread at home. It had been a wedding gift from GrammaLee. "Ted will love it." Angela added the new bedspread to the pile. It came with a dust ruffle and pillow shams and was definitely a bargain at sixty percent off.

Her life would be forevermore fairy-free. A thud of panic slammed her chest and Angela gasped for air.

"Are you all right?" An older woman in line patted her back. "Choke on a piece of saliva? It happens to me all the time, sweetie. You'll be fine."

"Thanks." Angela gave the aging woman a feeble grin and pushed the thought of life without fairies way to the back of her subconscious. Hopefully Ted would fill her void.

Wearing a worn and outdated fairy costume every Halloween and filling her house with porcelain fairy figurines was one thing. Dreaming that she really was a fairy — that there actually was a fairy queen — and that they needed her for an important mission that must be completed by Halloween? That was something entirely different. *Sorry, Mom.*

The term certifiable nut-job came to mind. Quirky was just a polite way of saying the same thing. She, Angela Anderson, would give up the fairy nonsense. And she would prove it to her family on this very day. Her children needn't worry any longer about her embarrassing antics. Her subconscious had gotten it right. This was about gaining their respect — about their home being a safe-haven for her children and not a fairy den — about her finally growing up and moving on.

Back at home, Angela ran into her bedroom, grabbed all of the old sheet sets and the bedding from the floor and raced to the backyard. She piled them in the middle of the lawn, ran back to her bedroom, and with superhuman strength, pushed the old mattresses against the wall.

Their bed was magical. She knew it. To please her, Ted had bought it at a thrift store thirty-two years ago. It sported a relief of magical sprites carved along the headboard.

Angela pulled the metal frame off and lugged the aging headboard to the backyard. Nearing exhaustion, Angela tripped, dropped the headboard onto the pile and then fell to the top of the heap. She lay there for a moment trying to catch her breath.

The doorbell chimed. Ugh! Couldn't they have waited five minutes longer? Angela forced herself up and ran, or rather hobbled, to greet the furniture movers.

"You got here just in time." Angela dabbed the sweat from her forehead. "Man, it's a scorcher out there today." Scorcher was putting it mildly — the September sun was hot enough to melt the skin right off of some poor unsuspecting soul.

"This was a rush order?" One man, er, boy — let's face it, she had kids older than he was — tapped his pen against a clipboard. "For a Mrs. Anderson?"

"Yes. This is the place. Come on in and I'll show you where I want it." Angela led them through the house to her bedroom.

"Ma'am—" (Oh, how she hated that word!) "These mattresses need moved. We can't assemble the new bed with those in the way."

"I have an extra fifty if you'll take the old mattresses. Give them to charity." She grabbed her purse off the dresser and flashed a fifty at them while grinning hopefully.

"It's against policy." He and his helper eyed each other furtively.

"Let's make it an even hundred, then." Angela pulled another bill from her wallet.

"Those are good-looking mattresses. You sure you want to just give them away?"

"Charity." She eyed them sternly. "I want to give them to charity."

They took the bait and hauled the old mattresses to their truck saying they'd take them to a nearby charity shop, but Angela wasn't so sure they really would.

It wasn't their job, but they also assembled the new bed for her. Angela stared in amazement as, plank by plank, they put together an extraordinarily large bed — four wooden pillars ornately decorated with cast-iron vines and oak leaves shooting up from each corner.

Hmm. Angela pressed her fingertips to her mouth and looked it over suspiciously. She had said she didn't care about the frame, thinking they wouldn't bring one at all, not that they'd bring the most expensive frame in the store. The vines and oak leaves — well, she'd just have to pretend they looked more earthen than fairy-like.

Whatever. Stores didn't sell magical furniture. Angela smirked, and signed the receipt.

"Thanks." Angela led the way to the front door.

They stopped just inside. "We were told there was a tip in it for the quick delivery." They waited expectantly.

"Oh, yeah." Angela rolled her eyes and retrieved her wallet. There went her grocery money for the week — for the next two weeks. Sheesh!

After they left, she couldn't help but mumble about their greediness. "But I'm the one who offered a tip and double delivery," she conceded. It was the extra hundred for the old mattress removal that set her on edge.

Getting right to work, she pulled the geometric-designed sheets from their wrapper, made the bed with the new comforter and all, and then admired the room. It was beautiful. "I should have done this years ago."

It was getting late. Angela needed to dispose of the old stuff before the kids came home. Forget the kids, she wanted everything perfect for Ted and rushed up the stairs to Derek's room to get his lighter. She knew he had one. He knew he shouldn't. Angela wouldn't quibble about that little detail today; she needed that lighter.

She found it in his nightstand, grabbed it and rushed down the stairs, almost tripping in her haste, and ran out the back door.

The lighter flared to life with just the flick of her thumb. She touched it to a fabric edge soaked in lighter fluid, and stood back. Having six sets of buttercup yellow fairy sheets, her magical satin bedspread, the dust ruffle and pillow shams and then that headboard all wrapped in golden flame gave Angela a sense of satisfaction. It was bright — she should have worn her sunglasses — and it was hot.

The intense heat evoked memories of marshmallow roasting as a child. If only she had some. Wiping sweat from her forehead, Angela stuck the lighter in her pocket, put the lighter fluid back with the barbeque supplies, pulled a patio chair to the lawn and plopped tiredly onto the soft cushion. Intent on the blaze, she concentrated on breathing slow and even. After chasing around all day, it took a few minutes to calm her heart — it might explode — but she'd count it as her aerobic exercise for the day.

The headboard had nearly burned to ashes when Angela's ears perked to a new sound, something different than the crackling and hissing of the nearly defunct bonfire. The sound got louder and louder.

A siren.

What in the world? Hoping none of her neighbors were hurt or having a domestic spat, Angela ran through the house and threw open the front door to see the source of the emergency.

"Oh!" She found herself face-to-face with a man in a heavy fireproof coverall, black boots, and holding a red helmet in his hands.

"My name is Troy McCray, with the Gilbert Fire Department. We've had reports of a fire at this location."

Angela peered around his muscular frame and saw a fire truck at the curb, its siren winding down.

"Oh!" Angela's face flushed. "I'm having a barbeque," she lied.

"Ma'am, it's too big to be a barbeque." The man shook his head. "We saw the flames from our tower." He indicated the station several blocks away and across Guadalupe Road, and Angela saw the tower. Drat!

"I, I'm..." Angela didn't know what to say. She couldn't tell them the truth. *Sorry, I was burning my magical bedding, because I actually thought I was a fairy, wings and all.*

Yeah, not. They'd send a whole different truck after her then.

Maybe she could confess a portion and still appear reasonably sane. "I'm sorry, sir. I didn't know it was bad. I'm burning ... things. Rubbish." She hung her head and mumbled, "My sheets."

A smile formed across his face. He bit his lips closed as if to suppress a laugh, then put his fist to his mouth and coughed. "You're the nut, um ... woman who thinks she's a fairy." He couldn't hide the smile; it took up his whole face.

Angela blushed deeper. "I'll put it out."

"Let me help."

She didn't need his help but that didn't seem to matter.

Troy stood in the doorway. "Hey, Gabe, this is the fairy-lady's house," he called to the man in the truck. "I'm going in. You want to come?"

The fairy-lady? Great. All Angela needed was an audience come to witness the "quirky fairy-lady" and her latest stunt.

Troy stepped through the front doorway. Angela followed and noted with annoyance that as he walked he took in their living room and family room décor. The snoop.

"Your house is decorated ... normal." He sounded disappointed. "I thought it would look more magical, like a fairy kingdom or something." He looked to Angela for an explanation. That was a first for her, someone who didn't think a home sporting thirty porcelain fairies was crazy enough. Yeah, she ignored him.

Upon returning to the confines of her backyard, the strangest sensation came over her. Angela glanced toward the Helmans' house and frowned. The ends of a ladder disappeared over the wall. Had the emergency call come from the diseased rat next door? She wouldn't put it past her.

A flame licked high in her peripheral vision and Angela turned her attention back to the fire. It had gotten hot again while she was away—hotter than she had imagined it could. The polyester batting in the comforter had melted a large hole in the lawn. Angela went to the faucet, turned it on, and pulled the hose to the smoldering mass.

As she put the fire out, Gabe the fireman ambled next to her grinning, his white teeth accenting his tan skin.

"Selfie time, fairy chica!" He pulled out his cell phone. "What's your real name?" he asked, putting his arm lightly around her shoulder.

"Angela." She gulped, loudly, and looked at him horrorstruck. 'Click!' This couldn't be happening.

"My name's Gabriel Castillo Perez." He reached out and shook her hand. "Just call me Gabe, yeah. Everyone else does." He leaned in and showed her the picture. "You don't mind if we take another one. Do you?"

Angela nodded. Was this part of her dream? She tried to smile. 'Click!' How did these men know her? Did this make her famous — or infamous? Either way it was humiliating!

TWELVE

"Eight thousand dollars?!" Ted held the receipt in his shaking hands. "You spent eight thousand dollars on a new bed? Why, Angela, why?" He rubbed his hands over his face.

Tears streamed down her cheeks, (a new, yet hated skill of hers). She hadn't even thought to ask for a price over the phone and deserved his anger. "You were right." She finally whispered.

That seemed to take Ted off guard. His eyebrows pinched together. "Right about what?"

"I'm weird. I've been too caught up in this whole fairy thing." She sighed, feeling a hundred years old. "I've decided to make a clean start."

He nodded, slumped onto the new bed as though no longer able to hold his own weight, and then sank into the pillow-softness of the new mattress.

"This is nice." He stared toward the ceiling and swooshed his hands over the bed's surface. "You got a new bedspread too."

At the time of purchase, Angela had planned to pay for the mattress and linens herself, but she couldn't pay for the overgrown wooden structure in their bedroom. Admiring it, Angela touched the bedpost and bit back on her lip. How many trees had fallen to make this one beautiful bed frame?

When had things gotten so expensive?

Hoping the worst was over, Angela sat on the bed beside him. "There's more than just the bed and linens," Angela said timidly, knowing she needed to tell him everything. Really, he'd find out eventually.

Ted sat up on the bed, concern pinching his face. Angela winced back, bracing herself for a lecture.

Taking slow, sighing breaths, Ted asked, "There's more?" then clenched his jaw tight.

"I bought three new sheet sets and this new comforter set." She went to the closet and pulled out the large bag that held the other sheets. "And as you can tell, the mattresses are new as well."

His eyes flared, and Angela stood back a pace.

"How much?" He spoke with his teeth still clenched together. Angela had never seen him do that before. Maybe he was learning new skills as well.

"I have money in my Christmas account to pay for the linens," she murmured, "and part of the mattress set." She wanted to placate him, to make him less upset, so she added some cheer to her voice. "Just tell me, Merry Christmas, and you don't have to give me anything else this entire year." She grinned manically.

"How much?" Again with glaring and jaw clenching.

A burst of hysteria surfaced, and doing her best to push it down, Angela ran to her purse and pulled out the receipt. "Four hundred dollars—but that's including tax." She thrust the paper toward him as proof. "It was all on sale—fifty percent off." Her voice rose at the end, making her sound angry.

Anger warded off her tears. She pursed her lips together, heart beating a thousand beats a minute, and tossed her head up defiantly. This whole thing—anger, frustration, loud voices—yes, it was a fight—left her breathless. Angela tottered to the bed and sat, her eyes on Ted, and waited for the big explosion.

He didn't move—at all.

It was too much. The pressure would have undone even the stoutest heart, even the most determined not to cry. And, even though Angela was a strong woman, (caring for five children, a husband, and running a household is not an activity for the weak), and even though she hated this new crying habit of hers—cry she did.

"I did it for you." Tears flowed afresh, accompanied by gasping sobs. "I thought you'd be happy!"

Ted leaned toward her, then stopped. "Happy? We could have bought a car with the money you spent today. What were you thinking, making such a large purchase?" He stood and walked to the bedroom door. "Just let me go outside for a minute to get some fresh air." He started toward the backyard.

At his first step, Angela lunged off the bed and took two leaping strides toward him. Then stopped. Fingers shaking, she reached out timidly and touched his arm. "I ... have ... a-a-a-nother confession to make!" she sobbed.

Angela's whole body trembled. Ted was upset over the money spent, but would be downright angry over the lawn. This last confession could skyrocket their fight to monumental proportions. Although tight with finances, Ted never hesitated to pay a landscaper to keep their lawn immaculate. She hadn't thought of that when she set the sheets on fire.

She hadn't been thinking.

Like a stone, Ted waited for her to speak.

She couldn't, however, speak the embarrassing words—confess to him she had nearly obliterated his showcase lawn. They were hosting a neighborhood barbeque two weeks before Halloween. Angela silently took his hand and pulled him to the backyard.

Ted gazed at the large, charred surface of their once flawless green lawn, and gasped. He looked at Angela and then mumbled something.

Did he mean for her to hear, or not? She couldn't tell what he'd said. He put his arm around Angela's shoulders and they stood there quietly staring, and hoping that their lawn would magically reappear.

"What did you do?" Ted shook his head. "What happened?"

Angela took a ragged breath, trying to settle her nerves. She looked up at him, but couldn't meet his eyes. "I've been dreaming that I was a full-grown fairy—you know that." She glanced up again, but looked away. "Then last night, as you are also well aware, I dreamed I was attacked by pixies." She shrugged her shoulders while staring at the lawn. "You called me weird. I decided that maybe they," she indicated the charred earth, "the bed and bedding, were somehow responsible—that they were magical." The ridiculous assumption was embarrassing now. "The grass'll grow back—won't it?"

He didn't say anything, but Angela felt him shaking. She looked up to see if he was angry, or crying, and reluctantly met his eyes. He guffawed loudly, and laughed hysterically until his eyes were wet with tears. "Anj, life with you is never boring."

She'd rather he be angry.

He patted the top of the patio chair, and snickered. "Were you roasting marshmallows out here?" He laughed again.

"Hey!" How did he know she had thought of that very thing? Angela didn't know whether to be relieved or angry. Clearly, her sanity was still in question. She remembered the firemen and frowned—everyone thought she was a kook. A weirdo. Worse than quirky. She folded her arms and stared out at the night sky.

Ted sat back in the chair and pulled Angela onto his lap. "I think it's time you tell me about your day, Mrs. Anderson."

Angela snuggled into his lap. It felt good sitting there with Ted. When they were younger, he wouldn't have resisted the impulse to kiss her and then take her inside for dessert, as they called it. Apparently, that was no longer an issue. Who kisses fairy fanatics who think they have magic sheets?

"I had no idea they'd bring such an expensive bed frame," Angela muttered. "Maybe we can ask them to take it back." She looked at him hopefully. Ted liked order and he was good at it. He always took care of everything for her.

"Do you like it?" He stroked her hair and put a strand behind her ear.

She nodded. "It's a lot bigger than I expected, but it's pretty."

"Then we'll keep it."

"But how can we afford it?" She nuzzled into his neck, hiding her face.

"You don't need to worry about that." He pulled her away and looked into her eyes. "I'll take care of it."

Angela didn't believe him. Her eyebrows creased together. "I don't want us to be in debt because I did something crazy."

"It's a good crazy." Ted looked at her with his crooked smile.

"Take that back." Angela play-punched his arm.

"I could never." He smiled wider and shook his head. "And by the way, Mrs. Anderson, will you forgive me for being angry earlier. I'm so sorry. I had a bad day at work and it all took me by surprise. The bed is no big deal, really. I'll cash in some bonds—we'll get it paid for."

Angela stared at Ted, searching his eyes, his soul, and wondering what she'd ever done to deserve him. She knew the answer to that, and it made her nervous: nothing. To prove the point further, he pulled her face to his and kissed her. His understanding and his willingness to forgive her erratic behavior made her feel worse—but the kiss gave her an idea. With her arms wrapped around him, she kissed him again.

"Let's go in." Ted stood.

Angela slid off his lap with a grin. She was ready.

He caught and steadied her with his hands. "I'll get the kids and we'll talk. I'm sure they don't mind your interest in fairies."

"Talking?" No! Her idea had nothing to do with talking. Angela wanted more kissing—and lots of it. What she ultimately wanted involved the bed though, so she followed her husband to the house.

"I'm really tired tonight." Angela faked a yawn. "Perhaps we could talk tomorrow?" Angela loved fairies, but there was something, someone, she loved more.

She hesitated at the doorway and reached toward her back (just to make sure). Nothing but her shirt. Of course not.

THIRTEEN

Derek and Hannah, duly summoned, trudged down the stairs looking as though they also wished Ted would skip the family meeting. Wearing scowls of agitation they slumped into the sofa, crossed their arms, and waited for their father to begin.

"I wanted to apologize to you kids for raising my voice at your mother." Ted rubbed his forehead. "Your mom bought a new bed and things because she didn't think we shared her interest in fairies—that we didn't want her pretending to be one." He turned to Angela, appearing as though he'd swallowed that bug of Rebecca Helman's.

Angela gulped and looked at the kids.

"Mom, can't you just save the fairy thing for Halloween? It's embarrassing enough then." Hannah pasted on a fake smile. "But my friends' moms are all weird, too." She shrugged and looked down. "So, whatever."

"Yeah," Derek interjected. "We don't mind you being a fairy. Honest." He glanced toward his father. Ted nodded his approval of the comment, and Derek continued, "But it's all over school how you were in your fairy costume trying to fly off our wall two days ago."

"Who would spread such a vicious lie?" Ted stood, brows pinched together, and agitated.

"We don't know." Derek and Hannah looked at each other, shrugging. "Everyone called us fairies today at school though, and they didn't mean small magical creatures."

Angela knew who had spread the word and she probably used the Booster Phone Tree to get the news out by noon—that cantankerous shrew from next door. Her son, James, must be following in his mother's rumor-spreading footsteps. Angela shrunk back, feeling vulnerable. This was her fault. Somehow, she'd allowed her family to be exposed to someone who would hurt them, and had in fact.

"It was the Helmans," she whispered, goosebumps spreading up her neck.

"That's not fair." Derek jumped up. "Just because you don't like James' mom, you can't go around making accusations like that."

Derek would take the Helmans' side over his own mother's. Angela looked down at her hands. Her kids' disbelief and their glaring accusations wounded her spirit. Derek and Hannah had fought constantly until last year, when all of a sudden, they became close. They had a common enemy now—her. Angela looked into her family's faces, none of them believed her.

"Who said I didn't like Rebecca Helman?" Angela shrugged, righteous indignation rising in her. "I'm just being logical." Oh, how she loved feeling she was right and they were wrong. She reveled in it a little too long, though, and spurted out something she should never have divulged. "It had to be them," she said shrilly. "It was two in the morning, after all. The Helmans were the only ones up." She waved her hands toward the Helmans' home for emphasis.

"Two a.m.?" Ted looked as though he would pop an eyeball. "You were out in the neighborhood at two a.m. in your fairy costume?" The veins on his neck bulged, his neck reddened.

Oh, whoops. Ted hadn't known that little factoid—until now. She bit her lip, frustrated. That morsel had been better left unsaid.

"Angela." Ted's brows pinched together. "What were you thinking—what were you doing?"

Angela wanted to defend herself, wanted to believe she had real wings. Fairies were kind and bright and beautiful. They granted people wishes. Real or not, fairies were a part of her—always had been. But burning her bed frame and all of her bedding? Her behavior the last two nights? Dreaming the fairies had actually given her fairy dust and a wand—and wings—and that she had a special mission? That was not okay.

But wait.

Angela stood absolutely still—the kind of still that comes with an epiphany. If the Helmans had seen her wings, then maybe her wings were real. The rumor was that she'd been in her fairy costume, a blatant lie. Nonetheless, Angela held on to the tiny thread of hope that they had seen her real wings. Her lips turned up.

"Angela?"

"Hmm?" She looked up from her reverie.

Ted was beside her and they were alone.

"Where'd the kids go?" She looked around, confused.

Ted tilted his head and looked at her, seeming curiously frustrated. "The kids went to their rooms." He handed her some hot chocolate.

Angela stuck her finger in the brown liquid. It was tepid. Yuck. She set it down.

He knelt down and talked slowly, as though to a three-year-old. "Promise you won't leave the house in the middle of the night anymore. It's dangerous."

Had she been living a real version of Rip Van Winkle? Would she wake up a hundred years from now, her family all grown and gone, and have nothing to show?

"I won't," she said tiredly.

"It's a busy day tomorrow." Ted helped her up and led the way to their bedroom. "You're not forgetting the company party Halloween night, are you? I didn't see it on the calendar."

One look at the bed and Angela remembered her idea from before—the one that involved lots of kissing. "The semi-formal company dinner? The one where I get to buy a sexy evening gown?" She smiled. "I didn't forget."

They always came home from the event and had their special 'dessert.' And tonight could be a trial run. They could make their own kind of magic in bed. So, instead of wearing her sweats and T-shirt from the previous night, Angela put on an aging-but-still-nice nightgown, hurried into the bathroom, and brushed her teeth.

She glanced up, toothbrush in hand, at the reflection in the mirror. A mistake. The face looking back was old and wrinkled; the eyes drooping like a mudslide. That couldn't be her.

Angela widened her eyes and made her ears go back. She'd learned to wiggle her ears as a kid. Angela used that same muscle to stretch her face back, it made some of the wrinkles go away. If she could keep her face like that, maybe the wrinkles wouldn't be permanent. She would look younger and more attractive. Angela tightened her stomach muscles and pushed them in farther with her hands.

A little better.

She still felt like the enchanting twenty-year-old girl from so many years ago. That was definitely her problem. Angela blew out her exasperation in a huff. Like a deflated balloon, her body returned to its otherwise dreary state.

She was no longer twenty. The reflection in the mirror proved that unwelcome fact. She needed to grow up and start acting like the over-fifty, menopausal woman she was.

Angela pulled herself away from the Mirror of Horrors, and in an effort to regain her self-esteem, sashayed sexily to her husband.

Ted snored in greeting.

Refusing to give up easily, Angela crawled across the bed like a playful cat. "I wore the nightgown you bought me on our honeymoon," she murmured hopefully, enticingly.

"Snort, phhht ... snork, phhht."

Angela needed a better strategy.

"Do you feel like a little rumba?" Leaning close, she blew into his ear.

"Phlumt!" He swatted, and his finger brushed against her eyelid.

"Ow." Angela massaged her now sore eye, leaned back in bed and heaved a sigh.

"We need to quit meeting like this," she muttered sarcastically. Whatever. She turned toward her own slumber.

FOURTEEN

Angela viewed the gathering of fairies. Did she have no imagination—to keep having the same dream over and over? She was done with this one already. It had gotten her into too much trouble. Yet, as though in a trance, she walked toward the magical sprites. Freestone Park, a luminescent blue under the moon's silver glow. Vines she'd never noticed before grew along the water's edge. Their small flowers bursting through the darkness in vibrant color.

The fairies had started without her. Again. Meetings, and more meetings. It was a ridiculous way to spend a lovely evening. But this was a dream.

Some psychologist would probably tell Angela the repeated dream meant she had issues with being left behind, or had a fear of letting go of her past. None of it mattered. Tomorrow, she would work at gaining her family's respect. Tonight, she would enjoy this last escape before starting her new life.

"We have the fairy-human." Tatiana stood in front of the fairies. "While the pixies are distracted with her sheer size or her bumbling efforts, we will annihilate them."

Annihilate? That sounded dangerous—and what did Tatiana mean by referencing Angela's "sheer size and bumbling effort?" That was just rude. Angela hid behind a tree and listened.

"The pixies want to take over our homes, the lazy demons. Will we let them?"

"No!" the other fairies shouted.

"Will we budge?"

"No!"

Tatiana's voice squeaked angrily. "They have started this war. There are hundreds of pixies, and they have ruined our peace." Tatiana heaved a sigh and looked across her audience and into Angela's eyes. She shook her head wearily. "You may come out of your hiding." She beckoned with her fingers. "You are human. They have reduced our numbers severely. You can help us."

"Why don't you think more about a peaceful resolution?" She wanted to be a fairy, sure, but fighting wasn't her thing.

"There is no peace with pixies around." Tatiana squeaked in rage. "Let those pixies create peace with us!" Tatiana shot straight into the air, and with a flick of her wand zapped a neon blue substance onto an intruding pixie, which then burst into the sky like a messy firework.

Being a fairy suddenly didn't seem like such a great idea.

"Ah, you think you can break your vow to the fairies so easily?" Tatiana's eyebrows rose in question. "I will tell you now that you cannot."

"I want wings, would love to be a fairy, but this isn't my fight." Angela turned to leave. She had a husband and children. *"I don't want to war with pixies or with anyone."* She couldn't go around risking annihilation. It was absurd.

"But this is where you are wrong." Tatiana shook her finger at Angela. "You have vowed a vow, pledged your allegiance to our cause. We risked our whole way of life by showing ourselves and asking for your help." She spoke with eerie calmness. "And you will help."

A shiver slid up Angela's spine and her scalp tingled, but there was nothing to stop her from going back home; she could walk there if the fairies took her wings away.

"You only think you can walk away from our fight," Tatiana warned. "If you try, you will lose your family forever."

A picture flashed before her: She, Ted, and the kids at a beach in California. Yeah. Big threat. They'd vacationed there the past two years. Going there again wouldn't be a big deal.

Tatiana lifted the corner of her lip, indicating the vision once more with a tip of her head.

The woman she'd assumed was her, turned. It wasn't her! The woman—the home wrecker—peered through the vision, caught Angela's eye and winked, then put her arm possessively around Ted and smiled as if in victory.

Angela gasped, not wanting to see more, but the vision continued.

Ted savored the woman with a look of pure adoration, one Angela hadn't witnessed for years, then bent forward and kissed her.

Angela gulped. "*I will help,*" she said.

FIFTEEN

"A swarm of pixies!" Angela woke with a gasp and began swatting the noisy creatures away.

"Good morning, sunshine." Ted held her arm down and kissed her cheek, then reached over and turned off the alarm.

He was still there. Good. Relief washed over her and she clicked their lamp on.

"Looks like the mosquitoes got to you." He lifted her arm and looked at the welts.

"Ted, we need to talk," she said, reaching for his hand. "Fairies are real."

Ted tensed. "We don't have time for this."

"When, then?" This was an important discussion. Angela sat up. "These aren't mosquito bites." She lifted her arm. "The pixies attacked me the other night. And I've got to get you and the kids to believe in fairies before Halloween."

There was barely one morning ray coming from their window—what was going on? She blinked her dry eyes, trying to focus. Ted wasn't in his suit. Wasn't this a weekday?

"You can't leave!" She screeched, remembering Tatiana's threat. "They have to give me a chance. You can't move to California—I won't let you! It would break my heart," she said weeping.

87

"Anj?" Ted got up and turned on the bedroom light, shedding light to the room. "What's going on?" He turned off the lamp.

"That's what I want to know." She heaved several breaths, trying to calm down. "Why aren't you in your work clothes?"

"I've got a surprise." He sat on the bed and patted her hand. "What's this about California? We're not moving."

"Oh. Okay." She heaved one last ragged breath. She'd overreacted. It was embarrassing, but she needed to push forward. To stand up for herself. Her life was changing, and Ted needed a heads-up.

"I'm going to be a fairy." She placed a hand on her chest. "They need me, Ted." She pointed to herself. "Me. Angela Anderson." She smiled, determined to convince him. "The pixies have come in and they're trying to take over." She shook her head. "The fairies refuse to listen to reason." Climbing out of bed, she began pacing the floor and continued, "Surely you've noticed our own disharmony. It's the pixies! The fairies want me to restore peace and harmony to their world. Once I do, peace will return to our lives as well." She worried her bottom lip, remembering the annihilation part. "It could be dangerous."

Ted's eyebrow rose.

"I'm not sure how dangerous," she said, backtracking. The tenor of her voice rising as she tried to sound convincing. "In fact, I'm not so sure that it won't be the easiest thing I've ever done." She shrugged. "Pixies are small you know, and when I'm through, I'll have permanent wings right here." She turned to show him her back. "That is, once you and the kids start believing."

Ted frowned, peering around the bedroom

"Don't worry. No one will be able to see them if I'm not flying." Angela cupped her chin, in thought. "Pretty sure. Anyway," she brightened, "just say you believe in fairies, in me, and I'm good to go."

"Have you been drinking?" Ted's brows pinched together.

"I just woke up." She scowled.

"Did you hit your head on something?" He leaned forward, reaching. "Come here and let me feel your forehead."

"I didn't hit my head." She dodged his grasp. "And I don't have a fever," Angela said, annoyed. "I feel fine. Why are you trying to spoil this for me?"

"I'm not trying to spoil anything. In fact, I think I'm being remarkably patient." He latched onto her arm and tugged her gently to him. "Put your clothes on. We're starting the day a little early." Ted pulled her onto his lap. "I've fired the landscapers. We're doing the lawn-work ourselves from now on."

"No," Angela groaned. What was going on? Her life was so weird lately. "Why?" She croaked out, her brows pinched together, lips forming a frown. She didn't want to work in the yard.

"We need more time together as a family." Ted walked toward the door. "Get dressed. I'll go wake the kids."

Angela felt as though the fairies had pasted a big red bulls-eye to her back. Risk annihilation or lose Ted — it was a horrible ultimatum. She sat with her eyes closed wishing to rid herself of the throbbing in her head. Ted had completely dismissed her.

He banged at the kids' doors, telling them to get up. Ugh! Couldn't he just let the landscapers do their job? What would the poor guys do now, and how would they feed their families? It seemed a shame depriving the landscapers of the thing they loved doing most, just so the Anderson clan could have a little family time.

Ugh! And who was going to clean up after the Helmans' dog, Spanky? He did a number in their front yard every day. They denied it, of course, but Angela had seen Rebecca out walking the pooch — and seen the dog squatting.

Ted and the kids appeared at the base of the stairs about the same time Angela stepped out of the bedroom, arms folded across her chest, glaring. The kids also had scowls of resentment on their faces. Ted beamed as he led them all out to the backyard.

"Why can't we have family bonding time in the afternoon when everyone is awake?" she murmured.

"Here, Anj." Ted handed her a rake. "Start with the burned spot. After you get all the ashes piled up, put them in this." He handed her a large, black plastic bag. "The block party is coming up quick. We don't want the neighbors seeing this mess, do we?"

"No." Her voice went up at the end, giving away her annoyance. She grabbed the rake, stomping to the deceased bonfire.

"Derek, Hannah, I want the two of you to pick up trash and pull weeds. The ground is hard, so soften the dirt with some water."

"I'm going to trim the hedges." Ted plugged in the extension cord and then attached it to his brand new electric trimmer.

"Huh," she huffed. "This isn't about family time." Angela drew the rake across the ashes. "This is about punishing me for destroying the lawn to begin with." She scooped ashes into the bag.

The four of them worked in silence, with Angela becoming increasingly frustrated. What was up with her lately—and why was Ted making them work in the yard so early?

"Isn't this wonderful?" Ted smiled at Angela. "The air is so fresh and clean in the mornings."

Whatever. The air was warm and thick with pollutants. It was still September; the nighttime low had barely dropped to the mid-80's. They hadn't had rain since July and no noticeable wind for weeks. As a result, pollution had settled like a blanket of toxic fog across the Valley of the Sun.

Angela missed the fresh, clean air. She missed the smell of sage, creosote, and the pungent fragrance of the neighbor's eucalyptus tree. In all honesty, she missed her bed.

September was horrible—everyone sun-baked and waiting for the heat to subside. Spring was Angela's favorite time of year when the Palo Verde trees in the neighborhood were thick with yellow blossoms, the green-grey sage bushes were bright with purple, and petunias, poppies and other annuals lined the streets.

Angela looked at Ted curiously. He didn't seem to regard this as a punishment at all. Ted enjoyed being with his family, she had no doubt, but getting up early? She watched as he trimmed the bushes, pretending the electric hedge trimmer was a light saber, and teasing with the kids. She had misjudged.

"Say," Angela began casually. "I have a friend, and someone wants to take over her property —"

"Amy?"

"No, not Amy. Someone else."

Ted looked at her strangely, but Angela continued. "They claim it's theirs. What would you do?"

"All she has to do is take her deed to the city."

"Oh, right." So, talking in vague terms wasn't helpful. "Thanks."

None too soon for Angela, Ted was satisfied with their efforts of the morning. "This was great, guys. But we probably need to get going."

Angela made a mad dash for the door, but Hannah and Derek breezed past her easily. They stopped to open the arcadia door and, not able to stop fast enough, Angela bumped into Derek, slamming him against the wall.

"Oops! Sorry," she said, smiling apologetically. Derek smiled back and Angela knew all was forgiven. The small faux pas had given Angela just a moment to catch her breath and settle her thudding heart. She really was going to have to start exercising more. Maybe she could start walking around the block. If only she had a dog. Not.

Ted and the kids got ready and rushed out the door in record time. It only took twenty minutes for them to shower and dress. Ted grabbed a bagel and kissed Angela on his way out.

"I love you," he called.

"I love you more," she replied.

"Hey Anj," Ted called from his car, "there's a pile of dog doo in our front lawn. Could you pick it up and throw it in the trash? It's unsightly, and if the Homeowners Association Neighborhood Committee sees it ..." He drove away.

Sure. She'd get right on that.

They had a shovel somewhere. Perhaps she'd turn into Angela-poo-flinger and it would accidentally land back where it belonged — in Hellcat's yard.

Angela shook her head and walked to her room, exhausted. It was only six-thirty and she had already raked the yard until the black disappeared. The spot looked like a place where the grass merely refused to grow. Ted had loosened the dirt, planted grass seed, and turned on the sprinkler. Angela would turn it off in twenty minutes, and then back on again at noon.

Too awake for sleep, Angela jumped in the shower. Getting up early and working as a family was certainly not as bad as anticipated. She wouldn't tell Ted though, he'd expect her up every morning by five.

After her shower, Angela decided on a cup of frozen hot chocolate for breakfast. She found their tallest cup in the cupboard, poured a large glass of milk into the blender with some ice and a generous scoop of chocolate mix. She sipped her chocolate slush and looked at the container.

"That's odd." Angela hadn't paid attention before, but it was the strangest little box — midnight blue with a galaxy of stars as decoration. Angela turned it around in her hands. "Who would have given something like this to Ted?" She hadn't bought it.

The words, printed in a foreign language, read: *Gourmet chocolate caliente con nuez moscada.* She understood the gourmet part and the hot chocolate part, but she had never learned Spanish — and it looked Spanish. How had they come upon a homemade-looking box of hot chocolate mix from Mexico?

"*Producto de Acapulco,*" Angela read the words with an exaggerated American accent. They had never been anywhere out of the United States — even on their honeymoon. Was Acapulco the best place to get hot chocolate mix — did cocoa beans even grow there?

Angela went to the computer and typed the foreign words into a free translation program. "Gourmet hot chocolate with nutmeg." Yeah, she tasted it now. Nutmeg. A brilliant idea. She put the carton back into the cupboard. The nutmeg had an exotic taste as though from a foreign country. "The nutmeg is from Acapulco." Angela nodded. "Of course it would taste different."

Angela alternately drank and hummed while she went from room to room straightening the house. She had plans and needed to get to the mall before Ted got home.

SIXTEEN

"Wow. That was unexpected." Angela sat up and stretched. "Am I going to start sleeping during the day now?" She went to the kitchen. Tatiana wanted her to get the kids on her side. Cookies would do the trick, but they didn't bake themselves. She got the ingredients out and before long, the aroma of baking cookies filled the air. As she made yummy treats for her family, Angela thought about the weird happenings of the other night.

"Oh, Angela-Fairy-Human," Angela mimicked, not quite believing what had happened. "We need your help to annihilate pixies." Please. Fairies were fun-loving creatures. They didn't go around annihilating other magical creatures. If they did, they didn't need her help. What were those fairies up to?

The notion was crazy. And how had she, without actually knowing, vowed to help? "Is that entrapment? Should I hire an attorney?" Yeah, not. Angela smirked.

"What is your legal problem?" Angela asked in a deep lawyer-like voice. Speaking high-pitched, she said, "My fairy clan tricked me into vowing to help annihilate a group of pixies, and I need you to get me out of my contract." Her husband would have her gagged and bound, figuratively of course, before allowing a conversation like that to happen.

Fairies were kind and good. They'd sent her this dream to help encourage her to get the kids and Ted to believe. Inhaling deeply, she savored the sweet scent of chocolate chip cookies. This heavenly aroma was all she could enjoy of the treat she was baking for Hanna and Derek.

Despite popular belief, the scent of baked goods had no calories. And Angela was a rock — a rock on a mission. Angela needed to lose some weight, plus gain the respect of her family. She made them cookies, but breathing sweet air was the only treat she could afford, calorie-wise.

The buzzer rang. "Ah, the last batch." Angela pulled them from the oven. They were tempting. Her fingers twitched over the pan. She had never not tasted one to make sure they turned out well.

But the company's quarterly dinner was on All Hallows' Eve, and Angela had to look better than last year — not bigger. She shoved her hand behind her back to resist temptation. Grabbing the spatula with the other, she tried pushing it beneath a cookie. The warm cookie bent and crumbled. "I can't get them off the pan one-handed." She scooted the spatula under the next cookie, lifting her shaking hand to secure it. That one crumbled as well.

Serving broken treats to her family would not do. Angela licked her lips. It was a proven fact that the crumbs held significantly fewer calories than whole cookies. Scooping the crumbs into her palm, Angela savored each speck as a separate cookie and then licked her hand clean.

Whole cookies tasted different. Didn't they? She spied them on the pan — but wouldn't try one. She carefully scooped off the remaining cookies and placed them on the cooling rack until there was only one left.

Were the whole cookies any good?

Angela chewed her lip. She needed to make absolutely sure that the treat tasted good enough for her family. A crumb test didn't count. Angela scooped up the very last cookie, still debating. Then, instead of putting it on the cooling rack, she nibbled it like precious manna while straightening the house.

Standing near the door, Angela surveyed her cleaned-to-perfection home with satisfaction. It was cleaner even than Hell-woman's house. Angela knew this because they'd been friends ever-so-briefly a year ago.

She grabbed her purse and left to make that trip to the mall. Ted needed a distraction—something seductive to take his mind off of television—something sensual to help him remember he had once believed in fairies—something sexy to put his mind on her, the overgrown fairy of his dreams. She needed ammunition.

As she walked to the mini-van, Angela made plans for the evening, this time hoping to actually make her husband's eyes pop with desire and forget about work for once.

The obvious choice was Victoria's Secret, but would they have something in her size? In the car, Angela shivered excitedly and couldn't help but sing her own version of a favorite tune, "*I am woman, hear me roar, I am too large to ignore...*"

When she arrived at the mall parking lot, two twenty-somethings stared at her as she got out of the van, still singing. Angela tucked her head down and looked away. What did they know? They were freakishly thin.

"This is what a real woman looks like," Angela murmured, patting her waist and wishing she had nerve to say it aloud. She stepped toward them, as if to actually start a conversation, and tripped off the curb. Clinging to a water-starved tree, she saved herself from a face-plant on the pavement. It was good the anorexic snobs hadn't looked back. She peeled herself from the trunk and headed to the mall.

There was a beauty shop at the mall entrance, and Angela had a sudden change of plans. She hurried inside.

"Do you have any openings?"

They did.

An hour later, Angela strutted from the beauty shop and into the mall feeling much younger with her hair back to its original, pre-gray, auburn.

Now, to find the other store. Her cheeks warmed at the thought as she hurried to the directory. She read it, trying to act innocent as people walked by and then sneaked unsurely to section C-12.

Once there, Angela paced in front of Victoria's Secret, afraid to go in, (a good portion of her nerve having stayed back in the parking lot). She stepped to the store window, peering in while pretending to fix her new hairdo. There were plenty of bras and lacy panty-things. Her cheeks warmed just looking at them, but she didn't see anything for ample women. When had Small become the new Large? Maybe, hopefully, they had her size in the back.

Three women passed her and entered the store. Angela's heart sank to her toes. One woman looked like that meddlesome magpie from next door. Yikes, this was no secret! Everyone could see her. She took several calming breaths. Stores like this should have side entrances. She should have driven across town to Scottsdale—no chance of bumping into anyone she knew there.

It couldn't be Hell-woman though. What would she be doing at Victoria's? Angela meandered to the store entrance, peeked around nervously and saw the woman she'd thought was Rebecca Helman. Poor thing. She did look like the she-devil, but it wasn't her. Heaving a great sigh of relief, Angela stepped across the threshold of the store, heart thumping, hands trembling, and wondering: was it a sin, what she wanted?

A slender, petite woman greeted her, "Hello___." Her eyebrows raised in question.

"Angela," she filled in the blank.

"Hello, Angela. My name is Trish. What can I do for you today?"

What did people usually want when they shopped there? Wasn't it obvious? Besides, how could anyone who was still the size they were at fourteen possibly know how to help her?

"I'd like something nice. Something to please my husband."

Angela's voice came out as a cracked whisper and she wondered if she'd have to repeat her embarrassing request.

A friendly smile stole across Trish's face. "We have just the thing."

She led Angela to a rack of teddies — the unwarranted name they gave little strips of lace hooked together with two small snaps — teddy sounded like teddy bear after all, and implied something warm and cuddly. "Oh." Recognition dawned on Angela, her face burning with heat. "Oh, no," she coughed. "Oh, *heavens* no."

Angela looked at the young waif — maybe she really was fourteen, and made a mental note — talk to Hannah about appropriate employment opportunities for when she's older — way, way older, and certainly nothing ever in a lingerie store.

Angela smiled, and blushed again as she glanced at the rack of lace. "I need something with a little more fabric."

The girl was young — clearly she'd gotten a job straight from the womb. They now stood by a rack of satin nightgowns — most of them so slender they would barely fit over Angela's thigh. She sighed longingly.

"Um, Trish, do you have something larger, something possibly to make me look attractive? Desirable, even?" She pointed at herself with both hands. Undoubtedly Angela needed more than one hand to take in her ample mid-section.

A half hour later, Angela pulled into her driveway using the keyless remote to raise the garage door. Her shopping spree at Victoria's had been a humiliating experience. Angela pushed her new satin negligee further inside the tiny little pink bag, darted out of the car and into the house, not stopping until she lay sprawled across her bed, releasing her embarrassment in broken sobs.

After an hour of thoroughly warranted self-pity, Angela forced herself off the bed and into the kitchen. A mother's work was never done. She pulled the corn tortillas from the fridge, and home-canned chicken from the pantry.

SEVENTEEN

The door opened. Hannah and Derek marched straight to the kitchen.

"How was school?" Angela lifted a wet hand from the sink for a hug.

"Fine," they said in unison, grabbed several handfuls of cookies, and headed up the stairs.

"Did you see Dorky Dan today at lunch?" Derek said.

"What'd he do?" Hannah asked?

"It was genius." They continued to their rooms still discussing the apparent awesomeness of the Dork. Angela strained to hear. Twenty minutes later, they came back to the kitchen. Angela knew what they wanted — more food.

"Dinner's almost ready and your dad will be home soon. Don't fill up on snacks." Everything needed to be perfect.

The refrigerator opened anyway and out came yesterday's leftovers. Angela gave her son the 'evil eye' and wished she could do it as painfully well as that dream she kept having. They'd respect her after one of those. "I said no snacking." She tried the glare thing. It didn't work. She was lame for even trying.

"What?" He barely glanced in her direction. "This is food, not a snack, and I'm hungry."

"Did you have a good day at school?" She tried ignoring how her son ignored her.

"You already asked that." Derek grabbed a plate and piled it with food. "The answer was, great. I had a great day. Thanks."

"Do you have homework?" Her children needed to keep up their good grades.

"Don't know." Hannah shrugged, taking the large spoon from her brother.

"Derek?" She waited for his answer.

"Maybe. I'll do it later." He pulled his plate from the microwave.

The refrigerator door closed and both teens headed out the front door carrying plates of food.

"Where are you going?"

"To the neighbors' to study."

They closed the door and the house was once again silent. Angela wiped the splatter mess from the microwave.

"Thank you for the delicious food, Mom," Angela said in a falsetto-like voice. "You're such a good cook, Mom," she said in her best tenor. "Let me tell you about the funny thing that happened at school today, Mom." If only.

By six o'clock, chicken enchiladas—the real dinner—were on the table getting cooler by the second. Angela thrummed the counter with her fingers. Ted was late. He worked so hard. Too hard. How was she supposed to turn her husband into a believer if he didn't come home?

An hour later, Ted came in, grabbed a plate of the now glacial enchiladas and plopped in front of the TV. Angela couldn't help the large, wet tears that formed as she sat alone at the table.

"Thanks for dinner, honey," she said.

"What?" Ted called. "Yeah, today was a killer. I've been chasing around since noon."

"That's too bad, honey." She had wanted a 'happy family' moment, but her family didn't know she existed. Angela hated her stupid tears. She hated her plump and yet amazingly still flat-chested body. She hated herself.

If only her life was more like a fairytale.

In fairytales, Cinderella was never invisible. Snow White didn't long for a kiss. Peter Pan believed in fairies, and Prince Charming always saved the day.

Nothing like her reality.

Everyone around her was perfect. Ted — the women at work ogled after him like he was a Greek god. They loved his slightly graying hair, and he worked night and day making himself invaluable to his co-workers. Ted was great at everything.

Their adult children were all successful. Richard was the youngest lawyer accepted in his firm, Milford and Hanks. Their daughter, Leanne, a soon-to-be-mother, had played with the Phoenix Symphony for three years, and Benjamin recently entered ASU to become an architect.

The unknowing few tried to push her children's accomplishments onto her, saying she was a wonderful mother. Angela shook it off. Her children's accomplishments were their own. People acquainted with her didn't bother with false pretenses. They wondered how the Anderson children got to be so talented with a mother like her.

She was a housewife — nothing more.

When her family was small, Angela had immersed herself in her home and family knowing they were the most important things in her life, but now she only had two teenage children left at home, and they didn't need her. She embarrassed them.

Her husband, though she never doubted that he loved her, had become distant. Even now he sat in front of the television eating a meal that for all he knew the elves had made.

"Where does all this great food come from?" Angela said in a mimicking tone. "I don't know," she responded for her children. "Don't we have a maid or something? It was in the refrigerator when we came home."

"Can you keep it down in there?" Ted said. "What're you doing anyway?" Rather than wait for an answer, he turned the volume up a notch.

Invisible. That's how her family saw her. They didn't see her at all.

The kids ran to friends. Ted sat in the family room watching television. All she wanted was a little appreciation. Was that so wrong?

"Food was great." Ted kissed her forehead and strode toward the door. "Be back by ten."

"Where are you going?" He'd just gotten home.

"I've got a booster meeting," he said, and then he was gone.

"But, I had a special evening planned." She rested her elbow on the table. Ted hadn't even noticed her new hairdo.

The kitchen received an extra cleaning as she scrubbed counters and scraped the dishes. Angela planned several scenarios of how the rest of the evening might play out. Ted would come home from his meeting exhausted and nearly comatose as usual. What could she say — what could she do to put him in the mood?

Would she be able to pour herself into her new nightgown before Ted began snoring?

After recent comments, Angela worried that Ted might feel obligated. As much as she wanted him, wanted to feel his longing touch on her skin, she didn't want him to feel he owed her anything. It would crush her if he did.

Ted came in the door after only an hour, startling Angela.

"The meeting got out early." He smiled.

"No bake sales to plan this week?" She frowned, wondering if his eyes didn't look a little sad.

"The budget is full. We're waiting for our team to win regionals and go to state." He pulled her to him.

Angela snuggled in his arms, scheming quickly. This new turn of luck made her plans all the easier. He pulled her willing body to the sofa where she snuggled onto his lap and kissed him on the cheek. The time to strike was now.

"I have a surprise for you." She was as excited as a little girl at Christmastime. Angela felt a blush steal up her cheeks. Ted pulled her closer, kissing her. "Mmm, surprise me." She wanted to head to the bedroom right then, but they sat there, wrapped in one another's arms visiting about their day—Ted's day mostly.

"Do you like my new hair?" Angela asked, flouncing it.

"Very nice." Ted took in all of her, which made Angela's heart skip with desire. She liked curling up, talking and kissing Ted. It was comfortable, pleasant, but Angela wanted more. "I'll be right back." She whispered in his ear, hoping he'd get goose-bumps, and then she kissed his neck for good measure.

Their master bedroom was on the ground floor, just off the family room. She went there and changed into her new burgundy satin and lace nightgown.

Angela stepped out of their bedroom, and rested her hand sexily against the doorframe. Ted didn't notice. Her heart sank. He was in that zone of his somewhere between awake and oblivion and staring at his favorite cop show.

Being a workaholic and avid supporter of their son's football team, he got so few nights off. Angela hated to disturb him. But if not now, when?

Angela needed to strike while the opportunity presented itself. Her new gown was perfectly modest. Sizes for the "mature woman" as Trish had termed it, always came with lots of fabric, yet she walked timidly into the family room and stood in front of the television feeling conspicuous, naked, and unsure of herself.

A crooked smile spread across Ted's face. Angela's heart flipped with joy. This would work! She walked slowly, hopefully seductively, toward him.

"You guys don't mind if we crash here to watch a m—Mom!"

Angela spun, horrified, toward the voice. Derek stood in the entryway looking absolutely green. His three friends turned their faces away in shame, but all matched the color of her gown.

Okay, new family rule: No company over while Mom is trying to seduce Dad. Angela ran to the bedroom, mortified — screaming.

In less than the time it took Angela to calm down, Ted was lying beside her. "Everything's fine Anj. The boys are going next door to the Helmans' to watch their movie. Hannah came home and she's studying in her room."

"I'll never be able to go out in public again," Angela sobbed. "We have to move. Far. Away."

Ted smiled his quirky, amused smile. "I think we'll be fine right here." He nibbled on her ear sending a rush of chills through her body. She tried to shake it off.

"What must they think of me?" Angela had a hard time letting go of the look on those boys' faces.

"They think that Mrs. Anderson loves her husband."

"But ... but ..." He was distracting her and she knew it, but this was what she had wanted all along.

"Mr. Anderson loves his wife, too, by the way." He brushed her jaw-line lightly with his fingers. Bringing her lips to his, he kissed her softly at first and Angela melted into his gentle kisses, savoring each one.

Then he began kissing her with the passion that she'd been feeling herself.

EIGHTEEN

"The pixies' numbers are growing." Tatiana looked grim.

Wait? What was she doing here? Angela surveyed her surroundings. As much as she loved the fairies, she didn't want to be here. Not now. She wanted to be curled up with Ted. Her heart warmed at the thought of their evening. Ah, more Ted. That's what she wanted. Was there a way to sneak back home? Angela looked behind her. The fairies met her with impatient glances and silent motions to turn around.

Sheesh. This was another trick, right?

Tatiana's lips pressed into a thin line, eyes squinted, brows furrowed.

Before the brain glare began, Angela remembered her place. She would behave. "*The pixies, yes.*" Angela thought of the green and glowing eyes and her near disaster, and nodded her agreement. "*They need to move to Ireland.*" Wasn't that where most pixies lived?

"Fairies have to be close in order to use their dust or breath on a pixie," Tatiana said,

If that was the case, she hoped they brushed their teeth.

Tatiana lifted her brows and continued. "Close enough to die in the effort."

"*Die?*" Angela cringed. Why did magical creatures have to be so stubborn?

Tatiana glared at Angela. "Silence!"

The fairies turned toward Angela in unison with a soundless plea expressed on their faces.

"*Ouch, ouch. Okay, silent,*" she agreed. Angela could learn to be silent. She cleared all thoughts from her mind once more. All thoughts.

She didn't ponder the fairies' bad timing. Well, she did, but she was over it. Sort of. She tried not thinking of her purpose there. Because, really, what was it?

Her knees ached, and she did rub them but spared no thoughts on the matter. At all. Like, why Tatiana didn't make her small like the others — the fairy queen was magic after all — or why they couldn't sit on the nearby benches. Or, even why they couldn't develop better timing. Nope. Nothing. She refused to think about it. And she refused to be distracted with thoughts of Ted and their wonderful evening. Mmm.

"Silence, fairy-human!" Tatiana glared. "You need to stay awake and focus."

Angela rubbed her temples. She could stay awake. She would focus. And while she did, Angela learned Pixie 101 —

Pixies had pointed ears. (No surprise there.)

They were strong. (Whatever. How strong could a four-inch creature be?)

No one should wrestle a pixie alone. (Really? Was pixie wrestling even a nationally recognized sport?)

The pixies' green, glowing eyes were lethal to fairies at a close range. (Okay, that one had Angela a bit worried. Good thing she'd closed her eyes on that pernicious snit, Rebecca.)

Pixies had magical dust too. They used it on humans in order to get them to do a wide variety of things.

At the end of her lesson, a peaceful scene flashed into Angela's mind — Ted and her children were there. They knew she was a fairy, and they adored her! Angela felt confident, strong.

The beauty of it brought her tears of joy. She tried focusing on the sight, wanting to get closer, to share the occasion with them, but the moment was fleeting and chased from her view like a laughing child.

"Bring it back. Please," Angela begged.

"That was a vision of your future," Tatiana said. "But only if you fulfill your vow."

"But I looked for pixies like you asked. There's more?" Angela would do anything to have this most recent vision fulfilled.

"Fairies know one another's thoughts and needs. That's how you knew my name. That's how you knew your trial mission."

She bowed her head. *"Yes, O Queen,"* she said, and then frowned. *"Just to get this straight,"* Angela tilted her head, *"I have a mission, but you won't tell me what it is, and I have to accomplish it before All Hallows' Eve?"* The task seemed impossible.

"You have spent your life pretending to be one of us. I have granted you this opportunity. You can pretend no longer and must earn it on your own merits."

"By pretending, do you mean no more fairy costume?" Angela gulped. She loved that thing, but it was getting worn out.

"If you are meant to be one of us, you will figure it out."

"But you'll help me, right?" Moisture beaded around Angela's hairline. *"You'll plant the thought in my mind, like before, and then I'll hear it. Right?"* She chewed her nail. *"Is that how I'll know?"*

Tatiana didn't reply. She glared at Angela. The other fairies scattered.

"Clearing my mind of thoughts," she said to the growing pain.

"You must believe in yourself before others can believe."

"I believe in myself. I have the most awesome cooking skills. And," she paused, trying to think of something else. *"There are other things,"* she insisted. *"I'm a good wife."* Aren't I? She furrowed her brows.

"Enough of this whining. Now, I know from your thoughts that you want to share our magical life with your husband." She eyed Angela. "But you must not."

Oops! That ship had already sailed.

"What is this you say about sailing ships?" Tatiana's hands went to her hips.

"*My husband loves sailing, is all.*" What would happen if he'd been told? Angela forced into her mind an image of a couple sailing she'd seen on an ad.

"Show no one your wings. For a disbeliever to know of our world is certain destruction." Tatiana tilted her head to the side. "Your family would be destroyed."

Angela gulped. There were sure a lot of ways for her family to be destroyed while she was being a fairy. She'd always thought they were so peaceful and loving.

Angela closed her eyes as she joined her clan in the sky, but when she opened them, the fairies were gone. Her heart skipped a beat. She looked around. There was a flash of green beside her. A flash of pink. A flash of blue.

Angela fell from the air waving her arms, struggling and searching for her wand. It wasn't there. She needed to find that thing. How could she defend herself or the fairies without her magical stuff?

"Hellooooo, wings. You can start working any time now!" The ground was growing closer by the second.

Her heart was in a panic. Tatiana knew. "I didn't mean to tell Ted! I didn't know it was wrong! I'm sorry!" Angela screamed as she sank. "Save me!"

Only yards from earth, her wings finally decided to work and held her above ground. But before she could fly for cover, Angela saw another flash of green. It knocked her off balance.

Her vision spun out of control. She wretched, and spun wildly through the same vortex as before, wishing she could scream, and not being able to. Her head felt as though it was being stretched through a funnel. The loud drain noise echoed in her ringing ears and continued until Angela plopped down into bed.

NINETEEN

"Aag!" Those fairies' timing was horrible.

Ted stirred and then quieted. Angela couldn't relax, couldn't snuggle into his sleeping arms, couldn't risk accidently waking him.

The fairies were out there somewhere, and they were in danger. Angela chewed her nails, contemplating. What did Tatiana want her to do? Did she have a specific mission tonight? Was that why she kept bouncing back and forth between worlds like a yo-yo?

After having one of the nicest evenings in, *ahem*, well, to spare Ted we'll just say recently — after one of her most recent lovely evenings. Angela didn't want to leave her bedroom. She most certainly didn't want to annihilate pixies.

Her sense of urgency, however, made her skin twitch and crawl. Angela pressed her hands to her temples and squeezed her eyes shut. "Clear my mind of all thoughts," she whispered. After a moment, Angela peeked her eyes open. Her mind felt pretty empty, but there was supposed to be a message in there from Tatiana.

Join the fairies. It's what she felt compelled to do. Angela could not stay in bed, all peaceful-like, if the fairies really were in danger. She jumped up and off the bed. Sort of. Her foot stuck in the sheet and she toppled against her dresser with a thud.

"Ow."

"What're you doing?" Ted turned, scratching his neck and yawning.

"I'm fine." She hoped. "Go back to sleep."

He did.

Hey, what if there had been a burglar in the house?

With bubbles of anticipation jarring her perfect reasoning, Angela rushed to the arcadia door, opened it, and peered around the corner. The lights were off at the Helmans' house, a good sign—always a good sign.

"All clear," Angela whispered, stepping toward the grass. "Here comes bumbling gargantua to your rescue." She would keep the fairies safe and alive, fulfill her vow and get on with the fun part of being a fairy.

After walking onto the lawn and preparing to fly, Angela looked down at her nightgown. "Beware the sexy temptress." (Yes, Ted the husband of 35 years, had actually called her that). She smiled. However, she had already stunted the growth of her son and his friends. "Yeah, no. I'm not scaring the whole neighborhood."

Angela rushed back to the bedroom and changed silently, quickly, into the T-shirt and sweats she found on the floor by the hamper. (Ted never stirred.)

Huh! Amazing how that worked. Her wings came flawlessly through the cotton fabric. The urge to accidentally bump the bed, wake Ted, and have him see her beautiful wings—yeah, she wanted to, but the word 'destroyed' echoed in her memory. She wouldn't put him in jeopardy now that she knew.

Hey, she had worn this only slightly smelly outfit just the other night. Angela sorted through the pockets. Extreme jubilation! The miniature wand and bag of fairy dust were there. They were real. She wasn't crazy, or quirky, or eccentric, pathetic or any of the above. Woo hoo! Just in time. Laundry day was tomorrow.

Keeping hold of the precious items in her pockets, Angela ran back outside and stood in the shadows of her backyard. How far would she fly tonight? Ah, one more trip. Angela rushed to the laundry room for her keys—just in case—and set up and into the night sky in search of the magical war.

The fairies needed her help. Angela had no room for failure. Not when her family was involved.

Yet, after flying the length of her neighborhood four streets above and four streets below theirs, in her state of exhaustion, Angela had yet to see anything even closely resembling a pixie. Or a fairy. Her shoulders slumped in fatigue. Maybe her mission was a ruse.

"Pixies, hello? Where are you?" Maybe Tatiana just wanted Angela out of their way while using up her nearly defunct wish.

The fire station was in sight, and someone was on the tower. Angela flitted behind a tree to keep him from seeing her. Luckily the person's back was turned. It looked like that Gabe guy, or maybe that friend of his, Troy, yes that was his name. Those guys were way too interested in her and her house.

Feeling lost and utterly alone, she darted a different direction and then slowed, pressing her fingers against her temples in concentration. *Find the pixies.* The old command hung in her memory. "Should I still continue in that quest?" Angela asked the sky.

There was no response. "But are there any pixies?" The fact that she'd woken up in bed, and in her nightgown, was disorienting to say the least. Those fairies. Was this all a ploy to discourage her interest? Or were they actually being annihilated? It was such a strong word and belonged in a combat movie. Not in her fairy life.

Angela had seen a pixie herself though. Those glowing green eyes were hard to forget. She turned tiredly in the direction of Freestone Park. She had only thought her shoulders ached before. They were currently burning with the fire of the damned. Tired, and wanting — wanting? — no, needing a rest, Angela's wings gave out. She landed on someone's roof with a thud. An alarm went off somewhere inside the house. Reluctantly, Angela the overly-tired-fairy-human scooped herself up and off the roof.

It would be no good, no good at all, if the police or that nosy fireman who was currently staring her way, came and escorted her home to her husband. Angela shuddered. One of the neighbors, bless them, had a full-grown pine tree in their yard, a desert oddity, and Angela struggled to the nethermost branches ready to collapse. She hadn't been in a tree for over forty years.

Ted would not approve.

"You're a grown woman," she murmured in tenor. "Get down from there. You can't fly. You'll hurt yourself!" Angela shook her head — she was doing just fine — and leaned against a branch.

Ah, the bliss of it. Angela felt like a rebellious schoolgirl, ignoring Ted's imagined tirade as she did. The nosy fireman had finally found someone else to spy on. She strung her arms around an upper branch and rested there as though sitting in a hammock, dangling a leg and twirling her hair. Yes, pure bliss. It was delicious.

After ten minutes, Angela felt rested enough to continue her search. Those pixies needed to go. She stood on the branch, leaned forward, and then stepped into the air. After she was in the sky, her wings did the rest.

Pixies were destructive and into annihilation, and Angela knew at least one pixie. Rebecca Helman. She didn't know anyone who enjoyed the misery of others more than that devious snipe. Their light was on. It must be nearly twelve o'clock.

Angela would win the biggest coup ever if she was able to knock that malicious mole out of the fairy war. Angela swooped down for a closer look.

TWENTY

A large picture window exposed the Helmans' family room. "Just give me one reason to call the police." Angela peered inside. Two could play at her game.

Derek was still there. She blinked back. Were they holding him hostage? It was a school night, after all. Angela moved closer to make sure. The scene appeared very innocent, tranquil even. But it was late, too late to be out on a school night. The Helmans and Derek were sitting and staring with blank expressions. Had they hypnotized him or something?

Oh, they were watching a movie. That was, they were watching a movie until the flood lights came on.

In unison, they turned their heads toward her.

A horror-struck Angela, surrounded in a blast of white light and hovering a foot off the ground near the patio, blinked.

She wanted to picture herself charging into the air, like Superman on a good day or Mighty Mouse even, and tried to concentrate. But the surprised, then angry, and then disgusted look on her son's face rendered her immobile.

After what seemed a lifetime, Angela's stunned body slunk to the earth. The Helmans' reaction only took a second longer. They stormed into the backyard like charging bulls. Angela wanted nothing more than to picture herself up and over the fence and lifted onto her tiptoes. It was no use.

"What are you doing back here?" Jeff Helman demanded.

"I came to check on Derek." A simple answer, and yet not actually true until she had entered the backyard, had seen him there and realized he required checking on—but there was no need to mention that.

Rebecca glowered. "We tried to get Derek to come talk to you. He wouldn't do it. You're a disgrace. An embarrassment to your family. Why don't you give up this farce?"

Rebecca knew Angela all too well. She was an embarrassment to her family. Angela knew it was true by the look on Derek's face. The viper's words cut deep into Angela's soul, but Rebecca Helman wasn't playing fair, using her son to wound her like that. It made her angry—and angry fairies were dangerous—especially gargantuan fairies with magic fairy stuff.

Angela grabbed her toothpick-sized wand from the waist of her pajama pants, and held it between her thumb and fore finger, flicking her wrist like she'd seen done in movies. Nothing happened. Well, nothing except it seemed to agitate Rebecca even more.

Angela growled in frustration.

Rebecca blinked and took a step back. "What are you doing?" she asked in high-pitched complaint. Then turning to Jeff, she said, "Did you know she blew in my face after I brought her soup?! She hadn't brushed her teeth yet either. Her breath smelled like she'd been drinking raw sewage."

"She was trying to poison me by bug." Hey, it sounded good. And it was just wrong to tamper with food.

Rebecca harrumphed. "All lies," she accused.

Angela pointed the miniature wand at Rebecca, flicking it over and over again, trying to zap Rebecca back to her homeland. But nothing happened. Not even the tiniest of electrical currents came through the tip. Squinting, she looked more closely. It didn't appear broken. Her shoulders slumped, then she pinned the wand back into her pants.

"Is Derek still here?" she asked impatiently.

"No. He stormed out after ... this." Rebecca flung her arms in an outward expression and directly at Angela.

"May I go home?" Angela felt weary. She didn't know how much more of this she could stand. Her life was one fairy disaster after another. Each failure gave the Helmans more fuel to their fire — each failure sending her farther away from her family.

"Just let me through the gate. I'll go home." She reached in her pocket and dangled the key. "I have a key this time." Angela smiled a defeated smile, then slipped the key back in her pocket.

The Helmans looked at each other, a secret communication passing between them.

"Well, she hasn't taken anything or done any damage," Jeff said to his wife. Rebecca answered with a curt nod.

Mr. Helman looked at Angela. "You've got to promise you won't break into our backyard anymore. We want to be good neighbors, but we'll call the police if this happens again."

Angela slunk through the Helman's gate like a puppy caught peeing on the white rug, head hanging, tail between her legs.

There wasn't any point in pretending now. Angela knew what had happened — Derek had stormed home, pounded on the bedroom door until Ted had answered it, and then complained to him about his embarrassing mother. Really, couldn't he have just laughed it off as an eccentric moment?

Angela felt her back. "Good." At least the wings were gone. She could make up a believable story without the wings. What a disaster. Hopefully the wings would come back, and hopefully they weren't damaged. Angela had an irresistible desire to get it right. She had been a wife and a mother for as long as she could remember, and nothing else. Was it too much to ask that she at least be successful in living a life she had fantasized since childhood?

The front door was unlocked, and Angela walked over the threshold. Ted sat in the living room waiting for her. What must he think? She closed the door, but stood there timid and uncertain as to what she should do.

"Come sit down." Ted patted the cushion beside him and Angela meekly went to his side. He took her hands in his but didn't say anything for the longest time. Instead he looked into her eyes, searching and concerned. "Derek's really upset," he finally said.

Angela nodded. She knew that part.

"Anj, he says you had your fairy costume on, and that you were pretending to fly in the Helmans' back yard. Do you know what this kind of behavior could do to my credibility at work? They're considering me for senior partner this year."

It took Angela a while to respond, and Ted didn't press her. She'd never lied to him before, but what would he think if she told him the truth?

Rebecca Helman is an over-sized pixie. I was trying to defeat her for the fairies' sake.

Yeah, she couldn't say that. She couldn't say anything about her fairy life. But even if she did, he had never believed her before.

Her body was changing and she had no control over it. She hung her head and put her face in her hands, once again feeling like an aging centurion.

"It's all just a misunderstanding." Angela kept her face in her hands and spoke in low murmurs. "You can see for yourself. I don't have my costume on." She peeked at him through her fingers. He was looking at her severely. She closed the gap between fingers. "I was just checking on Derek and dressed just like I am now, but the Helmans didn't answer their door. I went around back, is all."

Never mind that she hadn't gone to check on Derek like a good mother should have. Never mind that the Helmans kept their gate padlocked, and never mind that the Helmans would dispute her story in the morning. She glanced at Ted again.

All the tension that had bound his body together since she entered the room visibly dissipated. "I thought it was something like that." He took a deep breath and blew it out slowly, leading her to believe he hadn't thought anything of the sort. Still holding her hands, he lifted them and kissed each separately. "I'll go get Derek. He needs to apologize."

"No." Angela looked at him desperately, hoping he wouldn't press it.

"I don't understand." Ted looked at her, eyebrows pinched together. "Derek came home—you—no, I won't get into it with you. Anj, you said you weren't in the Helmans' backyard in your fairy costume." Exasperation peeked noticeably out of his controlled façade.

"I wasn't." Angela met his gaze so he'd know she told the truth. But the real truth was she just didn't feel up to witnessing her son's look. Not tonight.

"Then he should apologize."

"Please. Ted. It's not necessary, and I don't want him to." Angela put her head on Ted's shoulder. She felt comfortable there.

The fairies said it would destroy her family if Ted knew. She'd already told him once. How long would he stay once he discovered she was telling the truth? People got divorced all the time nowadays for way less. Would Ted's realizing she was a fairy turn her into another divorce statistic? Unable to bear the thought of life without Ted, she listened to his heartbeat. He absently ran his fingers through her hair.

"Please."

"I can't condone his talking about you like that." He was not going to let go of this.

"It's just that, well, I can see how it might have looked." Angela made it up as she went along. Her family was at stake. "I was in the Helmans' back yard, and I shouldn't have been. I already apologized to them. Their flood lights went on, and it startled me." Angela looked at him sheepishly. "You know I'm a little clumsy sometimes. I fell, and it probably looked," she thrummed her fingers against her lips, "I don't know." She shrugged. "I can just see his view is all. I don't blame him for being upset."

Ted smiled. "You are an amazing woman to be so understanding."

Amazing, yeah, right. Angela rolled her eyes. "Oh, please. The air's getting a little thick in here." She pretended to make a couple of gasping sounds, and then some liquid stuck in her throat making her change from pretend gasping to coughing fits.

Ted patted her back. Like he thought that would help. "Let's get to bed. I've got an early day tomorrow." Ted led the way to their bedroom. Angela tagged along, worrying. If Ted would be gone early, that meant she'd be there alone to deal with the remnants of Derek's anger. Could she convince him as easily that nothing had actually occurred? Angela doubted it. Derek had in fact seen her wings holding her above the ground. And, smoothing things over with teenagers was not her strong point.

That was all Ted.

If she went to bed, hmm. Angela looked at the clock on the nightstand. It was only 12:30. What if her wings returned? She needed some sleep and didn't want to risk leaving the house again. Not tonight.

What did fairies do to make themselves sleep? Angela twisted and turned in bed worrying over and over again. Why would any sane and rational person put themselves through this?

The answer was clear — Angela was neither sane nor rational. She never had been.

TWENTY-ONE

"Believe in yourself." Angela sat up in bed, the pillow beside her vacant. The house hauntingly quiet. Ted wasn't there. Angela touched the hollow space near her heart where she kept her husband's annoyingly cheerful, 'Good morning, sunshine,' and winced. "How can I ever believe in myself? Ted is still upset." Maybe after a long day at work. Maybe then he'd forgive her.

Ordinarily, Angela would be grouchy. Who was she fooling? She was grouchy. She hadn't slept well. She had issues to resolve with the fairy queen—and with Ted—and with Derek. Let's face it, she had issues. She didn't relish witnessing the look in his eyes. What a coward, afraid to talk to her own son, to see him even.

Angela remembered his total disgust from last night and shuddered. He'd been upset. Over the top. Worst of all, she didn't blame him. The barest hint of her peaceful dream flashed in and out of her memory before Angela could grab hold of it.

Could her family ever believe in her? Would they?

Opening her bedroom door, Angela peeked out. It was her responsibility to prepare a good breakfast for her children, but she would be just as happy if they had left early for school. Yet, just as she dared to hope, they clomped down the stairs and into the kitchen.

"Good morning," Angela said timidly.

Both of her children stood in the doorway, glaring at her.

"Would you like some breakfast? Let me cook you an egg." That was a nice motherly thing. They would forgive her after a good meal. And, to be honest, food was Angela's world—something she excelled in.

"You know we don't eat breakfast." Hannah scowled.

Since when? They ate breakfast almost every morning. "It's the most important meal of the day," Angela coaxed. She knew from years of experience that eating breakfast made life much easier for everyone. "It wakes up your brain cells so you can do good in school."

Hanna rolled her eyes and flipped open a can of soda. Derek scowled and moved beside Hannah.

Was Angela a blood sucking leech or some horrible monster that her children couldn't bear to be in the same room with their own mother—all over supposedly fake fairy wings? Tears trickled down Angela's face. She hated that every conversation had to end in tears—but her frustration, her anger with the tears only made them flow harder.

"I'm ... sorry ... it was ... a big ... misunderstanding," Angela sobbed.

"If only fairies were real," Derek growled, "then you could have had fairies for children instead of us."

Angela gasped. "I don't love fairies more than you!" She moved fluidly toward him, reaching out to touch his face. He shrugged away, which brought on a new wave of sobs.

"Sheesh! The tears, Mom. Do you always have to manipulate every situation with tears?" Derek shook his head. "It's just not right."

"Yeah, Mom, you're always crying all the time, and this fairy stuff is so, ridiculous." Hannah rolled her eyes again. "You have no idea what it's doing to our social life. You are so out of line."

Hannah's words shot poison into Angela's already wounded

heart. Her children had been so cute as babies too. They were cute now, but why had she ever wanted them to talk?

She had to fight back. Not a fight in the true sense of the word, she would talk to them, reason with them, and help them to respect her fairy life. Unfortunately, her hormones dictated a different approach.

"I'm your mother!" she bawled. "I've loved you your whole lives, but I've loved fairies my whole life. It's who I am, and you've known it all along. Now go to school and get good grades!" What else could she do? It wasn't like she could sprinkle fairy dust on their heads and make everything better.

"I love you," she said as the door slammed shut.

TWENTY-TWO

Angela stormed to her closet and pulled out the plastic tub with all of her fairy collector's boxes. "I do not like fairies more than my own children!" The dream she'd had—the one of her family falling apart, pinched at her as she trudged to the living room carrying the large tub.

"While I'm with the fairies at night, they seem so real," Angela complained. "But here, now ..." she looked around her living room and sighed. "In the daylight, I'm left feeling like a fool."

Each porcelain fairy had its own box. Angela took them one-by-one and wrapped them carefully in the original tissue paper. "Let's recap," she said to Tu'illa, her favorite porcelain. "Whether my dreams are real or hallucinations, it seems that you guys have got to go." She placed her on the coffee table and wrapped Ni'na, put her into her box and then into the plastic storage tub.

"Do the fairies want me to fail?" She wrapped Tu'illa. "If not, then they should give me something, a sign of some sort." Angela put Tu'illa into the tub with all of her other porcelain fairies, and closed the lid. "How am I supposed to know I'm a real fairy if Ted or the kids can't see my wings?"

Angela walked into the kitchen and pulled out the can of chocolate drink mix. There was a sticky note on the lid. "Enjoy a cup for me. Love, Ted."

"How sweet." She pulled out the blender and made a cup of frozen hot chocolate. "Tatiana had said this was about gaining my family's respect. Maybe that's all it ever was—a warning that things are getting out of control."

She sipped her frozen hot chocolate. "There's no need in even trying to pretend I actually have a fairy mission. My family will never believe."

The doorbell rang its new and boring, *Ding Dong*. Angela hated that characterless sound. She pushed herself up and went to answer it anyway.

A slightly familiar face greeted her. Gabe the fireman. Why did she remember his name when she'd only met him once? She'd pretend it was only the trauma of their meeting and that his good looks had nothing to do with it.

"I haven't started any fires today," she saidv, her arms folded across her stomach. She should tell her friend, Amy, about this guy though. He appeared single. No ring anyway.

He smiled. "I'm not here on official fire department business."

Angela tilted her head and looked him over—navy blue shorts. T-shirt with the Gilbert fire department logo embossed on the chest (a very firm and muscled chest, she noted before quickly glancing away). Angela put her fist to her mouth and fake-coughed to hide her discomfort, and looked down—black shoes and black socks.

"Oh?" She said. "You look pretty official." She tried acting nonchalant, but she didn't have handsome firemen come to her door very often. Married, remember? She definitely needed to hook him up with her friend. If he was single.

Gabe put his fist to his mouth and coughed, too. Was he mocking her or did he also feel awkward? But if so, why?

Angela looked at him again. It was the kind of look that asks a question, like, why are you at my door if there's no fire? "May I help you?" She raised her eyebrows.

"Well, the guys and I." He chewed at a soul patch under his lip. "You know. Over at the station." Gabe indicated with a nod. "I've seen you flying, and I ..." Gabe tilted his head down and glanced at her through thick black eyelashes. "I wondered if you were okay. Yeah?"

What? Why? Why had he given her one moment's thought? She chewed on a fingernail, pondering. Had he not seen her—she was old. She was saggy. She was the mother of five children, for crying out loud. Even her husband didn't find her that attractive.

"So, can I come in?" Gabe looked hopeful and peered into her house.

As if. "No one else is home." Angela moved behind the door. Was Gabe some stalker fireman? Weren't firemen supposed to take a psychological evaluation? "I'm fine. Anyways, no need to worry." She started to close the door but then something he said finally sank in and she opened it back. "Did you say you've seen me flying at night? As in, flying, and more than one night?"

"Yeah. Yeah, that's it." He smiled again, looking relieved.

"Weird." Angela shook her head in disbelief. "That's just so weird." She stepped inside the house and closed the door while still mumbling. It was all so unfair. The fireman had seen her flying—on more than one occasion—and he didn't mean in an airplane. Angela opened the door again and Gabe was still standing on her porch. "Did you see any wings?"

"Yes, I—"

Angela closed the door absentmindedly. Ted's inability to see her wings and Gabe the fireman's ability to see them was, indeed, puzzling. According to Tatiana, humans weren't supposed to see them. Or was it just Ted who wasn't supposed to see them? Why had the fairies made such a big deal out of Ted seeing her wings and knowing she was a fairy-human if other people could?

Angela opened the door again—and yes, Gabe was still on the porch. This time he looked worried, hopeful, incredulous? Really, Angela wasn't paying attention.

"So, you believe in fairies, then?"

"Yes, I—"

And, Angela closed the door again.

Amid more door-chimes, and knocking, she walked trance-like into her bedroom and floated down into her bed. This was her sign. She was a real fairy. It wasn't a dream—never had been.

Gabe could see her wings but Ted couldn't. Gabe believed in fairies and Ted didn't. This whole scenario smacked of irony. After all, what did she care if some strange fireman believed in her?

In the interest of family peace, Angela would keep her porcelains in their boxes. For now. But eventually, her family had to believe in order for her to earn her wings.

Without intending to, Angela fell into a deep and fairy-less sleep.

Angela glanced around the room—and looked at the clock. Whoa. She'd been asleep for hours. What was up with her lately? Sleeping during the day, again?

The house needed cleaned. Dinner needed fixed. They were her only acceptable interests now. "No kid of mine will claim I prefer fairies over them." Angela pushed one leg off the bed, and then the other, and stood. Her head was woozy like she'd been drinking. She hadn't. Was she being drugged? But Angela hadn't been anywhere near that malignant wart next door.

It would have been the fulfillment of her life's dream to spread her wings and fly around town. Perhaps take in the Phoenix art gallery—if her flying was acceptable. Her wings were real, though. Gabe had said so. It didn't matter, doing something like that in broad daylight was too risky. And it was apparent the Helmans weren't the only ones keeping an eye on her.

All Ted needed was the nightly news station at their door asking about his fairy-wife.

"I'm from KPAZ," Angela mimicked. "We have news footage of your wife flying around the Phoenix valley." She shoved out a pretend microphone. "How do you feel about that?"

Angela knew exactly how Ted felt about it and dropped her hand down. She needed to get busy with dinner.

Derek and Hannah stampeded into the house at three forty-five and began doing kid-like things, or rather teenager-like things—eating while alternately ignoring Angela. She was over it. Expected it even.

"Don't fill up." Angela stood in the doorway silently demanding respect. "You're dad will be home soon and I want us to eat at the table as a family."

"I'm hungry," Derek said, grabbing his overfull plate and heading upstairs.

"We've got homework." Hannah pulled her plateful from the microwave and followed her brother up the stairs.

That went well. At least they were talking to her. It was a start.

Ted came home at five o'clock.

Angela served Orange Chicken with homemade egg rolls and stir-fry vegetables for dinner with a no-bake cheesecake for dessert. She may as well have served them corndogs straight from the freezer. Angela prepared Ted a plate of dinner and sat it on the table. He grabbed it up and strode to his recliner, got comfy, and clicked on the television.

"No meetings tonight?" Angela scooped herself a plate.

"Naw." He settled into his show. "Dinner's great, Anj." Ted lifted a spoon to her miraculous cooking ability while keeping his focus on the television.

"It was nothing." Angela shrugged. What else did she have to do with her life until her family gave their consent? But this dinner, with the citrusy sauce? Even the fairies would believe in her.

She savored her food, alone, at the table and then went to the kitchen and cleaned up her mess. Her mess, only because everyone else ignored it. "It doesn't matter," she told herself over and over again. It didn't matter that she cleaned the kitchen twice a day with no help. She didn't have anything else to do, no other "approved" interests according to her family.

Then, as she thought that last little thing, the tiniest of ideas came to mind. The teensiest of memories warmed her heart. It definitely wasn't a hot flash this time. Angela remembered that pretty little burgundy satin and lace nightgown tucked into her drawer.

It had been a respectable amount of time. She wasn't a nymphomaniac. Nope. It had been days, weeks, even years since their last interlude. Sometimes ideas of this magnitude are subject to exaggeration.

"I do have other approved interests." At least she hoped Ted approved.

Angela hung the dishrag on the sink to dry. She folded the hand towel over the oven door and turned out the kitchen light with only one thing on her mind: Putting on her sexy nightgown and seducing Ted. Okay, that was two things, but whatever.

She slipped into her bedroom feeling lighter than she had in ages, having lost a pound and a half already, and slipped into her nightgown. Slippery fabric made that whole thing way easier.

Once she was dressed, or rather undressed, Angela peered out of her bedroom door looking for kids. The house was clear. She stepped from the bedroom.

"What do you think of this?" she whispered, too nervous to say it any louder, and walked seductively, exaggerating the swing of her hips and rubbing her hands down her thighs.

Ted didn't look but his show was a rerun. He just needed a little encouragement and he'd be all hers.

"Hey good-looking." Angela sat on Ted's lap and gently took the remote, clicking it off.

"Hey!" Ted frowned.

"It's time for bed, Mr. Anderson," Angela cooed. She stood and took his hands in hers.

"I'm watching a show." Ted pulled his hand away and grabbed at the remote.

Duh! She knew he was watching a show—he was always watching a show! And with that, Angela spun around and stomped to her bedroom.

Once? She had spent $80 on a sexy nightgown and it had only worked once? She should ask for a refund. In mere seconds, the gown was in the corner and Angela was wearing her old knit shorts and T-shirt.

After only a minute or two, Ted came into the bedroom. Probably during a commercial.

"Hey, Anj. Forgive me." He climbed onto the bed and lay beside her.

He took Angela's moist hand—she hadn't had anything else to wipe her tears with—and kissed it. She wouldn't look at him. Undaunted, he kissed each finger.

Didn't he realize he had spoiled everything?

Ted started nibbling up her arm. She didn't respond—or rather she didn't say anything out loud.

Angela pulled her arm away. Her thoughts were pretty loud as she silently screamed at him for finding the television more interesting than her. Her body language spoke loudly as well when, although she hadn't wanted to, she turned away from Ted, pretending to sleep.

You can't reject the delivery and still enjoy the goods. It didn't work that way.

However, rest didn't come. Not for Angela, anyway. The silence between them became a large megaphone screaming, *You're old and wrinkled and Ted doesn't find you desirable!*

For Ted, the silence must have whispered sweet nothings because after Angela pulled her arm away, he turned over in bed and was asleep within five minutes.

Agitated, Angela tried counting sheep in order to fall asleep. It didn't work. Who ever had passed that off as an effective cure for insomnia—well, Angela hoped he'd never been paid for the idea. Ridiculous.

TWENTY-THREE

The fairies danced and played on the lawn under an Arizona ash at Freestone Park. Their dresses were made of fabric so delicate that Angela was sure it had no human equivalent. The colors were in beautiful jewel-tones and light pastels of blue, orange, pinks and greens.

Yeah, she went willingly after that fiasco at home. This was where she belonged. Gabe had figured it out. Why couldn't Ted? Angela walked to them—and thought of her dear fairy-mother. If only she was still alive. Her mother would know what to do and how to get Ted to believe.

"Angela!" The fairies welcomed her as though they'd been waiting for her, and she danced with them. They doted on her and she was finally happy. After a time, they opened their ring of dance and Angela glanced around to see what was going on. It was a vision of Ted and her children. They entered their circle laughing and dancing and celebrating together. Angela couldn't imagine anything more life-fulfilling—to actually be someone—to be seen with her family offering love and support. The scene however, wasn't real. Rather than bring her comfort, it made her feel empty.

Tatiana appeared, and when she did, the other fairies disappeared. Tatiana squinted her eyes, glaring. "Where have you been?"

Angela cupped her head between her hands. *"Ouch already."* She much preferred the dancing and peaceful visions.

"Angela, fairy-human, you act as an impetuous child, abandoning us as you did! And why do you hold your wand upside down? These bumbling efforts are one more example of why you didn't get your wish sooner. Do you want to lose your family?"

Wait, what? *"Upside down?"* Her cheeks warmed, then embarrassment turned to frustration. *"Lose my family? I was attacked! And I would have used my wand correctly if I'd known how to use it at all. Why didn't you teach me?"*

"We taught you on the night we gave you the wand. Were you not paying attention?" Tatiana's eyebrows lifted.

"Oh." That was a recent problem of hers. Focusing. Angela folded her arms and set her jaw.

Tatiana scowled. "I will teach you once again how to properly use the wand." She took her own wand and demonstrated.

"I did that." Angela removed her wand from her sweatpants and followed suit.

"You are holding the wrong end!" Tatiana took the wand from Angela, turned it around, and handed it back.

Okay, then. Angela could hold it that way. Now that Tatiana showed her, she did notice one side was narrower. Angela was bigger, so naturally her hands were bigger, and her gargantuan fingers held the wand imperfectly. Now that she knew, she would pay closer attention.

"You must not use our gifts without knowing how," Tatiana said with forced patience. "You must have a proper hold on the wand, and your intent must be clear—no daydreaming about waterfalls or fairy dresses." She gave a thin smile.

How could Angela have been any clearer? She loathed Rebecca Helman and wanted to zap her away like a pesky fly. The woman was a menace.

"Leave your neighbors alone. Focus on turning your family into believers. That is chore enough. Learn your responsibilities. You, fairy-human, are only to use our tools on pixies. This is the reason we shared them."

Right. Only use the wand on pixies. Whatever. Rebecca Helman was a pixie—just oversized like Angela. Besides, what good was all this stuff if she couldn't use it effectively against her enemies?

Tatiana's eyes narrowed. "Angela, fairy-human, time is drawing near—your time is measured in weeks—and you have not fulfilled your vow."

Angela scrunched her eyes closed. *"I can't. It's no use."*

"Find a way, fairy-human. If you refuse us now after we've welcomed you into our clan and blessed you with our most precious gifts, you will lose your family forever!"

Blah, blah, blah. How many times were they going to threaten her? She knew already. Instead of threats of losing her family, what she needed was her family's support.

Tatiana glared at Angela and shouted something quickly. It sounded like an angry buzz.

Well, that hadn't worked like she had hoped. Angela spun uncontrollably, wishing she could scream, and being unable to. She would never get used to stretching thin like spaghetti while spinning through a whirlpool. The loud flushing noise echoed and continued until she plopped down into her bed.

TWENTY-FOUR

"Good morning sunshine." Ted startled her with a kiss. "You weren't here earlier."

"Yeah, I guess not." Feeling instantly guilty, she blinked, hoping to give a viable answer.

Ted, clad in a towel, went to the closet. "So?" he said. "What's the occasion?"

"Occasion?" She got up and went into the toilet room hoping he'd forget the conversation. When she came out, he was there, staring curiously—like she was a new stamp in his collection.

"You're never up at this hour," Ted continued, buttoning his shirt.

She resembled that remark. "I went to check on the backyard." It wasn't a lie. She had been back there.

Ted scoffed. "Doing the yard work once a week isn't enough?" He raised his eyebrows. "Since when did you care about the yard?"

"Since I burnt a big hole in it, I guess." She shrugged. "What's the big deal?"

"None, I guess." He pulled a tie off his rack. "What do you think about this one?" He smirked.

"It's not green, so I like it just fine," she said, and walked to the bedroom door.

"You're funny," he said, following her. "What's for breakfast?"

"Fruit salad." It was the first thing out of her mouth.

Ted frowned.

"And eggs?"

"Okay. Yeah, I could go with that." He nodded thoughtfully.

"I'm trying to introduce new fruits into the kids' diets." Her mouth watered at the mention of fruit. "I don't want them turning into food snobs."

Ted smiled. "Yeah. They're such picky eaters and all." He smirked.

He sat at the bar and they shared easy conversation as she got things ready for breakfast.

"Here." She handed him an apple. "Peel this, please." Then she plopped a few blueberries into her mouth. They were sweet and good.

Angela whipped up the eggs, poured them into a skillet and added the fruit and some shredded cheese to the top, and then put a lid on the mixture.

"What in the world?" Ted's face scrunched. "Why'd you do that?"

"It's a fruit-tata." She smiled at her clever twist.

"The kids won't eat that."

"It's time for breakfast," Angela called up the stairway. "The kids, or you?" she asked him, getting out the plates and silverware and slamming them to the kitchen bar in front of him. "Don't stick your nose up. Don't be a food snob. You haven't even tried it yet."

Derek and Hannah came down the stairs like a heard of charging elephants. Angela served them each a slice—including Ted.

They stared at their plates and then at Angela.

She led the way by tasting it first. "Mm, this is good," she said. It was one of her more brilliant food inspirations. "Try it."

"I think I'll pass." Derek pushed his plate away.

"Me too." Hannah sat her fork tidily across her meal. "Apples and blueberries in eggs? It looks gross."

"It's not gross!" Angela stood and took her empty plate to the sink. "I work hard every day providing good meals for you guys, with no thanks at all. I think the least you could do is appreciate it once in a while." She turned away and began scrubbing at the dishes.

"Come on." Ted lifted his fork. "Let's try this together." With his coaxing, the kids and Ted finished their one slice of breakfast.

The extremely helpful Anderson family wasn't helping Angela at all. Derek and Hannah kept her too frustrated to concentrate on her mission, and Ted the dear man, thought she'd turned into a lush and had quietly removed all the liquor from the house.

What would Tatiana do to her family if she didn't figure out how to help them? The fairies had tricked her into making the vow. In truth, she would have promised to help regardless. And, although she didn't really understand what to do, she hoped to do it soon. She hoped to make her mother proud by being of service. Most importantly, she wanted her family's respect and support.

Ted stood behind her, nuzzling her neck. "Why are you so moody lately?" he asked.

"*There is such a thing as fairies, and I am one.*" Angela wanted to say, but she didn't. Sometimes silence really is best.

He touched his hand to her shoulder, looking concerned. "I think you've started menopause." He kept a straight face for only a second, then grinned like a hyena.

Gag! Why did he have to say it? After eight months of night sweats and moodiness, Ted, the observant man, finally had a clue.

"Really? Funny man?" Angela shot him a glare, then without thinking, she pulled the spray attachment from the sink and squirted him in the face.

He gasped and sputtered.

Angela laughed. "You're so cool," she said and put the attachment back.

Ted grabbed it quick. "Take that!" He squirted her, then put the hose away. "I'm sorry," he said, rubbing her shoulders. "I didn't mean to get your wings wet." He grinned at his joke.

"Dang straight." She shook her shoulders and her hair as though her wings were there. "They've got to be dry by tonight."

They laughed together. Angela knew Ted still didn't believe, but it was okay for now.

There was only one viable solution to her predicament. She needed to help her clan in spite of Ted's disbelief. The only way to keep her family from harm was to help the fairies while pretending she wasn't one. Angela's plan unfolded something like this:

"You are aware I'm not pretending to be a fairy anymore." *I no longer need to pretend,* Angela continued silently. "You, my family, are my life." She smiled, indicating them.

"You're so mature." Ted kissed her cheek. "I've got to go put on a dry shirt." He hummed on his way to the bedroom.

"Whatever." Hannah shrugged her shoulders.

"Right." Derek grabbed a soda from the refrigerator.

Ah, but their inattention wouldn't bother her today, wouldn't bring her to tears. They didn't want to talk about it? — that was fine. The less talk the better. Angela poured herself a glass of apple juice, gulping thirstily.

"Derek has a football game Friday night." Ted came back in, tying his tie. "Let's go as a family."

Hannah rolled her eyes. "I'd love to, but I've already made plans with Denise." She grabbed her backpack.

"I think you should cancel them," Ted said.

"We volunteered to help at the concession stand. I can't let Mr. Varner down like that, and Denise needs me there. I'll still be at the game just like a big, happy family. Plus it'll be helping the boosters." She gave her father a sugar-sweet grin.

Ted returned the smile warily, seemingly resigned to their daughter's perpetual busyness, and then turned to Angela. "I guess that leaves just the two of us."

"Yay." Angela waved a pretend flag. She loved football. Not. She did love her son though, so she tried to act enthusiastic. "High five."

Angela raised her hand but when Derek reluctantly raised his, their hands didn't meet.

"Awkward," Hannah said.

"Hopefully they let you play every round."

"Quarter," Derek said. "You play a round of golf. Football is divided into quarters."

"Oh, okay." Whatever. "I just like the game better when you're in it." Even though Ted got frustrated having to give her a play-by-play of the action.

"Come on, guys and dolls, we've got to get going." Ted kissed Angela. But if she was getting technical, chickens gave longer kisses than the one she received.

"Be safe," Angela said. And they were gone.

Well. Angela looked around her home. She needed to learn how to conquer the pixies today. She wanted this whole affair wrapped up by Friday.

First, she cleaned the kitchen and dried up her and Ted's water fight. It took only a few minutes. Now she was ready for the main feature of her day—learning to use her fairy dust and her wand.

Angela went to the bedroom and pulled the magical objects from their hiding place. She opened the bag of fairy dust. Would it make her smaller? She stuck her fingers in, but it was hard to only get a small pinch when her fingers were so big compared to the bag. With a quick idea, she licked the tip of her pinkie finger and then touched it to the gelatinous dust.

That could prove dangerous. She looked at the sparkling mass. What if she had too much and it shrank her to a speck? What if she didn't get it over herself evenly and only half of her shrank?

"Definitely too dangerous." She wiped the dust back into the bag. Her fairy porcelains were the perfect substitute for herself. They weren't alive. They couldn't die. And, although she'd miss them if something bad happened, like being transported to their homeland in Italy, better them than her.

Testing the waters of her theory, Angela went to her large, walk-in closet and took out one of her storage boxes. Sitting it on the sofa, she pulled out all of her porcelains until she settled on using Breena, Raisa, and Faylinn for her experiment.

"This is your chance to do something great," she said, hugging them to her chest and taking them to the kitchen. "You always wanted to fly." At least she had pretended they did.

She placed them on the kitchen island near the fairy dust. Would they shrink? They were already fairy-sized. If they shrank, they'd be nothing but a speck. She moistened the tip of her pinkie finger with her tongue, touched her finger to the fairy dust and tapped the nail over the fairies, sprinkling only a few granules over her porcelains.

The precious knickknacks began spinning and flying crazily about the room like a feline on catnip. "Aak!" She didn't know what she expected, but not that!

Angela leapt forward, trying to catch hold of Breena, and missed. She heard a crash. Raisa had bumped into their hand-spun glass vase in the entryway, an expensive heirloom. It lay in shards across the floor. She ran toward the fairy hoping to subdue the porcelain figurine, tripped over the coffee table and bruised her shin. The fairy porcelain flitted away.

Had she used too much dust?

Faylinn flew across the living room and touched one after another of the other porcelains bringing them into action. Before Angela knew what to do, sixteen porcelains were causing havoc throughout her home.

"You crazy things, get back in your boxes!" Angela leaped after the blonde Kre'lyn, caught her and put her into her box. The porcelain bounced inside.

It took hours of chasing, jumping, and leaping to catch them all.

Really, she felt like a ballerina. Not. None went willingly. The boxes popped around the living room like jumping beans.

"That was weird," she said. Having found, captured, and boxed most of the fairies, Angela fell back onto the sofa exhausted and bleeding from stepping on glass shards.

The original three remained in hiding but at least they were no longer destroying the house. Angela hoped they had run out of fairy dust and were lying somewhere.

"So, turning myself fairy-sized isn't an option." She wouldn't risk a scene like that.

Walking on her heels, Angela hobbled to her bathroom and pulled out the first-aid supplies and her tweezers. One by one, she pulled the remaining shards from her feet and replaced them with bandages. Unwilling to mess up her bed, Angela hobbled to the family room sofa, slumped into its soft cushions, and closed her eyes.

For all the destruction throughout her house, not one of the porcelains had broken. Unless the three missing ones were damaged somehow.

After gathering strength, Angela got up and swept up the vase remnants, and finished just before Derek and Hannah came home from school. Although usually extremely unobservant, today they noticed the storage box of fairy porcelains the moment they entered the room.

"You brought the fairies back?" Hannah rolled her eyes and groaned.

"Ha!" Derek laughed. "I knew you couldn't do it."

"Do you see them anywhere?" Really, did they? "I was just looking at them is all." She picked up the box and lugged it to her closet.

"Whatever." Hannah rolled her eyes again and bounded up the stairs. "What's this?" She shouted. "Get this thing out of my room!" Hannah stormed down the stairs with a statuesque Faylinn and plopped it into Angela's hand.

Ah, so at least one of them had gone upstairs.

"I'm not a fairy." Derek opened the refrigerator. "So if one's in my room, you'd better get it out or I'm throwing it in the trash." He pulled out the leftover spaghetti and heaped some on his plate.

"There's nothing wrong with my porcelains," she grumbled. "You'd probably rather I decorate with sculls and crossbones."

"Would you?" Hannah looked hopeful, as if that was an option.

"It's all in the perspective, Mom." Derek turned to face her. "You going to get a skeleton costume and start parading around the Helmans' yard?"

Really, why had she wanted them to learn to talk? Angela hobbled up to Derek's room. Raisa was on his chessboard standing in victory around the toppled chess pieces. She snatched it up, stuffed it unceremoniously into her pocket, and descended the stairs.

"You need to clean your room," she said.

Derek picked out a couple more meatballs and placed them on top of his noodles, then put it in the microwave oven. "You're not going to start annoying the Helmans again, are you?" He carried his warmed plate toward the family room.

"No, Derek. I am not going to annoy the Helmans," Angela snapped. "Regardless of what you think, it's not my plan to annoy you either." Children could be so cruel. Angela wiped her eyes and fought her silly tears.

TWENTY-FIVE

"I'm home," Ted said, walking in the door.

"Oh, dear, yes you are." Angela peeked behind the toaster for the still missing fairy porcelain, and gave Ted a peck on the cheek. "Did you have a good day?" The laundry room door was open. Maybe it went in there.

"It was long and hard," he said loosening his tie.

"That's nice," she said, not listening—she hadn't looked in the laundry room yet. She walked past him and did a quick search. The fairy porcelain wasn't there. She shook her head and came out. "Dinner's ready. You want some?" She'd butter Ted up with his favorite meal, discuss fairies—and after he fell asleep, she was off to see the fairies.

"Um, yeah." He took his coat off. "You okay? You seem a little distracted—and why are you walking like that?"

"I brought out my fairy porcelains, and my beautiful vase broke."

"Did it break under your feet?"

"No, it didn't break under my feet." That was ridiculous. Angela scowled and then went to the bottom of the stairs.

"Time for dinner," she called.

"Not hungry," shouted Hannah from her room.

"We're losing these kids," she told Ted. "Have you noticed how we never eat together anymore?" She had. "The kids fill up after school and then they're either up in their rooms or over at a friend's house."

Ted met her at the bottom of the stairs. "Get down here," he shouted. "We're eating together as a family." The corner of his lip lifted when Hannah stomped down the stairs followed by Derek. "You just have to let them know you mean it. Teach them to respect you and they won't walk all over you like they do."

"Why hadn't I thought of that?" Angela muttered.

"Pardon?" Ted stopped and waited.

"Nothing." Angela shook her head. "Never mind."

"I was just trying to help."

Yeah, his criticisms were super helpful. Angela folded her arms and followed her clan to the dining room.

It was nice having dinner together. Angela smiled serenely. Her children scowled and glanced at one another. She had discovered a new talent—annoying her children. Ha! Maybe they'd have dinner at the table from now on. They'd learn to enjoy it. Eventually.

"I've been thinking about what you said." Angela sighed and scooped herself a bowl of fruit salad. She had outdone herself tonight. It looked and smelled delicious.

"What?" Ted stuffed a bite of meatloaf into his mouth and stared longingly toward the television.

"Remember? You said something about keeping things in perspective." Angela gave him a hopeful look. "Back when you wanted me to join the Happy Hookers?"

"What?" Derek stood. "No!"

"Sit down. It's a crochet group." Angela lifted her eyebrows. "It's a play on words. A pun."

"Still." He sank into his chair. "You can't join a group called *that*," he muttered. "What would people think?"

"Imagine when that gets all over school." Hannah pursed her lips.

"I'm not joining the group," Angela said shrilly. "If the *Hell-mans* would stop spreading lies, none of this would be an issue." She started again on her fruit salad knowing her emotions had gone too far.

Ted put his hand on Angela's arm. "What about perspective?"

"Well." Angela cleared her throat. "I know that you and Derek and Hannah feel threatened by my interest in fairies." She waved a hand against his denial. "You know it's true. And today, when I had the porcelains out, Derek threatened to destroy one of them."

"I told you, teach the kids to treat you with respect." Ted glowered at Derek and Hannah.

"I didn't have any problems with the first three," Angela said defensively.

"Still here." Hannah stabbed a fried potato wedge. "You put the fairies away and said you loved us more—and then you had them out today. What does that say?" She shrugged her shoulder. "It hurt." She ducked her head and returned to her meal.

Angela leapt from her chair. "Honey." She squeezed Hannah's shoulders. "I do love you more—but this isn't a competition." She looked up at Ted. "I was trying an experiment. And," she shook her head. "It got out of hand is all."

"I'm sure that the kids don't mind your fairy porcelains as much as you think," Ted insisted.

"That's right." Derek put his fork down. "We were just surprised you brought them out again so soon. That's all." He smiled. Angela loved that smile but suspected Derek's reconciliation was more for the benefit of his newly acquired driving privileges. "And I was teasing about your doll," he added.

Hannah nodded. "Yeah," she agreed.

"So." Angela gulped down the 'doll' reference. "Everyone is okay with me having a little fun with the fairies?" Angela knew they would misinterpret her meaning, but it was all for the best.

Eyebrows furrowed and no longer eating, Ted appeared suspicious.

"Derek was teaching me about perspective earlier, and I will. I'll keep it in better perspective this time. I promise." Angela smiled, wide-eyed and hopeful of her plan. "No porcelains in the living room." She ticked her fingers as she recited the list. "No walking around out front in the middle of the night. No annoying the Helmans." Although the Helmans were so easy to annoy, and were so, so, annoying themselves. Angela kept that part to herself.

The part of her flying around the neighborhood was also her little secret—definitely on a need-to-know basis. And her family definitely did not need to know. Not yet. By the weekend though, or at least eventually, her family—especially Ted—would believe.

While her family watched television, Angela kept a close eye on the clock as she flitted around the kitchen, putting the food away, loading the dishwasher, washing the counters—and becoming increasingly anxious for her nightly, "Good night, dear," from Ted.

The time finally came. Ted stood, he stretched. "It's a school night," he said and clicked the television off. "Time to hit the sack."

"Wahoo!" Angela threw her dishtowel in the air.

Ted and the kids stared at her.

"Um, I mean, yeah." She nodded. "Bedtime." She yawned. "Man, am I tired."

While her unsuspecting husband prepared for bed, Angela pulled the fairy treasures from her underwear drawer and put them in her pocket. Tonight, she would fly to Freestone Park and see what all the pixie fuss was about.

She then walked nonchalantly to the bathroom where Ted was brushing his teeth. "Maybe I could pamper you by rubbing your back tonight." She got her toothbrush. "You did say you'd had a hard day. It'll help you sleep."

Ted tilted his head quizzically. "Oh, yeah," he mumbled. Then, instead of following his usual routine that evening, he grinned mischievously and left the bedroom without a word. He returned with something behind his back.

"I brought you a cup of hot chocolate." Ted carefully revealed the steaming cup with a smile so big that all Angela saw was the dimple in his left cheek. She loved that dimple.

Twisting her mouth to the side, Angela looked at him, puzzled. Hot cocoa? Didn't he understand her raging body temperature? Was he totally oblivious to her night sweats? Besides, Ted didn't cook—not even hot water.

"What's this all about?" Why would anyone in Arizona think of drinking hot cocoa before January unless they were camping?

"It'll help with your sleepwalking." Ted urged the cup toward her. "You like hot cocoa, don't you?"

Angela took the cup reluctantly. She loved all things chocolate. Ted knew that. But she didn't plan to sleep, let alone sleepwalk. Ted didn't know that. "I brushed my teeth, and I'm trying to lose weight," she hedged. She had her questions about that chocolate mix. Something was suspicious, but Angela couldn't quite put her finger on what it was.

"Hey, I'm trying to be a good husband here. Just drink it and see if it helps."

This was terribly sweet of him. Maybe Ted was trying to apologize for hurting her feelings. Angela put the cup to her lips and drank her husband's peace offering. The hot liquid coursed its way through her body, warming it. With that warmth, her body made its own heat with an unwelcome hot flash that flowed through each cell like a well-rehearsed aria.

The cocoa tasted a little off. Angela made a mental note to check the expiration date.

"Sweet dreams." Ted took the cup from her and placed it on the nightstand.

"Sweet dreams." Angela lifted Ted's T-shirt and put her fingers to his back.

Ted flipped over, and moaned with pleasure. Less than two minutes later, he gave a little snort and Angela knew he was asleep

TWENTY-SIX

"Rise and shine, sleepyhead." Ted leaned down and kissed Angela's forehead. "How's my sunshine this morning?"

"What?" Angela propelled herself to sitting. "Oh," she groaned, and fell back down, her head spinning. "Think I'm coming down with the flu?"

Ted felt her forehead. "You don't feel warm."

That was a lie. Angela scratched her head. "You're dressed for work." What had happened to her last night? "Did you have breakfast?" After rubbing Ted's back, everything had gone blank.

"I had a bagel. The kids and I cleaned the yard. They left for school." Ted shrugged. "You're free for the morning."

"Yeah, I'll have to take that into consideration while I'm doing the laundry and cleaning the bathrooms." It was an endless cycle. She smiled. "Have a good day at work." Would Tatiana do something to her husband? Would her family be safe from pixies? It was a worry. "I love you," she said. Climbing out of bed and pulling Ted into an embrace, she gave him a kiss to remember her by.

"I might have a few more minutes before I've got to get out the door." Ted grinned and kicked the bedroom door closed behind him.

Angela dressed quickly. She went from room to room humming nervously as she straightened. They'd had a beautiful moment before Ted went to work—but that porcelain fairy was still missing.

The doorbell chimed around eleven.

"It better not be that fireman," Angela muttered as she made her way to the door. "Or that cantankerous cat from next door." Angela slowed her pace. Let the woman wait.

"Oh!" Angela said, opening the door. She peered at the familiar face standing there. "Amy?" Angela threw her arms around her friend. "Amy Baker, it's so good to see you!" She pulled away and looked her short, slender friend over. "You've changed your hair."

"I cut it at the beginning of summer," Amy said.

"I like it." Angela eyed the basket in her hands. "Are you selling something?" Amy had been recently widowed but Angela hadn't realized her friend needed to work.

"I was hoping you'd be home," Amy said lightly. "I've got enough food in here for both of us. Come on." She took Angela's hand and pulled her toward the sidewalk.

"Wait. What's going on?" Angela frowned. "Did I forget a lunch date?" She felt horrible.

Amy smiled. "I got lonely and thought we could have a picnic."

Angela gulped down her guilt. "I'm so sorry," she said. "I should have thought of you being cooped up alone in your house—it should have been me inviting you for a picnic."

"Nonsense." Amy waved the protest away. "Let's go to Freestone Park. I love watching the ducks and waterfowl." Amy looked hopeful. "Is that okay?"

"That's great." Angela smiled, suddenly grateful for the opportunity to leave the house. Sharing a picnic with a friend, checking for pixies, and possibly becoming hero to the fairies all at the same time, Angela loved multitasking. And Amy believed in fairies. She could help. "Let me get my purse." Angela ran inside, threw her magical tools into the inner pocket of her purse, and came back out. "Let's get on the road," she said.

The two of them got into Amy's car and headed west with the car's air-conditioning on full blast. The first week of October compared easily in heat to August—hot, always hot. Sometimes the weather didn't get a break until November, but on this day, a warm autumn breeze played in the air as they stepped out onto the Freestone parking lot.

Angela surveyed the landscape. It looked differently during the day. It appeared so ordinary Angela couldn't imagine fairies here.

"I remember when Phil and I first moved to Gilbert," Amy said. "You and Ted made us feel so welcome."

"We didn't do that much." Angela smiled at the memory. "You guys are easy to like—and you're the first, and only, person I've ever met that loves fairies as much as me."

"You decided we should call ourselves the "Double A's."" Amy laughed as they walked over the wooden pedestrian bridge.

"That was you," Angela insisted. "You thought it matched our bra size." She hefted her breasts mockingly and laughed.

"It was because both of our names start with A." Amy brushed across the top of her breasts. "Clearly my bra-size isn't a double-A."

Angela looked her over. "Me thinks they've grown a size or two. Do you care to explain?"

Amy wiped a strand of hair off her forehead. "No." The corner of her mouth lifted. "Only that Phil left me a little extra. I thought I'd put it to good use."

They both laughed. It was good catching up with Amy. They chatted non-stop and ended at their favorite spot near the waterfall. They had privacy there to talk.

"Did you remember Leanne is expecting?" Angela couldn't wait for the arrival of her first grandbaby.

"Of course I remember." Amy grinned. "I haven't been that out of it."

"It's a girl. They're naming her Zoey Grace—Grace is Rusty's mom's name."

"How do you feel about that?"

"It's a beautiful name." Angela shrugged. "Any name would have been fine, really it would." She pushed her hair back. "She's my first granddaughter. To me, naming her after the other mom is like saying, 'We like her better.'"

"You're thinking about it all wrong." Amy patted Angela's hand. "That's not their reasoning at all. I'm sure of it."

Her friend was probably right. Angela smiled. She loved that Amy was here, and filled her in on all the details surrounding the upcoming arrival.

"It shouldn't be much longer," Angela said. "We just hope Zoey will wait for her dad to get home."

"It must be tough being a military wife."

"Yeah," Angela agreed. The bubbling sound of water rippling over rocks in the manmade stream serenaded the friends as they chatted and set up their picnic at the concrete table.

"I miss how we used to come here more often," Amy said. "Of course with Phil, and the summer." She waved her hand dismissively. "Even so, it's been a while."

"Remember how we'd go along the sidewalks pointing out everywhere we thought fairies lived?" Come to find out, they actually did. Angela peered over her shoulder.

"We were so silly." Amy wiped her brow. "It's way too hot here for fairies or pixies, or even humans for that matter."

"Silly?" That stung. Angela held her hand against her heart. "There are so many beautiful—magical places in this large metropolis that would suit them. Freestone Park is just one of them." She tried keeping the shrill tone from her voice, and indicated the water. "The lake and the waterfall feeding into it has attracted hundreds of migrating waterfowl each year. Why not fairies?"

Amy didn't say anything for a time. She pulled a bag of breadcrumbs out of the picnic basket, picked a couple pieces from the bag and tossed them into the water. "So, what have you been up to lately?" She asked as the ducks glided to the water's edge.

A direct change of subject, but why? The question seemed innocent enough, and it was a question to be expected from reuniting friends. But somehow, something in her voice, the inflection maybe, made Angela wonder if her friend had heard rumors. The timing was too coincidental.

Angela rolled her eyes, imitating her children. "You don't want to know."

"Hey, I thought Double A's always stuck together." Amy prodded her friend, smiling encouragingly. "What's up?"

Okay, she had definitely heard something—but what—from whom? Angela watched her friend, chewing her lip and pondering exactly what to say.

"I've become a giant fairy, wings and all, and I have a special mission to perform. If I don't, the fairies will destroy my family." Apparently that wouldn't go over well.

"Well," Angela started, "Ted and the kids are tired of the whole fairy thing." She glanced at Amy to appraise her expression—one of encouragement, and not surprise or disbelief, which would be her normal reaction. Ted—yes. Her husband must have called. "I think Ted's worried about me. I've been having a rough time this past month."

"Oh, sweetheart, that's terrible. Tell me all about it." Amy kept an open countenance.

Angela didn't know any other way to be sure who had spoken

155

to Amy except to come right out and ask. "Did Ted call you?" She tilted her head a little, hoping Amy wouldn't think she was rude. Good friends were so hard to come by.

Amy looked away seemingly embarrassed at first, then she turned back and looked at Angela with concern. "Ted called me the other day. He's very worried. He said you burned your bed and linens in the backyard?" Her tone indicated she couldn't believe Angela would do such a thing.

Angela nodded. It wasn't as bad as it sounded. A glimmer of shock washed across Amy's face and then smoothed back into a friendly smile. She was a good friend.

"I was having a bad day—the kids were being terrible. I overreacted. That's all." Angela sounded defensive even to herself.

"What happened?" Amy leaned against the table, ready to listen.

"It all turned out okay, and I met someone—someone for you." It was kind of odd setting her friend up, but it felt right.

Amy grimaced. "I don't know that I'm ready. It hasn't been a year."

"There's no set time you have to wait, and it's not like you have kids to keep you company." That was harsh. "I'm sorry," she said. "I didn't mean it like that. It's just Gabe—his name's Gabe—handsome, muscular." Angela lifted her eyes toward heaven and sighed. "He's a fireman or an EMT or a fireman EMT—something. He works for the Gilbert fire department." Angela chewed her lip, and then plowed on with the rest, "He's hunk-a-licious man-candy, and you've got to date him—keep him in the family so to speak." Angela looked away. That was too much sharing. She gulped guiltily, and watched her friend.

Amy tilted her head as though considering. "I came here to help you," she finally said. "Tell me what's going on in your life, and I'll consider it."

Angela couldn't ask for a better deal than that. "Okay," she said, sorry that she'd gone on about a complete stranger like that, and anxious to move to a different subject—but she hesitated, not knowing what to say. Would Angela believe her own fairy story if someone were to tell her? Let's see. She drummed her fingers against her mouth.

"Hey, guess what! I'm a fairy, but my wings only come at night when no one's looking. And I had the craziest experience yesterday when I used fairy dust on my porcelain figurines."

Angela twisted her mouth to one side. Yeah, probably not. She glanced up appraising Amy's expression. She did pretty well actually, trying very carefully not to show the least bit of disapproval or impatience.

"Is there more?" Amy asked apprehensively.

"More? Of course there's more." But even Angela-fairy-lover couldn't vocalize the experience. "How about let's eat instead."

Angela eyed the picnic basket on the ground beside the table. A small squeak left her mouth as she stared in blank astonishment. A pixie sat on the wicker lid.

Angela hadn't ever seen a pixie—pointy ears, translucent, papery wings like a dragonfly—green eyes.

"Eek!" She slammed her eyes shut. It was a pixie all right. Angela jumped up, fumbling in her pockets for her wand or fairy dust. They weren't there. Her purse. They were in the pocket of her purse. She peeked an eye open and grabbed it.

"What's going on?" Amy searched around under the table. "Did you see a spider, or a mouse or something?"

"It's in the basket." Angela held her purse on her lap, calculating what to do.

"A mouse?"

"Or something."

"Well, I'm not getting it out!" Amy jumped away from the picnic table.

"Go get a cup from the trash, and some paper towels from the bathroom, and I'll get it."

Her friend rushed off.

Angela opened her purse and jumped back. The porcelain fairy flew at Angela's face, holding Angela's wand in one hand, the bag of fairy dust in its other.

Angela grabbed the bag and tried for the wand. The porcelain darted out of Angela's reach.

The pixie jumped out onto the basket lid. Angela sucked in a lungful of air, and blew.

The pixie flitted out of her way.

Angela blew again, and again. Each time, the pixie moved and stuck her tongue out at Angela.

"Just hold still." Lightheaded, Angela stopped to catch her breath.

The fairy porcelain flitted to the top of the basket and began dueling the pixie.

This was too much! Couldn't she just have a nice visit with her friend and start annihilating pixies another day? Angela kicked the basket. The two creatures fell inside.

The pixie climbed onto the basket's lid and stuck her tongue out. *Pffft!*

The porcelain figurine flew out and pushed the pixie, trying to get it to fall backward.

Angela was so startled by the scene, she forgot to blow her fairy air on the creature while it was distracted.

"What's going on?" Amy walked up with a handful of paper towel and a couple of plastic cups from the trash. "Did you find it? What is it?"

"Ants." Angela smiled guiltily, her fingers thrumming nervously on the table. She'd waited too long. She couldn't open the lid and try catching the pixie in front of Amy. "What did you bring us for lunch?" she said, trying to change the subject. Oops. Big mistake.

Amy reached for the basket. The pixie would hex her.

"No!" Angela screamed, lunging forward, knocking the picnic basket from Amy's grasp. She had to send that pixie back to its homeland — and that porcelain fairy had cost her $60!

The basket slid across the pavement, the pixie and fairy porcelain no longer in sight. Angela stumbled toward it, intent on getting that pixie. She'd zip it inside her purse, and then sprinkle fairy dust on it at home when no one was watching. Apprehensively, she lifted the lid.

The pixie and porcelain weren't there.

Angela crawled around, looking in the rocks. She crawled under the table. "Nice pedicure, Amy."

Angela crawled back to the basket. They must have hidden behind the sandwiches. She reached to lift the lid.

The whole thing slipped from her grasp.

"Don't worry girlfriend. I won't let you starve." Amy hefted the basket onto the table.

Angela started to get up and bumped her head. "Ow!" She sat back in the dirt holding her spinning head, her tan slacks a filthy mess, until finally she was able to heave herself back onto the bench.

"Still as clumsy as ever," Amy said. With a forced laugh, she started pulling the contents from the basket. Angela held her breath, staring wide-eyed each time her friend's hand went in, and exhaled each time Amy lifted something out. Fresh sandwiches made with homemade-looking bread, fruit, two sodas and a plastic container of sugar cookies. Angela sat at the edge of her seat ready to pounce at the first sight of either a pixie or her porcelain.

When all the contents were on the table, Angela slumped back giddy with relief, and then stood up, grabbing the basket between her hands. Lifting both lids, she looked inside, staring at the empty basket with a scowl. Where had they gone?

"What? Didn't I bring enough?" Amy's brows furrowed, her lips pursed.

"No, um yes, the lunch looks lovely. I ..." Angela broke off at the sight of the cookies. Amy made the best in town. They were tempting, but she put the basket under the table and forced herself to take a sandwich.

"Have you ever wondered what it would be like?" Angela eyed the luscious red, yet out-of-season strawberries, and the honeydew cubes. She had read once that fairy urges toward fruits and sugar were real and nearly impossible to resist. Without any further thought, she picked up a ripe, green chunk and popped it in her mouth. "Mmmm," she breathed, eyes closed.

"Wondered what it would be like, to what?" Amy asked between bites of sandwich.

"To be a fairy." They used to have similar conversations. Angela acted casually uninterested and took a bite of her sandwich. She tried savoring it appropriately, but then grabbed a strawberry and ate it at the same time, while keeping an eye on her friend's expression, gauging it.

Amy didn't say anything for a long time. Angela wondered if she would have to repeat herself. She took a couple of pieces of bread and tossed them to the waiting mallards.

The pixie was there—glaring triumphantly on the back of a bright male duck, and sticking out her tongue. Again. Was she trying to provoke Angela? The porcelain fairy was on the shore, lifeless. Angela jumped up, raced to her miniature knickknack, grabbed it, and walked with forced calmness back to the table.

"Do you see that?" Angela asked, slipping the porcelain into her purse's zipper section and zipping it shut.

"The mallard? Yes, of course."

"Is there anything on his back?"

"What do you think is there Angela, a fairy?" Amy folded her arms across her chest.

"No," Angela agreed. It definitely wasn't a fairy. "No, of course not. There's nothing there. I just wondered, you know, if you ever pretended anymore." She tried to appear sane, thoughtful.

Angela's forehead beaded with sweat. Maybe the picnic wasn't such a good idea. She felt the rushing waves of another hot flash building. Grrr! Why did her body have to be her enemy? She hated it—she always had to a degree—but now the reasons were far too numerous to list.

Taking deep, calming breaths, Angela looked away from the pixie, and away from the duck. If she could only calm her thrashing heart. Angela placed her opened soda on her neck careful not to spill any, rolling it around, laying it on her chest just above her cleavage (or where it would be if she had any), and then on her forehead. It helped.

Hot flash averted, she looked back to the lake. The duck, apparently bored from waiting for more bread, had drifted away. The diminutive pixie was also out of sight. Those miniature imps really were taking over the park, and in a big way.

"Girlfriend," Amy said, "if anyone deserves to be a fairy, it's you." She smiled sadly. "We did have a lot of fun pretending."

"Yes. Pretending." Angela agreed, noting her usage of past tense.

"But it's not real." Amy opened the container of cookies and handed one to Angela. "We need to remember the world we live in. It's no good getting caught up in a make-believe world. Fairies, magical creatures, they aren't real." She looked at Angela, concerned. "You need to stop this nonsense right now before it gets even more out of hand."

"Of course." Angela smiled. What, exactly, had Ted told her friend?

Her cookie eaten too quickly, she chewed her nails and eyed

the container. How long did propriety insist she wait before taking another? Angela opened the lid and whiffed the heavenly aroma of sweetness, her thoughts becoming unmanageable. "Mmm." But she glimpsed a movement out of the corner of her eye and looked up—had the pixie returned?

Amy patted Angela's hand. "You really need to give up the fairy thing," she said. "There are so many better ways to fill your time." She looked at Angela with bright eyes. "You love doing crafts. You could make some of those wooden angels to give as gifts at Christmastime. If you gave me one, I'd hang it on my tree. Promise." Amy smiled. "Or, you could emphasize your cooking skills—maybe start a muffin business—or something. But whatever you do, don't keep going on about fairies. We should be so over that at our age."

"Is this some sort of fairy intervention?" Angela laughed nervously. She knew that "we" was code for "you" as in, you should be so done with playing fairies at your age. Angela was glad she hadn't said more. No, she wouldn't say a thing about the fairies and pixies plaguing her world lately.

It was bad enough having her husband think she was weird—but to set her best friend and fairy-loving *compadre* against her?

"Are you finished with these cookies?" Angela pulled one from the container.

TWENTY-SEVEN

Water and bubbles filled the tub. Angela turned the Jacuzzi jets on. Bubbles floated to the top, and she switched the jets off. Neither Amy nor Ted had any faith in her. Seeing that pixie at Freestone Park had her rattled. Had they taken over in Angela's short absence? And why had she had an absence at all? Was Tatiana still angry, had the fairy queen given up on her?

A bubble bath, she decided, was the best way to kick back and get over her negative feelings. A little time moping, pampering herself with candlelight and a little soft music, was the perfect solution for frazzled nerves, a broken ego, and the sheer exhaustion of her pixie-chasing debacle at the park.

Angela felt like Audrey Hepburn—if only she had Audrey's looks and grace. Angela brought a book to read while she soaked but soon became bored with it and set the book aside. Who was she kidding; she couldn't see the words on the page in that dim light.

She began playing with the bubbles, piling them on her arms like great bubble-muscles, dabbing some on her nose, and staring at them cross-eyed. The bubbles didn't last long near the candle flame although the prism colors shone through brilliantly.

A few bubbles stuck to the faucet, and a drip of water wound its way through them to land soundlessly on the bubbles below. A new drop formed, and Angela stuck her toe there to catch it, letting the water run down her foot.

She emptied her mind of all thoughts other than her toe, the water drops, and the bubbles and put her toe a little farther inside the faucet. Her toe was a miniature dam. When she pulled her toe free, it released a larger amount. A bubble crater formed.

"How about a bubble Grand Canyon?" She put her toe in again and waited for water droplets to collect on the other side. When she pulled her toe out—Angela felt a sharp pain on her toe—and her toe didn't come out of the faucet.

Her heart lurched with alarm, but she would remain calm. So, thinking skinny thoughts and willing her toe slender, Angela tried again. It didn't budge. Her bubble Grand Canyon forgotten, she tried again, and again.

Her heart beat faster, and Angela was decidedly un-calm. She couldn't go into shock over something like this. Could she? She took a few deep breaths to make sure she didn't, and continued pulling at her toe. She lost her balance and swirled around the water-filled tub like a monkey on a waterslide.

"Agh! This can't be happening!" She grabbed hold of the faucet. "Who gets their toe stuck in the faucet? No one, that's who!" If there was even a remote possibility of it happening, wouldn't the manufacturers put a label there? 'Warning! Sticking your toe in the faucet could be hazardous to your health.'

She wasn't a ballerina or a contortionist. Bending her body far enough to get a good grip on her toe and the faucet was hard. It hurt. Angela tried another way. Sitting sideways in the tub, she leaned her left leg out over the edge. "Ow, ow, ow!" The movement hurt her knee. The sharp metal inside the faucet cut into her toe.

After a time, she quit. Gave up. Her joints hurt from trying to maneuver them. Her knee felt like she had knocked it out of its socket. The water was cold, the bubbles gone, and she couldn't even reach a towel. Angela had to sit there with her extremities curling up like prunes, waiting.

This wasn't a good time to cry, but she did. A few salty drops joined their chlorinated cousins.

They had no clock in the bathroom. She always wanted one. Ted hadn't seen the need. Nevertheless, it seemed like hours before she heard the kids walk into the house.

She hoped it was them.

"Hannah?"

Nothing.

"Hannah? Is that you?"

The refrigerator opened and the TV came on. It was the kids. Angela waited for the quiet between commercials, and then shouted, "Hannah!"

"What?" She opened the bedroom door. "Ew! Mom, put some clothes on."

That was the one drawback to their master bedroom. In an effort to make it seem luxurious, the builders had put an archway from the bedroom to the bathroom—no door. Anyone standing at the bedroom doorway could see straight into their bathroom, with the glass-enclosed shower and their Jacuzzi tub straight in the line of vision.

Until now, she thought their large, walk-in closet more than made up for that little flaw.

"I'm stuck. Close your eyes and bring me a towel."

"Mom! Ew!" Hannah repeated. "You're naked!"

Angela tried calming herself with a couple of deep breaths. It didn't work. "Get in here right now and give me a towel!"

Derek appeared at the door. "What's going on? Oh, gross!" He winced back as if he'd burned his eyes out.

"Yeah, tell me about it. Mom wants me to go in there." Hannah scowled.

"What for?"

"She wants a towel—says she's stuck."

"I am stuck!" Angela shouted.

"Well, take her a towel then, if she says she wants one."

"She doesn't have any clothes on," Hannah hissed. "You take her one."

Derek scratched his temple and frowned. "No. You're a girl. Take Mom a towel." He turned and walked away.

Hannah put her hand over her eyes and kept her head down as she walked through the bedroom and into the bathroom, muttering, "I don't know why I have to do this. It's so unfair. It's going to stunt my growth—burn my eyes out. Sheesh!"

"I can hear you." Angela's voice wobbled. She was losing it. "Derek, call your dad," she shouted. "Tell him I'm stuck in the tub. I can't get my toe loose. My leg has gone numb." Hysteria climbed up her chest and escaped in a mixture of screams and sobs. "And it hurts!"

Hannah turned with her back toward Angela for the last few steps to the tub. It didn't do her any good though because of the large mirrors at the sink. Hannah gasped, threw her hand over her eyes again, grabbed the towel off the rack, stepped back, inadvertently dropped it onto Angela's head, then dashed out the door.

"Thanks," Angela muttered, and let the water out. She dried herself off and draped the flimsy towel over herself as best she could, surprised at how chilly it felt to be damp with no clothes on.

Her toes and fingers were pink and wrinkly from extended exposure to water. Her thigh had a sharp, shooting pain from holding it up for so long. Angela tried to brace her right leg by putting her left leg under it, balancing her foot in the corner of the tub. She slid, bum first, to the drain. "Ow! Ow! Ow!" She'd be in traction for a week just to get her joints straightened.

"Dad wants to know if it's an emergency." Derek stood at the door with his eyes cast downward.

"Yes, it's an emergency!" she shrieked. "Tell him to get home as soon as he can! My leg feels like it's going to fall off!"

Derek disappeared from her sight while talking to his father. When he came back, he'd hung up the phone. "Dad's calling 9-1-1—the fire department should be here in a minute."

Angela screamed.

"Call him back. Tell him NOT to call the fire department!" Angela jerked frantically on her toe again. Raw and swollen from her other attempts, blood oozed from under the steel, but her toe didn't budge.

Derek left the room again, when he came back, his face was pink, he coughed, then he coughed again. "It's too late. Dad already called." He wanted to laugh, Angela could see it on his face.

"Don't you dare." She glared at him, hopefully shooting fire-daggers at him with her eyes. "I'll haunt you from my grave if you laugh at me!"

Derek shifted his face until it appeared sufficiently contrite. "Sorry mom." He left then, to answer the door.

"Tell them to go away!" Angela shouted. "Your dad can help me when he gets home!" Angela heard the door open. She heard Derek explaining that she didn't need their services after all, and she relaxed a notch.

"Mrs. Anderson, what seems to be the problem here?" Gabe and Troy walked in the bedroom door dressed in complete fireman attire. A policeman stood behind them.

"Get out! Get out!" Angela screamed and tried to duck. She lost her balance and slipped awkwardly, shrieking with pain. Gabe and Troy rushed to the tub. Troy put his hands under her armpits and lifted her back into a sitting position.

"Towels, I need more towels," Angela gasped.

Gabe opened his tool bag and pulled out a hacksaw. "This isn't going to hurt at all," he said. "If it does, let me know, but I'm sure we'll be fine."

The only thing that hurt was her pride.

Angela clutched at her towel, feeling amazingly lucky that the saw was sharp and the fireman strong because she didn't know how long she could wait to have her nervous breakdown. But whatever the cost, she wouldn't have it here, with witnesses.

"Hannah, bring me my T-shirt and sweat pants," Angela shouted.

"There you go," Gabe said.

And her toe was free from the wall.

With his gaze averted, Troy offered his hand. "Can I help you, ma'am?"

"I've had all the help I can tolerate for one day," Angela responded. She needed desperately to get the situation—and her dignity—under control. "I want you all out of here. Now!" She huddled behind the protection of the tub.

"We still have the matter of the faucet stuck to your toe," Gabe said.

"Out!" Angela pointed to the bedroom door.

"We'll wait outside the door while you get dressed." Troy nodded at Gabe. The two walked to the doorway. Troy put a hand on Derek's shoulder, and asked, "How about you bring us a large pan with ice?"

"Here's your clothes, Mom." Hannah stood behind the bathroom arch-way and dropped the requested clothing onto the sink before disappearing through the bedroom door.

Angela struggled to maintain emotional control while grasping onto her clothing. Her toe bumped unmercifully against the cupboard base—making her want to shriek with pain. Angela clenched her mouth shut instead. She didn't want any more rescuing than absolutely necessary, and leaned against the sink counter for balance while putting her clothing on.

"Okay," she shouted. "I'm ready." She hobbled back to the edge of the tub.

Gabe and Troy, and her children, and the policeman, came back into the bathroom. The two firemen EMTs helped put her faucet-encased toe in the ice.

Her toe got really cold wrapped in metal. "Uncle," she said. "Are you trying to freeze it off?"

"Sorry," Gabe said. While holding her foot, he smeared thick grease around the edge of the spout and twisted it around her toe. "This should do the trick. Yeah?"

In one smooth motion, he pulled as he twisted and the metal protrusion slicked right off.

"There you go." Gabe grinned, handing her the faucet.

"I don't want it. It's not like I'm keeping souvenirs." Angela frowned. "Get rid of it."

"Okay." Gabe chuckled. "But it won't burn, you know."

Angela flushed with embarrassment, and stood.

"Hey, we're not finished yet." Troy reached for her arm.

She sat back on the tub edge. Troy wiped her toe clean of the grease, then rubbed liquid antiseptic around the wound, wrapped it in gauze and taped it snugly. "Keep the dressing clean or it might get infected. If you notice swelling, or oozing through the bandage, contact your doctor immediately."

Oh joy.

Angela shooed the emergency crew out the door, and then leaned against it with her eyes closed. Her toe throbbed, her pride had been irreparably damaged, and not only did her neighbors think she was a kook, now the local police and fire departments could have a good laugh at her expense as well. She rubbed at a painful kink under her right buttock.

"Are you okay, Mom?" Hannah asked, giving her a hug.

"Yes. I'm fine." Angela sighed. "I just need to be alone for a while." She straightened and limped quietly to her bedroom closing the door behind her.

Life wasn't so bad — was it? Angela surveyed the faucet-less tub sprinkled with metal shavings. A movement in the mirror startled her — it was her own reflection. Peering at her aging self, Angela silently mouthed an A, exaggerating the movement to stretch the muscles in her face and neck. She followed the same procedure with the other vowels. If only she could bring back time, tighten the skin around her face so she at least looked young again.

That skin sagging under her arms — gross. They'd called that glob of useless flesh "wings" in high school — her 7th grade English teacher had them. Angela and her classmates had laughed behind her back — Ms. Baxter — Angela remembered the time clearly. Ms. Baxter liked to wear sleeveless blouses and when she wrote on the chalkboard, her wings wiggled from side to side like gelatin.

A cruel trick of nature that Angela had them now.

Angela lifted her arms and swung them back and forth. Her flesh-wings followed suit, wiggling spinelessly in an automatic response. If only they were functional in any way. The irony. Having useless, flabby wings instead of the beautiful fairy wings she had been briefly blessed with. Angela turned and climbed into bed. She would never wear sleeveless blouses again.

An hour and a half later, Ted entered the room, though Angela didn't follow him with her eyes. Tears fell unchecked and dripped off her nose. She waited, unmoving. Waited for Ted to laugh, to poke fun of her ridiculousness, to call her weird. Her breathing had slowed, but her heart beat a little faster as she waited.

"Angela."

It sounded like music the way he said her name — like when they were newlyweds. Angela hadn't heard that musical longing in his voice for a long time — hadn't realized it was missing from their life, but she remembered the sound of it now as though it had always been there.

Ted slipped into bed with her, and Angela came out of her stupor to focus on his face — warm, loving, handsome. He kissed her wet nose, and then wrapped his arms around her. She snuggled in, absorbing his strength, his comfort. He embraced her fervently, kissing her neck, her cheek.

Angela didn't fully respond at first — Angela with the English-teacher-wings — she wasn't desirable. Yet his lips were hot when they met hers, convincing her otherwise. And she gave in.

"What about the kids?" She asked breathlessly.

"Chinese takeout." Then his lips were on hers and there was no more discussion.

Menopausal *fairy* Mischief

172

TWENTY-EIGHT

A miniature honeymoon—that's what their evening had been like—with Ted wanting her, not only because of his yearnings, but because of his love for her. She felt beautiful, desirable for the first time in forever.

He pulled on his pajama bottoms and snuck out of their bedroom. He came back with a plate of warm leftover Chinese food and two forks.

"Hot Mama, you gave me quite a workout. I thought you might be hungry." Ted grinned and Angela couldn't help but smile back.

"Tell me about your day," Angela said.

Ted climbed back into the bed and sat beside Angela, filling her in on some of the high and low points of his workday while they ate.

"So, now, tell me about you—are you all right?" Ted looked at her with a playful smile.

Angela rolled her eyes mockingly. "I'll live, but really, I don't want to talk about it." She pulled her injured foot up where he could see it and tried to wiggle the bandaged toe. "You can kiss my boo-boo, though."

"Your wish is my command," he said, using his best genie voice.

She laughed lightly as he leaned over, and starting with her toe, began kissing her foot and on up her leg.

They were in no hurry. The kids were old enough to fend for themselves for the evening, and Ted somehow understood her need to be alone, away from everyone else. It was a night where only the two of them existed — until around ten p.m.

Ted took the dishes and excused himself and came back with a cup of hot chocolate cradled in his hands.

"Here." He offered it to her with a dopy grin.

Angela frowned. The offering of the drink, instead of pleasing her, made her feel silly — like he was merely humoring her — a pathetic old woman who needed coddling like a toddler.

"I don't want it," she said, turning away.

"But, it's the gourmet kind." He sniffed ivt. "It's wonderfully rich, the way you like," Ted coaxed as though she were a three-year-old needing medicine.

She looked at his handsome face and intended to explain ever-so-kindly where he could put that special gourmet cocoa — right down the sink — and how she didn't need anything to help her sleep. "I'm not your grandma. I'm perfectly capable of getting to sleep without a hot toddy."

Ted sat next to her on the bed. He leaned forward and placed the cup on his night table. "Anj." He pulled her to his chest, rubbing her back while his lips were in her hair, his breath warm. "Anj, babe, I didn't mean to upset you. It's just that you've had such a hard time sleeping lately."

And, although his words were kind, she ended up feeling more juvenile with each one.

"Yes. Of course," she said. "It has nothing to do with the fact that I'm a helpless incompetent." She waved at her toe. "A woman so ridiculous that I can't even take a bath without the paramedics coming to my rescue."

"Why do you have to be so difficult?" Ted asked. "I was trying to be nice — doing you a favor." He shook his head. "Just forget it," he grumbled, and walked into the bathroom.

Angela rubbed her cheeks, resting her elbows on her legs. Had she overreacted? Ted did love her. Why was it bad for him to bring her a drink? Why was it bad for him to want her to get a good night's sleep? She had overreacted. She leaned over, and grabbing the cup, chugged the warm drink down.

"Bleck!" Angela made a face and shuddered. That stuff was awful. It tasted as though Ted had put a whole tablespoon of cayenne pepper in her cup. The cocoa was currently burning a new tunnel inside of her throat.

"Good night," Ted mumbled when he crawled back into bed, his back to her.

"Thank you for the hot chocolate." Angela didn't dare mention its vile flavor. "I really do appreciate the thought and I drank it right down," she continued. "I'm sorry I got upset."

"Don't worry about it," Ted said, then reached to the stereo and turned it on. He laid back down still facing away from her, and Angela did worry about it. They'd had such a wonderful evening. A stark contrast from her afternoon.

She had ruined it.

Ted started breathing heavy right away, so Angela knew he hadn't given it much thought. Angela wanted to stew and worry about how she always ruined everything, but she blacked out again and didn't wake until morning when the alarm blared.

There was no Ted. No "Good morning, sunshine."

Maybe Ted had worried about it a bit more than he'd let on. Maybe this time he was the one who needed to get a grip. She heard him and the kids out in the backyard and forced herself to sit up. Her head spun and Angela paused until she could get up without knocking anything over. Why did she feel so loopy?

"Hmph." Angela hadn't even needed to get up to use the restroom during the night. "Who would have figured?" she mumbled. "Hot chocolate, the cure for both insomnia and my perpetual empty-the-bladder-in-the-middle-of-the-night syndrome."

These unexpected blessings did not trump the miserable fact that her dreamt-of wings were once again MIA. She felt her back. Had the fairies really given up on her? Were they even still around? Angela had no way of contacting them.

Putting a pretend phone to her ear, she sang, "Tatiana, where are you?" She pictured her wings on her back, trying to summon them. It didn't work. "Hello? I can't help you if I can't contact you." Yeah, if she did ever see them again, she would demand an extension on the All Hallows' Eve thing.

Just because she had seen a pixie at the park, and just because she hadn't annihilated it, didn't mean she didn't want to help. Surely her magical friends hadn't given up on her that easily.

At the doorway, Angela watched Ted push the mower across the lawn. Derek had the weed eater edging against the patio and Hannah raked. The yard looked perfect other than the one brown spot of dirt where the grass seed refused to grow. How much longer could this go on? Ted had already put the landscapers to shame with his obsessive-compulsive need for perfection.

She turned toward the kitchen to make them a nice breakfast, and something glimmered in her peripheral vision. Something was in the tree. Was it a pixie? Angela moved closer. Dangling like an ornament about half way up, were her keys. She hadn't even missed them.

How could she ask Ted to get them for her?

"Remember that night when you were angry with me?" Angela muttered in her pretend conversation with Ted. "Oh that's right, you're angry with me now — and over a stupid cup of hot chocolate." She slammed the gallon of juice and the milk onto the counter. "Well, it was the time before that when I broke into Helmans' yard and scared everyone with my fairy wings." She threw bagels into the toaster. "You know me—ridiculous Angela—I accidentally flung my keys into the tree. Ha, ha," she said. "Yeah. Could you get them for me? Pretty please?"

That wasn't going to happen.

This wasn't a fairytale. She wasn't a damsel in distress. Angela was a perfectly capable woman who was perfectly capable of getting her own keys, thank-you-very-much. After the tub incident, she should have known better.

Her loving family left for the day, and Angela took a chair to the base of the tree. She pushed up with her toes, and tried forcing herself up and into the tree. It didn't work. A stick might do it. She ran into the house and retrieved the broom, whacking the branches above her head. Angela never was a good shot.

Firemen rescued cats from trees—it happened on television all the time. Maybe they would rescue the keys for her. Although not a living thing, those car-fob thingies were expensive. And it would be ruined if it rained. Yeah, regardless that it was October and the soonest they could expect rain in the Phoenix metropolitan area was November, the fob could ruin in the sun.

Angela found the non-emergency number for the fire department. A different station than had rescued her yesterday. One that was several miles southeast of the station whose tower eclipsed her property—and called.

"Hello? Do you rescue things?"

"Yes, ma'am," replied the woman on the other end of the line.

"Oh, good." She sighed with relief. There was no way she'd ask to borrow Helmans' ladder. "I have something that needs rescued. Could you send someone? And bring a ladder? This is not an emergency," she added.

Three minutes later, the doorbell rang. Gabe and Troy stood in the doorway.

Angela slammed the door shut. How had they answered her call? She didn't want those two rescuing her keys—they had seen her naked.

The doorbell rang again.

Angela gritted her teeth, opening the door fully aware of her overheated cheeks, her gaze focused on the door's threshold. Why hadn't men from one of the other stations come?

"We got an emergency call—something about a rescue?" Troy said.

"It's not an emergency. I told them it wasn't an emergency." Angela shook her head, still gazing downward. "Bring your ladder and come around back."

She stepped outside, the firemen following behind her, and went to open the gate. It was locked, and her keys were in the tree. In the backyard.

"Shall we use the boot? With the arm extended it'll reach to the backyard."

"No, don't use the boot! All I need is a ladder." Ted was getting one for Christmas whether he liked it or not. "You'll have to bring it through the house." Keeping her eyes averted from the firemen in case they were smirking, she headed to the front door. The firemen followed her through the house.

"Well, if it's a cat," Troy said, "sometimes they get worried and climb to the top of the tree before we can catch them." He scratched his temple.

"It's not a cat." From the edge of the back patio, she pointed into the tree. "My keys are stuck."

They bit back on their lips. If firemen kept scrapbooks, they'd have a jolly time making a book of her crazy stunts, but doggone it, she needed those keys.

"Why didn't you just fly up and get them," Gabe murmured in her ear.

"Right." With hands on her hips, Angela looked at the keys, and then at Gabe. "If I could get them, don't you think I would?" Although she hadn't really tried summoning her wings for the occasion, she had just assumed they wouldn't work.

Why was that? This was all too embarrassing. Not in the same way as yesterday's fiasco, but still frustratingly horrible. Her life was not meant to be normal. Even Gabe could see that. To make things worse, she felt completely abnormal without her newly found wings, and completely lonely without her fairy clan.

"You'll figure it out." Gabe took the ladder from Troy and set it against the tree. He climbed up without a word and tossed her the keys.

"Is that all for today?" Troy retracted the ladder.

"That'll do it," she said. "Thanks."

Angela walked them through the house and stood at the door smiling dreamily as they drove away. That was the nicest thing anyone had ever said to her. *You'll figure it out.*

"I will figure it out," she agreed.

TWENTY-NINE

Angela put away the leftovers from dinner, turned out the light and grabbed her keys, toying with them and thinking of Gabe as she joined Ted in their bedroom. Why hadn't she even tried flying into the tree? She might have rescued the keys herself and spared herself a lot of frustration. Had all these years living with a family of disbelievers slowly changed her? "You must believe in yourself before others can," Angela muttered Tatiana's words.

Was that why Angela kept sleeping through the night? Had Tatiana quit calling for her? She glanced up at Ted. He'd been surly all evening.

"Will you make me a cup of hot chocolate?" Angela batted her eyelashes. Ted's pouting over hot chocolate had gone on long enough.

"No. Apparently my wife doesn't like me doing nice things for her." He glowered briefly then left for the bathroom.

"Ted, I already said I was sorry. Please, *please* make me some more."

If groveling on her hands and knees worked, Angela would do it. But she knew Ted. The gesture would get her into more trouble. Sometimes he was such a baby. It was hot chocolate, after all. And nasty hot chocolate at that. It had nearly turned her stomach last night. Here she was, having to beg him for another cup of it.

The extra 'please' had done the trick. Ted left the room to make the drink.

"Don't put quite as much cayenne in it this time," Angela called.

"I didn't add any cayenne." Ted set the drink in her hands. "I didn't add anything but water."

"Oh, good." She chugged it down. The liquid burned all the way. She turned away from Ted, her stomach convulsing. The face she made was involuntary as she shivered with revulsion.

"Is it too hot?" He took the cup and set it on the nightstand.

"I wonder if cocoa spoils." Angela tried to hide her second bout of shivers. She ran to the toilet and slammed the door shut.

THIRTY

"Don't forget we're going to Derek's football game tonight." Ted handed Angela the hose to water their navel orange tree.

That explained Ted's good mood. He loved football.

"It's too bad you can't sit with us, Hannah." Ted smiled encouragingly at his daughter. "But at least we'll all be at the game."

"Yeah, too bad I'll be working the concession stand all night," Hannah mumbled, grinning peacefully.

Yeah, Hannah felt real bad. Angela had hoped that all of the mornings spent on lawn work would be enough family time for Ted, but apparently not. No, really, she would go and support her son, but how much punishment must she suffer? She loved her family, but she hated football. And yard work. And getting up with the sun. If only she could talk him into playing a sport she enjoyed.

"Derek, you've got such a light spring in your step, I bet you'd be great at basketball." Angela loved basketball.

"The seasons overlap."

"Couldn't you just quit football early or start the basketball late? Then you could do both."

"I'm varsity, Mom." Derek made a face. "Besides, why would I want to?"

"Maybe we could go bike riding together this weekend?" Angela smiled sappily. Riding a bike was a stretch. She hadn't been on one since she was twelve.

"It takes bikes to do that, dear." Ted looked quizzically her way.

"We could go to the museum — or the library?"

They ignored her.

"A camping trip would be nice." Angela loved the outdoors. Still no response. In Ted's defense, they had just sold their camping supplies.

Her family cleaned up and left for the day.

Angela closed the door behind them and went to the kitchen, pulling out the box of gourmet hot cocoa mix. That vile poison needed a closer look. She pulled off the lid and jerked back. Just seeing the sugary brown powder sent Angela's chocolate cravings into orbit, but the smell turned her stomach. She put the lid back on.

Perhaps it was all a coincidence how every time she drank the stuff she fell asleep. Or how Ted had acted so guilty when she mentioned it. Yeah, maybe it was all a coincidence. But probably not. Her husband knew more about the origins of the cocoa mix than he let on.

She pitched it in the trash.

Then she pulled it back out and dumped the powder in the disposal, rinsing it down.

Although today was game day, Derek would come home after school for his favorite, game-day dinner. It was tradition. Angela needed a few things for the pizza, so she grabbed her purse and headed to the store.

Two famous Anderson family pizzas were on order. She plopped the ingredients into her cart one-by-one. Her family loved the buffalo wings that she often made to go with pizza, so Angela pushed the cart to the meat section of the store. She picked up a family-sized pack of chicken wings and started to place them in the front-seat of the cart.

"Oh!" She sucked in a breath. Two dozen little wings stared back at her — her hand went to her mouth. "The poor chickens." How many of the birds had lost their ability to fly, just to satisfy her family's lust for hot sauce and ranch dressing?

"No, no." Angela shuddered. "It just can't happen." She threw the package back into the cooler and hurried away. She had never before considered the precious nature of flight, and blinked back her shame, picturing a dozen wingless chickens running around the chicken yard. Angela shivered down to her toes. "I'll never eat wings again."

Trying hard to cast the picture of the bird-less wings from her mind, she paid for the groceries and ran from the store. "Oh!" She put her hands to her cheeks. "Oh!" Those bird-less wings reminded her too much of her current wing-less state. It seemed like an eternity since she had flown, and forever since she had heard from Tatiana. All Hallows' Eve was only three weeks away.

Would Angela really lose her family? Wouldn't they at least give her a chance to fulfill her vow? In truth, Angela did bungle things up a bit. She should have discovered a way to help her fairy clan before losing her wings. But how could she have known?

If only Ted could help her.

"Pizza smells great, Mom. Thanks." Derek came in wearing his black spandex pants and his gold uniform shirt, with Hannah several paces behind. "Did you make the wings too?" Derek snooped in the microwave and in the oven looking for them.

"Uh, no. I'm sorry, Derek. Not today." Not ever again. "I did make some fruit cobbler though."

Derek needed to be back at school before Ted got home from work, so Angela scooted him out of the way and took the pizzas from the oven so he could eat. Angela loved times like this when her children were happy, and pleasing them was as easy as homemade pizza.

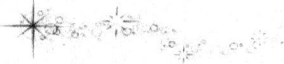

At five-thirty on the dot, Ted stepped inside the door. "You ready to go, Babe?"

"Ready." Ready as she would ever be. She twirled her finger upward with fake enthusiasm.

"You having those mood swings again, honey?" Ted grinned.

"Lookie here, buster—" She glowered, ready to tell Ted right where he could put his funny jokes.

"What?" Ted threw his hands up.

"Nothing," Angela muttered. Now was not the time.

Ted took her at her word and rushed into the bedroom to get ready. Angela waited by the door with her current read, tempted to take it, though Ted would not like her doing anything but enjoying the game with him. Her enjoying football was all part of Ted's fantasy world. She set her book on the table.

He thought that because he loved football, she did too. She only watched it for Derek. The mind-numbing tedium of the game was hard to tolerate for two whole hours. It wasn't that she didn't know what was going on. Ted had explained the game to her over, and over—and over. She just didn't get why anyone cared.

Ted came out donning his Gilbert Tigers hat made with a design that included angry tiger-eyes, tiger ears, and a tail in back.

"It's time for us to go if we want good seats," Angela teased half-heartedly. There were no good seats at a high school game. The best they could hope for were seats not already sticky with spilled soda or any other number of snack items sold to high school students and their younger siblings at the games.

"Go Tigers!" Ted chanted on his way to the car.

"Denise is giving me a ride home," Hannah informed them on

the way to the game.

"Are you sure, honey?" Angela glanced back at her daughter. She was nearly a grown woman — where had the years gone?

"Yeah." Hannah glanced from her dad to her mom and smirked.

As it turned out, they did get good seats — three rows up near the center of the bleachers. Ted didn't like sitting on the front row where people constantly walked past. It made it hard to focus. Three rows up kept them close to the action and in view of the game.

They brought their team blankets, not because the weather had cooled off, but as protection against all things grimy that had settled on and around the benches. They had purchased them to celebrate the first year Derek made varsity. Ted and Angela brought them to every game.

"Do you think Derek will start tonight?"

"I don't know this new coach." Ted shrugged. "He doesn't seem to encourage the boys' growth like Coach Weirhauser did."

If Derek wasn't playing ... Angela settled in for a long, boring night. Ted got into football with the kick-off, shouting his encouragement to the team, chanting along with the cheerleaders, and jumping up and down with excitement at every opportunity. *And Ted got embarrassed with her behavior? Truly.*

Angela perked up. Derek had the ball, running toward the goal. There was a skirmish — and the game stopped.

Time to measure the field.

Boring.

Tons of people Angela knew were at the game. The Finleys, the Madisons, they walked back and forth retrieving sodas, popcorn, and snow cones from the snack bar. "Hi." Angela waved.

No one seemed to see her. Of course not, she was invisible to neighbors and family alike.

"Hey, Gloria." Angela waved as the HANC board member walked past.

Gloria looked through her, smiling. "Pam! Patrick! It's a great game, isn't it?" The Waldens, sitting two rows behind them were highly visible, apparently.

Gloria had to have seen her—she waved again—Angela was between the two. Neither of them looked. Angela slumped to the aluminum bench. Many of these people had been her good friends until the Hell-woman moved next door. What that rabid rodent had said to prompt everyone to ignore her, Angela dared not imagine.

With so many time-outs, huddles and measurings of the field, Angela had too much time to dwell—on wings—and fairies—and pixies. Turning her mind away from the game and her non-friends, she pictured the purplish-blue luminescence of her wings, when she'd had them—remembered herself floating for the first time in her backyard—remembered patrolling her neighborhood for safety. Angela let out a deep sigh.

Those were the good times.

"Mama, look!" screeched a frantic young girl.

Angela turned her attention back toward the game only to see the girl pointing directly at her.

"Angela. Sit down. It's impolite," Ted said without taking his eyes off the game.

Only then did Angela realize she was hovering about a foot in the air.

"Oh!" she gasped. She grabbed hold of the bench and pulled herself down to the seat.

THIRTY-ONE

"You okay? Ted glanced at her, then jumped up. "Wahoo!"

"Yeah," Angela mumbled, feeling slightly different than okay—more a combination of shell-shock and exhilaration rolled into one. She grabbed the blanket from the bench and wrapped it loosely around her shoulders—yes, she was feeling a little shock-ish.

And the wings, they must be there on her back. Angela reached underneath the blanket, her mind going a million miles a minute, and felt their velvety softness. Her wings were back. She'd been given another chance as a fairy.

Extreme elation! Joyful news! Angela smiled. Except ...

"Um, I need to go get a drink." Angela stood abruptly and squeezed past Ted to the stairs. "Can I get you something?" Angela asked, her eyes wild with the implication of what just happened.

"No," he muttered, impatient.

She couldn't have her fairy wings. Not here. She wanted them, of course, but a rivalry football game was an extremely public and unforgiving place to make a fairy debut. Almost tripping on the bottom step, Angela rushed to get herself out of the limelight. Wings and fairies—this was something she had done by herself for over forty years and no one else had ever gotten involved.

It was dangerous to change that now.

Luckily for Angela, the snack bar was nearly deserted. Hannah, Denise, and a boy with long strands of stringy black hair stood at the back near a stack of soda cases, laughing. Most of the audience had come to see the game and it appeared to be exciting. Near half time the score was fourteen to twelve, in Gilbert High's favor.

"Mom! What are you doing here?" Hannah had a strict and yet unspoken, no-parents-invading-my-space policy. Tonight the concession stand was supposed to be off limits. Hannah rushed to the service counter, and whispered, "Why are you wearing a blanket? It's embarrassing."

"I need the blanket tonight," Angela said, sweat beading at her hairline. "I'm cold." She had hoped the blanket wouldn't cause suspicion or make her daughter uneasy—that hope went down the drain. She pulled the cover tighter. "Can you get me a drink?"

"What do you want?" Hannah leaned halfway over the counter whispering loudly. "This place will be flooded in just a minute."

Angela knew what this implied—steer clear when Hannah's peers were around. She didn't mind that. Teenagers made her edgy. How had she ended up having five of them?

The spectators jumped and cheered at something, and the band played the school song with gusto. A touchdown possibly. Turning back to the concession stand, Angela tried choosing between root beer and orange soda—she liked them both. Then a glimmering movement caught her eye.

"Mom? Are you going to order?"

"In a minute." Angela walked to the side of the building. What were pixies doing at a football game? They really were a menace. Did they have no boundaries at all? She felt her pockets but already knew she hadn't brought her fairy dust or wand with her. Who would have expected she'd need it?

Angela rounded the corner just in time to see something luminescent fly around the far side of the building, behind the

190

bathrooms. She hurried after it. Her best option was to get close enough to grab it and blow in its face.

"Stay away from me." The angry pixie hovered nearby.

"Go back where you belong, and I will." There was a small patch of lawn behind the concession/restroom building. Angela stepped onto it, took a deep breath and blew toward the delinquent pixie. Amnesia was the only option.

"This is war," the pixie bellowed.

How absurd. War? This magical sprite was getting on Angela's nerves. She lunged forward and grabbed at the pixie.

That was the last thing she remembered.

When Angela awoke, she was lying face-up and staring toward a gathered crowd—Ted and Hannah among them.

"Are you all right?" Ted's brows furrowed with concern.

Angela tried opening her mouth to speak, but her chest felt caved in. No air.

"Anj?"

Angela scrunched her face—it hurt. "Mmm," was all that came out. Everything was blurry. What had happened? Where was she?

"Witnesses said you fell out of the tree." Ted's voice sounded high-pitched and incredulous.

"Did I catch the pixie?" she muttered.

Several bystanders giggled. Ted frowned.

"She must have hit her head pretty hard." Someone pushed to her side and shined a small flashlight in her eyes. Paramedics. They communicated quietly, then one of them put a whiplash collar around her neck.

"Mmph!" Angela winced.

"Anj, sweetheart, they're taking you to the hospital to do some tests," Ted whispered in her ear. "I'll be with you the whole time." He kissed her forehead. "It'll be all right. Everything will be all right." His voice was soothing and Angela relaxed into it.

But they wanted to haul her away. What if she went to the hospital and they amputated her wings like they did on sci-fi movies? Angela caught her breath and leaned forward. "Don't let them take me, Ted." She rubbed against a headache and slumped back. "I just had the wind knocked out of me. I'm fine."

The two paramedics pushed their way to her side and lifted her onto the transport cot. It was almost level with the ground, but as soon as they secured her onto it, they pushed a lever and she shot up, waist high. It was a startling experience.

"Ted," Angela protested. "I'm fine, really." Her eyes closed as she shook her head in disbelief. No one listened to her. Ted was busy telling Hannah not to worry, and to go home after the game. The paramedics were busy saving her life — not that she needed it.

They wheeled her to the ambulance and jerked her inside the closet-like vehicle with Ted holding her hand. Amidst the blurry confusion, a hazy blue object hovered just outside the vehicle. Angela closed her eyes against the pixie's luminescent green eyes. "Get that pixie." She reached toward it, but the door closed and it was lost to her.

The ambulance started moving. A paramedic was on one side keeping track of her vitals. Ted was on her other side pressing himself close. Taking calming breaths, Angela tried staving off her claustrophobia.

Did she still have her wings? Angela couldn't feel them. Hopefully they had disappeared before anyone saw. If not, surely they wouldn't amputate without her consent.

Why had someone accused her of climbing a tree? She wasn't crazy — she would never climb a tree at her age. It had to have been the pixie.

But what had really happened — why would pixies be at a football game — why hadn't anyone else seen the little green-eyed demon in blue?

How had the pixie knocked her out?

THIRTY-TWO

Angela listened to the monitor's beep, watched the continuous line on the digital box go up and down as it registered her heartbeat, smelled the sterile antiseptic, and waited.

"The doctor will be in soon." The nurse smiled and left the ER's curtained exam room. Angela was tethered to the bed via the heart monitor, wearing the hospital's ever-so-fashionable airy gown, and still waiting for a doctor's permission to leave.

Ted sat by her side, holding her hand. "You'll be fine," he whispered.

What was he thinking? She would be a lot better without their insurance's hospital deductible looming over their heads.

"I wish you would've listened to me. I'm fine. I don't need to be here." Barely more than a headache for all the embarrassment she had suffered.

"We'll let the doctors decide." Ted kissed her forehead. "You could have a concussion."

While they waited (and waited) in the chilly room, two men appeared at the foot of her bed. They were brawny and wore navy-blue T-shirts that held tightly to their muscled chests. Their concerned frowns were contradicted by the friendly up-turn of their lips. "Are you all right?"

Ted stared at them.

"The three of you haven't ever met. This is Gabe and Troy from the fire department." Angela smiled. "What are you doing here?"

"We heard you were here and came to check up on our favorite fairy-lady." Gabe smiled pleasantly now, the concern at least momentarily gone.

With the term, "fairy-lady," the color drained from Ted's face. He looked to Angela.

"Ted," Angela smiled, "these are the firemen who graciously helped extinguish our backyard." She motioned toward them, feeling a tad embarrassed by the memory.

Ted stood and reached his hand out to shake theirs. "I guess thanks are in order." He nodded, then sat back down and took Angela's hand in his. "My *wife* and I appreciate your help."

Angela repeated his words in her mind. Had he emphasized the word wife? Was Ted acting possessive? She smiled. This was good. It felt a little like high school — and Angela liked it.

"You forgot to mention the time we cut the faucet off your toe." Troy grinned broadly.

Angela flushed with embarrassment. "I was trying to forget about that," she murmured, and glanced away.

"Yes, of course. My apologies."

Troy could make any woman swoon with the brassy blond locks curling around his ears, accompanied by his tall, lean body well accustomed to hard exercise — definitely eye candy.

But it was Gabe with whom she had an unexpected connection. After all, he believed in her. He believed in fairies.

Gabe was pushing six-feet, but a full three inches shorter than Troy. His ebony hair, short and straight, had flecks of grey. His well-toned body was stockier than Troy's, but not an ounce of waste. Very handsome, both. Was that a prerequisite for the firemen/

EMTs? Angela couldn't help but enjoy the view — she was human, after all.

"Yeah," Troy said after an awkward silence, "we sit around the station wondering what our fairy-lady is going to do next. We didn't get a call on this one. I wonder if it counts." He glanced at Gabe, who shrugged his shoulders with an innocent expression on his face.

"The chief has talked about adding a few more men just so we can keep up with your antics." Gabe then tapped his nose with his finger, and Angela instinctively knew they were joking.

"I'll bet," Angela said wryly. She hadn't been in that much trouble.

"Seriously, Anj," Gabe said, "you gonna be all right?"

"The doctor hasn't been in yet," Ted interjected.

"I'm fine. A little humiliation does a body good."

"So we hear." Both firemen smiled.

They left shortly afterward, and when they did, Ted left the folding chair and sat on the edge of her bed, holding her hand and studying her eyes. Angela wondered what he was thinking. It was kind of an expensive trip for some one-on-one time with her husband. Good thing they had insurance.

"Anj? You let strange men call you Anj?" He said, his voice even, his expression calm.

"They were just being friendly." Angela shrugged, realizing for the first time that they'd used Ted's pet name for her. "I've only met them a few times — they must have heard you use it." She bit her lip and shrugged again, feeling pleased. After thirty-two years, it was nice to have Ted acting even slightly jealous.

It almost made the humiliation of lying in the grass with a zillion spectators gawking at her, someone accusing her of climbing trees, and the subsequent ride to the hospital, worth it. Yeah, not really. It did lend a sweetness to the situation, however.

"I don't think I like you having men over so regularly while I'm at work." Ted smiled, yet his voice sounded strained.

Angela couldn't help but smile. He was jealous!

"I think they're sort of my protectors now." Then, feeling his chasm of disapproval deepen, she amended, "Only while you're at work, of course." His scowl didn't lessen so she added, "You'll always be my knight in shining armor, though." And it was true.

"Of course." He looked at her through his eyelashes and kissed her hand—the one without the I-V.

The doctor came in then. "Let's see what we have here."

He examined her briefly, and Angela wondered how he'd work in the phrase, "You're no spring chicken anymore," into his diagnosis. As long as he didn't send in a psychologist, Angela would count herself lucky.

After the doctor's exam, they waited another eternity to be wheeled to X-ray. Why the X-ray techs said they were ready, and then made her wait another forty-five minutes was beyond her. But, after all the hoopla, the waiting and the tests, they pronounced Angela was fine and they let her go home. It only took the medical community six hours to realize what she had known all along. No broken bones. No concussion.

Ted held her hand but remained silent on the trip home, and Angela was too tired to speak. He woke the kids up enough for them to get off the sofas, assure them Angela was okay, and send them to their rooms. He then led the way into their bedroom.

"So, why were you climbing a tree?" Ted sounded tired and frustrated.

"Whoever said I was climbing a tree, lied," Angela said matter-of-factly. "Honestly, why would I climb a tree during a football game?" It was ridiculous.

"How'd you get hurt then?" Ted eyed her, as though weighing the evidence for himself.

Angela thought about it for a while trying to figure out what had happened. She certainly couldn't tell him what had really happened. *"I tried grabbing a pixie and it must have knocked me out."* He'd send her to the hospital again, this time to have her brain examined. Something occurred to her then.

"I didn't get hurt. Remember? Anyway, someone pushed me down—it wasn't on purpose and I don't know who." Angela went on quickly before he started on a tirade and insist the whole school line up for her to identify the juvenile delinquent. "I was knocked pretty hard too, and lying there trying to catch my breath. Everyone gathered around and started making a big deal out of nothing."

It sounded good. She would believe it, and it was a good idea—one of her better ones—to turn herself into the victim of everyone's overreactions. Ted would believe her. What choice did he have? After all, what guy wanted to think their wife had gone out shopping and come home a few marbles short? A shiver of worry wiggled up her spine. Their happiness depended on it, but could she ever convince Ted that fairies were real?

"It seemed like you were saying something about pixies when you were in the ambulance." Ted pressed his lips into a thin line.

Angela rolled over onto her side. It was nearly two a.m. and well past time for bed.

Ted's breathing soon became heavy and even.

Angela hoped her wings would reappear. When they did, she would be ready. Those pixies were going down!

THIRTY-THREE

"Nutmeg? Chocolate mix? I have no idea where it came from." Angela sat on a tree root, explaining her experiences of the past week to Tatiana.

"Nutmeg puts fairies to sleep, but the more you ingest, the more poisonous it becomes." She gave Angela a knowing look. "Stay away from it."

"Thanks." Yeah, she needed that advice. As if she would drink hot chocolate ever again. And her pumpkin pies at Thanksgiving would be forevermore nutmeg free.

This was no coincidence. The nutmeg-spiced chocolate and that soup with nutmeg—Angela knew who was responsible—the spiteful sprite that lived next door.

"Your time as a fairy is drawing to a close." Tatiana lifted her eyebrows.

"No, no, no, there can be no closing." Angela's heart sank as her blood pressure spiked.

"So far you have been no help at all. Why did we think you would be? Your mother was incredible. Extraordinary." She shook her head. "You have proven less than exceptional." She sighed. "I cannot alter the decree. You have until All Hallows' Eve and then your family is lost to you forever. We are lost to you forever." She

199

looked out over her fairy clan, jaw clenched.

"*It wasn't my fault. The neighbor poisoned me.*" Angela lowered her head. "*I need an extension.*"

Dozens of fairies were on the familiar, tightly mowed lawn across the river from the cascading waterfall, the melodic rushing of water over rock resonated through the air. The wooden walking bridge was to her left, the gently sloping landscape to her right.

"All Hallows' Eve," Tatiana said. "That's final."

Pixies were freakishly strong. Angela didn't want to go against them again. She had no desire to spend another second in an emergency room. She needed a peaceful resolution.

"You think we shouldn't fight for our property?"

Fighting was not Angela's favorite hobby, although it seemed to be a driving factor for the fairies and pixies. Hands on her hips, Angela let the foul mood broiling under her surface take over and spill out into her voice. She was getting good at this. "*I was trying to help when I got hurt. A pixie was at the football game.*"

Tatiana gave her a disbelieving look, and Angela continued.

"*They're horrible, like you said. I tried catching it and the miniscule monster attacked me. But who wouldn't —*"

"You tried to catch a pixie?" Tatiana bellowed.

Angela stepped back, but then her jaw set and she glared at Tatiana.

"*If you haven't noticed, I'm considerably larger than a pixie.*" Angela crossed her arms. "*A pixie would fit in my purse — I could grab a pixie with one hand — two fingers.*" She demonstrated a pinching motion.

"You were instructed otherwise." Tatiana glared at Angela. "They are stronger than you think."

Angela had to give her that one. The pixie had been stronger than she anticipated. After all, she'd ended up in the ER.

"The pixies hurt Angela fairy-human," Tatiana squeaked. "We must seek revenge!"

"*I, um, no. I wasn't hurt. I think we should —*" Angela wanted them to see reason. She didn't want the fairies hurt because of her little inconvenience, but Tatiana swirled fairy dust over Angela's head and she felt its transforming power.

"*Let's do this thing,*" she hollered. Tonight was as good as any to fulfill her vow. And she would do it. Losing Ted was not an option.

The fairies charged into the night sky.

Angela leapt into the air after the others, shouting, "*Wait!*" Angela was in no shape to compete with the tiny fairies' speed.

She hurried in their direction, and saw flashes of green, blue, and pink — like a miniature fireworks display. The word, "annihilation" stuck in her throat and she paused. Something nut-sized struck her chest. "Ow!" She cupped the spot with her hand, and a full-sized Angela headed downward. Flapping her arms in unison with her wings, she worked at getting back into the sky.

A whoosh of air sped past, knocking her sideways. A horde of green eyes glared at her. Angela put her arms over her head — oh she hated this — and started sinking once more. Then, recovering emotionally, she took out her wand. "*Tatiana?*" Angela needed backup. She felt another whoosh of air. "*Tatiana!*" she shouted over her shoulder.

Angela's heart thumped wildly. She repeatedly pointed her wand toward the green eyes. Nothing happened. She looked at the end of the wand and then turned it over in her hands.

Another whoosh and a buzzing sound bumped past. "*Tatiana!*" Angela's breathing came in large gasps. Where had they all gone?

"I am here." Tatiana showed herself. "However, we must get you over there." She pointed. "The fairies need you." She tugged Angela's arm.

Angela flew closer, aiming her wand. A bright jolt of electricity slammed into her chest. She flailed her arms wildly trying to gain control. "*Help!*" she shouted, and then began slipping back to her room. "I can't go yet! I've got to obliterate the pixies! Tatiana-a-a-a!" She fought against the gravitational pull. "Stop it! Stop it! Stop it!" She writhed and tried freeing herself.

"Anj, are you all right?" Ted had his warm hand on her shoulder, but his voice echoed like he was in the tunnel with her. "Are you having a bad dream?"

"A bad dream?" It took a moment for her to get her bearings.

"You were thrashing around pretty hard — it woke me up. Who's Tatiana?"

Angela woke the rest of the way, but she didn't move. "Tatiana? Hmm," she pretended to muse though sick with worry. "I have no idea." What was happening to the fairies in her absence?

"Ouch!" Ted felt for her hand. "Is that a toothpick? Why're you sleeping with a toothpick?" Ted took the wand, leaned over her, and placed it on her nightstand. "You could hurt yourself with that." He kissed her on the cheek. "Night." He rolled back over.

But Angela couldn't sleep. She worried. Her heart thudded with disappointment. Had she missed her only chance? That whack in her chest, Angela rubbed her hands over the spot. That had been forceful. Had a pixie knocked her back home?

Beads of hot moisture drenched her from head to feet. Who knew toes had sweat glands? Angela took slow, deep breaths trying to delay the onslaught of her nightly sauna. Night sweats — aggravating! Trying not to wake Ted — frustrating! She climbed out of bed and hobbled into the bathroom, the room she spent half of her life in, and grabbed a clean washcloth in the semi-darkness.

Water from the Phoenix valley didn't get cool until December, but it had cooled some since August, and it felt good against her smoldering flesh.

She glanced at the large mirror. A shadow rested above her shoulders. Her wings! *"Thank you Tatiana!"* The fairy queen must expect her back in the foray.

Angela threw the washcloth down and limped to their closet. Last year for Christmas, Ted had given Angela a pair of satiny black slippers with a little bow on top. Old lady slippers. No, she hadn't ever used them. Until now. They were the perfect accessory for fairy wings and they kept her from going barefoot. She slipped them on, grabbed her wand from the nightstand, then stormed hurriedly across the dark family room.

It had been too frustrating of a day, what with the emergency room visit, that ornery pixie, Ted not trusting her, fighting with Tatiana — oh, the list went on forever.

What kind of a pantywaist let tiny fairies fuss at them and couldn't even take control of one miniscule pixie? Angela stood in the backyard. There were dozens of pixies at the park. She needed courage, and glanced through the glass door and into the home where her family slept — they were her life — her strength. Her family was the only thing she needed.

Stepping away from their back porch and onto the lawn, Angela inhaled the sweet scent of grass and smiled agitatedly into the darkness. Her wings fluttered and, Angela noted, they seemed happy. Maybe wings did have their own personality.

After the porcelain fiasco, Angela wouldn't risk sprinkling fairy dust over herself. She had to stop those pixies once and for all, and leapt purposefully into the night sky. Hovering in the air, however, her plans changed.

The Helmans.

Having been zapped from the pixie fight before she was ready, Angela was uncharacteristically grouchy and inordinately anxious. She could not be losing her family forever, and she needed to get those pixies out of her life. Now.

Conquering her human nemesis was a necessary evil for Angela to ultimately reign victorious. The poison cocoa mix? That was just wrong, and so un-neighborly. No longer would she sit around and let everyone else control her life.

"Heh, heh, heh." Besides, it would make her feel much, much better. "Put a bug in my soup, will you." Angela hovered over Helmans' lawn trying to decide on her target. She needed a little training. Nothing too grandiose, she wouldn't blow their roof off or anything drastic. Rebecca Helman's vehicle was parked outside of their garage.

A hole in one of the tires of that fancy Lincoln Navigator would be a good place to start. Just a slow leak. Something so natural they wouldn't get suspicious. Angela pointed her wand at the back tire and focused on what she wanted to happen. It didn't take long before she heard a small stream of air escaping the tire.

"Oh, yeah, that's what I'm talking about." Smiling with satisfaction, Angela wondered what she should do next. Flattening their tire had been too easy.

She flicked her wand.

A burned spot appeared in their lawn.

She flicked it again.

A small bush withered.

"I've got the power." At long last.

Angela flew down the street to the Madisons'. "Those fakers need a switcheroo." Angela pointed her wand.

It didn't take more than a second for the weeds to start sprouting in the front lawn. She checked the back lawn. Perfectly neat.

"This is actually a good deed," Angela muttered. "HANC can finally see the problem and make them correct it. They'll thank me. Maybe let me back on the committee."

This new feeling inside her chest—the desire to do lash out—was different. Of course Angela knew the things she had done were wrong, but she gulped down the guilt, the corner of her lip turning up to a crooked grin.

"This isn't a night for feeling depressed. This is a night of liberation from tyranny." Or something like that. She shot her fist into the air, ignored that nagging inner-voice telling her to right her wrongs, turned around and flew away.

"I am the gargantuan fairy. Moa-ha-ha! No one can stop me now," she said, flying with zeal toward the park, zapping little spots in the landscape and weaving a path of destruction. She would obliterate those pixies and save her family in the process.

Why hadn't Tatiana sent Angela her mission? The fairy queen had said it would come via her thoughts. "Believe in yourself," Angela said against her leaden stomach.

On the north side of Guadalupe Road, it was city life epitomized, but the south side still had the one — and five-acre farms Gilbert had become known for.

Night vision had become a problem the past year, and since she couldn't see well in the dark, Angela flew to the north side of Guadalupe. Staying in the neighborhoods with the streetlights was safer.

At least she now knew how to use the wand properly. This was how she appeased the guilt bug crawling up her neck.

"Oh, yeah baby!" Angela's wings bristled. "Believe in yourself and embrace that bad-girl feeling." It was much better than ignoring it.

But the fire-station's tower came into view, and the fire under her bad-girl persona fizzled.

"I thought it was farther away." Before she could modify her direction, she recognized the man standing at the tower. Gabe.

"He can't see me." She darted across the side street and hid behind a palm tree in someone's back yard.

Had he seen her? Angela scrunched her shoulders together trying to draw in her wings and be small. But, sinking to the earth, she extended them out again. Luckily, her wings hadn't disappeared all together. Yet. How would she explain that one? She peeked around the tree refusing to consider.

Gabe stared in her direction, a curious expression on his face. He'd seen something, but Angela hoped he didn't know what it was — or didn't believe his eyes at least. She didn't want company. At all. And, although Gabe said he believed, and said he'd seen her flying, Angela was suspicious.

"He's a total stranger," she said. "Why does he believe in me before Ted?" After all, what business was it of Gabe's? The tree trunk became a mini-oasis. Angela would wait behind it until he left.

Until a barking dog startled her.

These people had a pool in their backyard but no fence. "There's a law against neglect of this nature," Angela muttered. "I should turn them in." Someone should.

The Rottweiler worked its way around the pool, lunging at her feet. The heat from his nose warming her ankle as he nipped at her.

"Stupid dog." Angela flitted up and out of the dog's reach.

Of course she'd end up in a backyard with a dog. If she had a home that backed up against a main street, she would probably want a killer beast to protect her property too. Nope. Not ever. She hated dogs. Nothing could tempt her to own one.

The filthy beast continued barking.

Gabe didn't turn away. Great. The whole neighborhood could hear. Why not Gabe? If he would realize it was just a dog and go back to work, then she could leave. He wasn't looking away though, and lights in the house popped on one at a time.

"This is just great." She peeked around the tree. "Go away, Gabe."

When the patio light came on, Angela had no choice. She flew over the pool to the roof, and hid behind a gable. "Stay with me wings." It was a miracle they hadn't gone into hiding, as they were prone to do.

The dog kept barking.

Angela peered down.

The dog stared in her direction, barking harder.

"What a good doggie." Angela pointed her wand at his stubby tail.

"Yipe!" Fido yelped and dashed out of sight.

"It's about time." Angela gazed toward the fire station.

Gabe hadn't lost interest.

"I don't have time for this. I've got to get back to help the fairies." Angela flew to the neighboring roof, and then to the next until the nosy fireman was out of her sight. Her heart raced as though she was truly a six-inch fairy.

"It's unwise to have a heart attack right now," Angela told her heart, heaving several breaths, and picturing the headlines: *Woman found dead on random roof a mile from home. Foul play suspected.*

What would Ted or her children think? What time was it? Angela looked at her wrist. She needed to start wearing a watch to bed. Ted woke up early in the mornings. Not wanting to drop like an expired fly into a stranger's backyard, Angela rested on the tile roof of the two-story home waiting for her heart rate to settle.

She was thirsty. Next time she would bring a water bottle; Angela didn't want her skin to shrivel up from dehydration. Next time?

"I've got to settle this tonight."

THIRTY-FOUR

There was still water in the Arizona Canal. Angela landed on the dirt road next to it, exhausted from her stressful flight, and walked to the overgrown ditch. Was there some magical force at hand keeping her from Freestone Park? Or did she just need more exercise?

Angela found the built-in steps on the side of the concrete canal, pulled off her slippers and stuck her toes in. The water felt good on her overheated feet.

She enjoyed the solitude. It was a bright, starless night (stars in the city were a rarity), and a pleasant 75 degrees outside. During the day, the temperature had finally dropped below 100 for the season.

Regardless of the fact that she hadn't received any mission instructions, Angela needed to get back to her fairies—she did not need another lecture from Tatiana regarding her absence—and lifted her feet from the water.

A creepy feeling nagged at her spine and tickled its way to her subconscious. She was not alone. Had the pixies come for her here? Angela grabbed for her wand and turned her head toward the sound. Instead of her four-inch archrivals, Gabe ambled toward her. A smile twitched at her lips, making her immediately worried.

She looked around again, unsure whether or not to put her wand away, and tried to spot anything magical. Had Gabe seen something amiss and come to rescue her again? But he didn't have his fire truck or his colleague, Troy.

The aloneness of her situation frightened her more than if she were facing a swarm of pixies. Gabe seemed to take an interest in her and her fairies, and he was good-looking—but she was married. And she didn't know him. Not really. Even so, she put her wand away, put her slippers back on and stood, hands on her hips.

She felt her back. She was wingless, and sighed with relief. Did her wings instinctively hide at the sight of humans? It seemed ridiculous, but why then? Why did they seem to come and go as they pleased—and not at her command? And why did they come and go at all? Normal fairy wings didn't.

"Anj" Gabe stopped several yards back, his hands outstretched as though making a peace offering. He must have noticed her eyes bright with panic, though this gesture didn't stop the racing in her chest. He was so out of place wearing his blue shirt, but no fire, no emergency, no fire truck. It was like meeting your gynecologist in a dark alley—awkward.

"What are you doing here?" Angela tried to smile, to act friendly, but her voice cracked. Did he notice how nervous she was? She took a deep breath, but would have to quit chewing her nails in order to convince anyone she was calm. She clutched her hands together behind her back, worrying her bottom lip.

He turned his head to the side and shrugged his shoulders. "You're quite a ways from home." Gabe walked to the bank of the canal. He bent down, picking up a small rock, and chucked it into the water.

Angela couldn't think of any reason he would be here unless he had seen her from the tower and watched as she escaped from the dog, and then saw her come here. Angela took a step backwards. This was either a very good thing or a very bad thing. Was he stalking her? She shook her head. What was he thinking?

"I haven't done anything wrong. And, and I'm not in any trouble."

Gabe smiled but didn't say anything. He stepped forward.

Her heart thudded its warning. Angela couldn't let him get too close. What if it was a bad thing? He hadn't said why he was there yet. Gabe had been friendly, too friendly. Angela didn't want to hurt his feelings, but she couldn't trust this man, and stepped away while he wasn't watching.

In doing so, Angela felt herself stepping on air. She fell backwards, screaming.

Gabe rushed forward, catching her before she fell into the canal.

"Let me go, let me go!" she screeched. Struggling to escape his grasp and scrambling to get away, she almost fell into the canal again.

Gabe, growling his frustration, picked her up as though she didn't weigh anything, and stood her on safe ground. "Jeez, Anj, after all we've been through, and you're afraid of me?" He crossed his arms, scowling, and stepped back.

Well, so much for not hurting his feelings.

"I—I'm not afraid." Angela took a deep breath and tried steadying her knees. Why should she be afraid? Just because she was away from home in the middle of the night. Just because she was in her pajamas and slippers. Just because she was standing next to a handsome rescuer? "Did Ted call you?"

"No." Gabe grinned. "I have a feeling I'm the last person your husband would call in an emergency. Yeah?"

Okay, so that didn't reassure her. "Why is that?" She asked lightly. But really, did Ted know something about Gabe that she didn't?

He smiled, looking bemused.

"Aren't you supposed to be at work?" Angela took another involuntary step back and then peeked behind her to make sure the canal wasn't too close.

"I'm on lunch break." His shoulder lifted as though that explained everything.

Had she been too involved in being a fairy to see the obvious—that Gabe was dangerous in some way? He had come to the house uninvited. He had also shown up at the hospital. She could be in real danger.

Angela gazed toward Guadalupe Road, her safe zone. If she took off running, could she get there? No.

He was closer to the street.

Gabe was in top condition.

Angela didn't run. Ever.

She had never been good at that kind of thing even when young and so much smaller, and lighter, and in way better shape than now.

Gabe plopped onto the canal bank and removed his boots. "I won't hurt you, Anj. Come sit down." He patted the dirt beside him.

Was he dangerous? She chewed a fingernail. What would he do if she ran?

"They'll be draining the ditch in a couple weeks," Gabe said, his feet dangling in the water.

"Why are you here?" She eyed him. He didn't appear threatening.

He looked at her, his eyebrows raised.

Angela could tell he wouldn't say another word until she sat back down. She heaved a sigh and dropped onto the embankment a respectable distance away. Pulling off her slippers and splashing her feet in the water, she repeated her question, "Why are you here, Gabe?"

Clearly if he was some deranged fellow, he wouldn't let his guard down by removing his boots—he'd have hauled her off by now. However, his silence gave Angela plenty of time to let her imagination run wild. Her heart raced again and she worked to keep calm.

When he finally spoke, a tingling sensation moved up her spine.

"We firemen see things from our tower." He said it as an ordinary statement—some lame ad for a billboard. "Things we never talk about to anyone. Not if we want them to think we're sane, anyway." He rubbed his soul patch thoughtfully.

He had indicated as much before, but for whatever reason it hadn't seemed real. Until tonight. What should she say to that? Gabe reached over and closed her gaping mouth, his fingers lingering on her chin. Their eyes met, and she swallowed. Hard.

Did he expect her to confess, to tell him about her fairy life? If so, then what? No, even though it seemed that he already knew something, she wouldn't say anything. She couldn't.

He responded by casually taking his index finger and stroking one finger of the hand she was using to prop herself up. "Let's just say that, unlike your Ted, I'm a big fan of fairies, yeah?"

Angela jumped up with such force it cramped her knees and made her head spin. "Ow, ow, ow," she complained, hopping in circles and rubbing her knees. Trying to ignore her dizziness, Angela chugged on her slippers and rushed away. Well, she considered it a rush, but Gabe kept up easily with his practiced strides.

In order to get home safely and quickly, Angela had to find a private place to turn into a fairy. She couldn't do it in front of him. She wouldn't.

Where was a telephone booth when she needed one?

"Anj, I won't hurt you." Gabe walked beside her. Easily, Angela noted. It made her angry because after having another hot flash, she was drenched in sweat.

"Let me drive you home," he pleaded.

Yeah, there was no way that was happening. Angela tugged at the bottom of her T-shirt, wiping her face with the hem.

Most of the neighborhoods in Gilbert were separated by brick walls and it was the same along Guadalupe road. The sidewalk meandered in and out of strategically placed trees and bushes, as though designed and built by some drunk.

Unfortunately, the city landscapers had trimmed the area recently. There was no place to hide between bushes and brick wall. That would be a good thing if she weren't so desperate for an overgrown bush to dash behind—just long enough to persuade her wings to come out.

Angela headed east toward home. Gabe followed in an old truck.

"Get in Angela," he coaxed. "Let me give you a ride."

"I would," she growled, "but my mother taught me not to get into cars with strangers." She stopped on the sidewalk and glared at him. "Go away, Gabe."

"I'm a fireman." He sounded offended. "I'm not going to let you walk all the way home alone. It's dangerous."

"You're dangerous," she growled in response.

In truth, he could have stopped her if he'd wanted to. Apparently his only goals for the evening were to totally freak her out and then keep her from flying home.

THIRTY-FIVE

Five-thirty in the morning—that's what the clock read when Angela dragged her aching legs across the threshold—and one less day to fulfill her vow.

She had walked the whole way. Gabe followed her and waited in his truck until she went inside. What a gentleman. She closed the door and leaned against it with her eyes closed.

What was that all about? Why had Gabe been there? Angela had run off so quickly that he had never explained. Maybe she overreacted. Ted said she had a tendency to do that. It's just, his touch seemed so personal. She could still feel it on her skin.

Her legs ached and her body felt the heaviness of being up all night. Angela went quietly into the master bathroom and took a couple of vitamin tablets hoping they'd help her twitching legs.

It was kind of weird going to bed wearing the same clothes she'd had on all evening. She should put on something else, but Angela slipped under the covers while hoping not to wake Ted. His alarm would go off in fifteen minutes.

"Where have you been?" Ted's voice didn't sound sleepy, but then his voice didn't get all groggy while he slept like hers did.

"I was in the bathroom taking calcium for my legs." Please, she just wanted sleep. Angela closed her eyes hoping to doze for half an hour, and dreamt of the nap she'd take later.

"No. I mean the rest of the night, Angela." His voice sounded weary, like she felt. "Where have you been the rest of the night? Since you left the house?"

Oh, Ted knew. He was usually such a sound sleeper. Angela had never expected him to notice her being gone. Now he was upset. She would be too if her husband of thirty-two years had taken off in the middle of the night and hadn't come home until morning.

"It's not what you think, Ted."

"Well then, why don't we start with you telling me what I think." Ted sat up against the headboard, folded his arms across his chest, and glowered.

Angela sat up and rubbed her face in her hands, her half-asleep brain working and trying to decide what to tell Ted. "*I was going to Freestone Park, to get rid of the pixies and to fulfill my vow. Do you believe in fairies yet? Do the kids?*" She was a failure in every aspect of the fairies' request.

"I couldn't sleep?" She looked up. Ted's eyebrows pinched together, still waiting. This was going to be hard.

"I went outside." These two confessions did not soften Ted one bit. He wanted a long explanation. "I know you don't want me outside by myself after dark. I'm sorry." She wanted to say she wouldn't do it again, but what was the point? Angela had every intention of continuing her fairy life.

"Yes, well, this is the part I'm interested in—the part after you went outside. Then what did you do?" His jaw set and he watched her carefully.

"I went for a walk." She hung her head, which was better than having it bitten off.

"Angela! Don't lie to me." Ted pounded the bed with his fist. "I woke up and saw that you weren't in bed, so I looked around the house. I went in the backyard." He swished his hand in that general direction. "You weren't there. So, I got in the car and drove around the neighborhood. Do you hear me, Angela? I drove around the neighborhood looking for you at three-in-the-freaking-morning."

So much for not having her head bit off. The strain in his voice revealed several feelings at once — distress — worry — anger — disbelief — with betrayal prevailing over the others.

Angela was the woman who never did anything to upset her husband, the woman who always did her best to appease, the woman who always said "sorry" to everyone for everything. But, Angela wasn't that same person anymore. Who was she then?

She was a woman who loved her husband, so she would go with that.

"Ted, I'm sorry that you're upset, but I assure you, I wasn't doing anything wrong. I was, well," she braced herself and continued, "I was on fairy business." This really wasn't cheating.

She caught the accusing glare — the one she had seen a thousand times — the, I'm-so-tired-of-hearing-about-fairies glare. It made her angry, but they could still discuss this rationally. Except that when she opened her mouth, her overactive hormones made it sound a little differently than rational.

"Yes, yes. I know you don't believe in fairies, but I do. I am one! Like it or not, Ted, you are married to a human-sized fairy equipped with wings and all." Angela pulled her toothpick-sized wand out and shoved it in his face. "Fairy wand," she snapped. She jerked the miniature bag out from under her shirt, drawing it to the end of its tether. "Fairy dust." (Okay, that was cheating.)

In showing Ted her priceless treasures, Angela hoped that the physical evidence would calm him down.

Ted barked an ill-humored laugh. "A toothpick for a fairy wand — where'd you get that junk? Do they have a fairy store in town now?" Ted got off the bed and paced the room, combing his fingers through his hair. "Angela, you're too big to be a fairy and you're too old to keep pretending." Ted closed his eyes and rubbed his forehead. "This isn't funny anymore and it's no longer cute."

Waves of tears crashed over Angela's face and cheeks like a hurricane breaking over the sandbags in New Orleans. "I'll lose weight ... I promise ... I've been trying. But I'll never get any younger." They didn't have magic for that. She turned in bed, curling her knees to her chest as best as she could, and cried, wishing upon wish that she could fly away from his cruel remarks.

"Anj." Ted climbed back in bed and put his hand on her shoulder.

"Don't!" She shrugged his hand away and continued sobbing. "I'm sorry I can't be the wife you want me to be. I'm sorry I'm too big. I'm sorry you don't find me attractive anymore."

"No, Anj, please, I'm sorry." He kissed her hair. "You know I didn't mean it like that." He petted her shoulder. "You know I love you. I've always loved you. I'm so sorry." He nestled his face into her neck and his warm breath sent chills down her arms. "I didn't mean it like that. Please forgive me."

It wasn't fair.

She wanted to be mad at Ted for not believing in fairies, for not believing in her, for thinking she was more oddball than fun. However, even though all those things were true about Ted, it was also true that he loved her, was concerned about her, and that his remarks hadn't come out the way he intended. Because although she did have her share of middle-aged flab, that didn't matter to Ted. He loved her for who she was. (As long as she wasn't being a fairy, of course.)

Ted left then to take a shower.

Angela sighed with relief, closed her eyes and settled into her pillow, thinking the worst was over.

It wasn't.

After his shower, their conversation went something like this:

"So, where'd you go last night?"

Angela opened her puffy eyes. She didn't want to fight anymore. "I was going to Freestone Park, but only got as far as the canal." Had Gabe intended to keep her away?

"Oh, what stopped you?" Ted rubbed his hair with a towel.

"The fire station and a Rottweiler." There was a story.

Ted put the towel down and looked at her from around the corner of the bathroom wall. "People have been murdered near that canal."

Angela shuddered.

"You said you were safe." He combed his hair but kept an eye on her.

"Gabe followed me home." Her shoulders slumped, instantly realizing that little factoid might make Ted angry.

"*Gabe?*" He turned and glared. "Gabe the hunky fireman was with you? In the middle of the night." He rested his fists on his hips. "You're on a first name basis with him now?"

What was she supposed to call him? "I didn't get in his truck." Surely he wasn't dangerous. Angela bit her lips together, having already said too much.

"The Gabe that calls you Anj?" Ted stormed into the bedroom. "He's seen you naked!" Ted dressed in the closet and came out adjusting his tie. "How dare you go cavorting with him in the early hours of the morning!"

That's when they heard the front door close. The kids had heard them arguing.

THIRTY-SIX

"You have to put an end to this Gabe thing." He scowled. "I can't believe you'd leave home in the middle of the night, and after spending the evening in the ER. Is that when you made plans to meet up with him?"

"It's not like that. I told you it was nothing. And we didn't make plans to meet. He was just there. He works at the fire station, you know. He saw me." Angela climbed out of bed. "What will it take to convince you?"

"The guys at work," he said, pacing, "some of them are seeing a marriage counselor." Ted grabbed his phone and texted a message.

"We don't need a marriage counselor." Angela reached for him.

Ted jerked away. "Oh, we need a counselor." He looked down at his phone. "I've got the name and number." He called it and left a message.

"Maybe they're too busy." Angela tittered.

"No. They're not open yet. I've got an excellent referral. They'll see us." He shoved the phone to Angela. "They sent the name and number for a personal counselor as well. I want you to call him."

"What?!"

"You heard me." He shoved the phone forward again. "Call him."

Angela took the phone in her shaking hands. "Please, Ted, this isn't necessary."

"It's necessary." He clenched his jaw. "Call."

She punched in the number. "They probably aren't open yet either." One could hope.

"Hello. Doctor Brunell's office."

"I ..." she looked up at Ted. "I, um ... I'd like to make an appointment." She blinked back her tears.

"Tell them it's an emergency!"

"Um, my husband says it's an emergency."

"Is the appointment for him?"

"No. He wants me to come in."

Ted grabbed Angela's hand, speaking into her cell. "Your soonest available."

"Have you been in before?"

"No. This will be my first appointment."

"But not her last," Ted shouted to the phone.

Angela went to the dresser and found a pen and paper.

Ted's phone rang. "Hello, Doctor Franklin." He turned his back to Angela, mumbling as he left the room.

Doctor Brunell's assistant came back on. "Okay, I have you all set up for February fourteenth. Come in forty minutes early and bring your insurance card."

"Okay. Thanks," she said, writing the information down.

A counselor. Really? Angela winced.

Ted came back in the room. "His first available isn't until the end of January. You can stay out of trouble until then can't you?"

Angela glared at her husband. Anything she said at this point would only add fuel to their bonfire. To Ted, her lifelong belief in fairies indicated a deep-rooted need for therapy. She could humor him until then.

"I ..." Angela shook her head, turned, and walked to the toilet room.

Why did her life have to be like that? If Ted had asked her to believe in fairies, she would believe with all her heart.

"Let's do something," he said when she opened the bathroom door.

"Like what?" She washed her hands.

"Let's have a picnic." He raised his eyebrows and gave her a goofy smile.

Where had this man been? Was he not in the room during their fight? She thrust her fingers into her hair. "Um, okay." Angela was tired of fighting, and they needed to show a united front for the kids. It wasn't often the children heard them argue.

"You want to go to Freestone Park, then?"

"No," Angela shouted, and then was embarrassed with her outburst.

Ted looked at her questioningly. "You said you were on your way to Freestone Park last night. We should go as a family."

"Yeah, but maybe another day." She rubbed her cheek.

"We should picnic on the fire station lawn. Show that fireman that you have a husband and children." He worked his jaw around with a scowl. "I'm sorry. That was uncalled for." He rested his hand on Angela's shoulder.

"How about Usury Pass? We haven't been there in ages."

Ted nodded. "We could take the rifles with us and do some skeet-shooting."

Practicing for the kill was not Angela's favorite pastime, but it was a much safer activity for her than taking her family to Freestone Park — war zone for magical creatures.

As it turned out, it was the only activity that persuaded Derek and Hannah to accompany them.

The Andersons had a wonderful time. It was dusk when they

finally made their way down Power Road toward home. The setting sun left the horizon a blazing orange-red and a few porch lights already decorated the homes, a graying silhouette, like diamonds. Angela took a deep breath. "Look at that view." Gazing at the Phoenix valley from this slightly higher elevation was beautiful and peaceful.

"It's gorgeous," Ted said, "and so are you."

"Thank you." She smiled at the compliment but didn't take her eyes off of the desert landscape until it disappeared and they were inside the city-jungle with stop-lights, and traffic, and activity blurring everywhere along the streets.

"How about some dinner." Ted turned the steering wheel and pulled into Min Chow, their favorite Chinese-food restaurant.

The kids were on their best behavior. It was a welcome surprise.

When they got home a few hours later, Derek and Hannah bounded up the stairs.

"Where you going?" She asked.

"To our rooms." The doors shut behind them.

"Well, I guess that's about all the family togetherness they can stand for one day." Angela smiled at Ted.

He was a million miles away, already in his recliner clicking through the television stations with the remote.

"Well, I guess that's about it for everyone," she mumbled to herself. She went in the kitchen and unpacked the leftover picnic supplies, cleaned out the ice chest, put it away, and then wondered what to do with the rest of her evening. "Can I watch TV with you?"

"Sure." He patted the armrest.

Those counseling sessions had her a little nervous. They were opposite of the respect and belief Tatiana requested she gain. Maybe she could soften him up by being the best wife again—at least during their waking hours. After trying to talk to him several times though, she finally gave up. He hated being interrupted during TV time even if it wasn't his favorite show.

Angela had been silently begging for ten o'clock to come for an hour before Ted finally agreed that it was bedtime and clicked off the television.

She hurried into the bedroom. Putting on a clean set of pajama-shorts and a nicer T-shirt, she went to the bathroom, took out her wand and dust, and slipped them into her pocket.

Ted stood in the doorway. "What happened to the hot chocolate?"

"Oh, yeah." Angela shot him a dirty look. Their heated discussion wasn't over yet.

"I suppose you don't want any more." Ted shook his head. "No, of course not." He walked into the bedroom.

"I pitched it in the trash." She rested a hand to her hip. "Where'd that stuff come from anyway?" She lifted her eyebrows.

Ted looked guilty. "You don't want to know." His face reddened as he walked to her side.

"Oh, but I do." She already had her suspicions. Ted just needed to say it.

"Don't be mad." He reached for her hand, but she avoided his grasp. "Rebecca Helman brought it over." He tried for her hand again.

Angela reached for the bedcovers, flipping them down. "You secretly fed me something from my worst enemy?" It was much worse hearing it out loud. She turned to face him, her hand clutching her heart. "How could you do that?"

"Come on, Anj." Ted flopped onto the bed. "It was a gift. They picked it up as a souvenir for us in Acapulco."

"Souvenir, my foot. She was trying to poison me. And you let her." Angela breezed past him and paced the room.

Ted got up and tried catching her hand.

"I never thought she'd go that far." Angela's insides trembled with anger. She pressed a closed hand to her mouth, thinking, and sat on the bed.

"No, no. It still had the factory seal." Ted came and sat beside her. "It might have been a reaction to one of the ingredients, sure, but it wasn't anything she had control over. It couldn't be."

"Why didn't you tell me she brought it over?" Her eyebrows arched.

Ted squirmed uncomfortably. "She brought it for, you know, a sort of peace offering." Ted shrugged. "You love chocolate, and Rebecca thought that if you knew the stuff came from her, you'd throw it away." He smiled haplessly. "I agreed that you probably would, so I didn't mention it."

"How is it a peace offering if I don't know who sent it?" Angela rubbed her hands over her face.

"I'm so sorry. I wanted to tell you." Ted tried putting his arm around her but she pushed it off and stood. Ted stood too. "I mentioned to Rebecca that you'd been having a hard time sleeping. That's when she brought over the chocolate mix." His head tilted down in contrition as he looked up at Angela, his voice lowered. "She did also suggest Tylenol PM if the drink didn't work."

"Well, I threw the poison away, and I'm not taking any sleeping meds."

"It's just as well." Ted nodded and pulled Angela onto the bed beside him. "I know that it seems really bad now, and it is." He rested his hand on her thigh. "But it was chocolate. I didn't know it was dangerous. Will you forgive me? I'm really tired of fighting."

Ted had done wrong. But, he'd been manipulated. In truth, Angela was more upset with that putrid rodent than with her too trusting husband. She was ready to move on to a better subject.

Angela had one in mind.

"How about some special husband and wife time?" He owed her big time for this. "I've heard that we're supposed to make up after a fight." She wiggled her eyebrows hoping he'd get the hint.

"Ah, that sounds great." Ted flopped over, facing away from Angela. "So, you'll scratch my back?"

THIRTY-SEVEN

Almost as though her intelligent-wings knew the second of Ted's slumber, they appeared on Angela's back.

A grin crept across her face. She sighed and lay there for a moment reveling in her magical wings, listening to Ted's breathing, and then got up.

Ted would be upset if he awoke and found her missing once again, so she wrote him a note.

Dear Ted,
Don't worry,
I'll be back soon and I promise to stay safe.
Thanks for understanding.
Love Anj.

She hesitated with her pen but couldn't make herself write: I won't be with Gabe. She wouldn't be, but the mention of his name was like pouring salt in a big gaping wound. Angela put the sticky note on the mirror and left the room.

Angela's shoulders ached. She rubbed them, then stepped onto the patio and floated up into the night sky. She was only able to fly up to roof-height, but it was late. No one would see her.

The Helmans' Saguaro cactus loomed large. The unscrupulous hussy next door had actually tried poisoning her with chocolate. That was hitting below the belt. Dare she do something devious? One easily repaired tire certainly didn't make up for the bug in her soup, nor did it make up for being poisoned.

Angela pointed the wand at Helmans' prized cactus, concentrating. It was hard. The cactus was a large target, but she didn't break her focus until the saguaro started to wrinkle and then wilt.

The Helmans might get a fine for that. Angela put her fingers to her lips suppressing a laugh. Saguaros were protected by the government. Neglecting one ... well, that would be frowned on.

The tall palm tree in their backyard was also a good target, but after flying toward it, Angela decided to move on. If everything went wrong at their house at once, Rebecca would be suspicious.

And, enough of that Gabe. He'd gotten her in trouble with Ted. Jealous Ted. Angela grinned even though it wasn't funny, but his jealousy felt good to her. Angela flew south to Elliot Road to avoid the fire station — not having realized until she got there that Elliot was more populated than the last time she had ventured down the road.

In regards to time and effort, Angela should have flown through the middle of the neighborhoods like she did on the north of Guadalupe. At this height, she could see into people's second-story windows. Not something she cared to witness. And, not knowing this side of the highway well, she didn't dare. With her luck, she would end up at the fire station's rear parking lot.

With this reasoning, Angela flew west down Elliot Road. She didn't do well with the bright headlights — part of her night vision thing. She was long overdue at the eye doctor's office, but hated the thought of what he might say. "Women over forty ..." Ugh! "You're old, so it's only natural for your body to fall apart," Angela mimicked. Didn't they have any women teachers in medical school? Just one person to tell the hundreds of male doctors that rubbing peoples' ages in their noses wasn't polite? Doctors. They angered her.

228

Once again, Angela felt that uncharacteristic bad temper bubble forward. She pulled out her wand and pointed it at the tire of a parked car. "Mo-ah-ha-ha!" She laughed evilly as it deflated, and then she flew away. "Oh yeah, bad girl Angela is back!"

Angela entered the intersection heading west. "What other tricks can I do with my wand?"

She was startled by the blinding lights of an SUV in front of her, someone honking, and then by the force of a hard object slamming into her. A telephone pole, Angela realized, as she slid down it and onto the hard sidewalk.

Everything was black, and Angela was unaware of her surroundings. Then, in the distance, she saw a bright light. Was she dead, then? Was she supposed to walk to the light? She took a deep breath and tried moving herself forward.

The light moved.

"What in the world?" She tried to follow it. It moved again, and Angela heard voices. "Mama?"

"It's me, Gabe."

Angela opened her eyes. "Gabe?"

He was kneeling over her, looking in her eyes with a small flashlight.

She moaned. "What are you doing here?" Ted was going to be furious.

"The fire department is on their way, but I was close, so here I am."

"Get me out of here—quick!" Her heart skipped a beat. Angela raised herself onto her elbows, but her head spun, and she closed her eyes.

"You're hurt."

"No. I am not hurt," Angela hissed through clenched teeth. She refused to be hurt. She had promised Ted—how many minutes ago?—that she would be safe. She could not have Ted waking up to a visit from the police. "Sir, your wife is in the hospital. Again. Shall we rent you out a room?" She could not have the fire department there.

Angela heard someone talking in the background—a young woman, possibly in her twenties.

"It was like the weirdest thing." The girl must be talking to Gabe, but Angela's eyes were shut so she could only assume. "It looked like she fell from the sky. People don't do that, do they?"

Angela peeked an eye open.

Luckily it was late. How late she didn't know, but there were no crowds and only the one spectator. That was fortunate. However, if the fire truck and an ambulance showed up, and a police car. Ugh! The horror!

Angela jumped to her feet, but her equilibrium was off. Her head spun violently and she started back down for another visit with the sidewalk. Gabe caught her and stood her aright. Angela had hit that pole harder than she thought.

"Get me out of here," she repeated, pure desperation raging in her soul.

THIRTY-EIGHT

"Don't worry, miss, we're friends. I'll take her home." Gabe held Angela's arm by the elbow.

"I was going to the park," Angela muttered into his shoulder. What unseen forces were keeping her from that stupid park, anyway? It shouldn't be that hard to fly four miles.

"What about the fire department?" The girl followed beside them. "Don't I get to give an official statement?"

"I'm a member of the local department. Your statement will be recorded once I get back to the station." Gabe flipped open his cell phone and called off her rescue while escorting Angela toward his truck, a vintage Chevy with a custom paint job.

"You're a fireman? Cool." The girl squealed and clapped. "I'm going to tell all my friends." Okay, maybe she wasn't in her twenties yet.

Angela's legs turned to rubber and she started toward the pavement again. Gabe picked her up, cradling her in his arms like a child. "I really should take you to the emergency room to be checked out." He held her with one arm while opening the passenger door. The door didn't squeak, and he didn't drop her. It was a miracle.

"I won't go to the ER. I'm refusing treatment." Angela peeked at a bag-full of frozen dinners on the seat between them. "Dinner for one?" She had been right, he was single.

"The bachelor's life. Yeah?" Gabe shrugged and put the key in the ignition.

Angela felt perfectly rescued until the moment Gabe started the engine. "I, um, maybe I should just go home," Angela stuttered. Tatiana hadn't actually given her another mission.

Being alone with Gabe made her nervous, especially after his weird behavior of the other night. Angela laughed a manic laugh at her private joke—she was a human-sized fairy on a mandated fairy mission—and accusing Gabe of weird behavior. And according to Ted, she acted weird most of the time. Gabe had so many more nights of acting weird in order to catch up with her.

Angela looked at her wrist, willing her watch to appear. It didn't. How long would it take her to either obliterate the pixies or convince them to leave the park? She didn't even know how many pixies there were. How long could she be gone before Ted awoke? Because honestly, that was all the time she had.

"It's just after eleven," Gabe said. "Do you mind if I stay with you for a while?" His voice was soft.

Angela quickly closed her eyes and rubbed her eyebrows. Gabe made her nervous. If she looked at him, he'd see the crazy-with-fear look in her eyes. He'd said they were friends, though, so she should have no reason to feel nervous. She could be cool—her kids didn't think she could—but she could. She used to be cool. She would be again. Tonight. She opened her eyes and smiled, maybe it was more of a wince, so she moistened her lips preparing to say something.

"I need to make sure you're okay before I leave. Yeah?" He patted her hand and got out of the truck. Oh, they'd parked.

Angela sat, still inside of the truck, feeling embarrassed with herself. Gabe thought of her as a friend and only a friend. She had no need to fear. But then he opened her side of the door, took her hand and helped her out.

Ted used to open the door for her when they were dating. Her chest fluttered. That didn't help her focus on her mission at all. Aware of Gabe's warmth still on her palm, she wiped her hand on her pants leg. She loved her husband.

Before Angela could gather her thoughts, she and Gabe were sitting at a picnic table across the lake from where she and Amy had shared lunch. But Angela and Gabe were alone — the two of them with acres of green lawn, trees, and water between them and civilization.

Although she was nervous being there with a man who wasn't her husband, the thought of being alone with only herself and a hoard of pixies made her even more jittery.

The whole park was empty. No sign of the traffic, if there was any, on Lindsay Road. No sign of the hundreds of people who lived in nearby homes behind the mile of block wall. The park lights turned off at ten p.m., but the city never got completely dark, and the moon was up.

It felt like another world. That's probably why the fairies liked it. The landscape had a blue sheen cast from the moon. The lake was black with silver highlights.

Yes, Angela believed in magic, and it was precisely her fear of pixies that put her on edge. It had nothing to do with the magical intimacy of this place — being here or sharing it with Gabe that made her nervous. Gabe was merely keeping her company. He was nice. That was all. Why would she even consider the thought that he liked her inappropriately? It was absurd. After all, he had just told witness number one that they were friends.

However, finally conscious of his hand moving back and forth smoothly across the top of hers, she pulled her hands into her lap.

Angela was sadly aware of how she appeared to others — a haggard, overweight, overworked housewife and mother. Older than dirt, according to her kids.

"So. You haven't asked me why I'm here, and I haven't asked you why you're here. Does that mean we both know?" Gabe smiled.

What? Angela frowned. She knew why Gabe was there — to make

sure she didn't have a concussion. It wasn't any of his business why she was there. But she had come to really appreciate that smile of his in the short time she had known him.

"I wanted to ask ... oh, never mind." Angela shook her head. It was all too embarrassing—sitting there in the middle of the night, talking to a member of the male species. She hadn't talked to another man since Ted—not alone. She felt like a little school girl.

Angela smirked at that absurdity.

"What? You can ask me." Gabe reached across the cement table for her hand.

She pulled away from his touch.

The corner of his lip turned up. "You're still afraid of me aren't you?" he taunted.

"I am not. And, why were you at the canal last night?" She could act cool. Luckily Gabe couldn't hear her hard-and-fast-beating heart, it would discredit her reply. He would laugh at her for sure.

"Why were you there last night, and better yet, why are you here tonight?" He gave her a challenging smile. "Your husband isn't with you—you must be up to no good. Lurking in the neighborhoods, scaring guard dogs. Hey, I'm sworn to protect the city." He lifted his right hand as if to give an oath. "I've got to keep an eye on you and make sure you don't vandalize something.

Angela scowled. "No I wouldn't. I'm not a vandal." Then remembering all the yards and the tires she had ruined, the blood rushed from her face—a vandal is exactly what she was.

"Oh, yeah?" Gabe smirked. "Well, tell your face."

Her lips pushed together in a thin line. Was he teasing her? She looked him in the eyes, deciding to be as honest as she could. "I've got business here."

"Fairy business?"

Angela gasped and stood.

"I told you, we firemen see things when we're in the tower." He stood up and grasped her hand.

"So you've said." She looked down at his hand firmly holding hers. Would he have her arrested? Angela couldn't get her eyes to blink — and she couldn't get her heart to quit pounding. His hand was warm. Hers felt like refrigerated hotdogs comparatively.

"I'll leave you to your business now, yeah? But what I'm saying — what I want to say is this. I believe in fairies." He watched her face. He wasn't arresting her. Angela held her chest and coughed, and then she sucked in her breath. What was he getting at? "I think you deserve to have someone in your life who appreciates your gift."

"Ted appreciates me," she insisted, pulling her hand free. How she hoped that was true. She wiped her hand on her pants leg. After thirty-two years, sometimes it was hard to tell. After all, she had spent a half an hour talking to him just this evening before realizing that he hadn't heard a word.

"Well," Gabe said. "Think about it." He touched her shoulder and turned to leave, then looked back. "I assume you'll be able to get home safely?"

Angela nodded, watching mutely as he climbed into his truck and drove away. Her knees buckled and she clutched the table. So much for her cool persona.

THIRTY-NINE

"Everyone thinks I'm invisible," Angela muttered. "Why doesn't Gabe?"

Why did he have to be different, and what did he want her to think about? She was there, hoping for a face-to-face with Tatiana — hoping that in doing so, Tatiana would go ahead and give Angela the details of her fairy mission. Details that were frustratingly absent from her mind. And time was running out.

Why had Tatiana put such pressure on her? Rather than giving encouragement, the timed ultimatum stressed her more with each ticking minute of the clock. Nevertheless, Angela sat on the park bench quizzing her mind on Gabe's exact wording, something about him believing in fairies, and her needing someone to appreciate her gift.

Angela rolled her eyes and whacked her forehead.

"I'm so dumb!" She needed to get out more — eccentric Angela — severely delusional Angela — her heart had jumped and sputtered thinking that a handsome, muscular man was interested in her. If he wasn't arresting her, that could be his only motive. Right?

She had hemmed and sputtered, not knowing how to get away or even how to let him down easy. Angela whacked her forehead again as the realization of his true motive dawned on her — to be there for her and hang out with a fairy. Like a friend.

Everyone could use a friend, and Angela hadn't had anyone other than Amy for a while. She patted her hand over the cement table. Now that puzzle was solved, this old woman needed to get to work. *"Tatiana, I'm here. What do you want me to do?"* Why did the fairies have to be so secretive? If they wanted her to do something, why didn't they just text her? She had no idea how to listen for fairy thoughts.

Angela took a deep breath. If she helped solve the fairies' problem, maybe her life could get back to normal. She could start spending nights with Ted again.

Angela chuckled—a weird sound nearing hysteria. The noise echoed in the surreal nighttime glow, frightening her. She jumped, and then almost started to giggle again at her nervousness, but bit her lips shut instead.

Angela looked around apprehensively. She was all alone. Well, alone except for ... didn't she see something moving? Just over there? Her blood pressure shot up and her heart beat furiously in her throat.

"This isn't the kind of thing I signed on for," she muttered. Fairies were kind and good. They didn't go skulking around in the middle of the night in parks, alone, looking for pixies. Hm. Well, apparently they did—but how was she supposed to have known that?

"Fly, wings fly," she whispered over her shoulder, wanting to sprout wings and go home. They weren't there. "Any time now." Angela rubbed her hands together nervously. Verbal commands wouldn't work. They hadn't before. She scrunched her shoulders together, similar to the bust-improvement-exercises of her youth— the in and out movements turning into the flying motions that had kind of worked in bringing out her wings before. Still nothing.

"You've got it all backwards," she hissed to her invisible fairy wings. "You're not supposed to shrink back and hide when I'm afraid." She shook her head wearily. "You're supposed to open up and fly me the heck out of here."

Something made a sound.

Angela glanced toward the ramada. Something moved in the nearby bushes. She jumped up and raced behind the table, moving her shoulders back and forth. Nothing.

"Why, oh why, can't you get it right?" She plopped back down on the bench, and then sat up straight. "*You have a dangerous sense of humor, Tatiana.*" Recruiting Angela's help had proven disastrous. For herself anyway.

She heard a rustling sound.

"*Tatiana?*" Angela sneaked behind a tree. It didn't matter that she was twice as wide as the trunk, or that it didn't hide her, or that anyone a half a mile away could see her cowering behind it. The tree was her security blanket.

A twig snapped. The bushes fluttered.

Her heart thudded perilously loud. "*How many hundreds of pixies are after me?*" Tatiana could at least give her a head's up. She looked around to where the sounds had come from. They, whoever they were, were surrounding her. "Hello? Is anyone there?" She smashed her hand against her forehead, concentrating on picturing wings.

"*Tatiana? Where are you?*"

If one pixie had sent her to the hospital, she dared not contemplate what a dozen or more could do. Angela pulled her wand out of her waistband with shaking hands. "*Come out, come out, where ever you are.*"

But what if it was a human? Some creep?

"Gabe," she whispered loudly, knowing he'd left. "I'm going for a little walk." Pretending someone was with her made her braver.

What was the rule with pixies—just point the wand, right? It would be like the tires and the cactus, pointing while concentrating on her intent would send the pixies back to their homeland. If she could concentrate.

"*Can't we just talk?*" Angela waited, her wand ready. "*There must be some way to work this out.*" She had a general idea where they were, but another noise would make her sure. "*Just leave and everything will be okay.*"

The bush rustled again.

Phooey on diplomatic discussions! Angela leaned left, flicked her wand at the noise, and then bobbed back behind her wooden shield, her heart beating excessively fast. She was not cut out for strategic warfare.

The noises from the bush were not the sounds she had anticipated and the pixies didn't fly in a counterattack. Instead, she heard a loud squawking noise. "Do wounded pixies squawk?" She asked outloud. And then the sounds of ... swimming?

Had she scared the pixies off with just one flick of her wand? Or was it a trick?

Angela slowly peeked around the tree. Feathers fluttered out of the sky, resting near a feathery pile already on the grass. A half dozen waterfowl were swimming angrily across the lake.

The lump on the lawn worried her. Angela peered, wand in hand, for creeps or pixies, and then stepped from the safety of the tree and into the open. She hurried forward to assess the scene.

A semi-featherless duck lay near the water's edge. Her heart flipped and then sank to the pit of her stomach. Had she killed a duck?

Before Angela had time to react, several differently colored bodies of light hovered nearby. The pixies looked at the duck in unison, and in unison, they shouted angrily at her. She should run. She should hide. She should use her wand for zapping. But Angela was stunned motionless.

Several things happened simultaneously—one pixie knelt

beside the duck and began trying to revive the creature. Brown, white, and luminescent feathers floated eerily toward it, reattaching themselves to their owner. The duck remained limp.

In her peripheral vision, the other pixies edged closer, wands extended.

A sparkling bolt of lightning flashed past her head.

Angela broke loose of her shock and scrambled for the tree. Sitting on her haunches, she gasped for air. She had killed the duck. She loved ducks. And now the pixies wanted revenge.

A malevolent odor tweaked her nose and Angela felt heat near her left temple. She lunged downward, her head on the ground, patting the flame from her hair with dirt.

The pixies, momentarily distracted by her smoking hair, edged forward again. Angela jumped up, hair still smoldering, and ran toward the parking lot. "Get me out of here!" She shouted to her hiding wings, then rushed to a bush and leaped to safety.

"Oomph!" Angela brushed herself off and grabbed her wand. She pointed it at the pixies, but didn't want to see what happened and squeezed her eyes shut as she flicked.

A bright light shone, getting brighter.

"Eep! There's more?" She fumbled with her wand. "Will I be forced to destroy them all?" Angela could never live with herself if that happened. They were living magical creatures.

Angela couldn't destroy them.

She wrapped her arms around her knees and tucked her head in the opening there, and sobbed. Her whole frame shook while she waited for retribution. But whatever happened next, she wouldn't use her wand again tonight. She couldn't. Her only regret was not getting to kiss Ted goodbye one last time.

She had killed a duck with her magic—and possibly a pixie or two. Angela had never killed anything in her life. The image of the lifeless duck haunted her. Angela was glad she hadn't watched herself zap the pixies. Having that horror on her memory's instant replay would be unbearable. At least this way she didn't know—not for sure.

Maybe they got away

"Are you okay? I hope my being here is okay. No pressure, I promise. I saw lights flashing and needed to make sure you weren't hurt."

Angela looked up from her tear-stained pants. Gabe was almost beside her, approaching slowly, his head tilted questioningly.

Angela didn't understand. What was he talking about? Why was he there again? How did he know something had happened?

"The tower." He reminded her, but then seemed embarrassed. "I was worried, yeah. Believers can see everything on the tower. Magic is visible in the night sky," he said, and sat beside her. "So, is it okay—my being here?" Gabe looked expectantly and appeared nervous.

"No. It's good." She needed a friend. "I'm glad you came." Angela rested her head on his shoulders feeling instantly comforted and exhausted. "It's a relief to have another human who knows." Her eyebrows pinched together. "You *are* human aren't you?" She looked up. His eyes weren't green.

Gabe puckered his face and casually placed his arm around her. "Of course I'm human—probably a touch more so than the fairy-lady." He grinned and flipped her hair.

"Oh, right," Angela conceded. "You've got me there."

Gabe acted so different when they were alone—and different now than earlier—unsure of himself and a complete opposite of the confident fireman. How cute. It was so old fashioned of him to ask to be her friend. No one had ever done that before, except that once in fifth grade.

Maybe he asked because of her age, or because she was a fairy. But really, Angela was exhausted from her ordeal and didn't have the mental strength to care.

"Let me take you home. It's almost two a.m." Gabe stood and offered his hand. She took it, and he pulled her to her feet.

"No. I need to fly home," she said. "I'll be fine." The stress of the night left Angela groggy and it was hard to stay awake, but she knew better than risk having Ted see Gabe bringing her home. Even though they were just friends. "How old are you?" she mumbled as he steadied her.

"Fifty-seven."

Angela kept her eyes closed as she let this sink in. He was older than she was, but not by much. The same age as Ted, but Gabe had weathered even better. She hated men and their easily muscled physiques. Why couldn't they be the ones having babies?

"Come on. Let me drive you. The truck's right here." He motioned toward the parking lot. The truck's bright lights faced them.

"I killed a duck." Angela looked toward the lake, ashamed of herself. "I should take care of it before I leave." She didn't want to do it, but the thought of some toddler coming across it in the morning, well that would be unforgivable. Then, she realized there might be pixies still out there, waiting. "Will you come with me?"

He nodded. "Of course."

FORTY

Angela pulled off her slippers and tiptoed through the house and into her bedroom.

Ted was on the edge of the bed, note in hand. "Where have you been?" With his elbow resting on his knee, Ted rubbed his forehead and then swept his hand up and over his hair, resting on the side of his neck.

Angela learned something that night—the pre-dawn hours were not a good time for a serious discussion with an upset husband.

"Um, I was at Freestone Park."

"The park is closed." He lifted his eyebrows. "I asked if you wanted to go to the park. You said, no." He crumpled her note. "Or did you just not want to go with me?"

"I want to go to the park with you. I want to go everywhere with you. I love you," she said.

"Was Fireman Castillo Perez there with you?"

"Who?" Angela wrinkled her nose.

"Gabe."

"Oh." She took a deep breath. "I was mostly alone," she said.

He dropped his hand to the bed. "You said you were being safe." His brows pinched together. "What does safe mean to you, because to me, it doesn't mean going to the park, or anywhere, alone and after midnight." He lifted his hand to her singed hair, frowning. "What would I have done? How would I have even known where to look for you if something bad had happened?" He brushed his fingers through his hair. "This is the big city, Anj. There are gangs and thugs right here in our neighborhood."

"Gabe wasn't with me, but he did know where I was." She lifted her lips.

The news didn't appease Ted. "I knew it!" He stood up and paced the floor. "You'd better stay away from him, or I'm filing a restraining order. I'll punch his lights out."

"Make up your mind," Angela demanded. "Do you want me alone at the park, or don't you?"

He didn't seem to want either option.

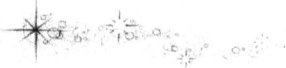

During the following nights and regardless of Ted's insistence to the contrary, Angela went faithfully to the park. Each night brought stronger feelings of desperation. Time was running out. Ted was angry. The fairy queen was angry, and it seemed that Tatiana was keeping her promise to destroy Angela's family. Angela's first effort to fulfill her vow after the duck incident went something like this:

Angela waved her hand over Ted's face, making sure he was sound asleep, and then she snuck out the back door. She looked to her left, checking to make sure the Helmans weren't around. They weren't. Angela's wings lifted her into the night sky. It was about eleven p.m. Gabe was in the tower. Since she had met her fireman friend, it seemed there was no way to avoid him, so instead of avoiding him, she landed on the tower beside him. She couldn't have her non-believing husband bossing her around all the time.

"I'm going to the park to settle this thing with the pixies," Angela said. "Can you come with me?" She was afraid to go alone.

"The rest of the team's out on a call." Gabe seemed to be standing closer than necessary. "I'm sorry, but I can't leave unless there's an emergency."

Angela peeked behind her, (just to make sure she didn't fall off the edge) and took a step back. "I've gotta go." Friend or not, Gabe's physical nearness still made her nervous.

At the park, Angela sat at the cement table closest to the waterfall, heart thumping, nerves jumping—until she heard a sound.

"Who, goes there?" No one answered, and she fumbled for her wand. "Be ye friend, or be ye foe?" Her fingers shook, her knees shook. Honestly, was there an earthquake? With her wand at the ready, she demanded, "G—g—g—go away and I won't hurt you."

"I'm going to have to ask you to leave, ma'am." A police officer stepped into view. "The park is closed, and we've had complaints from the neighbors about people lurking here after hours."

"I'm sorry, officer. I didn't realize the time." Giddy with relief, Angela headed toward the shrubs before he could ask where her car was.

"Kook," he mumbled.

A gentleman wouldn't call her names, so Angela pretended he'd asked if she could cook. "Yes, I can," she shouted over her shoulder as she speed-walked toward the parking lot.

Every time her eyes closed in slumber, the fairies were there. These magical nights had a bizarre rhythm. They had big banquets and danced. The pixies would come. Chaos would ensue. Angela would try to help, but the moment she saw a pixie or a wand pointed at her, she hid. Tatiana would save her, and then scream at Angela for not taking charge. "You must believe in yourself!"

Angela nodded and concentrated harder. If she could just hear Tatiana's thoughts like she'd done before, she would believe in herself. But she probably wasn't meant to be a magical creature. She was too old. *"How old do fairies live, anyway?"*

Tatiana zapped her back home.

Going alone to the park each night was hard. She hated doing it. Time was running out, however, and so she went night after night, hoping to somehow save her family in the process. Yet her fairy missions seemed to have the opposite effect.

It was easy getting Ted to sleep so she could sneak out, something else Angela had learned, but it was way more difficult getting back into the house without his notice.

"Why are you sneaking around every night?" Ted's jaw clenched. Yep, he was angry.

"I'm trying to chase the pixies away from Freestone Park." Angela had already discussed in earnest detail her fairy mission, contrary to Tatiana's wishes, yet when she reiterated this simple truth, Ted nearly exploded.

"Agh! Why can't you just be honest with me?!" He stood, thrusting his hand outward. "No wife of mine—"

"Oh yeah?" She didn't like his tone. "Well, I am your wife, and I WILL!"

Needless to say, occasional visits with Gabe became a much needed refuge from the storm raging at home. Everyone needs a friend, especially during difficult times.

She and Gabe found a common bond talking about fairies and the things he'd seen in the night sky. "The fairies want me to believe in myself and to quit pretending." Angela shook her head, tears welling in her eyes. "But it's so hard when I can't figure out what they want." Even with Tatiana right in front of her, she hadn't heard. A set of hearing aids were looking like a good idea.

"You should believe in yourself. You're amazing."

Gabe's comfort didn't come without a price.

"You've been with that fireman again!"

Angela didn't lie about it, she loved her husband (although he made her crazy), and Gabe was just a friend. Ted just refused to see it that way. This jealousy of his wasn't cute anymore. So, although she needed to talk to someone who understood her situation, and although Angela desperately needed a friend, she finally decided to avoid Gabe as much as possible.

The pixies must fear her human-sized self. Angela the fairy-human hadn't seen them again. And despite the lack of evidence regarding the mallard—it having disappeared—Angela feared she had hurt that duck. It freaked her out. She didn't want to hurt anything or anyone ever again. She wanted out. Tatiana wouldn't allow it. Angela tried every night.

"O, Queen, please release me from my vow. You had to have known I would fail."

Tatiana didn't see it that way.

She was exhausted, her shoulders ached with the pain of a thousand flames—all of her muscles ached—her legs constantly twitched from overuse—and she was having a hard time keeping up the house. Ted, the dear, had pointed that out.

Angela tiptoed into her bedroom. Her only goal, to collapse onto her pillow-soft mattress and disappear for the few remaining hours of nighttime.

"Ah," she groaned in satisfaction while sinking into comfort almost as complete as a Jacuzzi. Buying the mattress had been a good decision.

"You've been out again," Ted griped.

Oh. Ted, the man of her dreams—her knight in shining armor. If only he would believe in her. He was so good at solving problems he could easily help her with her current situation.

It was impossible for Ted to help since he didn't know, or rather refused to know anything about her situation. Ted couldn't believe in anything that wasn't on paper, not even if it—she, was lying in bed right beside him.

If only he believed in fairies.

Too tired for an argument, Angela rubbed his shoulders. Ted rolled over with a satisfied moan. She could barely lift her arms as exhausted as she was, but he was soon asleep and she turned toward her own slumber, or rather toward another heated argument with the fairy queen.

"Why do you not believe?" Tatiana thundered. "Can you not see us? Can you not see yourself? The pixies are invading our world. Rather than help, you are blundering about wishing for the help of an unbeliever."

"*Ugh*," Angela pursed her lips. "*You just don't get it. My family is crumbling apart here. The fairy and pixies' squabbling takes second place. Besides, Freestone Park is huge.*"

"Traitor!" Tatiana's eyes bulged with rage. "Traitor!"

Angela twirled through the atmosphere spinning so furiously that her head still swam in circles when she bolted upright in bed.

"Good morning, sunshine," Ted said, though his voice was not as chipper and sounded unsure. "Are we still having the block party this afternoon, or do you want to call it off?"

Ugh! The party. Angela pulled the covers over her head.

"Anj?"

Angela tossed the covers down. "Why wouldn't we have the party?" She wouldn't admit her discomfort at having the whole neighborhood over. "Are you not feeling well?" she asked, unbelievably smug with her witty comeback. Cancelling the party wouldn't be on her shoulders.

"No, I'm feeling fine. I just thought that you might be too tired." He wrinkled his brows together.

"I feel fine." She hugged her pillow. "No need to cancel the party on my account, dear." Okay, the 'dear' part had been a little over the top. It probably gave away her annoyance. Angela would try to be nicer. "Mind if I sleep a little longer? I know there's a lot to do, but just one more hour. Please."

Ted mumbled something. Angela didn't like the tone of it, but couldn't tell what he'd said. She was feeling particularly charitable though—or tired. Deciding to ignore the infraction, she turned over and enjoyed a blissful hour of rest.

FORTY-ONE

Angela stood at the glass door peering outward. Two grouchy-faced teens picked up errant trash that had blown in overnight. Her serious-faced husband trimmed their shrubs, and then disappeared into the garage.

The large dirt-spot in the middle of the lawn was a glaring witness to her absurdity. The grass hadn't grown back. Truth was, Angela kept forgetting to keep it watered, even though having a green lawn meant everything to Ted.

She pushed her lips together in self-disgust. She should be a better wife. And then, tapping a finger to her lips, an idea came to her. Hmm. She was good at making weeds grow; why not grass?

Angela walked to the backyard and opened the miniature bag of fairy dust tethered to her neck. She moistened the tip of her pinkie finger and barely touched it to the glittering mass. Using her finger as a type of shaker, she tapped it with the finger of her other hand, sprinkling glitter over the dirt.

Sprouts of grass magically appeared and then matured.

"That was awesome," she muttered, and she felt a little better about herself.

Ted approached with an armload of turf. He set the turf on the ground beside Angela and looked at the new grass, puzzled. "I'll be doggoned." He scratched his head. "I thought … did you see this, Anj?"

"Yeah, it's amazing isn't it?" She couldn't help but smile. The repaired lawn was her gift to him. She was the one who'd ruined it, after all.

For this first block party (Ted planned on having one every year) they were furnishing hamburgers and fruit punch. The neighbors were each assigned salads, vegetables, buns and desserts. The Wilsons from next-door (opposite from the Helmans) hung a large white sheet on the garage-side of their house, had an extension cord to their projector, and were providing movies for the youth.

There was a knock on the gate, and then Amy came into view. "I thought you might need some help." She went to Angela with outstretched arms. "And a little moral support during the party," she whispered.

Not long after, Ted went to the gate. "People should be coming any time now." He propped it open with a brick. "Let's get this party started."

The Helmans walked into the backyard. "Have you seen my dreadful saguaro?" Rebecca put the back of her hand to her forehead dramatizing her feelings. Of course they would come first. Rebecca probably hoped Angela would do something foolish, but she wouldn't give that venomous toad the satisfaction.

"We've been busy preparing all day. Did something happen to your cactus?" Angela did her best to sound innocent.

"I haven't heard." Amy, the sweetheart, grabbed Rebecca by the elbow. "Tell me all about it," she said, leading her away from Angela.

Olivia and Cody Wilson came over then with their three little ones, and the Madisons—poor Royce kept complaining about his wayward lawn. It had developed some sort of fungus that grew weeds. He had called in an expert to help him with the situation, and to get back into the good graces of HANC.

A twinge of guilt crept up Angela's spine.

The Burgs from across the street had four kids, from seven to fifteen in age. They couldn't afford the cost of removing their old lawn and soil in order to replant, but HANC had rules about unruly weeds. If they didn't have the problem under control within the month, the Association would take them to court.

Each neighbor came with their own confusing tale about weeds that sprouted as soon as one was pulled — the cacti — the flattened tires — and knowing she was responsible, Angela felt worse and worse. Tears welled in her eyes, and she dashed into the kitchen — she was a terrible person. Angela turned her back to their window, massaging her face with her hand.

Braced against the counter, Angela saw her blurred reflection in their stainless steel refrigerator. The woman looking back at her had some horrible secrets and Angela had to wonder — was she a fairy or a pixie?

Ted would come after her if she didn't get back, so Angela heaved one last sigh, patted her cheeks, and went to greet their guests with forced cheerfulness.

Jake and Sylvia Palmer met her at the gate. "I made it fresh this morning." Sylvia placed a cake, topped with strawberries and whipped cream, into Angela's hands.

"Thank you. This looks delicious." Angela lifted the cake to her nose, inhaling deeply, her eyes fluttering with pleasure at the succulent aroma of sweet-tart strawberries. "You've outdone yourself."

"It was nothing." Sylvia's eyebrows dipped.

Angela lifted her nose from the confection. "I'll put it right over there on the table." It wouldn't be polite to dive, head first, into a cake meant for everyone to enjoy.

Three families that Angela had never actually met before

walked, unsure, into the back yard; RJ and Dianna Rogers with a son Derek's age and a fourteen-year-old; Johnathan and Christina Ingersol came; and Adam and Naomi Buck and their young daughters, Lillie, Brynlie, Maelie and a new little one. "This is Evie."

"How do you do?" Angela bent down with her hand extended. Evie responded by hiding behind her mother's leg.

Angela remembered when her children were little, and smiled. She found herself relaxing and actually having fun while getting to know the neighbors. Ted was always right. The neighbors were nice, and nearly all of them came. Yet, Angela had the constant need to push to the background of her mind the shame and guilt of her previous magical actions in order for her to enjoy their company and to be a good hostess.

She couldn't go groveling at their feet, confessing her deed and begging forgiveness. "*I'm a bad fairy. Please forgive me. I won't use magic on your lawns again. I promise.*" No. That would never do, but Angela would rectify the situation. Tonight.

Amy proved to be a great support in steering Rebecca Helman out of Angela's way, and less supportive in other areas. Slender Amy who ate at will with no apparent worries of bulging in all the wrong places kept tempting Angela beyond her ability to refuse.

"This punch smells really good. Did you make it with fresh fruit?" Amy poured herself a cup from the five-gallon insulated container, took a sip and then poured a cup for Angela while leaning forward to utter a conspiratorial whisper, "Bat woman is headed this way."

What was Angela supposed to do? She downed the drink and tossed the cup in the trash. Before she could take a step away, Amy brought two large pieces of cake forward. Standing near the dessert table really wasn't a good place to avoid sweets.

"This cake is delish. Did you try it?" Amy offered her the larger piece.

"Um, yeah." The scrumptious-smelling treat had tempted Angela since its arrival and seemed to call to her from every corner of the yard. Angela had already succumbed to temptation twice and was trying, with iron-clad determination, to avoid more cake. The fairy-temptation toward fruit was undeniable — but there were those extra fifty pounds that Angela wanted to lose.

"You brought me some just a few minutes ago." Angela pushed away the temptation of another piece of heaven. "How do you stay so trim?" Really. She needed tips because so far this block party was not going well with her diet.

"Sylvia did her best on the cake." Rebecca stepped forward, took a miniscule taste of the cake in Amy's hand, and then threw the plate and all in the nearby trash.

Angela watched in wide-eyed horror.

"A little too sweet for my tastes. Have you tried my dessert?" She slid a tray of cookies off the table, offering them to Angela and Amy.

Angela forced her gaze from the trash receptacle and reluctantly took one of the offered cookies. They were brownish orange.

"Did I mention there's been another rash of vandalism in our neighborhood?" Rebecca's eyebrow arched.

"Do tell." Angela peered suspiciously at the cookie while waiting for her to explain. Certainly the caustic cougar wouldn't poison cookies.

"These are very tasty," Amy said, and then chewed her last bite. "I'd better not have another, though." She patted her mid-section. "What were you saying?"

Angela watched out of the corner of her eye to see if her friend showed signs of being poisoned. Orange was a weird color for cookies.

"Someone ruined the tire on our Lincoln." Rebecca's voice took on a scandalous tone. "We woke up last week with a flat tire. Jeff tried inflating it, but it wouldn't hold air. When he took it to the shop, they tried a plug—it wouldn't stick," she said shrilly.

Holes made with a magical wand couldn't be repaired. Interesting.

Rebecca leaned toward the women. "They said they'd never seen anything like it. It was as if someone had melted a hole in it with a laser."

"That's terrible," Angela and Amy said simultaneously.

At least the Helmans could afford a new tire. She didn't feel the same level of guilt for Rebecca's problems as she did her other neighbors, but everything needed repaired or replaced, including the Helmans' tire.

"Jeff hates mismatched tires on his vehicles, so we had to buy a new set." Rebecca scowled down at Angela's hand. "Don't you like my cookies?"

Angela still held it delicately between thumb and forefinger.

"Oh, yes," Angela replied nervously. "I was simply involved in our conversation." Angela plopped the small cookie in her mouth and chewed.

Only too late did she realize they were pumpkin cookies—spiced with nutmeg. The familiar burn seeped its way down her throat.

"Are you okay?" Amy's questioning face looked near panic.

"Water," Angela gasped, feeling her throat swell.

"Someone help! Call 9-1-1! Something's the matter with Ms. Anderson!" Rebecca shrieked as she lunged to Angela's side and forced her onto the lawn.

Amy rushed back with a cup of water. Angela grabbed it to her lips, and then everything around her went black.

She awoke to blurred and fuzzy sounds, like someone talking

underwater. Her eyes felt cemented shut. She tried gathering strength, tried making sense of what had happened ... of the feeling ... something — no, someone was close — too close. She felt the heat, the vibration of space invading space.

It wasn't Ted.

Something pricked her arm. Her heart raced as though it would explode.

Weasel woman was trying to poison her again! Angela bolted upright and slapped her would-be attacker with all the pent up venom she had for the she-devil.

Several things came together for Angela in that second: Gasps! Nervous chuckles. All the neighbors standing back, their familiar faces bent toward her — and a kneeling Gabe, rubbing his jaw and looking wounded.

"Ouch!" he complained.

FORTY-TWO

"Just let me go home," Angela groaned from her private room with the little plastic rolling bed. Another heart monitor, an arduous evening in the ER, needles and tubes poking from her arm—she'd had enough.

"Sorry Anj, I've got to disagree," Ted soothed. "You should stay overnight for observation, just to make sure." He signed something and handed it to the nurse. He had finally won—he always did—and since their insurance allowed it, the hospital staff didn't refuse. "What if you have a delayed reaction during the night? I couldn't live with myself."

"I think my reaction was pretty instantaneous." She couldn't believe she'd slapped Gabe like that. She flexed her hand. It still tingled.

She glanced past Ted and through the doorway. Gabe and Troy were at the nurse's station looking over some papers. Troy muttered something to Gabe, who shrugged his shoulders. Troy gave him a push and the two walked away.

"Here." Ted poured her a glass of water. "Drink this. You'll feel better."

Yeah, a gallon of water just before midnight was just the thing she needed. "Thanks," she said, and took the cup.

"Look," he said. "I'm sorry about the way things transpired out there tonight."

"Yeah, me too." Angela closed her eyes and leaned back. "Did everyone just go home, then?"

Ted nodded. "Amy stayed and helped clean things up."

"What did the vulture do?"

Ted brushed his hair back. "I don't know. No one ever saw her again, you know, after you blacked out."

"It was her cookie that did it."

"She probably feels horrible." Ted looked up at the television.

"Horrible?" Angela smirked. "She's probably dancing around her dining room as we speak."

"I hadn't had a chance to talk to her yet. There's no way she could have known about your allergy to nutmeg."

"Oh, she knew." Angela watched his expression. "What I don't understand is why you don't believe me."

"Look," Ted said. "I don't want to fight. You were poisoned by Rebecca Helman's cookies. Can we just leave it at that?" He took her hand and kissed it.

Angela nodded. She was too tired to fight.

"Turn up the volume a bit. The UFC championship is on. I'll stay until you're out of danger." Ted scooted into the bed beside her, took Angela's hand in his, and watched the game.

Angela dozed off and on beside him.

"Woohoo!" Ted thrust his hand upward, waking Angela. "That was the greatest ever!"

"Game's over?" She yawned.

"That was hardly a fight at all. I'm not surprised you missed it."

Hard not to miss it with her eyes shut. "You'd better get on home. The kids'll want to hear that I'm okay and you'll need a good night's rest before work tomorrow."

"Yeah, you're probably right." Ted kissed her. "Things are coming to a head at work. I might make senior partner."

"How nice, honey. You've worked hard."

"I'll be in first thing. Hopefully, the doctor will be too."

"Love you."

Exhausted, Angela lay with her eyes closed waiting for sleep to come, but kept thinking about Gabe. He and Troy had finished their paperwork at the nurses' station, but hadn't come in. Was her brutal blow the end of their friendship?

A nurse peeked his head in. "You need to get some rest."

Angela nodded. She knew.

"Want me to close the door?"

"That'd be great," she said, closing her eyes.

Rather than sleep, instant replays of slapping Gabe flitted across the insides of her eyelids. What kind of person was she becoming?

"Hey, do you feel up to one more visitor?" Gabe stood against the partially opened door in a halo of light from the hall, and sporting a crimson handprint on his cheek. He held a bouquet of mums and baby's-breath.

"You still have a mark." Angela frowned and closed her eyes not wanting to see the evidence of her stupidity. "I thought maybe you'd never talk to me again."

Gabe walked in the room and placed the flowers on a shelf, then came and sat on the edge of her bed. "Never? That's a long time without my favorite fairy chica." The corners of his eyes wrinkled pleasantly with his smile.

He'd forgiven her. Angela turned her lips up.

"The nurses say you're doing fine."

"Yep, I'm merely here for observation." She pulled her covers up to her armpits. "Although Ted may insist I stay another week just to make sure." She smiled ironically at her joke.

"You'll be able to leave first thing in the morning." Gabe reached awkwardly for her hand.

Angela pulled back and fiddled with the blanket she'd cast aside.

"Let me in, Anj," he pleaded. "Let me into your life. I'm not going to bite you." He reached forward, grasped her hand and rubbed it gently between his fingers.

Invisible Angela. *"This isn't me. I'm old and flabby, and weird."*

A prickle of worry crawled into her heart, but she didn't pull away again. This was the twenty-first century, and men and women could be just friends. He was comforting her, though his touch made her feel anything but.

"I'm sorry," Angela sighed, looking toward the small window in her room.

"Me too." His fingers brushed across hers.

Angela tilted her head, trying to understand what he'd be sorry about. "For what?" she finally asked.

"For what?" He said nearly simultaneously. He gazed at her earnestly while chewing at the soul patch under his bottom lip.

"You know, for slapping you." Pulling her hands to her face, Angela massaged her cheeks wearily. She wanted to sleep, but tried shaking her fatigue away, and faced Gabe. "I'm sorry," she repeated. Apologizing seemed like a good thing to do.

"Make it up to me." He grinned then, a demon's smile full of mischief.

"How?" Angela felt too exhausted to be overly curious. But she had hurt him. It seemed only appropriate to offer condolence of some sort.

"Come fishing with me tomorrow."

He looked serious, Angela mused—as if he thought she would actually go. After a night in the hospital, Ted would expect her to spend the day at home. Besides, she was married. A fishing excursion with Gabe was not a good idea. Plus, Ted for whatever reason, didn't like her friend.

She shook her head. "I can't."

"Can't, or won't?" Gabe leaned forward. He was close.

Her heart thumped nervously, but she could never trust her emotions. Angela was overreacting as usual.

"Tomorrow isn't a good day," she stuttered — so much for not overreacting. "I'm sure the house is a mess."

"How about the next day then, or the next? Go fishing with me, Anj."

Fishing sounded fun, but she shook her head. The action made her dizzy. "I don't know how."

"Someone who loves the outdoors as much as you and you've never been fishing?" Gabe appeared shocked.

Angela regarded Gabe wearily, "How do you know I like the outdoors?"

"Fairy, remember?" He tilted his head sideways and smiled. "They love all things nature."

Angela closed her eyes and nodded. He knew so much about fairies.

"I won't press you anymore tonight. Think on it, though." Gabe brushed her arm with his fingertips then kissed the back of her hand and left.

Angela turned the light off and fell asleep, and didn't think more about a day trip with Gabe at all.

The next morning, sun filtered through the mini-blinds and shone onto her face. She wanted more sleep. Angela pulled the sheet over her head and tried to ignore the sun's rays. Then she heard Ted's familiar greeting.

"Good morning, sunshine." He grinned at her from the doorway, and strode the two steps to her bed. "Are you free to go home?"

"The doctor won't be in until later." Angela frowned. "He has to sign the release form." She hoped it would be soon, but the nurses gave her no real hope of being released before noon. However, they had been so kind to her that she refused to complain about doctors and nurses ever again.

"Today's the day we're voting on whether or not to build a firm in Sacramento." Ted rubbed between his eyebrows with his index finger. "They'll just have to meet without me." He took the cell phone from his pocket.

"Sacramento, huh? You don't have to stay." Angela laid a stopping hand on his. "I can get a ride home from Amy." She hated the idea of Ted missing an important meeting.

"Anj." He smiled, his dimple showing. "I wouldn't miss another opportunity to wheel my wife to the parking garage."

"That's it. I mean it," Angela chided. "You get on out of here. If you want to be senior partner, they'll expect your vote." She reached back for her pillow and threw it at him. Husbands weren't allowed to insist their wives spend the night in the hospital and then tease them about it.

He caught the pillow effortlessly with his left hand. "Now, darlin', don't get yourself all worked up." He placed the pillow back under her head.

Angela plopped down on it, pretending to be exasperated.

"Where'd you get the flowers?" It sounded more accusation than question. Ted frowned at the bouquet on the plant shelf, his jaw clenching.

"I, um." They'd been doing so well. Angela didn't want to lose that. She swallowed guiltily, and stammered. "Gabe brought them by last night." It would be wrong if she lied.

"So the hunky fireman brings you flowers in the hospital." Ted brooded, his voice low. "I don't like it. I didn't bring you flowers."

"I've told you a hundred times, we're just friends." Angela shrugged her shoulders, trying to keep her tone casual, hoping they wouldn't argue in the hospital.

Ted peered into her eyes—trying to find guilt there, Angela knew—but she met his gaze. She was innocent. "I think Gabe felt bad for the way our party ended, and I think he's lonely. I'm considering setting him up with Amy."

"An excellent idea." Ted took Angela's hand and kissed it.

Angela sighed with relief, and with her hand on his neck, pulled him down for a real kiss. After a few more kisses, Angela wished they were already home, but at least they arrived at a compromise on how to get her there.

When the doctor didn't come by eight, Ted called Amy before he left for work. Ted's meeting didn't start until 10:00 and he could easily get there by then.

The nurse came in and took out Angela's IV in anticipation of the doctor's release orders. Angela took the opportunity to put on her street clothes. It was all in the skinny little closet where she had left it—her clothes, her fairy wand and the fairy dust.

After putting the magical dust around her neck, Angela unpinned the wand from the waist of her pants. Feeling a spurt of silliness, she jumped out legs extended, and whipped her fairy wand in front of her as though it was a miniature sword, and pretended to duel with the air.

"Clever." Amy leaned against the doorframe smiling. "Any more of that and they'll keep you here another week."

"Hey, girlfriend." Angela pinned her wand back and sat on her bed. "I was wondering if you'd show up." Had someone turned the air off? The room was suddenly warm. She fanned herself.

"Not only have I come, but I'm armed as well." Amy grabbed a straw off the table near the bed and extended it as if in duel. "Take that, you Double A. I'll cut you down to size!" Amy swished the straw-sword a couple of times near Angela.

This was why Angela cherished Amy's friendship—they could goof off and act a fourth their age one moment, with no judgments, and then completely act their age the next moment.

"There's nothing there to cut back." Swish, swish, swish. "Take some of the belly flab instead." Angela loved having her old friend back and played her part with gusto.

"Who wants belly flab? Nay. I'll take some of those buxom bosoms and add them to my own. I'll finally have a full set, I will. Arg." Amy swished her straw back and forth.

The nurse's aide stood in the doorway, mouth gaping, eyes bulging—and the two friends began to laugh—a full bellied, tears streaming, almost wetting their pants kind of laugh. Angela's face was red (she saw her reflection in the little mirror over the sink) and she flopped across the bed, wiping the tears from her face. Amy joined her, still laughing.

"Ahem." The nurse's aide, Gloria, announced her arrival into the room.

"May I help you?" Angela sat up and tried to act as though nothing had happened. What else could she do?

"I ..." Gloria looked from Angela to Amy and back again. "I have your release papers." She walked into the room and set papers and pen on the rolling table. "The doctor doesn't believe you'll have any further complications—"

Amy chuckled. Angela shushed her.

"—If you'll stay away from pumpkin cookies." Gloria waited for the papers with clipboard in hand.

Amy shook her head. "He should have advised her to stay away from Rebecca Helman."

"I'm sure I don't know what you mean." Gloria frowned, and then addressed Angela. "Apparently there's something in the cookies that doesn't agree with you."

"Yeah, apparently." Angela handed her the signed papers.

The attendant came with a wheelchair, and Angela half expected Amy to race her at full speed down the hallway while popping wheelies in the aisle, but Amy behaved herself and walked beside the assigned hospital staff.

Once in the safety of Amy's car, Angela turned to her friend. "I need to tell you something, and I need you to believe."

FORTY-THREE

"Do you think Tatiana would allow me to be a fairy too?" Amy sat on the Anderson family room sofa.

Angela rubbed her forehead. "I don't know."

The two friends had spent an hour at the Anderson home with Angela explaining many of the events of the past month, Amy's face an ever-changing field of expression—surprise—shock—excitement—horror—knowledge, and acceptance.

"We've always done this fairy thing together. It would be a shame to break up the Double A's now." Amy rested her fingers on her mouth wistfully.

"You might regret it if you get wings." Angela looked at her friend's disappointed face. "It's complicated, but I'll ask next time I can."

"It would be fun. We could fly around the city together casting spells on unsuspecting bystanders." Amy chuckled.

"Yeah, well, it doesn't work like that—or it shouldn't." Angela then rehearsed all of the bad deeds she had accomplished with her magic and how horrible she felt about it.

"The hateful wretch deserved what she got." Amy smiled.

"I've been doing things I normally wouldn't." Angela winced. "I killed a duck." With a mixture of disgrace and disgust, she continued,

"I'm a kaleidoscope of emotion—happy, sad—I cry sometimes twice a day now—and I get angry. Poor Ted. I've begun wondering if I was under a pixie's spell," Angela finally admitted.

"Never," Amy insisted. "You're too nice to ever be a pixie. But just think, if we both became fairies we would be stronger. Together, we could do a lot of good." Amy grinned. "The Double-A Team," she said with a laugh.

Angela laughed too. "Thank you for this. It's been so great having someone to talk to." Angela sighed, then poured them each a glass of ice water from the refrigerator and sat back at the table. "I've told you things that I wouldn't even dare discuss with Gabe."

"The fireman?" Amy frowned, her fingers scratching against her lip. "That's why Ted was so angry at the party." Her eyes narrowed. "You've been having a midnight fling with the hunky fireman."

"What?" Denial propelled Angela to her feet. "I have not."

"Ted must think you are." Amy smiled crookedly. "He went berserk at the block party—the best entertainment ever." She chuckled. "He seemed to think Gabe had done something inappropriate to deserve that slap you gave him. He laid into him like nobody's business. Luckily there were plenty of other men there to pull Ted off and calm him down."

"What?" Angela eased back into her seat. Her gentle, understanding husband begging for a fight? It was nearly as implausible as tabloid fodder. "Unbelievable. Gabe is just a friend," Angela asserted.

The thought of Ted being jealous had seemed so cute at first— the off chance that Gabe found her attractive, so flattering. But she couldn't have her husband going around beating people up, or even wanting to.

"Yeah, yeah, I see how it is—just friends." Amy chuckled. "I could use a friend like him."

"Oh, cut it out," Angela insisted. She didn't like joking about this. "Look at me." Angela spread her arms out and turned around. "I'm old. I'm flabby. At first I worried that he had the wrong intentions, but he doesn't. Gabe isn't interested in me that way."

"I know you're a happily married woman and all, but don't sell yourself short." Amy frowned. "You're beautiful. You're talented. You're the best, most devoted wife and mother that I know — and you're loyal. Ted's a lucky man."

"If only he thought so," Angela murmured.

"You're in denial." Amy rested her hand on Angela's shoulder. "Ted adores you. But you'd better stay away from Gabe."

"You're right. I've got to end this nonsense," she said, though ending her much-appreciated friendship with Gabe pinched at her heart.

"I know why you wouldn't want to." She rubbed her hands together. "He's just so gorgeous!"

Angela glared at her friend.

"I know, I know." Amy lifted her hands in a sign of surrender. "Ted's the only man for you. But, I'm left to wonder why you aren't discussing your life with him."

Frustration mounted at the thought of Ted's unwillingness to understand. "That's part of my problem. I'm supposed to convince Ted and the kids to believe in fairies by Halloween." She threw back her head. "As if I haven't been trying to do just that for the past thirty-two years. Time's running out, and yet he refuses to believe."

"It could happen." Amy leaned forward. "You have to believe it's possible first."

"Weird. That's almost exactly what the fairy queen said."

"What kind of things have you been doing to get Ted to believe?"

"Well, I bought that fairy costume years ago and I've been wearing it regularly."

"Is that supposed to convince Ted, or you?" Amy smirked. "As cute as the costume is," she touched Angela's shoulder, "now don't be angry with me."

"I won't."

"You bought the costume when you were in your twenties. Right?"

"Yeah." Angela nodded. What was she getting at?

"Sweetheart, it doesn't fit anymore." Amy smiled sadly.

Angela had kind of gotten that hint from Ted and the kids, but had refused to consider it. She gulped guiltily. "I guess you're right. But I've tried numerous times just talking to him about fairies. I even showed him my wand and fairy dust."

"With the fairy queen's permission?"

"No." Angela shook her head. "But he wasn't believing me, and it made me mad."

Amy rubbed her hand over her mouth, contemplating.

"What?"

"Again, don't be mad at me, but it seems that you need to stop trying to force everyone to see it your way and allow them the freedom of discovering fairies, and you, for themselves." She chewed her lip. "And you need to listen more closely to Tatiana. Trying to get Ted to believe in fairies by going against the fairy queen?" Amy tisked.

"Yeah, it kind of backfired. Ted set me up with a counselor." Angela scowled. "Two of them."

"See what I'm saying? You need to play by the rules."

"But I don't know what the rules are." Angela folded her arms.

"What did the fairy queen say?" Amy's eyebrows pinched together. "Do you remember?"

"Of course I remember. She told me to believe in myself and to quit being a pretender — she didn't like my fairy costume either." Angela pursed her lips, and then added, "Or my fairy porcelains. She wants me to get Ted and the kids to believe in fairies, but doesn't want me to show them my real wings, or tell them anything." Angela rested her knuckles against her cheek. "Fairies often talk to each other through their thoughts. It's how they communicate, rather than yell, when they're out flying around."

"I didn't know that."

"Yeah. Tatiana is supposed to give me a mission via her thoughts. I'm supposed to hear it, and do it." Angela frowned. "Since she said that, I've been too panicked to hear anything."

"You heard her thoughts before?" Amy appeared incredulous. "That's pretty amazing."

"Except I've only got two weeks left, and still haven't accomplished anything. I'm going to fail, just like I've failed at everything else."

"You cut that out right now." Amy pulled her up and dragged her to the desk. "I want you to write a list of the things you're good at." She found a pen and handed it to Angela with a piece of computer paper.

"Well, I'm a good cook." Angela wrote it down, and then stopped. It was hard thinking of anything else.

"You're pretty," Amy said. "Though that isn't a skill."

Angela wrote it near the top anyway. "I'm a good housekeeper."

"Oh, please. Of course you are, but you've got to dig deeper than that." She prodded Angela with her hands. "Why was Ted first attracted to you?"

"He said I was fun." She wrote it down. "I don't feel fun anymore."

"It's in there." Amy smiled. "You're just not seeing it. And you're loyal."

"Ted doesn't think so."

"Yes he does. He just doesn't understand what's going on. You need to encourage their belief a little less forcefully."

Angela stared at the ceiling.

Amy put her arms around Angela's shoulders. "What is going on? What has happened to my caring and confident friend? I shouldn't have to tell you all of your good qualities."

"I'm going to lose them, Amy. I'm a failure as a fairy, and because of it, Tatiana is taking my family away." Tears streamed down her cheeks.

"That's not going to happen. Ted adores you."

"Except he thinks there's something going on between Gabe and me." Angela wiped her eyes. "Tatiana showed me what's going to happen. I saw Ted in California—he and the kids. And another woman." Angela sobbed.

"Okay, clearly that is not going to happen." Amy grabbed a tissue and handed it to her. "Let's focus on the list." She grabbed the paper and pen, and wrote, I am, at the top, and added caring and confident to Angela's list. "You believe in the impossible. You believe in magic. And, you believe in love." She added those to the list and handed it to Angela. "You're to read this twice a day. Three or four times if necessary."

"Doctor's orders?"

Amy raised her eyebrows. "Doctor's orders."

Angela looked the paper over. Those were some good qualities.

"Read it out loud. Please."

She glanced at her friend. "I am a good cook, pretty, a good housekeeper. I am fun." Angela turned up the corner of her lips ironically. "I am loyal, I am a fairy failure."

"That's not on there. Focus on the positive."

Angela heaved a breath. "I am caring and confident. I believe in the impossible. I believe in magic. I believe in love."

"There. That wasn't so hard. Was it?"

Not hard. It just didn't sound like her.

Amy snatched the paper away and wrote more things on the list and handed it to Angela.

"I am a good friend." Angela looked up. "Am I a good friend? You had to come and get me for a picnic."

"But you were there for me every step of the way when Phil died. You were the only one I had." Amy brushed at a tear. "You helped me with the services and even helped me decide on a headstone."

Angela looked down at the paper. "I am an original." That one made her smile. "You got that right. Finally." She gave her friend a hug. "I'm pretty original, all right."

"And that's a good thing."

"I am a good wife and mother?" That was debatable, but Angela decided to err on her side, for once. "Well, Ted and I do have five kids together and a granddaughter on the way."

"You're so lucky." Amy had a faraway look. "I'd love to have grandchildren."

Angela was lucky. She knew that fact better than anyone, but she hated the now melancholy sound of her friend's voice.

"Gabe is single." Angela raised her eyebrows hopefully. "You said you'd let me set you up."

"I don't know." Amy chewed her bottom lip.

"Don't tell me that you don't think Gabe's a delicious piece of eye-candy, because I won't believe you." Angela couldn't help the grin on her face.

"I can't deny it." Amy blushed. "Those muscles — and that adorable soul patch." Amy stroked a pretend soul patch below her lip.

Her friend talked big, like she was some kind of flirtatious metro-girl, but it was all a front. Phil's death had hit her hard. It had taken a long time for her to fully recover, and even now she barely dated. "It's settled, then. Gabe would be perfect for you." Angela lifted her eyebrows and nodded encouragingly.

Amy opened her mouth to reply, and then the door opened.

"Is there anything to eat?" Derek came in with Hannah close behind.

Angela looked at her watch. "Time flies," she said.

"Wow. We've spent the whole day together."

"I feel a lot better. Thank you." Angela folded the paper and put it in her pocket.

Angela's family meant the world to her. And Ted, although he was a bit one-sided, she loved with a devotion that had matured and grown over the years until her life with him was a beautiful patchwork quilt. Take one piece out, and her life would have a gaping hole, and render her life-quilt useless and plain.

Derek foraged in the refrigerator looking for something to eat.

"There's some of that strawberry cake in there," Amy said. "The

Palmers left it here for you."

"Thanks." Derek pulled out the cake and placed it on the counter.

Angela held her breath. It took a lot of willpower to resist the aroma of fresh strawberries and whipped cream. If she'd known about the cake earlier, it wouldn't be there.

"You've got your family here, and I need to get going." Amy stood and walked to the door.

"Stay for supper." Angela worried about her friend being alone all the time.

Amy waved her hand behind her. "Don't worry about it. I've got plans."

"With your television?" Angela shook her head.

"No, not with the television. I'm taking classes at the college."

"You know you can stay."

"No. I really do need to get home." She grabbed her purse, gave Angela a hug and left.

"You guys talked for a whole day?" Derek asked. "What about?"

"Fairies."

"It figures."

"Don't fill up before supper."

"I won't." He took his plate and headed up the stairs.

When Ted finally got home that evening, he looked like he had walked all the way from Phoenix—his hair tousled, his coat in his hands and his tie crooked. He looked worn out.

But Angela had prepared grilled Hawaiian hamburgers, oven-fried sweet potatoes, green beans and a tossed salad. She would nurse him back to his proper strength.

"How're you feeling?" Ted kissed her forehead.

"Better than you look. Hard day?" Angela took his hand and walked him to the table.

"The worst—and the best."

FORTY-FOUR

Why was he making her wait so long? "So?" Angela finally asked after finishing all but a few bites of dinner. "The best of days? The worst of days?" She waited on the edge of her chair.

"I got the position as senior partner." Ted looked cautiously up from his plate. "If I want it."

"If you want it?" Angela beamed. "Of course you want it. All your hard work is finally being appreciated." She leaned over and kissed him on the cheek.

Ted let his breath out in a whoosh. "I was worried you'd be upset." His eyebrows pinched together.

"Upset?" Was he joking? Really? "Why would I be upset? No one deserves this more than you." She ticked off on her fingers, Ted's qualities as an employee. "You're honest, dependable, a hard worker. You work sixty hours a week, and some weekends." Angela lowered her hands. "I'm surprised it took them so long to see the light, actually." She stood. Ted must be feeling insecure. "Gimme a hug."

"They've given me until the fall banquet to decide." Ted stood and hugged Angela. "They want to make the announcement there."

"I'll buy a new dress." Her favorite part of the pretentious gala. She looked around Ted's shoulder to address her daughter. "Will you help me find something nice, and fashionable?" Angela would buy an especially fancy dress this year.

"Sure thing." Hannah smiled. "I know just the place."

Ted took Angela's hand and squeezed it. "It'll be hard getting the house packed up by yourself. Maybe I can hire someone. But starting at a new school in the middle of the semester will be great for the kids." He looked over at them. "You can make friends easier during the school year."

Hannah and Derek eyed each other, mouths agape, and then shouted, "No way!"

"Wait, what?" Angela frowned, feeling confused. "Why would we move?"

"I can't commute from Sacramento." Ted smirked. "And I'm taking over the new office the following Monday."

Her knees felt weak. Unable to bear her weight, Angela slunk down into her chair. "I thought ..." She looked at Ted, who sat back down as well. "I thought you'd take over the office here, in Phoenix."

"They already have an office full of senior partners here." Ted stared at her—impatiently, Angela thought. "If I want to be senior partner with Braxton and Braxton, this is the only way."

"Oh, that's just ridiculous!" Angela pushed her plate to the center of the table. "You've proven yourself time and time again. How much are they going to take from you?"

"It's a big burden to put on your shoulders, I know. But we'll get through this." He looked into her eyes and patted her hand—like a child, Angela thought. "They're giving plenty in return. As senior partner, my current salary will nearly triple. No more worries about buying furnishings for the home, and you can get your hair done every week if you'd like."

"That's a cheap shot." Angela didn't care about things. "You said we could afford the bed."

"We can. It's paid for."

"Ted." Angela shook her head, incredulous. "We can't leave. Not now." Not ever. She gestured toward their home. How could he even consider moving at a time like this? "Our daughter?" She glared pointedly. "Leanne is due with her baby. You'd miss the birth of your first granddaughter?"

"Rusty'll be there. We weren't invited to the birth." He clenched his jaw.

Angela looked at her husband with a mixture of anger, frustration, and disbelief. "Rusty only has two weeks' military leave. This is her first baby. Leanne needs me." She crossed her arms and legs. "I'm not going anywhere," she said with a shake of her head. "You'll just have to come home on weekends."

"Be serious," Ted growled. "What did you expect—that they'd just boot Drulman out and let me take over his position?"

"Don't be ridiculous!" She wasn't some child that didn't know the workings of office politics. But there were six senior partners in the Phoenix office. One of them could go. "I expected that they'd make you senior partner—here in Phoenix—as a show of appreciation for the sixty hours a week you've given them for thirty years."

"Ha!" Ted barked. "I'm the slacker in the company."

Angela looked at Derek and Hannah, sitting at the table, her aching heart went out to them. "Derek's a senior next year."

"California will be a good experience for the kids." He looked at them.

Hannah scowled. Derek smiled nervously and opened his mouth to respond.

Ted piped in. "It's a cultural melting pot with tons of opportunities."

"What about the football team?" Angela asked. "Derek has a chance at team captain next year."

Ted stood and pushed his chair under the table. "I won't let this promotion slip from my grasp." He clasped the back of the chair. "Not when I'm so close." He glared at her. "This is my dream, my life," he said.

"Oh," Angela responded. Her heart hurt. She had wanted senior partner for him, but she'd also thought they had the same dreams—working together to build their family—build their faith—build their life as one. "I thought your dream was providing our happiness."

"This is providing for your happiness."

Ted would bail out on his daughter and his family for work? Angela rubbed her fingers over her chest and neck. The Ted she knew wouldn't be bought for two-hundred-forty-thousand dollars a year and a penthouse office. Would he?

Ted walked to their bedroom raking his hands through his hair and shaking his head, mumbling.

Angela cleared the table, put the food away, washed the dishes and cleaned the house—anything to keep from having to face Ted again.

The kids went to their rooms. No television tonight. For anyone.

It was late when Angela went to bed. She rested tenderly on the mattress so as not to disturb her husband's slumber.

Angela couldn't bear it—his talking about abandoning the life they had built together—thinking about leaving their daughter and their new grandbaby—or any of their children. It was too horrible—a nightmare.

She tried thinking of other things, happy things to keep her mind occupied, and pulled out the list from her pocket. I am a good wife, it read. She could cross that one right off the list because there was no way she was moving anywhere.

Her thoughts kept returning to the joy on Ted's face when he'd thought she would leave her children, her life, and move to Sacramento.

His dangling money under her nose by offering her more to spend made her cringe. Money was no consolation. She didn't care what kind of house they lived in or the type of car she drove, as long as her family was together. In all the years Ted had talked about becoming senior partner at his accounting firm, Angela only remembered his mentioning an out of state move once. She had slammed it down.

Although grown, their three adult children were still young. They had full lives ahead of them and Angela expected to be a part of every moment—happy or sad. She would not let Leanne down. Her daughter counted on her. Although Rusty was getting two weeks leave to be with her while she had the baby, Leanne would be alone after that. She needed her mother.

Derek and Hannah were easily swayed by dollar signs, but she knew if Derek found himself in a new school in California for his senior year, he would not be happy. "California," she whispered with sickening realization. It was her nightmare coming to life.

Angela looked over at her snoring husband. None of this would affect his sleep. He seldom missed his seven hours. A surge of resentment welled in her heart. It wasn't fair for him to come home, drop that news, and then sleep soundly while Angela fumed all night long.

It wasn't fair that he expected her to be happy about moving—it wasn't fair to leave Leanne, or Richard, or Benjamin. Angela sobbed silently into her pillow until she'd had enough misery, and then she slipped out of bed and walked outside.

She had the strength to do it now—summon her wings—and she did. Extending them fully, she admired their beauty from the reflection in the arcadia doors. Ted would never see them. He didn't believe her, didn't believe in her. Pure and simple.

Reaching back, Angela felt their soft, velvetiness. They were miraculous, and they were hers. A gift because of some unknown good deed of her mother's, or a visible blessing bestowed on her for a lifetime of belief?

It didn't matter. Angela was glad she'd had them even briefly. She stepped onto the lawn and let her wings take her into the night air.

Menopausal *fairy* Mischief

280

FORTY-FIVE

"One new saguaro coming up," Angela said, hovering over the bare spot in the Helmans' front yard. Her feelings for the odiferous old toad didn't make up for this behavior.

Angela gulped back her animosity, opened her bag of fairy dust and took out the smallest pinch, sprinkling it on the spot where the old cactus had been.

As the shimmering particles floated to the ground, Angela pointed her wand and moved it in a circular motion over the dust as though stirring an invisible stew. A saguaro formed—a small thing at first, barely inches tall, then as she circled her arm higher into the air, the cactus grew larger.

"Much better," Angela said, feeling the pleasure of her good deed. Her wings fluttered as though happy. "As if wings have emotions," she huffed, but she couldn't keep the smile from her face.

Angela examined the tires on the Helmans' Lincoln Navigator. "Already replaced." She flew down the street to the Madisons' lawn. Luckily they hadn't started removing the old lawn yet. Shame washed over her like a dust storm, seeping into the nooks and crannies of her soul. "I'm such a jerk," she said. "To cause so much trouble." She swished her wand, transforming the front lawn to its original splendor, and putting the dusty weed patch of a backyard to its original form.

"Fairies are kind and good," she said, with a certain amount of satisfaction. But just restoring the lawns to their original state didn't make up for the mess she'd caused. With a flick of her wand, Angela altered the backyard and turned it into a green oasis where the Madisons' children would love to play.

Her wings fluttered again, and then Angela knew. "Quit being a pretender," she whispered. Fairies were kind and good and in order to quit being an imposter, she needed to use her powers for good. "No more gargantua. No more terrorizing the neighborhood. No more killing things. Not even pixies."

After that revelation, she did all in her power to restore peace to the surrounding vegetation. Then, hovering at an incredible height, Angela surveyed the neighborhood, the glow of satisfaction warming her heart.

"Just one more thing." Doing good was addictive. She sprinkled fairy dust in many of her new friends' desolate backyards, bringing life and beauty to those lawns as well.

"*You are no longer a pretender.*" Tatiana's words floated into Angela's mind.

"Heh, heh. That's one accomplishment down, two to go." And with that, her heart sank. Ted wanted to move to California. Angela knew what awaited him there — another woman. She could not allow that to happen. But how could she stop it? She needed a quiet place to think. Maybe the answer of how to get Ted to believe would come to her there.

Her wings took flight, and she found herself landing near the Riparian Habitat next to Gilbert's Southeast Regional Library. Years back, they had built the new library in Gilbert and made the riparian habitat as part of the grounds. There was a lake with walking paths, desert trees, grasses and shrubbery. It was a perfect place to be alone and sort things out.

She hadn't been there in years. The kids were too old for the small playground, they didn't bird-watch, and none of them fished. Derek was an avid reader, but, being on the football team, he refused to go where someone might know him, so they drove the thirty minutes to Mesa's Public Library. Derek wanted to be a professor of Medieval Theology when he got older, but that information was also strictly confidential.

Angela walked along the sidewalk south of the parking lot and toward the lake. She had forgotten there was a steel walking bridge across the tip of the lake, but she went there and leaned against the railing, staring into the man-made pool of liquid. The library, with its massive rows of windows facing the lake, was closed, but the dim inside-lighting cast an enchanting golden sparkle on the water.

It hadn't yet gotten too cold to hear the crickets chirping in the grass. Angela smiled at the quiet plopping of frogs entering the water, their sound joining nature's chorus. She had always been a bright-light-daytime person, but being a strictly nighttime fairy brought her a new perspective. She had grown to love the luminosity of the night. During the day everything was rushed, loud, chaotic. The night was reflective, enchanting, and peaceful.

Angela finally felt calm enough to listen. And she did, but her mind was one big blank. It was empty. Nada. Zip. Zilch. And that frustrated her. She had known Ted for thirty-six years, why couldn't she figure out how to make him believe? It was maddening, actually. Angela crossed her arms in self-contempt.

"It's beautiful here at night, isn't it."

"Aak!" She screamed, her heart jumped into her throat and she twirled around ready to confront her attacker. "Gabe? You nearly gave me a heart attack!" She placed her hand over her pounding heart and tried calming down. "Didn't your mama ever tell you it's not nice to sneak up on people—especially at night when they're all alone?"

Gabe, grinning and unrepentant, moved to the railing and leaned forward, looking into the shimmering lake.

Angela stared at him. How, and why did he continue showing up? Was he her friend? If not, what was he? Because she was married and intended to keep it that way.

Gabe looked at her, puzzled, feigning innocence. "What?" He smiled then, looking anything but innocent.

Angela's heart jumped. "Do you have all-seeing eyes or something?"

"Only for you," he answered, looking smug.

"Stop it." Angela straightened, hands on her hips.

"Stop what?" Gabe leaned back, with his elbows against the railing and faced Angela with a cocky smile.

"We're friends—right?" She needed to get their relationship straight, yet when she asked, she was transported back to her junior high school years. She felt idiotic.

"Best friends, of course," he said, standing. He sounded sincere, yet when he stood, he was too close for Angela's comfort. She stepped back a pace. He smiled, revealing that he found something wickedly amusing.

Angela's shoulders drooped. It was her. He thought she was ridiculous. And she was.

"Look," he said, "I'm not stalking you or anything." He shrugged. "I was getting off-duty and saw you come here. You're too early though—the fish won't start biting until around five."

His silly attempt to lighten her mood was too much. Angela pressed her lips together and shook her head slowly. Her eyes closed as she inhaled deeply, trying hard to keep herself together. *I will not cry—I will not cry,* she said to herself as tears escaped her pressed eyelids.

"Anj, you're crying. What's wrong?" Gabe circled her in his arms.

Angela felt his warmth and leaned toward the embrace of his comfort, and then remembered Amy's words. "It's Angela to you." She bolted from his grasp and darted to shore, feeling entirely too emotional to stay.

Walking hurriedly down the path, she forced Gabe, and Ted, and moving to California from her mind and focused on the fairies.

"Tatiana. If I knew you were happy and safe, I might be more willing."

More willing to what? Leave her children to tag along while Ted fulfilled his life-long ambition? It was too much. Angela sat on a bench to think. What would she do there? Who would she be there? Her despair over moving had less to do with fairies, and everything to do with her family. She'd only ever wanted her family nearby.

Gabe walked slowly forward and knelt in front of her. "Are you okay?" All the machismo gone from his voice, he conveyed genuine concern.

This was her Gabe-friend.

Angela looked up, blinking several times to clear her vision, then feeling tiredness of soul, she wiped her eyes. "Ted wants to move to California." With one arm firmly around her stomach to control her emotional pain, Angela rubbed her forehead with her other hand. "They'll make him senior partner there."

In one fluid motion, Gabe sat next to her and took her in his arms. Neither said anything for a time. Angela had always found it difficult to speak and cry simultaneously. Not wanting to embarrass herself with that whole hiccoughing tearful exchange, she tried silently to regain control of her tears while Gabe stroked her hair.

"What are you going to do?" Gabe whispered.

"I don't know. I don't want to move. Ted knows that." Angela blotted her eyes with the hem of her T-shirt and then searched Gabe's eyes wishing he had an answer.

"There has to be a way," Gabe whispered. "You can't leave now."

"I pretty well have to if Ted accepts the position." Angela rested her head in her hands and stared at the ground. "They're offering him an obscene amount of money. I'll come back once a month." Surely Ted wouldn't begrudge her regular visits to her children. The thought of leaving them tore Angela apart inside, and her tears flowed again.

"No. Stay." Gabe lifted her chin, searching her eyes with his sincere gaze as he moved tentatively closer. "Stay here with me."

FORTY-SIX

What had almost happened?

Angela sat on her living room sofa remembering Gabe. The sound of his pleading voice echoed in her ears. "Please don't go," he had begged.

She went anyway—jumped into the sky and fled the scene like a bandit.

Now that she was safely within the walls of her home, with Ted sleeping in the other room, Angela realized Gabe had only moved forward to wipe her tears. He'd had a handkerchief in hand.

Angela had jumped up too quickly. Flown off too fast. And made a complete fool of herself. Thanks to Amy. If her friend hadn't spent the afternoon teasing her about Gabe's supposed adoration. Please. Gabe was probably still sitting on the bench. "Where'd she go?" Angela mimicked his tone. "Why'd she fly off this time?"

Angela was a trying friend at best. She knew. "I'm such an idiot." She whacked herself on the forehead. It seemed an appropriate punishment.

Forcing herself up, Angela wobbled into the bedroom and slipped under the covers beside her husband. It would break her heart to leave her children. No matter how old they got, they were still her babies and she worried over them. But her heart belonged to Ted.

They'd had thirty-two mostly happy years together, and Angela intended to tell Ted in the morning and make up. Then, after he got home from work, perhaps they'd make up for real.

Angela fell asleep smiling.

"*Watch out!*" Angela called as the pixies booby-trapped the fairies' nightly feast. "*Don't touch that!*"

But the fairies couldn't resist the fruit. It exploded in their faces.

The pixies held their stomachs and roared with laughter.

"*This is not right,*" Angela said. "*You deserve to live somewhere peaceful.*"

"Our home is getting too crowded here, and this is the pixies' way." Tatiana blew a lock of hair off her forehead.

"*If you stay here, living so close to one another, will you turn into pixies?*" In living too close to the cancerous toad, Angela almost had.

Tatiana scowled. "Pixies? Never! We do not change our natures as easily as humans." She eyed Angela. "A fairy wouldn't consider the notion."

"*Of course not.*" Angela gulped guiltily.

"You have learned tonight, how to be a true fairy," Tatiana said. "Bringing light and joy to an otherwise dreary world is our destiny. You did well, but there is more. You must believe in yourself. When you do, your family will also believe."

"*Ted will never believe. He is fulfilling your vision. He's moving us to California.*" Angela chewed her lip, her heart a leaden ball.

It was better for her to move to California. Because living here, close to the fairies but not being part of their lives? Yeah, it would be too painful.

"Your Ted already believes more than you know," Tatiana said.

It was a nice dream, but reality spoke differently. She had been a housewife most of her life. It wouldn't hurt her to continue her domestic regime. Angela did excel, at least, in that. She turned and flew toward home ready to salvage her marriage.

Angela rubbed her eyes. The sun was out. The house silent. She stared at the alarm clock. The glowing, three-inch-tall LED numbers were blurry, but the exact time didn't matter. It was light outside and Angela knew. Ted had gone to work. The kids had gone to school.

Bile rose in her throat. Sure, they had gone to bed without talking it out, but Angela still expected Ted to wake her with his usual, "Good morning, sunshine!" It was their thirty-two-year-old tradition. Even when he was angry.

Angela stepped out of bed and hurried toward the bathroom. Eau De Gabe, wafted around her as she walked. "The man must have bathed in cologne," she muttered. She reeked. Not that Gabe reeked. Quite the contrary. He smelled divine, but not at all like Ted.

She showered and shampooed her hair. After she dried off, Angela picked up Ted's bottle of cologne. It smelled heavenly. As a show of loyalty that Ted probably wouldn't even notice, Angela squirted a healthy dose of Ted onto her blouse.

Finally ready for breakfast, she went into the kitchen and saw a note on the bar.

"Know how much you hate being woken up and decided to let you sleep in. Love, Ted." Okay, so that gave her hope. Angela spent the day changing the sheets, cleaning, and making everything ready for when Ted came home. She even went to the closet and pulled out the containers with her porcelain fairies. They would give her comfort and strength in California. She straightened the fairies' boxes, making sure they were ready for shipping and then put them away.

When Ted came home late that afternoon, Angela was ready. Her new negligee was laundered and under her pillow; and she had kicked Ted's pajamas under the bed. The garage door opened and closed. Angela pressed her lips against a goofy grin and waited by the door with a plate of cookies and a glass of milk.

"You showered," he said, breezing past her and into the bedroom.

"I shower every day." She had spent a night and a day forgiving Ted for the move. He should appreciate it.

He grumbled something unintelligible in response.

Angela wanted to chase after him and rip his head off (metaphorically), but stayed in the kitchen. Neither of them had slept well the night before, and both of them had spent the day hard at work. She put the finishing touches on lasagna, tossed salad, fresh mixed vegetables, and bread sticks. She was serving her husband love for dinner. And then everything would be all right.

"Dinner's ready!" Angela called.

Derek and Hannah came bounding down the stairs and sat at the table.

And waited for Ted.

They filled their plates.

And waited for Ted.

"He must have gotten held up in the bathroom." Angela scooped lasagna onto her own plate. It needed cooling anyway.

And they waited for Ted.

Derek lifted his eyebrows. "Food's getting cold."

"Can we eat?" Hannah lifted her fork.

"Maybe he didn't hear me." Angela went to the bedroom.

He was sitting on the bed reading through some papers.

"Ted. Honey. Dinner's ready." (She really was a good wife.)

He didn't look up. "Go ahead. I'll be a minute."

"Oh, okay." In their new family dining ritual, he always said grace. She turned back to the dining room.

Ted didn't come. At all.

The kids ate their dinner. Angela forked through hers and ate a few bites in the awkward silence. Awkward because Angela was upset with Ted. Awkward because she was sure the kids could tell.

Awkward because of the large empty chair at the table.

"Dinner was great, Mom." Derek gave Angela a quick hug and then took his plate to the sink. He even rinsed it off.

"Love you." Hannah nodded head down, and took her plate to the sink, rinsing and stacking it.

Derek motioned to Hannah and the two of them escaped out the front door.

Angela sat alone at the table.

The thick tension bounced invisibly between her and the bedroom. Finally, she'd had enough. "I'll just have to go the extra mile. That's all." She sat her fork down and prepared Ted a plate of food, taking notice of the cold lasagna and warming it in the microwave before adding salad.

"I brought you some dinner." Angela offered him the plate.

"I'm not hungry." Ted glanced up only briefly. "We had sandwiches catered in."

"Sandwiches? Oh." He could have mentioned that little detail. Angela turned and left the bedroom. She strode to the kitchen and scraped the meal into the disposal.

It was hard to clean the kitchen with her vision blurred by tears. But she did it. Work helped relax her. Never mind that her hands shook and the dishes clattered noisily in the sink. Never mind that she accidentally cut her finger on a knife and had to storm past Ted for a bandage. Yes, it was relaxing because if she sat down, she'd have fallen apart in an explosion of tears.

Ted had rejected her dinner. He had rejected her.

An hour after that, Angela stood with her hands on the counter, her forehead against the cupboard, her eyes open, and just breathing. Breathing was good. But what next? She had no idea what to do with this.

Ted came into the kitchen. He put his arm around her waist and pulled her gently toward him. "I'm sorry," he said.

She turned into his shoulder and sobbed. Her body, not to be left out, drenched her in sweat.

He pulled her closer and sighed. He kissed her hair and neck—he was too warm though.

Angela stepped away, fanning herself with her hands. "Let's go to bed, shall we?" She led the way.

Although she couldn't pinpoint their exact quarrel, she had high hopes for some good making-up time behind the locked doors of their bedroom.

Ted seemed uninterested though. "I don't want you to get too hot," he said, and turned toward the wall.

As if either of them had any control over that, but no, Angela wouldn't beg.

FORTY-SEVEN

Big-as-life Angela flew into the air, her eyes puffy, and sniffling back Ted's latest rejection.

Gabe was standing at the tower. He looked sad, and so Angela landed beside him.

"Hey, stranger." She lifted her lips into what she hoped was a smile.

His brows furrowed as though surprised at her appearance.

"I'm the crazy fairy-lady." She lifted her shoulders. "Remember me?"

Gabe gazed into her eyes and stepped closer. "I didn't think I'd ever see you again." He rubbed his hands down her arms.

Angela stepped away. "The fairies," she said. "I've got to help them before I leave."

"Yeah," Gabe said. "I know."

Angela wanted to apologize for flying off the previous night, but what could she say that wouldn't make things even more awkward between them? "Do you have any idea what they might need? They haven't sent me the message and I'm afraid I'll have to leave before I can actually help."

"As far as I can tell, they don't need anything besides a little space, yeah."

It was curious, indeed. Had the fairies only pretended to need Angela's help? But what would be their purpose?

Gabe was gazing into her eyes. He must wonder the same thing.

He reached out, his hand gracing hers, and Angela leapt away. She didn't look back until after she landed at her front door.

"He should know by now that I'm not a touchy-feely kind of friend." She unlocked the door and walked inside.

"Good morning, sunshine," Angela muttered to herself.

Placing her hand to her chest, she rubbed against the gaping hole in her heart where Ted's greeting used to be.

Surprising. Angela hadn't realized until now that she had always counted on Ted's simple greeting to start her day. She stepped out of bed and into her empty bedroom.

Their lives went on like this for a week, dancing back and forth in a demented cat and mouse game. Apparently, by unspoken consent, they had agreed to disagree about the move. "If you would just talk to me," Angela said.

"I've got a booster meeting."

Angela clenched her jaw.

"I've had a rough day."

Angela heaved a frustrated breath.

"The big game is on tonight. Derek and I are going over to the Helmans'."

"Helmans? We need to talk." Angela put her fists to her hips. "Don't expect me to simply end up in California."

How long could his silent treatment continue?

Perhaps they had silently agreed not to speak about anything because Angela wanted clarification on a number of subjects.

Ted fell asleep in their bed each night with his back to her.

Angela went to the fairies each night and offered her support.

In an effort to get a clue about how to help the fairies, she did research on magic during the day. It was to no avail. There wasn't one review or article she could quickly read, and nothing specifically on fairies or pixies.

One thing Angela didn't do: visit Gabe.

Each night she flew straight past him. It tore her up. Seeing her friend suffering and not able to offer him the same support and kindness he'd shown. It was horrible. But Angela wouldn't allow Ted to use Gabe as an excuse or weapon against her. Not that he had. He'd merely quit speaking to her.

Angela couldn't know how she stood on never-discussed subjects, but one thing she knew for certain: Ted was not a believer. Things didn't look promising for him to ever be one.

Tatiana was wrong.

The other thing Angela knew for certain was that she had broken Tatiana's rules and told Ted about her fairy mission, and she could lose her family forever.

Things looked increasingly sure in that regard.

For thirty-two years she had cured their world with food. She had won her husband's heart with food, nurtured her children with food, and kept her family together. With food. She could do it again, and worked herself into a cooking frenzy.

Each evening, no matter her culinary offering, the routine went something like this:

"Dinner's ready!"

Ted pulled his tie off. "We had food catered in."

Really? Had the company invested in a catering business? But, Angela continued trying.

"Dinner's ready!"

"I'm too busy," Ted grunted from behind a manila folder.

Too busy to eat? That was just absurd.

"Dinner's ready!"

Ted rubbed his mid-section. "I have a sick stomach."

Whatever. It didn't stop him from making a sandwich later that evening.

On Wednesday, she decided to try a different tactic. Fast food tacos.

Ted didn't notice. He didn't notice because he worked late.

Thursday, she bought sliced beef sandwiches and dessert.

"This is fantastic!" Ted grabbed a sandwich and a cherry turnover. "I love these," he said, and ate the turnover before the sandwich. "I haven't eaten anything this good in a long time." He moaned with pleasure and grabbed another one.

Angela gulped back an irritable response. If only she had known the key to his heart was fast food and greasy turnovers. All those wasted years trying to perfect her famous cherry pie and pie crust recipes. Which emotion did she feel the strongest, hurt or anger? She couldn't decide.

Hannah broke the charged silence. "I hope you aren't planning to wear your fairy costume this year." She looked up from her curly fries.

Angela glared at Ted. Had he asked her to say that? Her heart thumped loudly and she was about to respond very loudly.

"No, Mom. It's not like that. I was hoping you'd let me wear it to school this year. I'm as tall as you — it would fit." Hannah's shoulders drooped and her lips formed a pout. "Just let me try it on. Please?"

Angela glanced smugly back at her unbelieving husband. *Ha! Take that! Hannah wants to be a fairy. Just like her mom.* Oh, yeah, it made her day slightly less miserable.

The confused look on Ted's face: Priceless.

Sweet satisfaction! Angela pushed away from the table, sprinted to the closet (as well as any over-fifty, out-of-shape person could), and brought back her costume, laying it across the family room sofa.

"You'll be careful with it — no rips or tears?"

"Yeah, yeah, I'll be careful," Hannah said between bites. "We're having a contest at school to see who can wear the lamest costume."

296

Angela looked at her daughter, open-eyed with horror. "It's not lame."

"J.K., Mom." Hannah smiled, signing the two letters. "J.K." Then she turned to Derek. "Lacy says her mom's got the most embarrassing costume of all time. I said, 'no way,' she said, 'way,' but I've got a free lunch riding on it. I'll win." She turned and smiled innocently at Angela.

Was it too late to tell her no? She couldn't have Hannah wearing her prized possession in a 'lame' contest. Her fairy costume was not lame.

She finished her dinner in silence and went to bed in silence—the kind of silence that speaks things no one wants to hear.

The next day, she once again awoke to silence.

"I am going to set this right," Angela said. "I won him over with food, I'll win him back with food. I just need to try harder."

This is why, early Friday afternoon Angela was busy making stuffed pork chops.

"This past week was just a fluke," she said, slicing into the side of a pork chop and pushing her filling into the pocket she'd created.

The phone rang. "Anderson residence," she sang into the receiver.

"Hey, Angela. Mr. Drulman made reservations for everyone at Ruth's Steakhouse."

"What time?" The one thing she liked better than her stuffed pork chops was a pricey steak at the company's expense.

"Six."

"Woo-hoo!" Angela did a jig around the kitchen.

"I won't be home beforehand."

"Give me the address and I'll look it up on the Internet." She grabbed a pen and paper.

There was a long pause on the line.

"I'm sorry. It's just for the partners," Ted replied. "We're going over some important stuff—legal documents and plans for the new office. You wouldn't have a good time."

"Yes, I would." For an expensive meal at an exclusive restaurant, Angela was willing to suffer through. She would be quiet, wouldn't offer a word of comment. If it was top secret, Angela would bring Hannah's iPod. So, for the opportunity of a melt-in-her-mouth steak dinner, she begged, "Ted, please."

"It wouldn't be proper," Ted insisted. "Pretty sure none of the partners are bringing their wives. It's employees only."

Pretty sure? "Fine." Angela hung up the phone. Agitated, and resenting how lonely and dissatisfied she felt with her life, she plopped down onto a kitchen chair.

"I have wings—I should be happy." She crossed her arms. "Fairies are real—I should be thrilled." She rubbed against the ache in her forehead. "How can I be happy when in a few weeks, visits with the kids will be budgeted into our vacation?" And her fairy adventures, nothing but a wistful dream.

Because Ted didn't believe in her.

"What's the point?" Angela stared at the half-prepared meal. "Derek and Hannah would rather have fast food."

The phone rang again.

Angela picked it up hoping Ted had reconsidered. "I can be ready in a half hour," she said.

"Anj?"

"Gabe?"

A flutter of joy surged through Angela. It made her nervous. It shouldn't be that way, but her traitorous self didn't listen. It felt like she was hearing from an old friend at a time when she was at her lowest—oh, wait, that's exactly what it was.

"Gabe!"

"Yeah. Hey, are we good? I haven't seen you lately. I miss my little fairy *chica*."

It was a combination of things that caught her off guard. His calling her little—his calling her *his* fairy *chica*—his calling her period. It lifted her spirits and made her feel beautiful.

She couldn't spend time with Gabe alone. Especially not while she and Ted were having problems. Angela could, however, spend time with him on the phone. So they talked.

After a respectable amount of time had passed, Angela decided to bring her other friend into the conversation. If Gabe and Amy were together, maybe Ted wouldn't be so jealous, and maybe she could be around Gabe without feeling so nervous all the time. That would be one small problem, or rather two problems solved, and would leave only the nearly insurmountable issue of the fairies.

"We ever going on that fishing trip?" Gabe asked. "I've got the poles ready."

"You know," Angela said, "I've got this friend—Amy. She's a really great gal and I think the two of you would hit it off." Did people even say things like that anymore? "Perhaps you could take her fishing."

There was a pause. "So, you're pawning me off. Ted put you up to it?"

"It's not like that." It wasn't. Was it?

"What's it like then?"

"Well, it's like this. I have a girlfriend and she lost her husband about a year ago. She's ready to move on, but doesn't quite know how. You could help."

"I'll pass." Another pause. "I wouldn't know where to go or what to do."

"Take her to the zoo." Angela smiled. Gabe might do this. "It's one of her favorite places, and the weather's great."

"I don't know," Gabe said. "I don't do blind dates."

"The two of you would be perfect together." Angela used her most convincing tone. "And besides, it's not really a blind date. You've met her before, sort of. She was at our party."

There was silence on the line.

Had he hung up the phone? "Hello?"

"It's a date," he finally replied, "as long as you come, too."

299

"Wait, what?" Angela grabbed hold of the counter to steady herself.

"Let's all go to the zoo. Today. Right now."

"O-o-k-a-y," Angela lengthened the word as she said it. "I'll call Amy and see if she's available."

Angela was excited for a chance to see Gabe and Amy together, and did a short victory jig, glad for the afternoon's possibilities.

They agreed to meet by the entryway to the Phoenix Zoo. It was a highly public place and along with Papago Park right next to it, the zoo was also a favorite spot of Angela's.

As soon as she hung up with Gabe, Angela redialed.

"Amy, I'm in deep here. I need your help."

"What's up, girlfriend?"

"Gabe wants to meet you in an hour. He wants us to meet him at the zoo. Will you do it? You said he was cute."

Angela banged her head on the wall in frustration. She wasn't good at setting people up, but when she heard Amy speaking, Angela put the receiver back to her ear. "What?"

"I said I'll go. Yes, I'll meet your Gabe."

FORTY-EIGHT

"There's a spot there." Angela pointed at an empty space in the zoo's massive, and yet nearly full, parking lot.

"I've got it." Amy zipped around the corner and parked.

Angela got out and waited by the car's trunk, surveying the distance to the entryway bridge with a grimace.

Amy pulled a couple bottles of water from the backseat and then tossed one to Angela. "Let's get this embarrassment over with."

"Do you have a wheelchair in the trunk?" Angela asked.

"Sometimes you say the funniest things." Amy laughed lightly.

"Heh, heh. It wasn't that funny."

"I'm just practicing for when Gabe joins us." Amy took a swig of her water. "Just a little nervous, I guess."

Angela raised her eyebrows. "You? Nervous? You and Gabe will get along so well, you'll forget all about me. I'll be stranded over in some remote trail, dying from exhaustion." Angela put the back of her hand to her forehead in mock drama. "You and Gabe will be having such a great time, you won't even be aware of my demise."

"Ha! I'll be clutching your arm the whole time," Amy said.

She did look nervous. "I told Gabe we'd meet him here,"

Angela said when they got to the bridge.

"There's enough people here today." Amy rested her arms against the railing and peered toward the turtles resting on a log floating in the water.

"He better not get lost." Angela faced the parking lot.

"It might be for the best." Amy scrunched her face. "Why do you think they have all this water here? It was probably expensive to build, even back whenever they built the zoo, and it's too shallow."

"Apparently," Angela lifted her brows, "years before the zoo, someone decided to build a fish hatchery here. Can you imagine?" Angela never wanted to know what happened to end the endeavor, but the thought of parboiled fish floating on the water's surface in the heat of an Arizona summer made her shudder.

"I guess the turtles are glad they did." Amy turned to face Angela. "Do you think he changed his mind?"

"See for yourself." Angela grinned.

Gabe walked toward them, wearing tan walking shorts and a midnight blue T-shirt with Gilbert's fire department logo on it. It was a good look.

"It's about time you showed up." Angela gave him a friendly bump against his shoulder.

"Traffic," he said. "You want to feed the fish?" Gabe went to the feeding machine and then filled Angela's hand with a quarter's worth of rabbit pellets. He went back and got another handful. "You're Amy, yeah?" He said, pouring pellets into her cupped hands.

"I'm sorry, where are my manners?" Angela made the proper introductions.

"Don't worry about anything," Gabe said after the pellets were gone. "This is my treat." He paid for their entry into the zoo and grabbed a map. "I haven't been here in a long time."

They walked through the main courtyard with Gabe in the middle, a woman on each side, and his arms around them both.

"You're loving this aren't you," Amy accused with a playful smirk.

"You have no idea," replied Gabe with a wicked, charming smile.

"Would you like to take the train?" Angela asked Gabe. "The place is massive, and the train gives a good overview of all the large animals." *Just say yes.* She had already used her energy walking from the parking lot to the main entrance.

"No." Gabe made a face. "You miss too much. Yeah?"

"Exactly," Amy agreed. She and Gabe linked arms and led the way deeper into the zoo.

"Don't mind me," Angela muttered to their retreating frames, and then hurried to catch up.

"There are bald eagles at the Mogollon Rim," Gabe said, resting his hand lightly on Amy's back. "Do you like camping?"

"We used to go camping all the time," Amy replied. "I still have our tent."

Gabe and Amy appeared to be walking leisurely from exhibit to exhibit. Why, then, was Angela speed-walking to keep up? She took a drink of water and then splashed some on her face.

"I have a friend who likes to hunt," Gabe said at the javelina exhibit. "He was out once, and a javelina chased him up a tree." He laughed. "That was his first and last javelina-hunting experience."

Amy laughed in response, leaned in and said something Angela couldn't hear.

They finished walking through the Arizona Trail, and walked through the African Trail. Angela felt like an overheated wet-nap — warm, sticky and moist.

"Would you ladies like a frozen lemonade?" Gabe pulled out his wallet and stepped up to the refreshment stand.

"I'd love one," Amy replied. "That's so thoughtful."

"Thank you," Angela said, placing the cool cup against her cheek.

"After you." Gabe extended his arm, letting Amy lead the way. The two looked pretty cozy as they walked around the main lake and approached Gibbon Island.

Angela tagged along behind, frustrated and worn to a frazzle, and almost wished she'd stayed home to finish the pork chops. Almost. She gulped down her dread of returning home to an empty house even though her muscles ached with the pain of a thousand flames. No, her current pain surpassed that by at least another thousand, or even a million flames.

"Hey, I need a rest." Gabe smiled back toward Angela. "According to the map, there's some picnic tables next to the island, let's go sit down."

"There are." Angela nodded. Gabe was probably just humoring her, but she didn't care. Just let the misery end already.

The zoo's train wheeled past, and Angela bit back her longing.

"I need to use the ladies' room," Amy said. "I'll only be a minute." Before Angela could ask to go with her, Amy trotted away.

"Let's go find some shade." Gabe motioned for Angela to go first.

Angela watched Amy disappear down the lane as she stepped onto the shrub-enshrouded pathway leading to Gibbon Island.

"Whoa!" With her foot half on the path and half off, Angela flailed her arms, frantically trying to regain her balance. It was futile, and she began her descent to the brutal pavement.

Two saving arms wrapped themselves around her. "Easy there," Gabe muttered good-naturedly in her ear. Her speedy tumble caused Angela's head to spin. Gabe held her, mercifully, until she caught her footing and was no longer in danger of a bruise the size of South Africa on her derriere.

"Here, let me help you." Gabe started to take her arm.

"That's okay." She wasn't a feeble old woman. Angela shook her head. It spun with the motion. That, combined with her tired and wobbly knees, sent her downward once more.

Gabe put his arm around her shoulder, holding her firmly, and guided her for the half-minute walk to the picnic area.

Angela looked up, embarrassed. "Thanks." She sat on the picnic bench leaning against the table, facing the lake and the monkeys, and wishing she could take a quick dip in the lake. After all, the monkeys wouldn't care.

Gabe slid in beside her, stretching his legs out comfortably in front of him. "If only I could take my shoes off and really enjoy the water." He grinned.

"Yeah, that's what we need around here is more water for the adults." It would be nice, though. Angela waited a moment, feeling the awkward silence, and then said, "So, how's it going with Amy? She's nice, huh."

"Very nice. She's agreed to go fishing with me tomorrow morning." He winked.

Angela laughed. "I guess I'll have to get Ted to take me now." She took a long sip of the lemonade wishing she hadn't made that comment and then pointed to the monkeys. "Look at that one."

"Angela Anderson!"

Angela's skin crawled at the sound of that voice. She turned to face her would-be oppressor.

"Imagine my surprise at seeing you here." Rebecca Helman stood in front of Angela, sporting a scowl. "And with someone other than your husband. You are a hypocrite and a cheat." Her fists went to her hips.

"We are—this doesn't—" Angela's heart squeezed with anxiety.

"Of course now you're going to tell me this isn't what it looks like." She smirked. "Except that I saw you hugging each other on the main path."

"Ma'am," Gabe started.

"You're that EMT!" Rebecca shrieked, eyes widened. "No wonder Ted hit you!"

"It was a misunderstanding." Gabe put his hand on the table and stood.

"Rebecca, please—" Angela wanted to explain. She was here chaperoning her two friends on their first date, but Rebecca interrupted.

"Please what? I'm not your judge. You want some tasty eye candy—want to walk the forbidden path—it's none of my *affair*." Her eyebrows rose, her face portraying a look of self-righteous indignation.

Angela opened her mouth to speak words of reason. Something to calm her malicious neighbor, but choked on the word affair.

Emotions and hormones surged to the front of her tongue and she shouted, "You evil-minded, vile speaking, ignominious ant. You've been following me!" Why else was this woman, this spiteful nag, at the zoo at the exact same time? And of the thousands of people there, how had Rebecca spotted her from behind the bushes surrounding the island?

"There's no proof in that. The zoo is a highly public place." Rebecca sniffed her nose into the air.

"You tried to poison me!" The bug, the soup, the hot chocolate, and the nutmeg-spiced cookies? It was no coincidence.

"I did not!" Rebecca scowled. "Can I help that you're allergic to nutmeg?" She pinched her lips together, one shoulder raised in a mock shrug.

"You put a bug in my soup!" Angela wanted to hurl at the memory.

"I was hoping you'd at least get a bite out of the poor guy before spotting him." She smiled with satisfaction.

"You've turned my family against me." Angela growled the words from her soul and glared.

"I didn't have to do a thing." Rebecca blew on the tip of her index finger as though it was a gun. "You're an absurd, pitiful excuse for a mother, and I have no idea how that saint of a husband of yours puts up with you."

"Stay away from me, and stay away from my family." Though she meant it with all her heart, she spoke the words as a defeated whimper. Angela knew too well how her fairy antics appeared to her family — and how this looked to the loathsome snake.

.

FORTY-NINE

Angela folded her arms on the picnic table and rested her head there, all life whooshed from her.

"Hey, you okay?" Gabe put his arm over her shoulders. "That was pretty intense. So, she's the one who brought the bad cookies to your party?"

"The one and only," Angela muttered. How was that vile woman always able to say such hurtful things?

"Don't worry about it. If she says anything, your family won't believe her gossip."

"Yeah." The problem was, they already did.

"What's going on?" Amy approached, and sat on the opposite bench.

"The 'ignominious ant' showed up," Gabe said.

"Oh." Amy patted Angela's hands. "Ted won't believe her. You'll see."

Angela wanted to believe her friend. "The damage has been done, but we can't let that shrew ruin our outing." She drew in a shaky breath, poking the unpleasant woman to the nethermost regions of her mind, and stood. "We can salvage this afternoon." For her friends, she would do it.

"Papago Park?" Amy asked.

"Why would we leave the zoo?" Gabe stood and offered a hand to Amy.

"Tradition," Angela and Amy said together.

"But neither of us brought a picnic." Angela chewed the tips of her nails.

"There's food here," Gabe suggested. "You still didn't answer my question."

"About that," Amy said, looking apprehensively toward Angela.

"Fairies." Angela lifted her eyebrows. "It's our favorite topic."

"It is," Amy agreed.

"So, I only have one question, yeah." Gabe smiled crookedly, rubbing his fingers down Amy's arm. "Would you rather eat here at the zoo or at the park?"

Amy looked at Angela. "Let's eat here," she said. "It would get cold and smushy hauling it over to the park."

The three dined on hamburgers and French fries in the shadows of the African Savannah.

"I'm surprised you haven't shown us a secret fairy lair," Gabe mused.

"There are no fairies here at the zoo." Amy touched Gabe's hand. "We think there are a few at Papago Park, though."

"Why don't we check it out?" Gabe stood and reached to help them up. "You ladies can show me this magical kingdom of yours."

"Don't be disappointed if we don't see anything. Now isn't the best time to see fairies." Angela wondered if her friends would still believe with no evidence other than herself. Was she enough?

"There's a specific time? When?" Amy asked.

"At dawn or at dusk when the sky casts golden shadows through the trees, and the air is static with the possibility of magic." Angela sighed at the lovely vision inside of her eyelids.

"Well, I can only stay until five-thirty. I have a class at seven." Amy frowned.

Gabe looked at his watch. "That means we only have another hour. We'd better hurry."

With evening on the horizon, the threesome made their way out of the zoo to search along the rushes and reeds around Papago Park for the colorful glint of fairies.

"The zoo could make a killing on golf cart rentals," Angela said as they hiked the expanse of the parking lot, her legs once more twitching from overexertion. "This is at least a half-mile walk," she complained. It felt more like ten miles as she trudged to the nearest picnic ramada.

The little rock hut, half hidden with cattail stems, was Angela's oasis. She stumbled toward it and sat down inside. Her two best friends seemed unaware. Made of river rock, the aging ramada almost looked like an abandoned dwarf house, except it was open on each end, with window cutouts in each wall and a cement table fused to the concrete floor inside.

"I need a rest," she groaned mostly to herself. "Yeah, my heart and legs and lungs might give out if I don't."

Gabe and Amy were down the trail, looking down into a shallow ditch.

"Don't worry about me," Angela muttered, although her lips turned up. Her two friends were hitting it off well. She had gotten something right at least.

The cattails along certain parts of the lake, like near the ramada where Angela rested, didn't look as though they had ever been trimmed. Other areas were thick with water lilies. Despite the greenery growing in the water, the surrounding land was bare— nothing but hard Arizona dirt and a few trees for shade.

Angela chugged the remnants of her life-saving water and chucked the bottle into the nearby trashcan. The cattails rustled. She peered around, worriedly. She heard the sound again and cringed. The eerie rustling reminded Angela of the night she fought the pixies (and the duck) at Freestone Park. She jumped up and bolted toward her friends. "Wait for me!"

"Look at the lights over there." Amy pointed to a place across the water.

With the sun's golden glow on the lake combining with the fuchsia, orange and purple of the sunset, it was hard to tell if there was something there other than a beautiful evening reflection. Angela squinted but it didn't make the sight any clearer. "I don't know — it's hard to tell."

"Why don't you fly over there and see?" Gabe asked.

"Is that a good idea?" Amy chewed her bottom lip. "I mean, if you think it's okay. There really isn't an easy way to get to the other side."

"Why couldn't I?" Angela peered across the water wanting to do it. Tatiana had basically forbidden her to use her wings in front of humans. But Gabe had already seen her flying away. And Amy wanted to. Angela needed someone to believe in her. And Tatiana's objections were mostly related to the area surrounding Freestone Park. Papago Park probably wasn't under her jurisdiction. Probably.

"I've never seen your wings before." Amy smiled. "Can you do it?"

Angela looked from side to side. "There aren't any phone booths for me to change in," she quipped.

"Har, har," responded Amy. "Show us your stuff."

She could do it, and she wanted to do it. Angela hesitated for only a moment longer. Fighting against feeling she was doing something wrong, she prodded her wings to the surface, allowing them to come.

"They're so beautiful," whispered Amy.

"Yeah, they are kind of cool." Angela smiled at the longing in her friend's voice.

"You're kind of cool," murmured Gabe. Then he leaned to

Angela's ear and whispered, "Ted's a lucky man."

That's all it took to have jittery Angela fly across an ocean just to get away, even though it was merely a shallow lake. She rose and made her way across it in search of fairies. Half way over the water, an image flashed into Angela's mind. Tatiana, angry and shouting. "You arrogant, disobedient human—you will be punished!"

Angela lost her balance and headed downward. *They're my friends, and they already believe in fairies.* She flapped her arms, and urging herself upward, made it to the other side of the water.

There were fairies in the rushes. Angela sensed them. She wanted them to like her—to see that she was friendly—to show themselves. She didn't need to prove anything to her friends. She didn't. Angela merely wanted to share with Gabe and Amy the fairies that filled her life. What could she say to get the magical creatures to come out?

"Here fairy, fairy," she sang. It didn't work. She tried a different approach. "Come out, come out wherever you are." No fairies appeared.

Feeling desperate, she physically searched among the reeds and overgrowth, and saw something glimmer.

"I come in peace," she said.

On second thought, Angela realized, she should have made sure they were fairies and not pixies. On third thought, she should have learned how to approach unknown magical colonies.

Angela lay flat on her back on the hard dirt shoreline, her feet sinking miserably toward the muddy undersurface of the water, and realized something all too late. She hadn't been thinking at all.

"Ow," she groaned, shaking herself awake and trying to sit up, but slumped back onto the hard ground.

Why, oh why had Angela been so foolish? Just because she had part-time wings, it didn't make her a real fairy. Her size proved that. She had a life of her own as a human.

Angela lay there, her head swimming, and the only thing keeping her from losing her dinner was the sight of her approaching friends.

"Are you all right?" Gabe and Amy finally made their way around the lake. "Your wing is bent — are you in pain?" Gabe took her wrist and checked her pulse. "It's a little fast."

Of course her pulse was fast, her wing was bent! Her wing? Why were her wings still there?

"Oh," Angela moaned. "I don't feel well." Her body sang its dismay by flooding her with heat.

FIFTY

Gabe felt her forehead. "You feel hot. Could you be getting a fever this fast?"

"I'll be fine." Honestly, couldn't she just sink into a hole never to be found?

"I'll take you home," Amy said.

"I can't go home like this." Angela glanced back at her wing.

"Freestone Park?" Gabe suggested.

"Maybe the fairy queen will fix them." Angela hoped.

"I'm coming too," Amy helped Angela to her feet.

"You have a class."

"You're more important than any class."

"I'll take her, in case she passes out or something. Yeah?"

Gabe drove straight to Freestone Park, Angela in the passenger seat. Amy pulled in right behind them. She jumped out of her car and helped Angela out of Gabe's truck. Amy and Gabe both helped support her as they walked toward the pedestrian bridge.

"You two wait here. I need to do this alone." Angela waited until they both agreed, and then hobbled across the bridge to Tatiana's kingdom.

This wasn't the way it had ever worked before, but Angela wasn't above groveling. She collapsed on the prickly Bermuda grass nearby. Her knees didn't bend right anymore. It was uncomfortable trying to sit cross-legged, and her legs wouldn't go behind her either. Finally, on her knees, her arms stretched awkwardly to the ground in front of her, Angela began.

"*Tatiana, I need your help.*"

It took several minutes before Tatiana appeared in her mind.

It wasn't a happy reunion. Moments later, Angela walked, dazed, toward her human friends.

"Will she fix them?" Gabe helped Angela to Amy's car.

"No." Angela's voice wobbled with the uncertainty of her situation. "Tatiana says I have to prove myself—whatever that means. Until then, the broken wings are here to stay."

"Maybe it's something simple," Amy offered.

One could hope.

It was eight-forty-five when Amy pulled to the curb in front of Angela's home and parked near the large moving van in the driveway.

Angela noted the time because it was the moment her life shattered. Ted hadn't mentioned his renting the van. They hadn't even resolved whether they were moving or not. She tried gulping back the pain in her heart. It didn't work. The truck was a sign—a huge two-ton sign with wheels.

The sign said: "*I'm moving to California with the kids whether you like it or not. You can come if you want to, but I don't care either way.*"

"You want to talk about it?" Amy's hand rested on Angela's shoulder.

Angela blinked at her tears. "Thanks for the ride." Her voice quavered, and Angela didn't say more, but wiped impatiently at her moist eyes and opened the car door.

Amy didn't say anything else. Nothing more needed said. Angela heard loud and clear the message her friend sent: "*I'm only a call away. I'm here for you.*"

Angela walked to the front door as to her own funeral. In

her mind, beyond the door could very well be the death of Mrs. Anderson. Heaving a ragged breath, she grabbed and twisted the doorknob. Their wicked witch of a neighbor — had she called Ted?

An ominous feeling crawled up her spine as she opened the door. One light revealed a dark and silent house, her husband standing at the sliding glass-door and staring into the backyard.

"I'm home," she called, trying to sound cheerful and not convey the panic she felt. Angela faced her broken wings to the wall and walked sideways toward the bedroom.

Ted didn't turn around or respond.

"I'm pooped — a lot of walking, you know." His silence was extremely loud and Angela's head began to ache. "I'm going to turn in early." She shouldn't leave him alone like that, go to bed without a word, but Angela couldn't very well go to him with wings stuck to her back and ask about his moving van-sign. Instead she sent him silent messages:

"*I love you, Ted. Believe in me — believe me. Love me back,*" among other unheard thoughts as she inched her way to her room, wings behind her as she went. These messages kept her from screaming the things in the other region of her heart: "*How could you rent a moving van when you know how I feel about moving? If you loved me, you'd believe in me. If you loved me, you'd talk to me,*" and things like that.

As soon as she got inside of their bedroom, Angela closed the door, trying not to slam it in her haste. Locking it, she rested against it for only a second, and then rushed to the closet searching frantically for something to cover her wings. She needed to talk to Ted, convince him of her love and fidelity.

Ted wiggled the knob. "Angela, open the door." He sounded weary.

"Okay. I'll be out in a minute." She tried calling the words cheerfully, innocently, but they came out as a screeched warble.

The discard pile on her bed grew larger as Angela made her way through her wardrobe. She yanked a blouse off its hanger and tried it on. Her wings penetrated the fabric. The once miraculous feat was now irritating.

"Angela," Ted said firmly. The doorknob wiggled.

"I'm almost there." With her desperation increasing, she tried on more blouses, and then started on her dresses. Each time, her wings penetrated the fabric. There had to be something. She stepped over the pile of discarded hangers and frantically, she started on her summer outfits, but ripped them each off her body as her wings came through the fabric. She gulped at the sight of her sweaters, and then pulled the first off its hanger.

Ted wiggled the doorknob again. Angela's heart jumped in panic.

"Angela, let me in." He sounded angry. "We need to talk."

"Sure. Now he wants to talk." She peered at the pile on her bed. None of her clothes hid the wings. What would she do? What if nothing hid these once-desired atrocities on her back? "I'm almost there." Angela's knees faltered and she grabbed at the wall for support. Her world was collapsing around her.

She hesitated for only the briefest second—all other choices gone—and started on her coats. Not that she had that many. Even in the coldest of most Phoenix-area winters, coats were merely a fashion accessory. It was here in the deepest recesses of the closet that Angela saw a white garment box with a bow wrapped around it.

The flurry around her stopped.

Angela took the gift carefully to the bed and stared at the white box with the gold ribbon. Ted didn't buy superfluous gifts. He gave her presents five times a year and she always knew what they would be—a card and a gift certificate for her birthday—a box of chocolates for Valentine's day—pajamas for Christmas—a necklace or other piece of jewelry for their anniversary—flowers for Mother's day.

"Curious, curious, curious," she muttered, and opened it.

Pulling back what seemed a copious amount of tissue paper, she discovered a garment of some sort. The fabric was soft like velvet and smooth as satin, yet much lighter in weight. Certainly nothing she had ever come across.

It looked like a dress—dainty cap sleeves—short bodice that might actually accentuate her nearly nonexistent bust line—flouncy, glistening bell of a skirt. Fabric pieces were attached to the skirt at angles like scarves each pointing to her toes. The main color was buttercup yellow, with shimmers of every color in the rainbow catching her eye.

Angela put the dress up to her. Something fell back into the box. "Tights." The color of midnight. She tried them on. They ended at the ankle. "New slippers." She pulled them out of the box and tried them on. "They're so dainty." Not at all like grandma shoes.

She slipped on the dress. "It's magnificently beautiful," she whispered. And it looked expensive.

The wings, of course, came through the fabric flawlessly. One glance in the mirror revealed Angela the fairy in a new costume. It was ingenious. The perfect way to disguise her wings was to make them part of a costume, but Ted couldn't see the wings while he was still so angry.

"We need to talk!" Ted banged on the door, impatient now.

Shaking her head, Angela brought herself back to her reality.

Yeah, they needed to talk all right. If he thought this costume, no matter how lovely, made up for his renting a moving van and moving away from their adult children, well he was wrong.

Angela rushed back to the closet and the coats. She needed to confront him, talk to him about this disaster threatening to break their marriage.

She pulled out her very last coat. It was a heavy one. She hadn't even glanced at it since their January snow trip to Mogollon Rim five years ago. She put her arms through the sleeves. It was this coat — the coat she had purchased at the thrift store, shabby but still warm — the coat made of down, the under-feathers of duck wings, that her own wings stayed tucked underneath.

Angela slunk to the closet floor, her body trembling into another hot flash under the heat of the coat. How to do it, she didn't know, but Angela needed to prove herself to Tatiana, quick.

"Ugh."

Ted wanted in. He wanted to talk. Of course he did, but only on his terms and never hers. Angela clenched her jaw. If not, then why hadn't he 'talked' when she'd initiated conversation this past week?

Angela forced her weight against the doorframe, pulled herself up and wobbled over to attack the mountain of clothing lying uselessly on the bed. She'd hang these up first. Yeah, she was being a coward.

There was a clicking noise at the door, and then Ted walked in.

He flipped the door shut with his foot and stood there, arms folded across his chest, glaring at her and the pile of discarded clothes.

"I was going to open the door." Angela, pretending to be nonchalant though seething and wounded inside, walked shakily to the closet with five blouses in hand. "I just wanted to clear the bed first."

"Why'd you change?" He demanded, stepping to the bed and searching through the pile.

"Do ya want it back?" Forgetting her wings, she pulled at the dress, though her coat was also in the way. "It's not going to change my mind about moving." Angrily, she pulled at the tights. They didn't budge in the slightest — it was like tugging on her skin. She gave up the endeavor. The outfit must be too small.

"No. You can keep it. I bought it to celebrate my new position — before you started acting all weird." He closed his eyes, sighing deeply, and raked his hands through his hair. "The coat?"

"I ... I was cold."

Ted glanced up, disbelieving, and scoffed. "Cold?"

Her overheated face and the sweat droplets on her forehead attested to her lie. He found the clothes she had changed out of and sniffed them.

(What? Was he a bloodhound now?)

He tossed the clothes to the floor and stormed from the room. Angela followed.

"What Ted? Talk to me." Angela pulled on his arm.

Ted shook away. "You've been with Gabe!"

"And Amy. I wrote you a note."

"Yeah, that's what you said. Evidence says otherwise. Rebecca sent me a picture with her cell phone of the two of you arm in arm." He pulled out his phone.

"*Rebecca?* You're on a first name basis with that belligerent biddy? How'd she get your cell phone number?

Shaking his head, he waved the thought away. "That's irrelevant."

"How are my questions irrelevant, and yours not?" Angela shoved her fists to her hips.

"Yours is a question of fidelity, and mine's not!"

"Who says so? For all I know, you could be cavorting with my worst enemy! After all, you believe her over me!"

"She sent photographs, Angela. More than one—and they're pretty damning." His voice choked on that last word, but fire blazed in his eyes. "You think I don't know where you go every night after I fall asleep?"

Angela felt her own fire. She'd been perfectly honest—too honest—told him about her fairy mission. He still didn't believe.

"Here, I'll show you." He turned his attention to the phone's screen.

"I don't want to see Hellcat's pictures." She could imagine how they must look, but that self-righteous snake had taken them. Ted shouldn't believe a snake over his own wife, regardless of photographs.

"She said the two of you were acting cozy at the zoo — sans Amy." He lifted his phone for her to see the picture.

"Would you like to call Amy?" Angela would never forgive him if he did. "You might think I'm a liar and a cheat, but you know Amy won't lie to you." She pushed the rest of the clothing onto the floor. "I'm going to bed now. Do what you want. Sleep in the stupid moving van for all I care."

"I think I'll go *next door* to sleep." He grabbed his pillow and took a sheet from the closet instead.

Angela screamed from anger and frustration as he stormed from the room.

It was then, during the worst time possible, a time when Angela felt her lowest, yet near to explode, that the phone rang.

She threw off the coat and yanked at the stupid fairy dress — Ted could take it back. The outfit refused to budge.

"Agh!" Angela screamed again. *Grief!* Her wings and the fairy dress — "Agh! Stubborn paranormal appendages!"

The phone rang again, and again.

Apparently Ted wasn't going to answer it in the family room.

"Why does my life have to be like this?!" she screamed at the wall. Then she cleared her throat and answered the phone by their bed as sweetly as possible. "Hello, Anderson residence."

"Mom, I think I've started labor." Leanne's voice cracked with panic. "You need to take me to the hospital. Doctor Smith said if you brought me, he'd do his best to make Zoey Grace wait until Rusty gets here."

"Shall I call an ambulance?"

"Just come!"

FIFTY-ONE

"I'll be right there." Angela hung up the phone and resentfully put the coat back on.

Ted was lying on the sofa watching television. Of course.

"It's Leanne," she said, grabbing her purse and rushing toward the garage.

"I'm coming too." Ted jumped up and followed her out the door, shoes in hand.

Sure Ted would come. Big manly man that he was, he hadn't been able to stomach the birth of any of their five children. No matter their preparations. He fainted during the births of Richard and Leanne, lost his lunch during Benjamin's birth.

When Derek was born, Ted was ready—until the head crowned. The nurse guided a swooning and queasy Ted from the room. Giving up on all pretenses, he paced the hallway outside of the birthing room during Hannah's birth. Yeah, he'd be a big help to Leanne.

Angela pushed her way to the driver's seat, forcing Ted to sit passenger. This was another of the reversals in their life. When they'd first met, Ted rode a motorcycle—fast. When they bought their first car as a couple, he still drove at mach-speed. It made Angela nervous at first, cautious driver that she was, but she grew to trust Ted and his driving. He hadn't had a ticket in over thirty-two years.

As an unconscious celebration of turning fifty, Ted began driving differently. Slower. He now drove like her grandma, pulling to a stop at yellow lights and driving a safe two miles under the speed limit.

It was now Angela who pushed the limits speed-wise. And it was Angela who would get them there before their first grandchild turned one.

"You should at least change your clothes," Ted groused. "You look ridiculous."

"Oh, okay." Angela shrugged out of the heavy coat and was instantly, gratifyingly, chilled. "Thanks. That's much better." She turned the ignition on and peeled out of the driveway and down the street.

"I meant the costume and wings, and you know it," Ted growled angrily.

"I think Leanne would rather her mother be there to help, than to have her sitting at home wondering the appropriate attire for childbirth."

"Whatever."

"You're starting to sound like Hannah."

"At least she doesn't traipse around town dressed as a fairy."

"Maybe she will one day. She did ask to use my old costume."

Silence.

Ah, silence was good. Angela used the silence to mentally scream all the things she had never said aloud. She shouted things like: *You make me so angry! Why can't we communicate anymore? And, You're not so perfect either — you snore when you sleep and you dribble on the toilet. Oh yes you do! You should clean up your own mess, but you don't. You always make me do it.*

Of course, she didn't rant about the things that hurt her most — the renting of the moving van, his refusal to eat with the family, his not saying good morning anymore — his willingness to believe the worst of her.

He might have been shouting as well, but Angela didn't want to hear his silent rant—he was wrong.

The drive to north Mesa didn't take as long as usual. Angela willed all of the lights to stay green, and by some miracle, they did. Whether it was by fairy magic or luck, Angela didn't know. She was just grateful.

When they got to the small stucco home, Angela was the first one to the door. She knocked once and walked in. "Leanne, it's us. Mom and Dad."

Their daughter was standing in the middle of the room on her way to get the door. She looked terrible—the color drained from her face with sweat dripping around her hairline. "Love your outfit, Mom." Then her knees buckled.

Angela ran forward and caught her daughter just in time. She should have called an ambulance before leaving home. This was not good.

"Ted."

Her white-faced and panicked husband appeared by Leanne's side, and the two parents helped their daughter into the bedroom.

"Let's get you off of your feet." They helped Leanne onto her bed and Angela began propping pillows under her daughter's feet and legs to elevate them. Rusty would be home soon—within twenty-four hours—to witness the birth of their first baby. She couldn't deliver before then.

Leanne screamed from the pain of a contraction.

She was at the screaming stage—definitely not good.

"I'm going to call your doctor, sweetie," Angela soothed, and hurried into the other room. Leanne kept her emergency numbers taped to the refrigerator.

"I'm calling an ambulance," Angela murmured to Ted. "She's pretty far along."

Ted rushed to Angela's side. "You'd better not call your boyfriend over here," he warned.

"Don't be ridiculous." Would he really have this pointless

fight with her here? Now? Angela dialed 9-1-1. "Hello, this is an emergency ..."

After the ambulance was on its way, she called the doctor while Ted went back to the living room sofa, grumbling.

Another shriek signified another contraction.

"Yes, Doctor Smith? This is Leanne Thornock's mom. I'm not sure she will make it to the hospital. I've called an ambulance, but I'm not even sure if she'll make it until they come. Yes. Okay." Angela hung up the phone, and called to Ted, "The ambulance is on its way and Doctor Smith says to keep her calm and comfortable."

Leanne shrieked again. Angela rushed to her daughter's side. Leanne's eyes were round with horror. "I think I wet myself."

"Let me help you to the bathroom." Angela put her arm around Leanne and helped her stand.

"I can't control it!" Liquid drizzled to the floor. It was just as Angela feared.

"You'll be fine, sweetheart. Your water's broken is all." The baby had to come now, there was no giving her meds to stop the contractions. Angela's heart skipped a beat. She had never been on this end of the delivery before, and she would just die if something happened to her daughter or grandchild.

With Leanne sitting safely on the toilet, Angela changed the sheets. She became a whirlwind, a rock—soothing, consoling her daughter, guiding Ted on what to do and how to keep out of the way, helping Leanne back on the bed, to be comfortable and calm, and guiding her through her breathing—all while hoping, praying that the paramedics would get there in time to deliver her granddaughter.

If they didn't, Angela would help the child into this world herself.

"It hurts!"

"Calm down. No more screaming, everything's fine." Angela wiped the hair from Leanne's brow. "Don't waste your energy on anything but getting our little girl here safely."

"I think I feel her." Leanne groaned.

"Remember your breathing. Everything will be fine."

Leanne began her childbirth-breathing again, her eyes focused on Angela.

"Okay, that's good." Angela then called to Ted, and he came running. "Let's help her scoot clear to the end of the bed."

"I thought I was going to the hospital." Leanne grunted and complained as they moved her.

"Sweetie, this is just a precaution." She hoped. "The paramedics will be here in just a minute." Angela smiled and nodded then turned to Ted. "Why don't you go ahead and wait outside for the ambulance? They have the house number, but it'll be nicer to have you out there so they don't have to wonder."

Ted grimaced. "Can't you at least take off those wings before the paramedics arrive? You look silly."

"I'll do no such thing," she shot back. Not that she could.

Angela lightly brushed Leanne's hair away from her face with her fingers. "Don't worry, sweetie. Don't worry. Mama's here and everything will be fine."

Leanne had another contraction, and Angela took her hand. "Don't forget to breathe. That's right. Calm down. Okay, that's one less contraction before our baby is born. Breathe. Good girl."

The paramedics were at the front door and Angela heard Ted giving directions on which way to turn. He appeared just behind them in the bedroom. They were in a light-hearted mood, laughing and trying to put everyone at ease.

"Are you on your way to a costume party?" one of them asked.

Ted glared at Angela.

"No," she chuckled casually. "My husband bought me this costume for Halloween. I was trying it on and I didn't have time to change."

"So, it looks like you're having this baby at home," one paramedic said.

"Rusty's not here yet," Leanne moaned.

Angela moved to Leanne's side and held her hand. "Everything's going to be fine. Don't you worry about a thing."

The paramedics got their equipment out and started taking her vital statistics, listening to the baby's heartbeat, and determining if the baby was in the birth canal.

Then they waited and waited, and nothing seemed to be happening.

It caused Leanne to panic. "Daddy!"

Ted rushed into the room and quickly came to his daughter's side. "That's my baby. That's my girl," he cooed. "Daddy's here."

After several more minutes, the paramedics counseled briefly and then one of them rushed from the room, returning with the gurney.

"You're going to deliver at the hospital after all." The paramedic assured as he helped her onto the stiff mobile cot.

FIFTY-TWO

"What's going on?" Angela chased after the paramevdics.

"No problem, ma'am." He closed tight the ambulance door with Leanne and the other paramedic inside. "It's just a precaution. The hospital has better equipment for situations like this."

"Situations like what?" Angela ran back into the house for her purse. Ted locked the house, and the two of them hurried to the car. Angela drove to the hospital.

"She'll be fine," Ted said, looking straight ahead as though comforting himself.

"Yeah," Angela agreed.

They ran through the hospital parking lot toward the ER entrance. Angela was acutely aware of her appearance—sweaty hair, wings, and a permanent fairy costume. Yeah, just an ordinary day. But she wouldn't rush home and hide in a dark corner. Angela was more scared for Leanne than she had ever felt for herself. What if things weren't fine? What if something happened to the baby? What if something happened to Leanne?

She couldn't take it, and blinked back tears.

"Only one of you can go in," the charge nurse cautioned, giving Angela a sideways glance. "You don't want to be in the way."

"You go," Ted urged. "You know I'm no good at that."

"Thanks." Angela ran through the double doors and into the ER.

"Mama," Leanne moaned.

Angela took her hand. "It's okay now. I'm here." Angela smoothed Leanne's hair, whispering encouragement.

"We're going to have to do a C-section." Doctor Smith and his staff wheeled Leanne from the room in a flurry.

Angela stared at the doorway. "C-section," she said, nearly comatose from fear. A few minutes later a kindly woman came in and ushered Angela to where Ted already waited in the surgical waiting room.

"You're daughter is in good hands," she said. "Doctor Smith is one of the best maternity doctors in Arizona."

It was hours of silence—heavy ominous worrying silence.

Angela hated it.

She hated the muted television in the corner. It played some mindless show, she didn't even know what. The silence in this room told of tragedy, worry, and guilt. It whispered of the hundreds of families who had waited there, unsure, while a loved one was in another room facing life or death. Alone. The room, ashamed, spoke hauntingly of many of those same families broken and going home, also alone. Their dreams forever altered.

Angela feared for her daughter, but she would be strong. She couldn't fall apart now, not when Leanne needed her. Her body had different plans. Tears fell from her cheeks. Angela couldn't do it. She couldn't be strong any longer. The silence, the aloneness weighed on her like an anvil, and forced her to crack.

A single hand reached over. Angela held it.

Ted looked at her, the smallest of smiles bending his lips, his eyes brim with worry. Angela fell onto his shoulder, sobbing. Then after a moment, as though no longer able to resist, Ted put his arm around her.

Although she no longer recognized this shell-of-a-person known as Angela Anderson, so changed with worry was she—both over her daughter and her marriage—she nestled in the warm comfort of Ted's shoulder. Exhausted.

There were no windows in this most despicable of rooms. Only a small inornate clock told of the passing of time.

It was after four in the morning when a woman entered. "You're Leanne Thornock's parents?"

Angela nodded, gripping her husband's hand tight, and almost afraid to hear the woman speak.

"How is she?" Ted sat up and strengthened his grip around Angela's shoulder. Together they prepared for the news, and hoped and prayed it was good.

"Your daughter is in recovery. She's doing fine."

"What about the baby?"

"The baby is doing fine. She's got a healthy set of lungs on her." The woman smiled.

"Thank heavens." Angela embraced Ted, relieved. Then she stepped back wondering if it was okay.

Ted took Angela's face in his hands and planted a kiss on her lips.

She smiled. "I love you," Angela whispered timidly as though it was her first time saying the words.

They waited another hour before someone else came and took the quiet couple to see their daughter.

"Thanks for being here." Leanne smiled weakly.

"We wouldn't be anywhere else. You know that." Angela rubbed her daughter's hand. "You've had quite a night. We'll let you get some rest now."

"Don't you want to hold Angela Marie before you go?" The doctor had finished with all of the tests and the small infant lay quietly on Leanne's chest.

"You're naming the baby after me?" Angela looked at her

daughter in wonder, and a slow smile filled her. "Are you sure it's okay with Rusty? Don't you want us to wait to hold her until after Rusty has had a turn?" Angela looked at her first granddaughter, Angela Marie, longingly.

"No, Mama. I want you to be the first one to hold her — and yes, Rusty will be fine with whatever name I choose."

Angela reached down and carefully picked up the small bundle and rocked her in her arms. "Angela Marie, we've waited so long for you to join our family."

Seemingly unaware of her wings, Ted stood behind Angela with his head slightly above her shoulder and with his arms around her waist. "She's got her grandma's auburn hair — such a pretty baby."

On the way home, Ted took over the position of driver. The two of them rode in silence. That was okay because Angela didn't have the energy for conversation, and frankly she was too blissful to argue. Leanne was in good hands at the hospital. They would see their little girl and their new granddaughter again after the kids got home from school.

When they turned down their street, Angela shut her eyes, refusing to acknowledge the large moving-van-sign in front of their house, the one that said Ted didn't care what she thought. Surely he did, because he'd been such a comfort at the hospital. But did he care enough to accept her the way she was now?

The empty van was ironically symbolic. Angela walked into her home feeling nervous.

"Did she have it?" Derek and Hannah met them at the door dressed for school.

"How about you kids take the day off of school today and we can all go visit Angela Marie?" Ted quirked a crooked smile.

"Are you not going to work?" Angela asked. Ted never took random days off.

"Work shmirk. We've got a new granddaughter to celebrate."

Ted squeezed Angela around her waist. It was an I-love-you hug, and Angela relaxed. Perhaps Angela Marie had helped change Ted's mind.

"Woot! Woot! Woot!" Derek shouted.

"Yippie!" Hannah cheered, jumping up and down.

It was a special day. A one of a kind day.

Ted called work. "I just had a new granddaughter," he said. "I'll be in late."

Angela called the school. "Please excuse Derek and Hannah Anderson. They won't be in."

"How about we take the kids to see their new niece?" Ted reached for Angela's hand, stopping as their fingers touched.

"That would be perfect." Angela bridged the gap and took Ted's hand in hers, where it belonged. With no need to speed, Angela let Ted drive — it soothed his man-ego somehow.

The four of them walked into the hospital foyer, interrupting a group of preschoolers. Apparently it was field trip day.

"Look!" said the freckled boy leading his peers.

"A fairy!" A brown-haired girl in pigtails said, pointing.

Ted groaned his disapproval and let go of Angela's hand. Derek and Hanna walked in a wide circle, pretending they didn't know her.

"Look," said Hannah, "the gift shop." The two teens hurried toward it.

The young children surrounded Angela, talking and giggling and asking questions while their teachers tried frantically to get them back on task.

"Can I touch your wings?"

"Me too!"

"I want to too!"

"I'm not sure." Angela smiled at them, but didn't know if she should let the children touch her wings. They were already damaged, and she knew how careless four-year-olds could be. Amid the excitement, Derek and Hannah came to the edge of the group, watching their mother interact with the preschoolers.

"We should charge a quarter a piece," Derek whispered to his sister.

Ignoring her children, Angela pulled out her wand. "How about if I give you a fairy blessing?"

"Give it a rest, Angela," Ted muttered.

There was that icy tone again.

The youngsters readily agreed, so Angela circled her toothpick-sized wand above the children's heads. "I, fairy-human Angela, bless you to grow up to be good, obedient children, to help your parents, and to always believe in fairies."

The children stood there unmoving as though waiting for something more.

"That's it." Angela shooed them away with her hands.

The children walked slowly toward their teachers. Really, what had they expected without a parent's approval?

"Stupid lady. I thought she was going to give us candy." A boy kicked at the carpet as they walked away.

"They probably have fairies confused with the Easter Bunny." Angela smirked.

"Is that why you wore the new costume Dad bought you?"

"It's as good a reason as any," responded Angela. She shrugged her shoulders and then not really knowing why (perhaps it was sleep deprivation) she told them the simple truth, "I'm a human-sized fairy."

"Mm-hm," Derek responded.

"Mom, you're so ridiculous," Hannah said.

Ted walked away.

The kids followed not knowing he was angry. Angela followed, knowing that he was.

"My wings are broken, so that's why you see them," she said, hoping to educate her children. "Otherwise they disappear during the day."

"Yeah, whatever."

"I went to the zoo with Amy and her new friend, Gabe, the other day. I wanted them to believe in me, and did something I knew I shouldn't. Now these wings are out here for the whole world to see until further notice."

"Wow," Hannah murmured, "I thought you were just being weird."

"Can you fly like a real fairy?" Derek asked. "You better show us that one." He stopped, eyebrows raised, and waited.

"I'm not supposed to fly in the daytime where everyone can see me," Angela said, exasperated. "That's what broke them to begin with."

"Uh, huh." Derek and Hannah muttered in chorus.

They walked down the hallway toward the elevator. Angela received weird looks from passersby and staff. The kids laughed wildly, and then rushed to the open elevator. A woman gave Angela a frightened and disapproving stare — immediately ushering her son out before the door closed.

Derek burst out laughing. "Good going, Mom. Way to terrorize the neighborhood!"

"We fairies do what we can to amuse." Angela sniffed her nose in the air.

Rusty was sitting on the edge of Leanne's bed holding Angela Marie. He had only missed the birth of his daughter by six hours. He glanced quizzically at Angela's wings but didn't say anything.

The feeling of joy and completeness in the room was a soothing balm to Angela's soul. It reminded her of a dream — one of her first as a fairy. Angela let the kids each have a turn holding the baby, and then snatched her up before Ted got his arms around her. Babies smelled so pure, like they were fresh from heaven.

"What's this?" Angela noticed a tiny bracelet on the baby's wrist.

"It's a fairy charm bracelet. I always loved those fairytales you told us as kids. I figured I'd keep up the tradition." Leanne smiled at Angela.

Rusty gave Leanne a guarded look, and she amended her comment. "I won't go as far as wearing a fairy costume all over town, though." She laughed lightly. "It's cute Mom—real cute. But really, you didn't need to do it. I would have bought Angela Marie the fairy charm anyway."

"You should have seen the way these little punks attacked her in the lobby," Derek said. "She's been freaking people out all the way here." He chuckled.

"The lady in the elevator was classic." Hannah laughed. "I thought she'd have a stroke." Then she looked at Angela and smiled. "You're so weird, Mom."

Angela fluttered her wings. "I am one of a kind, it's true."

Their teasing was all in fun, the way they teased someone they loved. Even Ted seemed to relax and enjoy the banter. Angela breathed deeply with satisfaction, but she couldn't leave it at that. It was an impulse, something in the back of her mind that she had always wanted to do but never dared try—Angela stared at Hannah and Derek.

"Silence," she said.

"Ow!" Hannah's hand shot to her forehead the same time Derek's did.

Derek frowned accusingly at his mom. "Did you do that?"

Angela smiled, feigning innocence. "Me? Do what?" Her hand went to her lips as she struggled to keep from laughing. It had worked! Fairy magic was wonderful.

"Wicked," a wide-eyed Hannah cooed.

"That's wack!" Derek's voice had a nervous edge to it. "You?—

no! — That was like a one-time thing, right? It's not like something you're going to do whenever you get mad."

"Fairies never get mad at their children — because their children are always well behaved," said Angela smugly.

Leanne and Rusty seemed to watch the exchange with silent curiosity, but Angela could tell her daughter was getting tired. "Well, we've got to get going. Your father needs to go to work, and the kids and I are going to spend the rest of the day at the mall shopping for my new granddaughter."

Ted gave her an anxious look.

"It's only money, honey." She smiled. Angela couldn't help it, she felt so happy that a smile didn't seem adequate to convey her joy.

Leanne took Angela's hand. "Mom, you've been such an inspiration in my life. Thanks for all of your help. I don't know what I would have done without it. I hope my daughter grows up to be just like you."

"You better watch out what you wish for." Angela scrunched her wings together making them flutter, and then she was so thrilled she just couldn't contain herself any longer. Stretching her wings, Angela floated up toward the ceiling. "I'm so happy, I feel lighter than air."

"Mom!"

FIFTY-THREE

"We are overcrowded and I'm repulsed by the pixies' continual pranks. Your mission is to annihilate them. We will help, of course." Tatiana's words floated into Angela's mind.

This was it. Her mission—figure out their overcrowding situation—and she could do it. Angela did a jig around the kitchen, then stopped. **"But I won't be annihilating any pixies."** Angela felt strong and confident. *"Hear me out,"* she said before Tatiana could give her a headache or begin one of her tirades.

Angela hurried silently past her TV-watching husband and to their bedroom, closing the door for privacy.

"Traitor!" The fairy queen appeared on their bedpost. *"Traitor!"*

"You wanted me to believe in myself." Angela sat on the bed. *"And I finally do."* Helping Leanne as she had, and now that Ted had come around, Angela knew she could do anything. *"Fairies are kind and good."* She lifted her eyebrows as though chiding Derek or Hannah. *"They don't go around annihilating pixies."* She would use her newfound confidence to help solve the fairies' problem peacefully.

Angela drummed her fingers over her lips as she planned. *"You could cast a spell to immobilize them and then I could blow in their faces and give them amnesia.*" She made a face. It wasn't annihilation, but it wasn't peaceful either.

"This will never work." Tatiana flitted around Angela's head. "The pixies refuse to leave," she said, resting back on the bedpost. "They love the beautiful lawn—the water—and consider themselves a type of guardian for the water fowl."

"*Or, you could —*" The answer was on the tip of her memory.

"The pixies are making our lives a misery and you had better stop them by tomorrow. Or else," Tatiana said and disappeared.

"Wait! I have it." Angela stared at the bedpost wishing the impatient queen would reappear.

As Ted prepared for bed, Angela prepared for something else. She came out of their bathroom wearing her new fairy costume (it still wouldn't budge) and thinking pleasant thoughts of her new little granddaughter while trying to keep away thoughts of how it would break her heart to leave.

"Seriously?" Ted glared at Angela. "Aren't you going to get ready for bed?"

"I've got to complete my mission." She thought he understood. "I finally heard Tatiana's message and I know what I need to do now." Angela finally had the perfect solution to the fairies' dilemma.

"I can't believe you'd do this."

If Angela hadn't been so tired, she would have noted Ted's frustration. "I have to." Angela yawned. "I've finally got their problem solved. Your wife, she's a genius." Angela pinned the toothpick-sized wand to her waist, pleased with her idea. "After tonight, the fairies'll fix my wing. And if that's the case," she patted her chest, "full time fairy here."

"Angela, I thought we had this resolved."

"Yeah, I did too." Finally realizing he was upset, her brows knit together pleadingly. "You know I've got to keep my promise, but this isn't a problem." She shook her head. "I've got it figured out."

"There you are, going on about the fairies again." His jaw clenched. "Angela Benoit Anderson, you know it's just an excuse to leave the house."

"Theodore Matthews Anderson." If he could use full names, she could too. "When will you trust me? When will you believe in me? When?" She put her hand to her forehead, feeling way too tired for this.

"There is no such thing as fairies. You're just going to meet up with Gabe."

"Doubtful, but what of it? If I happen across him, what does that mean? If he consoles me because my husband is being unreasonable—what? I'm being unfaithful?" Her voice pinched into a shriek.

"You don't know him like I do." Ted paced the room.

"How do you profess to know him at all?"

"Rebecca told me some things you'd be interested to learn." His eyebrows rose and he looked at her like the all-knowing parent.

"I don't want to hear a word that fiendish ferret has uttered from her noxious lips!" Angela trembled with fury.

"Don't go." It wasn't a plea.

"What do you mean, don't go? This is my last night. You win!" Angela didn't mean to cry, but her tears fell when angry. "You win," she repeated. "I won't get to be a fairy after all." *Because you didn't believe in me.* "This is my last night. My last hope."

"I mean," he paused, unaffected by her tears. Tilting his head downward, he gazed at her pointedly. "I forbid you to leave this house."

"What, am I two? Do you mean to give me an ultimatum?" Angela glared at Ted, her hands on her hips.

"I mean, I'm sick and tired of this." He thrust both hands toward her indicating her wings and outfit. "Choose tonight. What is it — full-time fairy — or human? You've got to choose either Gabe or me. You can't have us both. I won't have my wife *flying* off every night into the arms of another man. I'm not an idiot."

Oh yes you are. "I choose you, Ted. The problem is, do you choose me back?" And with that, she walked out of the bedroom and then through the arcadia door.

The October sky was clear. There were twelve stars out. Angela counted them as she flew toward Freestone Park. It was time for her to fulfill her mission. At least tonight she looked like a fairy (other than her sheer size). When she got near Greenfield Road, however, Angela stopped at the riparian habitat. Perhaps she could persuade the fairies to come to her.

The moon shone on the black water and the reeds rustled in a slight breeze as Angela walked down the path that circled around the main lake of the habitat.

With crickets chirping, thick grasses along the shoreline, and the sounds of frogs and small snakes entering the water, this place was magical — more magical than Freestone Park — and less occupied by humans and pixies.

Putting her fingers to her temples and closing her eyes, Angela concentrated and called, "*Tatiana!*" No response. "*I've solved your problem. I have a better plan than annihilation. Remember, fairies are kind and good.*" Freestone was nice with its manicured lawns and perennially trimmed hedges, but the fairies would like the riparian habitat better. Angela pictured it in her mind, showing Tatiana its raw beauty.

Tatiana didn't magically appear in her mind's eye and have a visit, nor did she appear in person. There was no response at all.

Had the pixies taken over — had they zapped the fairies back to their homeland? Angela felt very alone, and anything could be true. She no longer knew truth from error. The truth that her whole life was based on — that Ted loved her unconditionally — didn't feel true anymore. Angela had thought that truths, once true, were true forever.

There was a bench nearby. She walked to it and sat, but didn't cry. She was the Sahara Desert, dry, spent, and nearly lifeless.

After waiting for over a half hour, Angela thought that she may have to fly to Freestone Park and discover if the fairies were there for herself. She shuddered and started walking toward the library.

A familiar silhouette leaned against the bridge's railing.

"I see you're stalking me now, yeah?" Gabe chewed the end of a blade of grass. "That's okay. I was hoping you'd show up."

Angela walked to his side. "Hey, you." She nudged him with her shoulder.

Gabe didn't respond playfully like she had hoped. Really? He couldn't be upset with her, too. Angela gulped back.

"When's the big move?" He glanced at her.

Angela focused on the water and shrugged, not desiring to hash it over again.

"Is it soon?" Gabe turned toward her, his right elbow resting on the railing.

Angela gazed up to the heavens. She had risked it all for the fairies — for Ted — and for what? Apparently, they'd found their own solution and hadn't even bothered telling her.

Was Ted's mood a part of Tatiana's interference — her punishment for telling? Now the fairies were gone, would Ted go back to his old self? His trusting self?

"So are you moving or what?"

Angela didn't respond. After all, how would she know?

Gabe guided her face toward him with his finger. "Talk to me, woman."

"Talk? What is there to say? Sure I'll go. If Ted still wants me." Resting her elbows on the railing, Angela put her head in her hands and stared at the water. "I'm going to lose my wings. I won't be special anymore."

Gabe didn't respond, and Angela knew he believed it too. It was too much rejection in one night.

With a nod of finality, she left the bridge and headed south. The walking path wound around several receiving ponds and through acres of desert vegetation before making its way back to Guadalupe Road and eventually the parking lot. Angela wouldn't walk that far, they'd have to send an ambulance for her if she tried. She had had enough of that kind of fun.

"You are special." Gabe caught up to her. "I knew you were special the first time I saw you.

"Yeah, not everyone burns their sheets in the backyard." Angela smirked mirthlessly.

"No, it was before that."

Angela frowned, trying to figure out when she had seen him before.

"I was on the tower at the fire station." Gabe put his arm around her and rubbed her shoulder. Angela didn't pull away. As he massaged, she allowed herself to think back.

"I've been alone for twenty years," he continued. "My wife left me for another man."

Angela spun around, her eyebrows wrinkled in concern for her friend.

"Don't be sorry. We weren't good together, yeah." He turned her carefully back, massaging her shoulders again. "However, I spent a good portion of the time after that feeling bitter—hating women." He paused long enough that Angela thought he might not say more, but then he continued. "I transferred to Gilbert's Station 23, and something magical happened. We rotate guard on the tower but it seemed like I was always pulling the night watch."

Angela glanced back at him.

He scratched his head and grinned. "I started seeing things

that weren't normal—not humanly possible. Then, as I accepted the fairies into my world, you came." He turned her around to face him. Angela furrowed her brows, but didn't say anything. "I could see something from the tower so I got the binoculars, and there you were. Learning how to fly." He smiled crookedly. "Life blew into my soul at the sight of you." Gabe looked at Angela through his eyelashes. They were thick and long, his eyes pleading.

"I was driving the other guys crazy, pacing the floor, trying to figure out how to meet you." He smiled. "Then we got a call."

"I remember. Our lawn has just barely recovered." He was just trying to cheer her up, but his praise made Angela beam inside. They had become good friends, and in such a short time, too. He always knew just what to say to make her feel better.

"I thought I loved you, Anj."

"Wait. What?" Angela stepped away. He was going too far with his comfort. She scratched between her eyebrows and grimaced. Ted was right all along. She walked away from Gabe and to the lake's edge.

"Don't be angry." Gabe followed and held her arm. "Thought, Anj. I *thought* I loved you."

"But you don't?"

"I owe my life to you." Gabe ran his hands through his hair. "If you'd have given me one inch of encouragement, I'd have taken you into my arms and never let you go."

So this didn't comfort her. She frowned.

"Don't you get it? I didn't want to be that man." He worried his soul patch. "Not deep down. My wife ended our marriage with that man." He shook his head. "That one moment would have spoiled what we have." He clasped her arms. "I love you as a friend. As the woman who opened my heart." He smiled endearingly. "Amy and I—"

"You like her!" Angela clapped her hands together, a childlike exuberance, but new love is often childlike.

"What I wanted to say though, is that you are an inspiration."

"Yeah, that's me. I'm an inspiration to crazy ladies everywhere." Angela looked away.

"No." Gabe's eyebrows pinched together. "You and Ted, you work hard at making your marriage work. I admire that."

Ordinarily that was a compliment Angela would have loved to hear and would have accepted readily. Tonight it made her sad.

"Still upset about the move?" Gabe stepped closer and put his arm around Angela. She nodded. It was related to the move.

"I have a gorgeous and soon-to-be-spoiled granddaughter, by the way." Angela grinned and bit at her bottom lip. "I almost delivered her myself."

"Tell me about it, yeah?"

They sat on the bench and looked out over the lake while Angela told Gabe about the birth of Angela Marie, the sunset a distant memory.

"It's hard to believe we're in the middle of town." Angela sighed. "It's so quiet here."

"Look!" Gabe stood and pointed across the lake.

Sparkling lights drew near. Red — blue — green — pink — hundreds of lights, hundreds of varieties of color. Angela rose from the bench, and standing beside Gabe, they watched in awe as the fairies came to claim their new home, settling in the rushes.

A familiar ache pounded in Angela's head and then Tatiana appeared in her mind's eye.

"You have done well my child.

"*So, you like it?*" Angela was giddy with relief. "*I've done all that you've asked.*" Sort of. "*Do I get my wings full time? Can I fly to Chillers Ice cream for All Occasions for a German Chocolate treat? Can I use my wings whenever I want?*"

"Silence!"

"*Only for special needs. Right? To buy milk for breakfast?*" Come to think of it they were out of milk again.

"Silence!"

Angela cringed with pain. "*Okay, okay. So, only when there's a fairy need?*" It hardly seemed fair. "*But, no more secrets,*" Angela said. "*Ted can see them now. Right? Because he already has.*" Tatiana seemed strangely immobile. Why wasn't she agreeing to anything?

"My child, knowledge of the fairies is not for your world. You know that. Your Ted is not yet a believer, and tomorrow is All Hallows' Eve."

"*But I've been faithful. You said I did well.*" Angela's heart sank. "*Can I keep my fairy dust and my wand at least?*"

"You may. However, until midnight tomorrow, your wings will remain on your back in their broken state." Tatiana gazed up into Angela's eyes. "Each point of your mission must be fulfilled by then."

"*Or?*" She hated to know.

"You are already aware of the terms and conditions of your fairy life. I'll not repeat them." Tatiana sighed and shook her head. "I have failed your mother."

"*What?*" Her mother had been gone for years.

"I was there when she passed into the eternal world. You had already begun to doubt both our magic and your own abilities. I promised her I would help you learn to believe in yourself once again. I would help you believe in us." Her lip turned up.

"*You promised my mother?*"

"I thought that if you had to fight for your beliefs — you would believe in us once again."

"*I do,*" Angela insisted. "*I do believe in you.*"

"Yes. Our disagreement with the pixies helped to some extent." She straightened her crown. "But rather than take courage and believe in your own abilities, you faltered."

"*I don't understand.*" Angela frowned. "*I couldn't concentrate because of the stress of losing Ted.*" She may still lose him.

"I should have come sooner—when your love with the nonbeliever was new. Your Ted would have believed easier then."

"*Why didn't you?*" The fairies could have helped soften the blow of the sudden loss of her parents.

"You had already purchased that hideous costume and started that ridiculous collection." Tatiana looked away, her jaw set. "And that is where I failed you. If we'd have come and spent our time building you up, your Ted would have believed long ago."

"*He proved that at the hospital. But it didn't last.*"

"Your Ted is a stubborn man," Tatiana said and then disappeared.

Angela wobbled and stepped forward to keep her balance.

Gabe caught her. "What just happened?" Not privy to the conversation and not having seen Tatiana, Gabe's head tilted and he appeared concerned.

"Tatiana, the fairy queen granted me my fairy wings for helping find their new home," Angela said. "Until tomorrow, anyway. Ted still has to believe in fairies before they're permanent." She gulped back her disappointment.

"You are an amazing woman. Are you sure you wouldn't like to trade Ted in for someone who already believes?"

Angela glared at him. "You're not funny."

"I know, I know. I'm sorry." Gabe chewed his soul patch. "I really do like Amy and you're married to a wonderful, understanding and loyal man."

"Yes." *For now.* Angela needed to get home to ensure she stayed that way. "Thanks for making me feel better and for always being there, but I need to go."

"I probably won't be seeing you for a while."

"No?"

"Amy's taking me to Oregon. We're going to stay in a tree-house hotel, do a zip line. See the ocean." Gabe shrugged. "I have a lot of vacation days built up."

"All this after only one date?" Angela paused. "Behave yourself."

"You know it." Gabe smiled evilly, and then sobered. "Nah, I'm joining a singles group of hers. There'll be a dozen or so of us." He reached out and touched her fingertips. "This is it, huh? Your fairy mission is over. When will we see you again?"

"I don't know," Angela said, feeling nostalgic. "I don't have another fairy mission—and I like all my new sheets."

"Will you ever learn how to fish?"

Angela just smiled, shrugged and then flew toward home.

FIFTY-FOUR

Angela didn't like eating crow. So, hoping to avoid another argument, she snuck in the back door. Hopefully, Ted was asleep. As she tiptoed to the bedroom, Angela noticed one annoying thing—her wings were there. Shaking her head, she sighed at the absurdity of it all, and slipped into bed.

Ted leaned up onto his elbow. "You came back," he said.

"Of course I came back." Acting on impulse, Angela leaned down and gave him a quick hug. When she pulled away, her cheek was wet. "You've been crying?" She wiped a thumb tenderly across his cheek and cupped his face in her hand.

"I didn't know if my wife would come back," he choked the words.

"I would never stay away. Not as long as you want me." Angela sat on the bed beside him, toying with the curls on his forehead.

"I've made a terrible mess of things." He heaved a ragged sigh. "I meant to tell you how impressive you were."

"Impressive? How?"

"The way you just took charge and helped Leanne until the paramedics got there." Ted's lip lifted crookedly. "You were confident and self assured. You were great, and I've been horrible." He took her hand in his. "Is it too late to apologize?"

"Great, huh?" Angela's lip turned up into a smile.

"And you look adorable in your new fairy dress—wings and all." He lightly caressed the edge of a wing. "They're softer than they look. What're they made of?"

"Who knows?" Angela smirked, shrugging. It made her wings flutter.

"How do you do that?"

"It must be magic." She grinned, snuggling into his embrace.

"They're really real, aren't they?" His expression was that of a curious schoolboy. "Can I see?"

"Sure." Angela sat on the edge of the bed, her back and wings toward Ted. She felt each touch of his trembling fingers as he explored her wings, each kiss on her back as he saw for himself that the wings were a part of her.

"I love you, Angela Anderson." He pulled her backward onto the bed. Leaning forward, he kissed her.

"Fairy fixation and all?" Angela said, emphasizing the words 'fairy fixation' then bit her lip, waiting for his response.

"I love you for now and forever—fairy fixation and all." He kissed her hand. "And Gabe? You never cared about him?" He sounded nervous, apprehensive.

"You are the love of my life." She stroked his cheek. "Gabe was only someone who believed in fairies. A friend." Angela took Ted's hand and kissed it. "And now he's perfectly infatuated with Amy."

Ted sighed deeply, his eyes closed. "I'm so happy to hear that."

"And what about—" she indicated the Helmans' house, "you-know-who?"

Ted flexed his jaw. "She won't be bothering us anymore."

"Oh?"

He sat up and held her hands in his. "I overheard her talking to Ralph Begay, my Booster's vice president." He shook his head. "Anyway, she was telling him you were unstable and how they needed an emergency election for a new president because I'm connected to you. Of course, she offered herself as candidate for taking over as president. The nerve."

"I'm so sorry, honey."

"Ralph and I had a long talk about it. I've booted her out of the Boosters."

"Yeah?" Angela bit back her smile.

He kissed Angela's hand. "Anyway, poor Jeff came over and asked me about the whole deal. He about blew a gasket when I explained the situation. Said Rebecca was totally obsessed with you, and that he'd had enough. They're moving back to California."

"California?" Angela chewed her lip. Hopefully nowhere near Sacramento. "Do you know whereabouts in California?"

"What do I care?" Ted gazed into her eyes. "The point is, you're free. They're gone."

"Gone?" Her heart fluttered with hope.

"They filled their shiny Lincoln Navigator and left. Jeff's paying a company to pack the rest of the house and to list it."

It was a lot to process. Angela took a deep breath and let it out slowly—no more Hell-woman—no more devious snake. A smile lifted her lips.

"Let's not talk about the Helmans anymore." Ted rubbed his finger up her arm, a mischievous glint in his eyes. "That fairy dress is pretty darn cute, but you know what I like better?"

"What?" Angela asked, furrowing her brows.

"That sexy little nightgown you bought a while back. I haven't seen it again, but I'd sure like to." He wiggled his eyebrows up and down, as if she didn't get the hint.

Angela leapt off the bed and ransacked her drawer to find it. "You mean this?" Angela was tired, yes, but not too tired for that. She put the negligee up to her, smiling hopefully. "But, I couldn't get the dress off earlier." Would it be part of her forever?

"Here," Ted stood next to her. "Let me try." He lifted the dress up and over her head.

"You have the magic touch." Angela smiled.

The next morning was Saturday, and Halloween, and Angela was in an exceptionally good mood. She hummed while making breakfast for her family.

As soon as the mall opened, the Andersons went in search of more gifts for the baby because Angela remembered she hadn't gotten Leanne a baby book.

They spent hours at the mall, had lunch at the food court, then returned to the hospital and shared their gifts with the new infant. When Leanne grew tired, they headed home again.

"Tonight is the company dinner," Ted said.

"Oh, no." Angela whacked her forehead.

"You have plenty of time to get ready."

"I forgot to buy a dress. Do I have time to go back to the mall?" Angela looked worriedly between Hannah and Ted.

"Count me out. Rachael and I have plans." Hannah walked away texting.

"Wear the one from last year." Ted acted as though this made perfect sense.

"Maybe." Angela's shoulders drooped. It was Halloween. Time was up. And her wings were still protruding from her back, broken. Her wings would go through last year's gown. (She had tried it.)

Besides, the people in Ted's company were above the 'upper middle class' classification. Most of them had no children and none had more than two. They lived in posh houses, drove expensive new cars, wore designer clothing—and always, *always* a sparkling new evening dress at each gathering. It was an unwritten requirement among the wives.

Angela had a hard time keeping up with socialites. Not that she usually wanted to. At the company dinners, all Angela ever wanted was to *not* be a hindrance or a liability to her husband's career. It was hard for Ted to socialize with coworkers who bonded weekly at the golf course because he preferred being at home with his family or spending time helping at the high school, but it was harder for Angela.

The only thing she had in common with these women was the semi-annual dinner. Most of them had successful careers of their own as doctors or lawyers. They were businesswomen. Angela was a housewife. By choice.

They spent weekends at five-star resorts and relaxing at the spa. Angela spent weekends with dirty laundry and dust bunnies. They got their hair groomed and had monthly manicures at 'Le Chic,' one of the most prestigious salons in Scottsdale. Angela had her hair trimmed four times a year at Cheap Cuts. On the rare occasions when she had a manicure, she did it herself.

Angela could not face these women while wearing her dress from the last dinner, or while sporting full-sized fairy wings. She slumped onto the sofa.

"What's wrong?"

"I can't go with you tonight." Angela moaned. Despite all the pressure, she usually enjoyed the dinners to a degree. It was a chance to dress up, Ted usually danced with her at least once, and the food was always exquisite. "I still have my wings."

"Don't be absurd." He sat beside her. "Wings or no wings, I won't go without you."

Angela shook her head. "I'll just embarrass you. You need to go so everyone can congratulate you on your new position, but no one will miss me."

"I do need to go," Ted agreed, nodding, "but I'm not leaving without you. If you didn't come — I would miss you." He leaned over and kissed Angela on the forehead.

"Ted, really, the wings haven't repaired themselves." Angela turned to show her husband and then looked at him bleakly.

"People will talk."

"They probably will." Ted shrugged. "But who's afraid of talk?"

"Not me." Angela lifted her lips in a smile she didn't feel. "But the gown from last year doesn't fit and I don't have anything to wear."

Ted tilted his head to the side. "I think the dress I bought you looks stunning."

The fairy-dress. Angela looked down at it—her nonstop companion for two days. She lifted her arms one at a time and sniffed under them. Hmm. Maybe fairies didn't get body odor. "It does go perfectly with my wings," she said, feeling a little more encouraged.

"Go get cleaned up and fix your hair. We'll make it in plenty of time." Ted took his shirt off and laid it over the armrest.

Ted's clothing wasn't an issue. He had a black designer suit and a matching black tie for the occasion. It was a cruel gender-obsessed rule that allowed men to wear the same suit more than once—their only required change was their shirts. Tonight, Ted's would be buttercup yellow.

Angela stared at her calm husband. He acted like her being a fairy was no big deal. This was an abrupt change of heart for him.

"Do you think a shower will ruin my wings?" She asked, reaching back to see if they were still there. They were.

Ted puckered his lips, reflecting. "I thought fairies liked the water."

"They like it, but I don't know if they get in it," Angela responded.

"Well, don't they live outdoors?" Ted continued. "If they live outdoors near the water, it seems that their wings would get wet occasionally."

"I don't know." Angela worried her lip. Ted was always so logical, but nothing about her situation was logical. Could she count on logic?

Ted thought for a minute. "Take your dress off and I'll be back." He left the bedroom.

The dress had refused to come off once before. Angela looked down at it. "What do you say?" she asked the dress. "Can I have a shower?"

Feeling a little apprehensive, Angela tugged at the dress. The silly thing came right off. "My life is so absurd." She took it and hung it on a hanger hoping steam would freshen it. She sniffed the armpits. The dress looked fresh and still smelled fresh, but just to be sure, she hung it near the shower.

Ted came back into the bedroom with two black garbage bags. "I wasn't sure if they'd both fit under one." He opened the first bag and slipped it over Angela's right wing. "If I pull the other one under — is it okay?" He took the left wing and gently wrapped the bag around it as well, and then waited for her response.

"It's a little tight, but I think it'll be fine for a shower." Angela adjusted the water temperature and then stood under the water listening as the spray hit the plastic bag. It almost sounded like water hitting a tin roof. She hurried through her routine, and dressed.

"Are you almost ready?" Ted asked from the doorway.

She put the finishing touches on her hair. "Almost." In keeping with her fairy theme, she had curled her auburn hair. It laid in short, bouncy curls around her head. She felt like an overgrown and aging doll.

The down coat was on the bed. Angela put it on — she didn't want to make a spectacle of herself.

"You're not wearing that." Ted frowned.

"It hides my wings."

"You bought it at a thrift store, and it shows." Ted helped her slip out of it. "I don't want this old rag hiding your beautiful outfit. And besides, you'll have to take it off once you get inside anyway."

"You have a point there."

An hour and a half later, Angela walked nervously through the lobby of the five-star resort. She couldn't have been more nervous if she were walking through the door naked. She shivered involuntarily at the thought.

Bob Drulman, Ted's boss, met them inside and shook Ted's hand. "I'm glad you made it. And, I hear congratulations are in order on the arrival of a grandbaby?"

"Thank you. Yes." Ted put his arm around Angela's shoulder. "We have a new granddaughter."

Mr. Drulman glanced at Angela, took Ted by the elbow, and ushered him a few steps away. "Was your wife not aware that this is not a costume party?" he said, agitated.

Angela walked to Ted's side. "Hello Mr. Drulman. So happy to see you again." She offered her hand.

He glared at her.

She put her hand down and fidgeted with her ring. "I hope you don't mind my costume, but it is Halloween." She lifted a shoulder and smiled. "Ted bought it for me and it was so beautiful, I just had to wear it."

Mr. Drulman's chest expanded. His glaring eyes were green.

Angela closed her eyes, took a deep breath and let it out between nearly closed lips.

"What the—!" Mr. Drulman put his hands up, covering his face. "You'll be sorry about turning our semi-formal affair into a freak show, Anderson," he grumbled, then charged off in a huff.

"I should leave," Angela said, watching Ted's boss storm across the room. She turned toward the door wondering how much the taxi fare for an hour-long ride would be.

Ted caught hold of her arm and pulled her toward him. "We've been in this together for thirty-two years," he said, slipping his hands around her waist and nuzzling against her neck. "I've been recently reminded that I'm nothing without you. Promise to stay."

His whisper sent chills down her spine and made her knees weak. "But Ted—"

"But nothing. I'm married to an amazing woman and I want you by my side—forever." He placed his hand on her neck and pulled her gently closer, surprising her with a tender kiss.

Angela was ready to take Ted as her prize and turn for home, but he took her hand in his and guided her to one of the tables circling the portable dance floor.

Elaborate chandeliers hung above luxurious red carpeting. Each circular table draped in white linen, and the accompanying white china was accentuated with gold-ware. In the center of each table was a round faceted crystal bowl with an elegant arrangement of fall colors.

"Bryan, Mike, Dave—you remember my wife, Angela."

They each stood and shook her hand, and Angela smiled in greeting to them.

"My wife came as a fairy tonight. None of you have a problem with that do you?" He sounded gracious, but Angela heard the slight strain in his voice.

"The dress is beautiful," one of the women said.

"There's no problem at this table," Dave said. The others shook their heads in agreement. They only looked anxiously at her for a moment, then introduced their wives, Melanie, Kari and Kym.

The evening went smoothly enough—if she didn't count everyone gawking at her and whispering wildly—and the food was delicious. It was the type of event where there were lots of courses, each brought separately. Angela ordered shark steak for her main course. It was served with rice pilaf and fresh vegetables. She had Crème Brûlée for dessert. The waiter brought a mini-torch and set her dessert afire. Angela smiled at the memory of her own silly fire. She had grown so much since then.

Ted had just cracked the shell on his dessert when Bob Drulman stepped beside him. "Follow me," Mr. Drulman said, and walked to the CEO table.

"So much for dessert." Ted put his napkin down and joined his boss and the six partners that made up their firm.

Angela couldn't hear what was said, but she could tell they weren't happy about it. Ted looked firm and resolute. By the time he came back to the table, the other couples were on the dance floor enjoying the first dance of the evening. Angela was sitting alone.

"What's going on?" She worried the napkin on her lap. She should have gone home—she shouldn't have come at all. Her being a fairy for an expensive company dinner was crass. The bosses probably thought of it as a slap in the face.

"Let's dance. Shall we?" Ted extended his hand.

Angela allowed him to help her up. "I thought you'd never ask." She smiled at him as they walked to the dance floor. "You look mighty handsome tonight." It was true too, but to Angela he was always handsome.

Ted pulled her into his arms and Angela wanted to melt there. It was their best dance effort yet, but she couldn't relax until after the bombshell of California was announced.

"You never have to worry about coming to another of these company-sponsored functions again." Ted gazed serenely into Angela's questioning eyes. "I gave them my notice of resignation."

"What—why? No, Ted." Angela forgot to dance and stood in the middle of the floor. "This is your dream."

Ted scooped her into his arms and kissed her neck. "It just wasn't worth it anymore," he whispered. "It took a while, but I finally realized this isn't my dream." He swept his open hand toward the partners' table and then brought it to her face caressing her chin. "You are. You and the kids."

It took a moment for it all to sink in. She looked at him concerned. "We're staying in Arizona, but you don't have a job?"

"My fairy queen, you worry too much. I was offered a job yesterday by a smaller, more personal company." He placed his fingers over her mouth stifling a question, and then replaced his fingers with a kiss. "I didn't say anything because I didn't think I would take it.

And no, I won't make as much, but yes, we'll get to stay here. You were right, how could we ever leave that sweet little granddaughter of ours?" He looked into her eyes.

She saw and felt the same love—no, a stronger love than she had known before.

"This is long overdue, but Angela, my dear fairy-wife, I want you to know that I believe—"

She thought he was going to say something she had longed for her whole life. She thought he would say, "I believe in fairies," but he didn't. What he said surprised and pleased her more than anything he could have ever said, and she let the words ring musically through her mind as they finished the dance. "Angela, I believe in you."

The words made her feel tingly inside. At first, she just thought it was the moment and her joy. But then Ted stepped back, appraising her. "Do you want to tell me something, Mrs. Anderson?"

"They're gone, aren't they?" Angela wiggled with excitement. Her wings were healed! She had proven herself, and Ted had apparently won Tatiana's approval as well.

"Yes, they're gone. Will they come back?" Ted had her in his arms again.

Angela nodded, beaming with joy. She had finished her mission.

Ted pulled her close and they waltzed across the floor to the large French doors. He opened them and pulled her onto the balcony. Before Angela could utter a word, Ted kissed her passionately. "I've been waiting all night to do that," he said after he pulled away.

Angela smiled. He'd been kissing her all evening—but not like that. "Why stop with just the one?"

His lips were on hers again, and she forgot about everything else until he reluctantly pulled away.

They leaned against the railing and gazed out over the city lights. It was a serene moment filled with the joy of sharing it with someone she loved. She could go on now and live a normal life, yet Angela didn't want normal—she had always excelled at abnormal in every way. And she itched for something even better, something terribly eccentric.

"I have to know, Ted." Her eyebrows lifted in apology.

"What? I'll tell you anything." He held her elbow and searched her eyes.

"No, it's not that." At her silent request, Angela's wings appeared. She leaned forward, giving her husband a tender kiss for good luck, then climbed onto the ornate railing, her heart thumping in her chest.

Ted's eyes widened. "Get down. You're going to hurt yourself," he pleaded.

"I need to make sure they still work properly." She leapt forward and took flight into the night sky.

A frantic Ted lunged forward. "Come back!"

A cool breeze blew across her face as she swooped up and over a eucalyptus tree, the city lights gleaming. It was a heavenly pleasure. Even Tatiana couldn't blame her for flying tonight. Angela had everything an overgrown fairy could want—a loving husband—good children—a new granddaughter—and wings!

Angela couldn't stay away long though. She was drawn back to the balcony like a fairy to her nectar. Back to Ted, her knight in shining armor who believed in her at last.

BOOK CLUB QUESTIONS

How did you feel as you read the story?

What is the main conflict in the story?

Were Angela's motivations believable?

For what purposes does Angela use her fairy powers?

What does Angela learn about herself?

What are two difficult decisions Angela made? What influences these decisions?

What personality traits do you have in common with Angela? Discuss two of these.

Select and read a passage that you found meaningful. Explain why.

What might the author have been saying about family relationships? Use the story to back your position.

Where could Angela's story go after the end of the book?

ABOUT THE AUTHOR

Doesn't everyone believe in fairies? As a young girl, Tina Scott did. Her one wish, well, her one fairy wish was that she could fly. She dreamt about it often and during her waking hours, Tina was Tinkerbelle to her brother's Peter Pan.

Tina Scott loves writing about ordinary people in extraordinary circumstances—always with a touch of romance. Her husband is her main support and inspiration. They have seven children and a growing number of grandchildren. Other than large family get-togethers involving lots of food and fun, she enjoys writing, watercolor painting, long walks, ice cream, and traveling to Europe--especially to her father's ancestral home of Denmark.

Connect with Tina on social media:
http://www.facebook.com/TinasWritingAdventure
http://www.pinterest.com/tinascott161214
www.linkedin.com/in/tinapetersonscott
 Twitter: @authortinascott

Other Titles by Tina Scott:
Farewell, My Denmark
My Sweet Danish Rose
Surviving Denmark on a Bag of Peach Rings